TOLSTOY
AS PHILOSOPHER

ESSENTIAL SHORT WRITINGS (1835-1910)

AN ANTHOLOGY

The publication of this book was supported by the grant from
the Mikhail Prokhorov Fund.

 transcript

Published with the support of the Institute for Literary
Translation, Russia.

ИНСТИТУТ ПЕРЕВОДА

AD VERBUM

Special thanks to the Faculty Research Fund at The New School
for supporting this project.

TOLSTOY AS PHILOSOPHER

ESSENTIAL SHORT WRITINGS (1835-1910)
AN ANTHOLOGY

Edited, Translated, and Introduced by
Inessa Medzhibovskaya

BOSTON
2022

Library of Congress Cataloging-in-Publication Data

Names: Tolstoy, Leo, graf, 1828-1910 author. | Medzhibovskaya, Inessa, 1964- editor.
Title: Tolstoy as philosopher : essential short writings (1835–1910): an anthology / edited, translated and introduced by Inessa Medzhibovskaya.
Description: Boston : Academic Studies Press, 2022. | Includes bibliographical references and index. | Translated from the Russian.
Identifiers: LCCN 2022019766 (print) | LCCN 2022019767 (ebook) | ISBN 9781644694015 (hardback) | ISBN 9781644694022 (paperback) | ISBN 9781644694039 (adobe pdf) | ISBN 9781644694046 (epub)
Subjects: LCSH: Tolstoy, Leo, graf, 1828-1910--Philosophy. | Tolstoy, Leo, graf, 1828-1910--Translations into English.
Classification: LCC PG3366.A13 M43 2022 (print) | LCC PG3366.A13 (ebook) | DDC 891.73/3--dc23/eng/20220622

LC record available at https://lccn.loc.gov/2022019766
LC ebook record available at https://lccn.loc.gov/2022019767

ISBN 9781644694176 (hardback)
ISBN 9781644694039 (adobe pdf)
ISBN 9781644694046 (epub)

Cover design by Ivan Grave.
On the cover: The toys of Vanechka Tolstoy (1888-1895). Courtesy of The State Tolstoy Museum in Khamovniki (2010). Photo by Inessa Medzhibovskaya.

Book design by Kryon Publishing Services.

Published by Academic Studies Press
1577 Beacon Street
Brookline, MA, 02446, USA
press@academicstudiespress.com
www.academicstdiespress.com

For my father (the philosopher of kindness);

My teachers (who forgave me "seventy times seven");

My students (my keenest challengers);

And for Jared (when he is old enough to read).

Contents

*See Credits.

Acknowledgments

I would like to thank Academic Studies Press for inviting this project—specifically, Mark Lipovetsky, the Cultural Syllabus Series Editor, Faith Wilson Stein, the former acquisitions editor, and Kate Yanduganova, the current editor, under whose expert guidance I have brought this volume to completion. This text benefitted from the splendid comments by the four external reviewers. Sasha Shapiro, Ilya Nikolaev, Kira Nemirovsky, and Matthew Charlton took over the project at the production stage and worked with me patiently through the final edits. Galina Alekseeva, Jeffrey Brooks, Ellen Chances, Liza Knapp, and Donna Tussing Orwin wrote warm endorsements.

I would also like to express my deepest gratitude to The New School Provost's Office for granting me a Faculty Research Fund award and the Mikhail Prokhorov Fund. For the financial support of this translation project.

My thanks to the Leo Tolstoy State Museum in Moscow (GMT) and its Manuscript Division for many years of supportive collaboration. In the year of the centennial of Tolstoy's death (2010), the museum allowed me to take a picture of the toys of Tolstoy's youngest child, his son Vanechka, at its branch in Khamovniki. This image is on the cover of this book. To the Museum Estate of L. N. Tolstoy at Yasnaya Polyana and the division of Tolstoy's Personal Library at Yasnaya Polyana for twenty-five years of friendship. I thank the division of Tolstoy's Personal Library and its directorship for providing an image from Tolstoy's Bible at my request and for granting exclusive rights for its one-time reproduction. Thanks also to the Library of Congress and the British Library for their help with procuring materials from the newspaper The Daily Chronicle.

To the Society for Textual Scholarship (2019, 2021) and the International Congress of Translators (2020), my appreciation for the opportunities to share my work in progress.

Special thanks to Dr. Galina Alekseeva, the head of research at Yasnaya Polyana, for her unstinting care and friendship, and to Ekaterina Tolstaya, the director of the Museum Estate at Yasnaya Polyana. Thanks to Anne Adriance, Valentina Bastrykina, Carolyn Vellenga Berman, Rita Breidenbach, Jeffrey Brooks, Stephanie Browner, Jesse Clagett, Jackie Clark, Ilario Colli, Juan De Castro, Caryl Emerson, Laura Frost, Barbara Garii, Natalia Kalinina, Paul Kottman, Bruna Lago-Fazolo, Orville Lee, Eleni Litt, Melanie Mabee,

Marjorie McShane, Julie Beth Napolin, Tatiana Nikiforova, Svetlana Novikova, Caleb Oberst, Donna Tussing Orwin, Dominic Pettman, Rose Réjouis, Vitaly Remizov, Andrew Reynolds, Jen Roth, Elaine Savory, Justin Sherrill, Michael Schober, Val Vinokur, Marta Werner, Jennifer Wilson, and John Young. Vitaly Borisovich, your friends miss you already.

A special word of gratitude to my copyeditors. Thanks to Dr. Joel Thomas Paxton de Lara for sharing generous insights and innumerable inputs about the best quality of the English sound of the final text—for being my first reader, a stern censor, and a source of constant reinforcement and productive critique, and for his devotion to lucidity in presenting philosophical thought. And to Veronica Dakota Padilla for her fruitful commentary and advice. And to Sasha Shapiro, once more, for overseeing the whole anthology and its formatting.

Thanks to my students at The New School for Social Research and Eugene Lang College of The New School. Thanks to the librarians at the List Library of The New School.

And to my family, thank you for being so patient and compliant (again!).

Credits

Of the seventy-seven texts included in this anthology, all the translations are by me, Inessa Medzhibovskaya, except for the following four pieces, which I have corrected, annotated, and updated as and where necessary (they are earmarked with an asterisk on the table of contents and in the text):

Entry 46: Tolstoy's letter to Alexander Macdonald (July 26, 1895), which was translated into English by Maria Lvovna Tolstaya and Leo Tolstoy and was published in volume 68 of The Jubilee edition of Tolstoy's Complete Works in 1954 (68:123-27). Copyright-free publication.

Entry 48: Tolstoy's article known as "Patriotism, or Peace" (1896), was originally published as "Count Tolstoy on Venezuela. Characteristic Letter (specially translated for Daily Chronicle)" with translation by Vladimir Chertkov and John Kenworthy, authorized by Tolstoy. (Daily Chronicle, March 17, 1896, p. 3). Daily Chronicle ceased publication in 1930.

Entry 49: Tolstoy's preface to the Russian edition of *Modern Science* by Edward Carpenter (1896), which was translated by Aylmer Maude and published in *Essays and Letters by Count Leo Tolstoy*, translated by Aylmer Maude (New York's Funk and Wagnalls, 1904), 219-29. Defunct publisher; no copyright reserved.

Entry 52: Tolstoy's introduction to a short biography of William Lloyd Garrison in the form of a letter to Vladimir Chertkov. This text was translated by Vladimir Chertkov and Francis Holah and published as "By Leo Tolstoy. Letter To V. Tchertkoff," in Vladimir Chertkov and Francis Holah, *A Short Biography of William Lloyd Garrison: With an Introductory Appreciation of His Life and Work by Leo Tolstoy* (London: The Free Age Press, 1904), vi-xii. No Rights Reserved.

As regards entry 43, my translation of Tolstoy's talk "The Concept of Life" (March 14, 1887), I would like to thank the North American Tolstoy Society, the *Tolstoy Studies Journal,* and the journal editor Michael A. Denner for their permission to reprint this reformatted material from my book: Inessa Medzhibovskaya, *Tolstoy's* On Life*: From the Archival History of Russian Philosophy* (Toronto: Imprint of the Tolstoy Society of North America and *Tolstoy Studies Journal,* 2019), 354-61.

Illustrations and Image Credits

Figures 1 and 4, L. N. Tolstoy, *Polnoe sobranie sochinenii v devianosta tomakh* [Complete collected works in ninety volumes], ed. V. G. Chertkov et al. (Moscow: Gosudarstvennoe Izdatel'stvo Khudozhestvennoi Literatury, 1928–58), 38:283. Public domain.

Figure 2, *Biblia ili knigi Sviashchennogo Pisaniia Vetkhogo i Novogo Zaveta* (St. Petersburg: n.p., 1862), 441. Courtesy of the Museum Estate Yasnaya Polyana [Muzei-usad'ba L. N. Tolstogo Yasnaya Polyana-Музей-усадьба Л. Н. Толстого «Ясная Поляна»].

Figure 3, The Daily Chronicle, March 17, 1896. Courtesy of the British Library [The British Library Board, shelf item MFM.MLD10].

A Note on the Text

Transliteration

Except for traditional spellings, I have followed with some minor modifications the Library of Congress romanization system for transliterating Russian and Cyrillic, for example, "Nikolai Berdyaev," "Afanasy Fet," *The Death of Ivan Ilyich*, etc. Soft signs were not used in the spelling of personal names (for example, "Lvovna," not "L'vovna"), but were used in the names of institutions and organizations as well as in terms.

Dates

All the dates of events that occurred in Russia before 1918, unless otherwise noted, refer to the Julian calendar (Old Style, for short) then in effect across the territory of the Russian Empire. All the dates in the same period pertaining to the writings, publications, and letters of Tolstoy's correspondents, critics, and translators in the West adhere to the Gregorian calendar (New Style, for short). On occasion, both calendar dates were necessary to mention in discussion. On these occasions, the first date given is from the Julian calendar, which is followed by the date from the Gregorian calendar in parentheses.

The Use of Angle Brackets

"<I felt astonished and admired everything that I was saying.>" Following Tolstoy's own practice, *The Jubilee* editors use angle brackets—as in the example above—to enclose lines and whole passages in Tolstoy's manuscripts specially earmarked for future consideration, perhaps for a possible inclusion in the fair copy. I have retained angle brackets for such portions of text to reflect their use in Tolstoy's originals.

Capitalization of the Word "God."

Tolstoy's spelling of this word is irregular, sometimes lowercase (*bog*), at others using a capitalized Б (*Bog*). The editors of the *Jubilee* received vague and non-committal instructions in this regard, and they chose a lowercase spelling as the definitive style in most volumes of the edition. I have used a capitalized standard English spelling "God" throughout this volume, adding a note to the text where necessary to indicate a potential conflict of interest between Tolstoy's intention and the impositions of the top-down guidelines from the Soviet publishing apparatus for the handling of religious vocabulary in print.

Crossed-Out Text

On occasion, the reader will notice a crossed-out sentence or two in some of Tolstoy's articles, most often in his earlier writings and philosophical drafts of the 1870s. There is no typographic error to be assumed when crossed-out sections are encountered: these are Tolstoy's own deletions. Always informative, they alert us to his hesitations and to the dynamics of his thinking method that thrived on self-critique and self-rejection. They show us the artist and thinker who demanded much of himself even when jotting down drafts.

Major Sources and Abbreviated Citations

Most of my translations of Tolstoy's texts are from *The Jubilee* edition of Tolstoy in ninety volumes: L. N. Tolstoy, *Polnoe sobranie sochinenii v devianosta tomakh* [Complete Collected Works in Ninety Volumes], ed. V. G. Chertkov et al. (Moscow: Gosudarstvennoe Izdatel'stvo Khudozhestvennoi Literatury, 1928–58). The first volume of the *Iubileinoe izdanie* (*The Jubilee* edition; *The Jubilee* hereafter) was scheduled for 1928, to coincide with the centennial of Tolstoy's birth. Unless otherwise noted, all references in the present volume to Tolstoy's texts in Russian are to *The Jubilee* and cite the respective volume and page numbers, separated by a colon. Where corrections of *The Jubilee* texts against the autographs, manuscript copies, or journal variants occur, they are explained and referenced in the notes accordingly.

System for Citing Periodicals and Institutions

All Russian publishing institutions, titles of collections, and periodicals are referred to by their Russian name in transliteration, with English equivalents provided on first mention: for example, Posrednik for the Publishing House Intermediary; *Tsvetnik* for the collection *The Flower Garland*; *Vekhi* for the collection *Signposts*; and *Voprosy Filosofii i Psikhologii* for the journal *Questions of Philosophy and Psychology*. According to the guidelines of the 16th edition of the *Chicago Manual of Style*, only journal titles have been italicized, while newspaper titles are not (for example, Novoe Vremia [New Time]). Russian organizations are referred to in translation after having first been mentioned in the Russian original, for example: "The Society of the Lovers of Russian Literature" for Obshchestvo Liubitelei Rossiiskoi Slovesnosti; and "The Moscow Psychological Society" for Moskovskoe Psikhologicheskoe Obshchestvo.

Editor's Introduction— "The Magic Mountain": On the Textual Shape of Tolstoy's Philosophy

> —What benefit do you get from philosophy?
> —What could be a better benefit than philosophy?

It surely looks and sounds like one, but the above-quoted exchange is not part of a philosophical dispute. This is an opening of an unfinished vita of Justin the Martyr spoken in common parlance, which Tolstoy intended for one of his Russian Readers. Before he answers this provocative question, the hero of the vita (entry 70 in this anthology) has already disavowed the legitimacy of stoic, peripatetic, Pythagorean, and neo-Platonic schools. In his experience, they all fell short of providing basic answers about one's place in life. The dialogue takes place on a deserted seashore outside the city gates. Questioning Justin is a prototypical stranger who is about to introduce and then convert Justin to Christianity, and his question to Justin already implies that a kind of wisdom superior to any known philosophy exists. Stranded much like Justin in his searches, Tolstoy is forty-six years old when he writes these lines in 1874.

Five years after completing *War and Peace*, at an earlier stage of his work on *Anna Karenina*, Tolstoy too addresses himself to predecessor questors and sages, seeking the meanings of living that can satisfy and comfort. These open questions on an open shore—here the vita breaks—augur new beginnings for Tolstoy's durative preoccupations with harmonizing, or bringing into a mutually dependent and cooperative sphere, philosophy, science, art, religion, social and political life, and history: "I exist. My existence is the sum of me plus the infinite plenitude of the world known to me and of what is in the process of becoming knowable," writes Tolstoy in one of the numerous philosophical sketches from the year 1875 (17:340).[1]

The essence of the philosophical question is this: what is life and what is death? (entry 28 in this anthology). In November 1875, Tolstoy shared some of these new auguries with a close friend—the thinker and writer Nikolai Strakhov (entry 30 in this anthology). There, he compares the journey for meaning—armed only with a compass of true, religiously focused philosophy for a set of carabiners, slings, and anchors—with climbing the magic mountain of life (*volshebnaia gora zhizni*). Standing on the peak of one's life after a difficult ascent allows for a maximal vantage point on everything. The clock is ticking. But the prospect of traveling down the slope during the descent and gaining a look at what lies at the base of the other side of the mountain promises an inviting homecoming.

***

A year before his death (1909), Tolstoy imagined and sketched a vision of integral knowledge represented in a sphere, his remake of a more traditional pie chart. Clockwise from the top of the sphere are the following forms of knowledge: Natural Sciences, Life [I], Religion, Verbal/Literary Arts, Philosophy, The Social, Life [II], and Mathematics.[2] At the top of the sphere is natural scientific knowledge. Life knowledge is situated to the right and is followed by religion and then the verbal arts. Philosophy is at the bottom of the sphere. In an upward-moving rising direction and to the left of philosophy is social scientific knowledge. Life knowledge—Tolstoy explains this as "active life"—shows up "born again" on the left of the sphere across from religion on the other side. Mathematics is situated at the next upward-moving position on the left of the sphere, returning us to the top with natural scientific knowledge. According to such a scheme, the even (or harmonic) distribution allows for the natural sciences and philosophy to be connected through a vertical line that cuts through the center of the sphere. The "born again" active life of an individual connects horizontally to religion. The "first born" life—explained by Tolstoy as "social life"—between the natural sciences and religion is diametrically connected to the social. Cutting through the center of the sphere from the upper left corner, the remaining diameter connects mathematics with the verbal arts.

---

1 **"Editor's Introduction."** Here and elsewhere, unless otherwise noted, references to Tolstoy's texts are to *The Jubilee* edition, with the volume number and page number separated by a colon.

2 See entry 58 in this anthology.

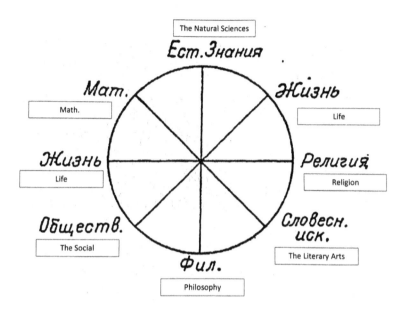

FIGURE 1. L. N. Tolstoy, *Polnoe sobranie sochinenii v devianosta tomakh* [Complete collected works in ninety volumes], ed. V. G. Chertkov et al. (Moscow: Gosudarstvennoe Izdatel'stvo Khudozhestvennoi Literatury, 1928–58), 38:283. Public domain.

All the participating elements of acquiring wisdom matter only if they cooperate; and without the right prioritization of them, there could be no meaningful application for either one's knowledge or one's search. Notice that on his diagram, Tolstoy does not grant the rank of the *Weltwissenschaft* (universal world science) to philosophy, the overweening queen at the university and the academies, the science of the sciences that obviates the importance of all the other disciplines. But none of its sister members on the circumference of the sphere are given queen-like status either. There can be no philosophy for philosophy's sake, just as there can be no art for art's sake, religion for religion's sake or science for science's sake. Philosophy is certainly at the bottom of Tolstoy's diagram: it is the convex base, the pillar structure, the foundation bowl. But one is born again to correct reasoning only after having passed through its crucible.

What Kant had styled *Der Streit der Fakultäten* [The Conflict of the Faculties] in his well-known eponymous book (1798) puzzles Tolstoy too. The inclusions in this anthology (for example, entries 20, 22, 23, 29, 29, 57-62) allow one to observe how decade after decade, by mostly painstaking judgment, Tolstoy struggles to regain the "university" of the disciplines. In their unyielding competition for dominance, the disciplines had lost the ability to cooperate and integrate knowledge. Tolstoy's sphere of redemption is neither a mere figure nor a scheme; it will surely have gaps and intervals (for example, entry 22) as if laid on a thread on which beads require constant readjustment. The truly universal knowledge gathered from essential sources blends with the vital sphere of integral being. "The narrow sphere of activity" can lead to catastrophic results (discussed using these exact words in entries 23, 57-62). Tolstoy admonishes and cavorts too: he was known to demonstrate in jest his principle of the pie chart on real cake stands, taking delight in doling out slices of only-what-you-have-deserved size to overconfident scientists and philosophers invited to his home for tea. He would literally cut back on their dessert portions to show them the proof and working rule of the pie.[3]

What is the good of philosophy—its benefit or utility? "Utility" (pol'za) is precisely the word used by Justin and the elder in the dialogue on the seashore. In 1907, the National Phonograph Company headed by Thomas Edison contacted Tolstoy with the stated intention of sending a phonograph to him should he, the greatest moral teacher on the planet, consent to using the machine to record his ideas. The dream machine from America reached Yasnaya Polyana in early 1908 and Tolstoy used it frequently to record his own and other selections of wise sayings—including the beginning of "I Cannot Remain Silent" (1908), his protest against capital punishment. Also sent from New York, a plea for help arrived suddenly in November 1908, which began: "Great Man! Lev Nikolaevich!" The message came from joiner Peter [Petr] Okhremenko, a starving Russian immigrant who was unable to find work in his trade as a metalworker.[4]

Spirituality for profit? Never mind. Without hesitation, Tolstoy asked Edison to hire Okhremenko in exchange for advertising his products, launching Okhremenko's career in the recording industry. The money-earning grooves on a sphere of a rotating record rarely provided such a direct barter for Tolstoy to spin his philosophical sphere. He frequently doubted whether it was too much

---

3   One such episode of "dessert austerity" policy during a tea ceremony with Tolstoy can be found in the reminiscences of Pavel Miliukov (1859–1943). As a young untenured lecturer in history at The University of Moscow, the future leader of Constitutional Democrats and the Minister in the Provisional Government fell victim to this policy near the samovar at Tolstoy's Moscow home. See Inessa Medzhibovskaya, *Tolstoy's* On Life: *From the Archival History of Russian Philosophy* (Toronto: Tolstoy Studies Journal, 2019), 55-56, 280. See Future Reading for a complete citation.

4   On the incident and the correspondence of Tolstoy and Edison, see "Perepiska Tolstogo s T. Edisonom," in *Literaturnoe nasledstvo*, ed. A. Sergeenko (Moscow: Izdatel'stvo Akademii nauk, 1939), 37-38:330–38.

or too little that is expected of philosophy, but he read it, wrote it, spoke it, and struggled for and against it his entire life. On the one hand, Tolstoy occasionally called professional philosophy an enemy of life and poetry; even the best representatives like Aristotle, Plato, Leibniz, Locke, Hegel, and Spencer did not deserve to be compared with authors of the true teachings on life like Zoroaster, the Brahmins, Buddha, Lao-Tzu, Confucius, and Jesus Christ.[5] On the other hand, Tolstoy participated in the work of Russian philosophical associations and published in their periodicals.[6]

The biography of Tolstoy's philosophy begins as soon as he begins to write: entries 1, "Childhood Fancies" (1835) and 64, "Apprentice's Writings" (1839–1941) were written by him as a prepubescent boy. In one reflection from 1847, the nineteen-year-old author was already looking back at his "cognitive history" as if it had lasted a lifetime, considering the contributions of philosophy to "welfare or happiness" (*blagosostoianiiu ili schast'iu*) along the route, never doubting that we might have been born for anything other than this:

> I here narrate my cognitive history since the time it commenced and prior to the time where its course was too simplistic and alike anybody else's. The striving that I discovered in myself was the striving for welfare or happiness, and that striving I could not understand otherwise than when these [two should] be manifest; they dissatisfied me when becoming manifest, however. Being delimited is not a concept but is consciousness: I am aware of the finitude and infinity, but I am [conscious of being] delimited and infinite. Having found many of the existing rules unsatisfactory, I have rejected them altogether and would accept for true only what I would draft for my own self out of what there were to be followed.[7]

---

5   See entry 61 in this anthology.
6   See further in this introduction and entries 43 and 45 in this anthology.
7   This reflection is a marginal comment added to an unfinished philosophical draft dated 1847 (see 1:227). "I here narrate": Tolstoy's phrase "ia izlagàiu" ("I here narrate"; "I set down here") is a canonical beginning for narratives of self-accounting in the literature of the nineteenth century featuring a young ratiocinating protagonist. Alfred de Musset's cultic *La Confession d'un Enfant du Siècle* [*The Confession of a Child of the Century*] published in 1836 (just nine years prior to Tolstoy's philosophical reflection quoted here) had solidified this fashionable formal habit among aspiring writers of Tolstoy's generation. De Musset uses "Je raconte" (Alfred de Musset, *La Confession d'un Enfant du Siècle*. Nouvelle Édition [Paris: Charpentier, 1867], première partie, chapitre premier, 1), which Robert Arnot translates "I here narrate . . .": Henri de Bournier, preface to *Confessions of a Child of the Century*, by

Tolstoy pauses, then continues:

> Activity is consciousness and is not a concept.—
>
> The cause of this is the activity that is in contradiction: if one of these original two elements did not exist, I could not even imagine activity to myself.—
>
> It follows from this inference that were it not for finitude, there would be no activity, and hence, the first consciousness is that of being delimited. (Ibid.)

The first consciousness is that of being delimited (*pervoe soznanie est' soznanie ogranichennosti*). There is nothing in the ready-made repertoire of philosophical science that the young Tolstoy would accept to help him extrapolate himself by force out of the deeply palpable limitations. He chooses the path of a long and difficult search for the fount of universal wisdom.[8] Discovering one's dissimilarity from others, one's uniqueness, is like creating one's own system of reference; that everyone who is finite and "delimited" is alike and yet not alike was an impetus for all of Tolstoy's future philosophizing in earnest. Of crucial importance for the appreciation of Tolstoy's originality since his youngest of days is his sensitive insight into the relatedness of consciousness to concepts: although he would later also use the other Russian word for "consciousness": *soznànie*. In his youth, however, he operated with the word *poniàtie* (notion), which in Russian is both a "concept" and a "conscious understanding." How do I relate to what is outside me? Do I impose my preconceived opinion on others? Do I allow myself to be imposed upon? This would be coercion, violence; what is needed is a conscious sense of integration with the life and the living that are outside me. On the ascent and descent of his long journey, Tolstoy learns and teaches others how to fuse the individual need for welfare and happiness with the same need but for all—the felicitous synthesis of purpose and presence in life, that for which we should live, and what he calls *blàgo*.[9]

Alfred de Musset, trans. Robert Arnot (New York: Current Literature Publishing Company, 1910), 1.

    In the most recent translation by David Coward, the phrase "I set down here" is also a very apt rendering. See David Coward, introduction to *The Confession of a Child of the Century*, by Alfred de Musset, trans. David Coward (New York: Penguin, 2013), 5.

8   Tolstoy would go on to write many other parables where this exact act is performed on the most resistant and obstinate non-believers by the magic and well-wishing hand of an external helper.

9   Henceforth, I shall frequently use this word in transcription from Russian into English and in italics.

**

For the first time in the history of Tolstoy scholarship, this book assembles seventy-seven essential texts that document the variety of the processes along the long route, from the very first records of Tolstoy's written *œuvre* that survive. There is, indeed, a cognitive history in place, the history of forming concepts out of the discoveries of one's consciousness. The seven-year-old author in entry 1 describes violent natural bestiary in contrast with the picturesque fineries of a domesticated barnyard. The last entry in the anthology is a lesson on vegetarianism that a hungry wolf teaches a hungry boy during their chance encounter when both are on their way to lunch.

The wolf discloses to the boy the cruel reality of the barnyard bucolics; chickens are separated from mother hens and slaughtered near the kitchen coop each morning to become soup ingredients. This tale from 1908 was composed by an eighty-year-old Tolstoy for his seven-year-old grandson (entry 77).

Totaling seventy-seven, the number of entries is a tribute to the principle of Tolstoy's sphere as the completed circle indicating the fullness of time. In chapter 9, verse 24 of the book of Daniel within his personal copy of the Russian Orthodox edition of the Old Testament, Tolstoy penciled in a blue vertical line in the right margin of the second column and underscored various individual words and phrases highlighting where Gabriel appears to Daniel in one of his prophetic dreams to announce the forthcoming remission of guilt: when the symbolic seventy-seven weeks shall transpire and the ram horn of atonement (*the yobel*, the jubilee) sounds to remit the transgressions and sins, at the time when the truth of the Messiah is established. (See Figure 2 at the end of "Editor's Introduction").

Throughout his critical study and devotional meditations, regardless of language, Tolstoy gave equal attention to the Hebrew Bible and the Gospels. In entry 47 in this anthology, "How Should the Gospel Be Read and Of What Does Its Essence Consist?" (*Kak chitat' Evangelie i v chem ego sushchnost'?*), written on June 22, 1896, in response to queries about his exegetic method, Tolstoy recommends that anyone reading the Gospels should underline with a blue pencil all that seems simple, clear, and comprehensible on the first reading. The words spoken by Christ should then be underlined in red to distinguish between the records of his direct speech and the narratives of the synoptics and John. He also recommends leaving unmarked all the words of Christ and the evangelists that appear incomprehensible on the first reading (39:115). Red underlining must be added in increments of increased understanding. As

Tolstoy further explains, his own copy of the Gospels bears his markings made "according to his understanding" (*sootvetstvenno moemu ponimaniiu*) (39:116).

The principle of seventy-seven arising out of his reading of the Old Testament is a great illustration of a sphere of knowledge. Tolstoy's underlining in blue pencil found in his copy also suggests his interest in the idea of forgiving to the end of time, which for Tolstoy is synonymous with living under the aegis of the eternal. Notably, Daniel 9:24 and 9:25 mentions the seventy years of desolation and despair during the reign of Darius, when Daniel feels deeply that the Jews of the covenant "have sinned" and "have gone astray." Daniel then begins composing a shamed apology to the Lord "for the trespass they committed against You."[10] Daniel later has a prophetic dream in which Gabriel appears and announces the remission of sins by explaining the symbolic meaning of seventy and seven. Unless interrupted by any new violations and transgressions, forgiveness will come after seventy-seven weeks of waiting (the human term for long, contrite, patient labor) and will continue in perpetuity (in the true eternity hinted at in the number seventy-seven and through the sanction of the arrived Messiah). The seventy-seven weeks of waiting will count (be sealed) toward the decreed moment. The book of Daniel sums up this mission as if "sealed to the time of the end": "(. . . Happy the one who waits and reaches 1,335 days.) But you, go on to the end; you shall rest, and arise to your destiny at the end of the days." (Tanakh, 1492).

The number seventy-seven also honors another resulting philosophical principle of Tolstoy's: a tenet about the number of the times we should forgive, which he borrows from Matthew 1:21-22 and puts in the epigraph sections in many of his works, including his last novel, *Resurrection* (and entry 62 in this anthology).

Tolstoy's open questions to philosophy and its sister disciplines in a wide array of philosophical fragments, drafts, notes, dated and undated personal reflections, dramatized dialogues, rare speeches made in public in the first 43 entries (parts 1–5) of the anthology (and entries 64-71 in part 8 containing philosophical fictions) account for the development of his thought before the age of sixty. The remaining 34 entries in parts 6–8 were written during the final two decades of Tolstoy's life, culminating in the very last lines about the quintessence of a meaningful journey through life in the proofs of his *Path of Life*, which were delivered to Tolstoy on his deathbed in Astapovo in November 1910 (entry 63).

---

10 *Tanakh, A New Translation of The Holy Scriptures According to the Traditional Hebrew Text* (Philadelphia and Jerusalem: The Jewish Publication Society, 1985), 1486.

***

When we say "Tolstoy and philosophy," among the first things to come to mind would be his major principles that are—in addition to the principle of forgiveness—very much enshrined in the history of thought: non-violent resistance and pacifism, vegetarianism and abstention from substances that cloud consciousness inducing hypnosis and self-delusionary entropy and from practices that whet excessive appetites;[11] the simplification (*opròshchenie*)—a variant of the future minimalism of today—of the conditions and habits of responsible living; the principle of non-doing (avoidance of what is wrong, useless, redundant, rash); the principle of non-participation in the life of the state and its institutions; conscientious objection; promotion of popular art and progressive education and their potential to unify people. These are philosophical principles that are supposed to be practiced in life and not simply theorized about, which is why they powerfully motivated important social movements of the twentieth century and their leaders, beginning with Mahatma Gandhi.

Based on what is currently available in English translation, readers might also associate with Tolstoy's philosophy some other time-honored things from his canon: the many philosophical digressions in most of his fictions and drama; the mesmerizing energy of *A Confession* (1879–1882); the recalcitrant aesthetics in *What Is Art?* (1897–1898); the progressive essays on education written in the 1860s; politically tinged pieces like the aforementioned "I Cannot Be Silent"; perhaps Tolstoy's response to the Holy Synod of Russia concerning its determination to excommunicate him in 1901 from the Russian Orthodox Church;[12] his collections of wise thoughts;[13] and perhaps even his diary, which has never been translated into English in its entirety, although it exists in a splendid two-volume selection listed in Further Reading. But most likely—and at worst for its author—one of those hefty tomes would come to mind: an intractable and hectoring treatise-length tract written in the old fashion, each individual chapter verbosely titled and foregrounded with domineering epigraphs from various scriptures.

---

11 "Why Do People Stupefy Themselves?" (1890) and "Non-Doing" (1893) are popular references in this regard.

12 The official pretext for this determination was Tolstoy's description of the liturgy to soon-to-be-sentenced prisoners, who were herded into a prison chapel for the purpose—something he described as a shameful farce in his novel *Resurrection* (1899). Also relevant here are the strongly articulated messages in writings such as "Religion and Morality" (1893); "Christianity and Patriotism" (1894); "On the Christian Teaching" (1896); "Thou Shalt Not Kill" (1900); and "On the Slavery of Our Time" (1900), to name a few.

13 *The Cycle of Reading* (2 vols. 1904–5; 1907–8); *Wise Thoughts for Every Day* (2 vols. 1907; 1910); and *The Path of Life* (1910).

Especially after he had reached the age of fifty in 1878, and entered what would become the last, thirty-year-long phase of his later life, Tolstoy did compose many of these momentous works of monumental size that also deserve new and improved translations before they can be properly judged, such as *The Harmony and Translation of the Four Gospels* (1880–81) with commentary, *The Critique of Dogmatic Theology* (1879–84), *What I Believe* (1882–84), *What Then Shall We Do?* (1882–86), *The Kingdom of God Is within You* (1890–93), *Christian Teaching* (1894–96), as well as long articles such as "The End of the Century" (1905).[14] What this anthology provides is different: the mostly unknown and untranslated, provocative, unexpected, somewhat "anti-literary" and yet delightfully artistic, playful, if a little arrogant and ironic and less iconic Tolstoy, an interesting, intense, absorbing thinker. This "other Tolstoy" is not a curious piece in a well-appointed scholarly vignette: it is an essential and, given the volume of it, an irrepressible part of him.[15]

Why is this part of Tolstoy—a huge part of him, really—still not well familiar to readers more than a century after his death? Despite the mass of literature that has been on the Tolstoy market in the West, his philosophy remains by and large *terra incognita*. Several factors are to blame. The first one is the sheer immensity of Tolstoy's written legacy.[16] The philosophical output proper occupies about sixty volumes out of ninety of *The Jubilee*

---

14 The best of these older translations are by Aylmer Maude, but these, too, require updating.

15 This side of Tolstoy recalls Gérard Genette's *Mimologiques: Voyage en Cratylie* (1976), the philosophy with shapes, voices, aspects, and sounds, the multidimensional world or several worlds at once. Gérard Genette, *Mimologics*, trans. Thaïs E. Morgan, foreword Gerald Prince (Lincoln: The University of Nebraska Press, 1995).

16 According to conservative calculations that I have recently conducted, Tolstoy wrote three long novels, leaving three others unfinished; some 140 short stories, sketches, and tales; twelve short novels (and novellas); seventeen plays and dramatic sketches; some eighty essays; 110 articles; roughly thirty protests and addresses; twenty or so drafts of non-fiction; about forty project notes for social causes and on methods of governance; some two dozen biographies of, and about as many prefaces to, the works of other writers; dozens of sermons and prayers; and he even composed poetry, even though he quickly understood that it would work best for him if he incorporated this poetry into his prose as embedded songs written by his characters or ethnographic specimens he ostensibly overheard during his travels. In addition to all of that, he wrote five travelogues; four sketches of reminiscences; gave four public talks; published two volumes of ABC books and four Russian readers; about a dozen collections of aphorisms and proverbs; and five books of worldly wisdom. Additionally, he wrote some ten thousand letters and—with the exception of the fallow years 1886–87, when they were sketchy or extremely short—Tolstoy kept diaries on a daily basis starting on January 27, 1847, until his departure from home in October 1910. His diaries occupy thirteen volumes out of ninety in *The Jubilee*. Inessa Medzhibovskaya, *L. N. Tolstoy*, Oxford Bibliographies (New York: Oxford University Press, 2021), https://www.oxfordbibliographies.com/view/document/obo-9780190221911/obo-9780190221911-0104.xml

(1928–1958). Even if we take *The Jubilee*, which is the most comprehensive existing edition of his works,[17] as our main source and the main indicator in one, it is itself very far from complete. And this is not to mention all the existing variants of the known texts. Entry 45 published in this volume, Tolstoy's article on the freedom of the will (1894), is simply absent from *The Jubilee*.[18] All the same, *The Jubilee* is true to its name, providing its own ram's horn of atonement for any of its sins, while remaining forever a monument of unparalleled achievement to the several generations of remarkable scholars and specialists on its heroic team.

Constituting the sole Soviet-era edition that did include the most complete array of Tolstoy's dangerous works in various states of expurgation and ideological massage, *The Jubilee* was initiated through a temporary truce between Vladimir Chertkov, the executor of Tolstoy's will (who died in 1936), and the writer's daughter Alexandra Lvovna, to whom Tolstoy entrusted his entire written legacy, its free dispensation, and interpretation, all of which were lost to the monopoly of Soviet power through its nationalization policies (Alexandra Lvovna defected in 1929 to the United States by way of Japan, never to return). *The Jubilee* edition neatly overlapped with the worst three decades of Stalinism and another five years that reaped its direct effects: continuous intimidation of scholars, systematic withholding of necessary resources, and the rush of the five year plans. All that the pressure from the *apparatchiks* "overproduced" were multiple errors due to the indefinite languishing of completed volume sections in the archives of party-controlled publishing institutions and to systems of ideological control that resulted in the publication of outdated or under-checked materials. The harsh realities of time necessitated the non-sequential release of nearly each of the ninety volumes from 1928 to 1958. Not until 1964 were the final revisions completed during the production of the Index.

On top of the sheer mass of material in Tolstoy's archive and the historical challenges that kept obstructing its release for decades, a "second blame" is attributable to Tolstoy. In 1891, he renounced all copyright, granting full rights

---

17 See Acknowledgments for a description of this edition.

18 The case with this entry is explained in note 304 (see annotations to entry 45). The history of *The Jubilee* edition is a complex story that I develop in a forthcoming monograph, *Tolstoy and the Fates of the Twentieth Century*, for Princeton University Press. My soon-to-be published chapter 34 on publications and editions of Tolstoy in *Tolstoy in Context*, ed. Anna A. Berman (Cambridge: Cambridge University Press, 2022: 281-88) provides a sufficient starting point.

to anyone who wished to publish their own renditions of his work in translation, without any consultation with him. He wrote:

> I grant the rights to publish free of charge in Russia and abroad, in Russian and in translations, as well as produce on stage all of my works that were written by me from 1881 and published in volume XII of my *Complete Works* 1886 edition and in volume XIII published in the current year 1891, as well as all of my works unpublished in Russia and all works that might henceforth be written following today.[19]

The result of this laissez-faire attitude was an unregulated dispersal of his work in English, about which Aylmer Maude, Tolstoy's best and most loyal translator, warned him more than once. Many of these flawed and downright erroneous translations are in fact those that a cursory reader is most likely to find when searching the internet for an example of Tolstoy's nonfiction available in the public domain. Still, this concern describes the situation with the better known, easily available works that could have attracted a few amateur transposers at one time or another.[20] Maude's own masterful twenty-two volume edition published through Oxford Classics (1928–1937)[21] for Tolstoy's centennial included both fiction and non-fiction (for the latter, he was never a devout annotator). Most of these volumes have been digitized. However, the catalogue of Tolstoy's works at Maude's disposal (who died in 1938) was restricted to the times prior to the release of the first volumes of the Soviet *Jubilee*. And thus, Maude simply did not get to see the vast majority of the original texts of Tolstoy's philosophy that are included in this anthology.

At the turn of the twentieth century, Tolstoy's fame in the English-speaking world rested on his radical political and religious philosophy, more so than his fiction. Echoing some common chords with Transcendentalism, Pragmatism, Buddhism, Confucianism, Taoism, and Fabian or Christian Socialism, the impact of Tolstoy's thought far outweighed that of his art. After his spectacular flight from home at 82 and a very public death in the spotlight of world media at the end of 1910, Tolstoy's reputation in the West as a thinker and theorist

---

19 *The Jubilee*, 66:47. Originally Tolstoy's disclaimer about relinquishing his copyright appeared on September 19, 1891 in Russkie Vedomosti [Russian News], no. 258 and Novoe Vremia [New Time], no. 5588.

20 Project Gutenberg and sites such as marxists.org are good examples of translations of this type.

21 *The Centenary Edition: Works of Leo Tolstoy*, 21 vols., trans. Aylmer Maude, Louise Maude, and J. D. Duff (London: Oxford University Press, 1928–37).

had been negatively affected by a combination of factors, starting with the partial and very unscrupulous adoption of his philosophy by the Soviet regime, and his lasting exploitation as a poster classic and a baptizing grandfather of the Socialist Realist canon. Because his teaching was engaged in the proportionate rearrangement in the hierarchies of the personal and the collective governance of life, Tolstoy was a dangerous and an intimidating rival to all systemic and totalizing orders. It did not help that émigré and dissident movements before the fall of Communism and the intellectuals of the post-Communist era are either deeply divided or very vague on how exactly they implicate Tolstoy in the two World Wars, the arrival of 1917, and their aftermaths. As a method of thought, such a characterization is reductive at best.

Whatever remains of the old pre-revolutionary sea of Tolstoy's radicalism in English are mainly the sporadic reissues of antiquarian editions. Tolstoy's hortatory and polemical literature, once so prevalent, is a noticeably less traveled terrain for today's readers because it did not recover from its sharp curtailment in the public sphere that had begun after 1917. In Soviet Russia and the Soviet Union, pre-revolutionary editions of Tolstoy's social and religious thought, themselves severely censored under the tsars, had been withdrawn from circulation and remained suppressed. Those who remembered enough of the real Tolstoy and shared this memory incautiously or, worse, persisted in living his way, were purged or silenced. Today, *The Jubilee* edition is digitized, albeit it remains unrevised, and Tolstoy's texts still wear a superimposed patina of Stalinism and post-Stalinism. The new one hundred-volume academic edition published under the auspices of the Institute of World Literature in Moscow has released nine volumes of Tolstoy's prose works since 2000, and one hopes that the Institute will gradually and eventually publish carefully verified texts of Tolstoy's philosophy (also see commentary to entry 11 in this volume).

***

What is included in this edition is—in the majority—the first-time publication in English translation.[22] My primary intention as translator and editor was to present the range, change, nuance, and continuity of Tolstoy's thought

---

22 Translated for the first time are entries 1-17; 19-29; 31-42; 44-45; 50-51; 53-54; 56-61; 64-70; 72; 77. Entry 43, "The Concept of life" is a slightly modified reprint of my translation from a very recent book (see Acknowledgments). Entries 18, 30, 43, 46-49, 52, 55, 62-63, 71, 73-76 have been translated anew and annotated. The four translations checked by Tolstoy but compromised by the publishing conditions of *The Jubilee* where they have been included have been corrected and annotated where necessary.

and, without any detriment to the amount or substantive input of annotations, to otherwise forgo excessive editorializing for the sake of allowing for a fuller presence—at long last—of the variety that is the philosophical Tolstoy, making this the fullest edition of Tolstoy's philosophy collected in one volume to date.

Selectivity was crucial. I strove to include whole shorter works that spoke to each other through every decade of Tolstoy's writing and opted out of "the bits and pieces" approach commonly employed in most existing anthologies where the wholeness of longer works is disrupted in favor of abridging the material selected from a wealth of incongruent lengths and fitting it into "themed" rubrics or topics. Instead, I pursued to present Tolstoy's discipline of thought that already possesses many philosophical disciplines within each text selection, such as economics, politics, education, psychology, or a subspecies of philosophy however broadly conceived [for example, hermeneutic interpretation, the human condition, the life of the mind, phenomenology of religion, epistemology, logic, moral philosophy, philosophy of religion, philosophy of history, political economy, political science, sociology, aesthetics, philosophy of education, philosophical anthropology, philosophy of life (*Lebensphilosophie*; a fashionable subspecies during Tolstoy's time), or one of the new directions of our time such as critical gender and race theories and ecological studies]. First among the reasons for rejecting the "topic-and- rubric" approach is that it violates Tolstoy's method of simultaneous concordance between the moments of truth in his "principle of the sphere." Second, as consultation of Tolstoy's diary, letters, and daybooks reveals, this approach is not how he tended to sketch his philosophical agendas. Instead, Tolstoy usually treats many topics and rubrics in one and the same writing sequence.

A good indicator of Tolstoy's fluid approach to rubrics and problems is his diary, which he kept almost without interruption from March 17, 1847 to October 31, 1910. Here is an entry made on March 24, 1900. Tolstoy is at work on two of his well-known longer essays, "Patriotism and the Government" and "The Slavery of Our Times." The surgery of his elder daughter Tanya overshadows what he was writing:[23]

> Tanya's awful surgery took place yesterday. I have understood quite certainly that all these clinics erected by merchants, industrialists, who have ruined and are continuing to ruin dozens of thousands of lives, are an evil thing. That if they cure one

---

23 Tatiana Lvovna Sukhotina-Tolstaya (1864–1950), Tolstoy's elder daughter, had to undergo an invasive surgery on her sinuses for a rhinological disorder. Tolstoy and lawyer Mikhail Sukhotin, Tatiana Lvovna's husband, were both present.

patient they will ruin hundreds if not thousands of the poor, it is obviously an evil, very evil thing. That they allegedly learn how to diminish suffering and to extend life is also not good because the means they are resorting to are such (they say "up until now" and I speak of the substance of it) that they can save and alleviate suffering of only a select few; and the main thing is that their effort is not directed at prevention, hygiene, the cure of the crippled—of whatever is going on constantly and incessantly.

He continues,

I am now writing *Patriotism* and *Monetary Enslavement* [*Denezhnoe rabstvo*].[24] I have much improved the former, but have written nothing the second day in a row. I am reading psychology. I am reading Wundt and Høffding:[25] very instructive. Their error and its source are obvious. In order to be precise, they wish to adhere to experience alone. This is really precise, but on the other hand completely useless. Instead of "psychic substance" [*substantisia dushi*]—I reject it—they posit an even more mysterious parallelism.

My simile has failed.

I should have said this: a man is riding a horse, he reins it in some, and the horse drives him on some. People watch on and think. Some say: "he reins the horse in"; others say: "the horse drives him on; his movement is the consequence of the horse's movement." The third ones, reproaching the former two, are uttering with self-importance: "there is parallelism between the movements of an equestrian and a horse: it trots, he bounces up and down from riding, the horse will stop, and he will stop." All of this may be, but the former two [explanations] and the third one all have zero interest. The only thing interesting here is whence and wither he rides and who has sent him on his ride.

---

24 See the full titles of the two works in the paragraph above.

25 Tolstoy was for a long time a curious, though mostly critical, reader of Wilhelm Wundt (1832–1920), the great physiologist, philosopher of science, and one of the founders of modern psychology. The other reference is to the Danish philosopher and theologian Harald Høffding (1843–1931), famous for his work on Darwin and Rousseau, but mainly for his studies on various topics of psychology. Tolstoy's spelling of Høffding's name (Koefding) is incorrect. The text of *Psychologi i Omrids paa Grundlag af Erfaring* (Sketches in Psychology Based on Experience) (1892) was available to Tolstoy in the Russian translation. For further details of Tolstoy's reading of Høffding, see 54:15, 18, 349, 413-15.

I have been thinking during this time:

1) fortune telling is *hypnosis* [*gadanie eto vnushenie*]: it is a promise that whatever you wish will come true and therefore the increase of energy for the achievement.

2) The striving toward unification, toward the liberation from division; love broadens the material and spatial confines; the activity of the mind destroys the limits of movement, the temporal ones.

3) There is no complete liberation (and therefore no complete freedom), but man gets closer to freedom the more unified he becomes with the infinite, free source of love and reason.

4) Hypnosis [*vnushenie*] is necessary and useful when it transmits to those who follow after us that of the more advanced content of what has been absorbed; but it is ruinous when the backward and the obsolete is transmitted to those who follow after us and is going to be further preserved in them.

5) All of our cares about the happiness of the people are much like what a man would do by stamping out young shots and crippling them and then tending to every tree and every blade of grass separately. This mainly relates to upbringing. Our blindness to the cause of upbringing is striking. (54:18-19)

This typically long reflection is far from finished: on the item numbered "6" Tolstoy switches to the topic of the conservation of energy and compares its patterns in nature and human activity. The day concludes on his reaffirmation of the universal connection of *I* and *All* (consider the 1847 fragments cited earlier in this introduction): "Consciousness that is reasonable is the consciousness of God. You only then understand yourself to be separate when you understand yourself to be universal. The concept of separateness could not have appeared without the concept of non-separateness. Consciousness destroys therefore the material limits through love, as it does the limits of movement through reason" (54:19).

And so, the thematic or subject divisions have proven themselves inadequate for rendering authoritatively in English such a mass of material—nothing truncated—in a single comprehensive treatment, through the process of conserving the energy and preserving the integrity of, Tolstoy's texts, the luxury of which for so long they have been deprived. Here, I have done this even though this was at times going against Tolstoy's own other grain in his rich anthologizing practice.[26]

***

In the 1860s, Tolstoy was busy putting together reading lists for his educational ventures. In the mid-1870s, he produced first readers, and, starting in 1886, was working steadily and constantly on creating anthologies with a specifically philosophical orientation. There are dozens of these, whether published in his lifetime or not, and all in a state of perpetual revision. In a typical letter to Nikolai Strakhov on November 16, 1887, Tolstoy informs his friend of a plan to compile a reader for school use out of Strakhov's philosophical works. These and similar editorial endeavors culminated with the more famous and later collections put together by Tolstoy in his final decade, for example, *Wise Thoughts for Every Day* (also *Thoughts of Wise People for Every Day*), *The Cycle of Reading*, and the magisterial *The Path of Life* published in the year Tolstoy died (1910).

In addition to compiling his books of world wisdom, starting in 1874,— in the mode of Justin's vita—Tolstoy wrote other cameo biographies of, and sketches on, the philosophers of antiquity, Buddha, Church Fathers, Pascal, Lichtenberg, Kant, Schopenhauer, Skovoroda, and Nietzsche, among others. He wrote words of commemoration summarizing the legacy of Russian philosophers (which was a nascent field in Russia, with first home-trained specialists graduating with professional degrees in this discipline from the mid-1870s). One of the highlights in this genre in the anthology is Tolstoy's note on Nikolai Grot, a longtime Chairman of The Moscow Psychological Society and editor of *Voprosy Filosofii i Psikhologii*,[27] the first professional philosophical journal in Russia.

It should not be forgotten that Tolstoy did publish his work in learned journals and philosophy journals, in particular: *What Is Art?* and two other shorter works first appeared in installments in *Voprosy*, which was edited by Grot. In addition to essays placed in philosophy journals, Tolstoy wrote informal reviews and responses about philosophical collections: for example, a review of *Vekhi* (*Signposts* [1909], entry 60), a legendary pre-revolutionary forum of the Russian intelligentsia.

Tolstoy responded to hundreds of correspondents with letters on diverse, encyclopedia-wide topics, providing his definition of revelation, the methodology and philosophy of science, pedagogical theory and practice, the concept of right, and so on.

---

26 On this, see my article "Tolstoy's Original letter Found: On Benedict Prieth, Ernest Crosby and Aphorisms of Immortality in *The Whim*," *Tolstoy Studies Journal* 22 (2010): 65-78.

27 See "A Note on the Text" in this anthology.

In all of these genres, but in his anthologies especially, Tolstoy felt—very strongly and vocally—that he could amend the texts of others through his own idiosyncratic paraphrase, and, beginning with his harmonization and abridgments of the gospels, frequently cutting, pasting, and rewriting them. He never thought of himself as a translator, but a transposer with authorial rights of his own in such endeavors. He also cared little if he was working off the originals perfectly accurately. It was more important for him to have a vision, and this, he believed, plain translations mostly lacked. What he shared with an acquaintance and temporary follower, Nikolai Ozmidov, captures this attitude: "Reinterpreters are inexhaustible, but so are true interpreters." Tolstoy puns on the Russian word "perevodit'sia" which can mean "peter out" and "be translatable." What matters, whether you translate or reinterpret, is to render accurately and in a readable way the core of the message that feels important.[28] As a translator, it mattered most for me to transmit with every accuracy the truth of Tolstoy's meaning in the sounds and phrasing that do justice to it in literary English to the extent that it allows Tolstoy to sound in his own voice, with no shortcuts or abridgments. In entry 58, "Religion and Science" (1908), Tolstoy mentions the detriments of a scholarly digest resulting in the loss of skills to read the grit of the originals (the healthy flour of knowledge being replaced with the unhealthy chaff passed off as flour, as he puts it).

For the scholarly objective, this anthology shall be supplemented by a monographic sourcebook on Tolstoy's philosophy, which will serve as a detailed survey of the disciplinary divisions, main themes, concepts, and genres of Tolstoy's thought, providing an in-depth, contextualized background, listing a rich array of sources for each entry, and plentiful cross-references. Including the main subdivisions that are important for the study of Tolstoy's thought, the monograph will explain his engagements with the big tradition; engagements with contemporary philosophy (Western, non-Western, and Russian); the reception of Tolstoy's philosophy in his lifetime; posthumous philosophical reception of Tolstoy; and Tolstoy's philosophical afterlife. Tolstoy on philosophers and philosophers on Tolstoy.

---

28 [*Re-interpreters ne perevodiatsia, no za to i ne perevodiatsia i istinnye tolkovateli*]. To Nikolai Ozmidov November 4, 1886 (63:405).

***

In practicing selectivity, preference went for the truly philosophical material that has never been translated, does not include what is longer than the set limit of words for each entry, and is not readily available elsewhere, albeit rarely with serviceable annotations.[29]

I have, however, included Tolstoy's commentary on Edward Carpenter's *Modern Science* (entry 49) in Aylmer Maude's translation, a text of a few pages that was truly essential in the 1890s for its connections with other entries on art and science throughout the anthology, not least for the fascinating backstory of its translation. While doing this, I have provided the first-ever commentary on this translation.[30]

Likewise, my retranslation of "Labor, Sickness, Death," "Three Questions," and "This is You" (entries 74-76) as one whole cycle is in keeping with Tolstoy's wish to donate all three of these tales—which he dubbed "Three Tales"—for the relief of the survivors and families of the pogrom victims of the Easter 1903 atrocities in the Bessarabian capital of Kishinev. Tolstoy wrote to Sholem Aleichem, the classic writer of Yiddish literature and compiler of the relief book collection *Gil'f* [*Help*], expressing a wish for the inclusion of precisely this composition of tales. However, Aleichem asked Tolstoy to swap "This is You" with a longer tale "The Assyrian Tsar Asarkhadon" (1903). Keeping the purpose of the collection in mind and the importance for the publishers of collecting the necessary proceeds, Tolstoy obliged.[31]

---

29 Not included in in this anthology is Tolstoy's "Letter to a Hindoo" (1908), a long and well-known letter available in a classic translation in public domain or a "Reply to the Synod's Edict of Excommunication," reprinted from older editions in the translation by Aylmer Maude in: Leo Tolstoy, *Last Steps: The Late Writings by Leo Tolstoy*, ed. Jay Parini (London: Penguin Books, 2009), 141-50. The same can be said of "The Destruction of Hell and Its Restoration" (1902–3), a longer philosophical parable, spectacularly translated by Robert Chandler in *The Lion and the Honeycomb: The Religious Writings of Tolstoy*, ed. A. N. Wilson, trans. Robert Chandler (London: Collins, 1987), 107-25. And of "Siddhartha, Called the Buddha, that is the Holy One . . . His Life and His Teaching" (1884–87), by Dragan Milivojević in his *Leo Tolstoy* (Boulder: East European Monographs/New York: Columbia University Press, 1988), 141-56.

30 Maude's reprints are customarily unannotated (e.g., *Last Steps*, 89-97).

31 Tolstoy wrote to Aleichem expressing his wish for the "Three Tales" composition on August 25, 1903. Eventually, Tolstoy published "This Is You" through the publishing firm Posrednik where it appeared as "Eto ty. Izlozhil s nemetskogo L. Tolstoy" ["This is you. Transmuted from the German by L. Tolstoy"] and published along with the story "Karma" in 1906 (74:168). Dragan Milivojevic translated the third tale as "It is You," having separated it altogether from the other two tales, which are not included in his collection (Milivojevic, *Leo Tolstoy*, 165-68). Parini published, uncommented, two tales of the three, as "Work, Death,

Concerning the brevity of some of the inclusions in this anthology, Tolstoy's love of the aphorism supports this decision. (At the same time, Tolstoy's own sentences are a great challenge to translators, for they often are exhaustingly long, and include multiple repetitions, frequent self-paraphrase, and various clauses bumping onto each other owing to a lack of conjunctions, correct punctuation, and other efficient, especially syntactic, reins). In one instance, he congratulates the English journalist John Kenworthy—he will figure in several texts and annotations for the 1890s—for his accomplished (and short!) critique of poverty by writing his own paragraph-long introduction to this work:

> "Excuse the length of this letter. I have not had time to make it shorter" wrote De Maistre to his King.[32]
>
> Nothing demands so much time and pains as brevity of treatment of a weighty matter, be it in a diplomatic letter or in a work of learning. Yet in the learned world, and consequently in society, an idea has found its way that only massive volumes can be works of authority.
>
> This little book stands evidence (sic) to the contrary. It not only offers the reader more solid matter than volumes upon volumes of works written on the same theme, but does what multi-volumed works on political economy do not do,—it states economic problems clearly and simply. Any one who reads this book with (sic) unprejudiced mind and sincere desire to find answers to the problems which confront people of our times, will find those answers, and will arrive at a clear understanding of things which most people imagine to be difficult and obstruse (sic). He will find also moral guidance and stimulation to good.
>
> We should all like our social arrangements better ordered than they are now. To move in this direction we must ourselves become better. It is the only way. There is no other.
>
> It is this simple truth, which, however, we always forget, that is with clearness and convincing power, set forth by the

---

and Sickness" and "Three Questions," both in the translation of Aylmer Maude (*Last Steps*, 192-99).

32 The political scientist, philosopher, and writer Count Joseph Marie de Maistre (1753–1821) is meant. "The King" must be the King of Sardinia.

present work. Yasnaya Polyana, LEO TOLSTOY. June 2, 1900. (O[ld].S[tyle].)[33]

***

Apothegmata, maxims, visions, pedagogic talks, programs and rules, and reminiscences are some of the multiple genres that represent the textual shape of Tolstoy's philosophy in this anthology. They often sport running theses, devices, similes—for example, the aforementioned well (or badly) milled flour for the healthy spiritual food—the oft-occurring phrase "this is astonishing!" that feigns surprise at the wrong practices of modern life; the already cited similes of the horse and the rider to describe the motivations and driving forces of a committed seeker, supplemented with those of the lantern and the walker, the sower and the weeds; the oars and the rowers. In nearly every text, we see the proverbial reappearances of adjectives and adverbs that describe as "indubitable" and "obvious" that which is only wishful. These are all the leitmotifs of Tolstoy's spiritual proprioception, his special orientation toward that unnamable and invisible "thing" beyond space and time. This proprioception finds its expression often in the private, non-mainstream philosophizing that is clashing against the immobility of the Cartesian *res cogitans*; that speaks most often face to face and behind the closed doors in his private writings with Kant and Pascal, but almost never with Schopenhauer, whom Tolstoy more gladly parades in the works that he hopes to publish. A lot of the inclusions in the anthology are referred to in Tolstoy's diary as "burnt," without having been shown to anyone. As Tolstoy noted in more than one place in this anthology (for example, entry 8), to form and cultivate his mind, manner, and style, a philosophical writer should know how to "scribble and strike out" [maràt']. (This thought is best

---

33 See "Introduction. By Count Leo Tolstoy" in John Coleman Kenworthy, *The Anatomy of Misery: Plain Lectures on Economics*, 2nd ed. (London: Trade Agents Simpkin, Marshall, Hamilton, Kent & Co., Ltd., 1900), 13. Several stylistic and grammatical comments are in order: "This little book stands evidence to the contrary" must be "This little book stands as evidence to the contrary" in standard English. Likewise, "Any one who reads this book with unprejudiced mind and sincere desire to find answers to the problems which confront people of our times" must be corrected to "Anyone who reads this book with an unprejudiced mind and sincere desire to find answers to the problems which confront people of our times ...." And now obsolete, "obstruse" must be replaced with "abstruse." These delightful infelicities must be indicative either of the state of Tolstoy's written English or of how trusting he was toward the accuracy and care of his English copyeditors.

expressed in his letter to literary biographer P. I. Bartenev [August 16-18, 1867; 61:176]).

The question of fragmentariness in these trial genres does not bother contemporary readers. This style presents an unusual side of Tolstoy that will hopefully be of interest to those who have read Kafka's *Blue Octavo Notebooks* or Wittgenstein's *On Certainty* and *The Blue and Brown Books* or who are interested in Borges's luminary anthologizing practices as exemplified in "The Aleph" (1949), or, to cite a more difficult attraction, Heidegger's quickly infamous ponderings and remarks in his *Schwarze Häfte* (*Black Notebooks*). Lovers of the genre of the human sketch will hopefully be stunned by Tolstoy's sleight of hand with the practices of the "nasty anecdote" in the vein of Dostoevsky of the post-Siberian decade in the 1850s and the 1860s, of Gombrowicz's grimaces from the tales of the times of immaturity, Kharms's incidents, Beckett's existential enigmas. I especially mean entries 68 and 77. Or, the truly astonishing amount of precis in the form of dreams and visions or hypothetical inquiries, entries 28, 29, 39, 66-67, 69.

There are many generic hybrids in the anthology, especially in the juvenilia part, as well as in the writings of the 1870s, the transitional decade to a bolder embrace of the religious art, for example, "A Conversation about Science" (entry 32) and "Interlocutors" (entry 36). We know that this trend will translate into Tolstoy's almost complete transition to shorter fiction and the genres of popular and legendary tale-telling from the mid-1880s going forward. This trend may either indicate one of the many lives of the reality of the novel in modernity recently advocated by Thomas Pavel[34] or it might reflect Tolstoy's assertion of the rights of alternative literary forms.

The question of the juvenilia must be addressed separately. Over and against the objections raised by Harold Bloom about judging the literary qualities of a young author,[35] I have included 12 selections by the young Tolstoy (entries 1-11 and entry 64). Here, with Tolstoy, we speak of the promises pretty much fulfilled. We can foretell in these writings the makings of the author of the future masterpieces. It is as if the boy Tolstoy enters into a room filled with cutout cardboard dummies and dainty *papier mâché* and breathes life into them.

The Barbos and Polkan diplomacy tale from 1839–1841 about two dog buddies leaping into a fight over a tasty bone thrown their way (entry 64)—they must be broken apart by a river of cold water—continue almost word for

---

34 Thomas G. Pavel, *The Lives of the Novel: A History* (Princeton: Princeton University Press, 2013).

35 Harold Bloom, introduction to *The Diary of Anne Frank*, by Anne Frank, new ed. (New York: Bloom's Literary Criticism, 2010), 1-4.

word in the drafts of Tolstoy's 1896 response (90:163-64) about the Venezuela crisis in 1896 (entry 48). The best buddies in question in the latter piece are Prime Minister of the United Kingdom Robert Gascoyne-Cecil, 3rd Marquess of Salisbury, and Grover Cleveland, the President of the United States. The fleshy part of the bone is Venezuela and its oil, the bone of contention in question is the Monroe doctrine invoked by Grover Cleveland to clash the "worthy rivals" and former friends should one of these friends suspect "a supine submission to wrong and injustice" that threatens "national sense of self-respect and honor." In this case, going to fight will shield and defend "a people's safety and greatness." [36] The thirst for fighting is just a "funny silliness" (*smeshnaia glupost'*) (90:163), as in the fight between Polkan and Barbos, for as long as it is only a playful perspicacity for starting a fray. But the invocation of patriotism as a holy principle calling on man to fight another man and on one nation to go to war against another is criminal. Before this criminal justification for war is eliminated, nations will keep fighting for a new bone. Hopefully, someone will be there watching with a bucket of cold water to separate them.

The childhood parable about a greedy beggar (entry 64) is developed in the mature statements on independence, love of work, charity and non-doing, the abstention from useless work (for example, entries 14, 15, 23, 24, 27, 39, 59, 62, 63, 69, 71, 72,73, 74, 75). Tolstoy's love of happiness and well-being that depend on the capacity of self-sacrifice and forgiveness show early in his description of the destruction of Pompeii, a devastating fire in Tula, and in the behavior of Marfa Posadnitsa (Marfa the Governor's Wife) who saves her political adversary Ionn from reprisal by an angry crowd (entry 64). Similar continuities can be traced throughout this anthology for other big themes of Tolstoy's philosophy. The index at the end of this volume will enable readers to identify and cross-reference these themes.

The Varinka tale (entry 65) is a great example of how Tolstoy translates the mundane into his pedagogic art. His coquettish seven-year-old niece—the prototype and the dedicatee—is mentioned more than once in Tolstoy's Moscow diary of the late 1850s. But the abundance of mermaids and water nymphs in the text aside, she is not a Nabokovian nymphette. What attracts us in this never-before translated piece—aside from its clear charm and the intimate tones of a tale written for the closest of kin—is its warmth of respectful, nonjudgmental care for everybody's field of vision. Not to mention that in the scenes at the

---

36 Grover Cleveland, December 17, 1895, Presidential speeches archive online, https://millercenter.org/the-presidency/presidential-speeches/december-17-1895-message-regarding-venezuelan-british-dispute.

theater and in the abandon of children's rituals and dreams we notice the shaping of the childhood scenes in *War and Peace* and *Anna Karenina*, of Natasha Rostova's visit at the opera, and the elaboration of the rudiments of Tolstoy's mature aesthetics, such as defamiliarization, alienation, the pros and cons of the hypnotic effect, and infection.

A quick word now on Tolstoy's satirical wit. In his bipartite historiographic tale-parable of the beehive (entry 73, "Two Different Versions of the History of a Beehive with a Lacquered Lid" (1888/1900), Tolstoy is hardly competing with Bernard Mandeville's *The Fable of the Bees* (1723) (see my commentary to entry 73). The tale relies as much on the Homeric epos. And on the contemporary detail. After a few years of heated arguing with composer Nikolai Rimsky-Korsakov about the art of the parasites and the exploiters, Tolstoy should not have missed an occasion to write a satire on Korsakov's orchestral interlude "Flight of the Bumblebee" ([Poliot Shmelia] opus 57) from the composer's newly finished opera "The Tale of Tsar Saltan" (1899–1900), a beloved musical tune ever since.

And another guess might be ventured in the same connection: that the name of the courtier Debe in Tolstoy's bee tale may have been prompted by a popular composition of Eugène Dédé, whose opus 562 on the theme of the bees and bumblebees in D major for the strings was a piece frequently performed at the turn of the century. It is not too far-fetched to consider Tolstoy's reason for acclaiming social justice through the means of his life-affirming satire on exploiters, slave-owners, and parasites, thanks to his perhaps becoming inspired by a lighthearted joke of a son of an African American composer from New Orleans.[37]

---

37 Tolstoy records his gripe against "an enormous number of people inhabiting this contemporary world of ours that have the arts and sciences for their permanent occupation (or what men call the sciences or the arts)," naming Korsakov's "Capriccio Espagnol" and "Scheherazade" among the parasites of art after noticing the announcements for new art performances and productions in Russkie Vedomosti [Russian News] for December 15, 1890 (30:234). During the final stages of the writing and editing of *What is Art?* Rimsky-Korsakov and the composer's wife paid Tolstoy a visit on January 3–4, 1898 together with art critic Vladimir Stasov. Tolstoy complained to his diary on January 4, 1898 about their "stupid talking about art" (53:176). Regarding Eugène Arcade Dédé (1867–1919), "Bees and Bumblebees," opus 562. The composer was a Paris-based conductor and author of popular music, son of the New-Orleans-born African American composer Edmond Dédé (1827–1901) who was trained and made a career in Paris. Dédé, Sr., was for many years assistant conductor at the Grand Théâtre in Paris. After marriage, he moved to Bordeaux where Eugène was born.

Tolstoy's composition glorifies the optimism of labor and creativity of the busily buzzing summertime of bees [*pchely*] and bumblebees [*shmeli*], and it does not pity the fate of the parasitic drones [*trutni*]. In this connection, Tolstoy's view on American and Russian slavery can be gleaned from entries 12-18 of the 1850s, entry 36 of the 1870s, and his preface to the American abolitionist movement in entry 53.

***

The structure of the anthology is simple and easy to follow. It illustrates a feature of every decade in which Tolstoy wrote: the central preoccupation of the 1840s are the self, freedom, searching for ways of engulfing the life of the All, testing as many forms as possible for self-expression, whether this be writing in French or Russian, taking notes on criminal law or critiquing the science of music, for confirming one's uniqueness. Tolstoy tests the internal motivation of freedom and the external motivation of violence, coercion. In the 1850s, Tolstoy is the self-proclaimed abolitionist (emancipator), the writings of this decade are characterized by an orientation toward social activity, they show Faustian tiredness with cold abstraction. The writings of the 1860s focus on progress, historical laws, and education as well as the issue of violence throughout everyday life and history. They signal the first mention of the direction given to history by Christ. There are records of Tolstoy's failed defense of the soldier Shibunin condemned to death. In the 1870s, we see a lot of unguarded searches for philosophical truth, unabashedly free in its expressions. Tolstoy's "sphere" is taking shape, especially after his having spent enough time with Kant in his room for faith. Philosophy is given direction, aim, purpose, task, and several urgent assignments. The 1880s are represented by texts that explain the importance for Tolstoy of the newly formulated law of religious action, which is not only about the literal *announcing* of the good news [*blagàia vest'*] in the gospels as would be synonymous with the meaning of the concept of the evangelical per se, but also the literal *making* of *blàgo*. Unlike the well-known longer works of this decade, the short selections in part 5 focus on the interior workings of Tolstoy's new Kingdom. The ethos of this decade is a forceful objection to a more traditional vision of organized religion and the gospels. The 1890s are mostly Tolstoy's responses to various commissioned requests which beg for his evaluations and stated opinion, often from overseas, in letters, prefaces, introductions—these are the *how-to* selections where Tolstoy explicates his own mature terminology, methodology, and position. The 1900s look back and sum up conversations from the preceding six decades: Tolstoy evaluates the problem of religious tolerance after his own ex-communication, compares his own method of doing philosophy with those of other sages, judges the methods of the new intellectuals, revolutionaries, and politicians for changing life. He outlaws certain models of social behavior, the desperate acts of suicide, addiction, bomb-throwing. He harshly calls himself to task and reminisces. How full of insanity the new century is. But live we must. Only about half of these articles Tolstoy shares or publishes, some of them are dictations into his Edison phonograph.

Finally, a quick note on Tolstoy's philosophical style. It is extremely dynamic, polyvalent, and pregnant with associations and connections. Yet, such style is rarely for the sake of playfulness and wit alone. Tolstoy impels words to illuminate the deeper meaning of what they designate; he lets them act beyond their narrow definitions. In entry 19, "On Violence" (1866), he begins by orchestrating a rhyming charade between the Russian words *sila* (meaning both "force" and "power") and *nasilie* (meaning both "violence" and "coercion"). This game is then followed by another charade with the double meaning of the Russian word *otnositel'no*, which can mean both "relative to/concerning" and also "somewhat," doing so to underscore the relativity of justice in human societies that leads them to violence. Tolstoy is not trying to disabuse his audience of the notion of justice. Rather, his disambiguation is different: despite its dialectical passages and transmigrations, this justice can never be absolute in human hands and, consequently, can be abused under the cover of justice. In another example in entry 50, "On Religious Tolerance" (1901), Tolstoy obligates both churchmen and laity to do as they preach within their ecumenical space. By choosing *ispovedniki tserkvi* (those who profess their belonging to a church, its adepts), he activates the polyvalent meanings of the Russian word *ispovednik* ("confessant, confessor," someone who professes something) to compel those who claim to be believers to choose religion as a form of open community representing the aspirations of larger society and human brotherhood over the church, which is only the institutional hand of the modern state (a closed commune of the like-minded and an example of a nationalistic and intolerant society).

Tolstoy's philosophical terminology is not scientific, its insights are not what we would consider traditionally philosophical. Justin the Martyr uses a lot of these terms in Tolstoy's vita of him: the seeing of the holiness of ideas, the knowing of the spiritual, the thinking of the divine, the believing in the "religion-faith," the practicing of reasonable consciousness versus rational consciousness. The purpose of this anthology is to call attention to these peculiarities through Tolstoy's immediate usage, the way he explained some of them to poet Afanasy Fet in the announcement of his new Christian worldview (Fet was then at work on the translation into Russian of Schopenhauer's *Die Welt als Wille und Vorstellung* [*The World as Will and Representation*] *Mir kak volia i predstavlenie*, 1881). Tolstoy writes, "Bentham the wise[38] states that only self-interest [*intérêt*] and pleasure [*plaisir*] will urge a human being to do anything. Christ has gone a bit deeper with this (according to my reason). The whole book with his teaching is called: the announcement of *blàgo*; it is all filled with only that which shows the features of an indubitable *blàgo*."[39] "What is the benefit of the gospel announcement" (*chto mne daet Evangelie*; 63:29), and "the foretelling of the good news?" Tolstoy asks (63:29). The good news of the gospels [*blagàia vest'*] is for doing good with submission and love. Regarding the philosophical dispute between Jesus and the devil in the desert, this is a dialogue of an open choice as Tolstoy sees it: "Neither Jesus has won nor the devil, but each has expressed their foundations" (63:27). Tolstoy agrees that there is no dialectics in the Hegelian sense in his choice of an answer, that his scheme for choosing the one and only *blàgo* amid the myriad of enticing pleasures on the cycle of life is really "the figure of a sphere" [*eta figura est' krug*] (63:26).

Circling back to where we started this discussion about Tolstoy's philosophical sphere: What is the utility and the benefit of having access to an artist's philosophy? On a simple practical level, teachers assigning their students "Story of One Appointment" (2018), a recent film describing Tolstoy's defense of Vasilii Shibunin, directed by Avdotya Smirnova, can now read the background texts in translation.[40] Similarly, students reading Tolstoy's great fiction can now consult his concurrent writings in other genres. But how should they relate to it on a more existential level, given when Tolstoy looks at his own writings and sees in them a form of activity that is part of his life's deed (*dèlo zhizni*)? The Russian word *dèlo* can have the solemn meaning of "vocation" or "calling," but it can also be translated neutrally as "thing." Or more practically, as "business." Lo and behold, despite his best effort, Tolstoy's parable about the three questions (entry 75) is used in the instruction of best practices at business schools in today's Russia.

---

38 "Bentham the wise" (*Bentham mudrets*) is Tolstoy's ironical appellation for the venerable father of utilitarianism.

39 A surviving draft of the letter to Fet of October 10–15, 1880 (63:25).

40 See entries 23 and 57 in this anthology. I mean "Story of one Appointment" (Istoriia Odnogo Naznacheniia), STV Film Company, 2018. Directed by Avdotya Smirnova; screenwriting by Pavel Basinsky, Anna Parmas, and Avdotya Smirnova; with Aleksey Smirnov starring in the role of Grigory Kolokoltsev, Filip Gurevich in the role of Vasilii Shibunin, Yevgeny Kharitonov as Tolstoy, and Irina Gorbacheva as Sophia Tolstaya. The appointment in question is that of Grisha Kolokoltsov (see entry 57).

All the arguments for and against the utility of the artist's philosophy and its consequences in an anthology like this are unlikely to rewrite Tolstoy's reputation as one of history's greatest artists. My best hope is modest: that the philosophical side of Tolstoy will be appreciated more by becoming better known. The reader could do with it what Tolstoy recommended in 1896 that we do with the gospels (entry 47): read it using red and blue pencils to mark what is good and suitable and strike out what does not appeal. We can alternatively take our cue from Thomas Mann who may have borrowed Tolstoy's metaphor of the magic mountain of life to write his masterpiece. There is the irritation about the "namby-pamby nonsense" inspired by the useless questions in the enigmatic "Russian texts." In a glorious ecstasy of the young shipbuilder and everyman Hans Castorp, curiosity becomes excessive and wins over. The Magic Mountain it is. Let it be.[41]

---

41 The explanation of this link belongs in my forthcoming book. See especially chapter 5 and its research ("Forschungen") into the "humaniora" about the life that we love to the utmost yet both know and do not know it. Thomas Mann, *Der Zauberberg. Roman* (Frankfurt-am-Main: Fischer, 2004), esp. 368-94. See also the following English translation: Thomas Mann, *The Magic Mountain*, trans. John Woods (New York: Vintage, 1995), 262-81.

ПРОРОКА ДАНІИЛА

у҃ма

ти въ зако́нѣхъ є҆гѡ̀, и҆́хже дадѐ пред̾
лице́мъ на́шимъ рꙋко́ю ра̑бъ свои́хъ про-
а҃і рокѡ́въ. И҆ ве́сь Ї҆и҃ль престꙋпѝ зако́нъ
тво́й, и҆ ᲂу҆клони́шасѧ є҆́же не послꙋ́ша-
ти гла́са твоегѡ̀: и҆ прїи́де на ны̀ клѧ́т-
ва, и҆ заклѧ́тїе впи́саное въ зако́нѣ
Мѡѷсе́а ра̑ба Бж҃їа, ꙗ҆́кѡ согрѣши́-
в҃і хомъ є҆мꙋ̀. И҆ ᲂу҆ста́ви словеса̀ своѧ̑,
ꙗ҆̀же глаго́ла на ны̀, и҆ на сꙋдїй на́шихъ,
и҆̀же сꙋди́ша на́мъ, навестѝ на ны̀ ѕла̑ѧ
вели̑каѧ, ꙗ҆ковы́хъ не бы́сть под̾ всѣ́мъ
нб҃се́мъ, по [всѣ́хъ] бы́вшыхъ во І҆ерꙋ-
г҃і сали́мѣ, ꙗ҆́коже є҆́сть пи́сано въ за-
ко́нѣ Мѡѷсе́овѣ, всѧ̑ ѕла̑ѧ сїѧ̑ прїи-
до́ша на ны̀: и҆ не помоли́хомсѧ лицꙋ̀
Гд҃а Бг҃а на́шегѡ, ѡ҆брати́тисѧ ѿ не-
пра́вдъ на́шихъ, и҆ є҆́же смы́слити во
д҃і все́й и҆́стинѣ твое́й [Гд҃и]. И҆ ᲂу҆бꙋди́сѧ
Гд҃ь Бг҃ъ на ѕло́бꙋ на́шꙋ, и҆ наведѐ сїѧ̑
на ны̀, ꙗ҆́кѡ пра́веденъ Гд҃ь Бг҃ъ на́шъ
во все́мъ дѣѧ́нїи свое́мъ, є҆́же сотворѝ
є҃і и҆ не послꙋ́шахомъ гла́са є҆гѡ̀. И҆ ны́-
нѣ, Гд҃и Бж҃е на́шъ, и҆́же и҆зве́лъ є҆сѝ
лю́ди твоѧ̑ ѿ землѝ Є҆гѵ́петскїѧ рꙋ-
ко́ю крѣ́пкою, и҆ сотвори́лъ є҆сѝ себѣ̀
самомꙋ̀ и҆́мѧ, ꙗ҆́коже де́нь се́й, согрѣ-
ѕ҃і ши́хомъ, беззако́нновахомъ. Гд҃и,
всѣ́мъ поми́лованїемъ твои́мъ, да ѿвра-
ти́тсѧ ꙗ҆́рость твоѧ̀, и҆ гнѣ́въ тво́й ѿ
гра́да твоегѡ̀ І҆ерꙋсали́ма, ѿ горы̀ ст҃ы́ѧ
твоеѧ̀: ꙗ҆́кѡ согрѣши́хомъ непра́вдами
на́шими, и҆ беззако́нїемъ ѻ҆ц҃ъ на́шихъ,
з҃і І҆ерꙋсали́мъ, и҆ лю́дїе твои́ во ᲂу҆кори́знꙋ
бы́ша во всѣ́хъ ѡ҆кре́стныхъ на́съ. И҆
ны́нѣ, Гд҃и Бж҃е на́шъ, ᲂу҆слы́ши мо-
ли́твꙋ ра̑ба твоегѡ̀, и҆ проше́нїе є҆гѡ̀,
и҆ ꙗ҆вѝ лицѐ твоѐ на ст҃и́лище твоѐ ѡ҆пꙋ-
и҃і стѣ́вшее, тебѐ ра́ди, Гд҃и. Приклонѝ,
Гд҃и Бж҃е мо́й, ᲂу҆́хо твоѐ, и҆ ᲂу҆слы́ши,
ѿве́рзи ѻ҆́чи твои́, и҆ ви́ждь потребле́-
нїе на́ше, и҆ гра́да твоегѡ̀, въ не́мже
призва́сѧ и҆́мѧ твоѐ: ꙗ҆́кѡ не на на́ша
пра̑вды [ᲂу҆пова́юще] поверга́емъ моле́-
ѳ҃і нїе на́ше пред̾ тобо́ю, но на щедрѡ́ты
твоѧ̑ мнѡ́гїѧ, Гд҃и. Оу҆слы́ши Гд҃и, ѡ҆чи́-
сти Гд҃и, вонмѝ Гд҃и, и҆ сотворѝ, и҆ не
закоснѝ тебѐ ра́ди, Бж҃е мо́й, ꙗ҆́кѡ и҆́мѧ

твоѐ призва́сѧ въ гра́дѣ твое́мъ, и҆ въ
лю́дехъ твои́хъ. Є҆ще́ же мѝ глаго́лю-
к҃ щꙋ, и҆ молѧ́щꙋсѧ, и҆ и҆сповѣ́дающꙋ грѣхѝ моѧ̑, и҆ грѣхѝ люде́й мои́хъ Ї҆и҃лѧ, и҆
припа́дающꙋ съ моле́нїемъ мои́мъ пред̾
Гд҃емъ Бг҃омъ мои́мъ, ѡ҆ горѣ̀ ст҃ѣ́й
є҆гѡ̀: И҆ є҆щѐ глаго́лющꙋ мѝ въ моли́твѣ, и҆
и҆ сѐ мꙋ́жъ Гаврїи́лъ, є҆го́же ви́дѣхъ въ
видѣ́нїи мое́мъ въ нача́лѣ, парѧ́щь,
и҆ прикоснꙋ́сѧ мнѣ̀, а҆́ки въ ча́съ же́ртвы
вече́рнїѧ, И҆ вразꙋми́ мѧ, и҆ глаго́ла ко мнѣ̀,
мнѣ̀, и҆ речѐ: Данїи́ле, ны́нѣ и҆зыдо́хъ
ᲂу҆стро́ити тебѣ̀ ра́зꙋмъ. Въ нача́лѣ к҃г
моли́твы твоеѧ̀ и҆зы́де сло́во, и҆ а҆́зъ
прїидо́хъ возвѣсти́ти тебѣ̀, ꙗ҆́кѡ мꙋ́жъ
жела́нїй є҆сѝ ты̀, размы́сли ѡ҆ словесѝ,
и҆ разꙋмѣ́й въ ꙗ҆вле́нїи. Се́дмьдесѧтъ к҃д
седми́нъ сократи́шасѧ ѡ҆ лю́дехъ твои́хъ,
и҆ ѡ҆ гра́дѣ твое́мъ ст҃ѣ́мъ, ꙗ҆́кѡ да ѡ҆-
бетша́етъ согрѣше́нїе, и҆ сконча́етсѧ
грѣ́хъ, и҆ запеча́таютсѧ грѣси̑, и҆ загла́-
дѧтсѧ непра̑вды, и҆ ѡ҆чи́стѧтсѧ беззакѡ́-
нїѧ, и҆ приведе́тсѧ пра́вда вѣ́чнаѧ: и҆
запеча́таетсѧ видѣ́нїе и҆ проро́къ, и҆
пома́жетсѧ Ст҃ы́й ст҃ы́хъ. И҆ ᲂу҆вѣ́си и҆ к҃є
ᲂу҆разꙋмѣ́еши: ѿ и҆схо́да словесѐ, є҆́же
ѿвѣща́ти, и҆ є҆́же согради́ти І҆ерꙋсали́мъ,
да́же до Хр҃та̀ Старѣ́йшины седми́нъ
се́дмь, и҆ седми́нъ шестьдесѧ́тъ двѣ̀: и҆
возврати́тсѧ, и҆ согради́тсѧ сто́гна, и҆
забра̑ла, и҆ и҆стоща́тсѧ лѣ́та. И҆ по к҃ѕ
седми́нахъ шести́десѧти двꙋ́хъ потре-
би́тсѧ *пома́занїе, и҆ сꙋ́дъ не бꙋ́детъ
въ не́мъ: гра́дъ же и҆ ст҃о́е разсы́плетсѧ
со Старѣ́йшиною грѧдꙋ́щимъ, и҆ по-
требѧ́тсѧ а҆́ки въ пото́пѣ, и҆ до конца̀
ра́ти сокраще́нныѧ чи́номъ поги́бельми.
И҆ ᲂу҆тверди́тъ завѣ́тъ мнѡ́зѣмъ сед- к҃з
ми́на є҆ди́на: въ по́лъ же седми́ны ѿи́-
метсѧ же́ртва и҆ возлїѧ́нїе, и҆ во ст҃и́-
лищи ме́рзость запꙋстѣ́нїѧ бꙋ́детъ, и҆
да́же до скончанїѧ вре́мене сконча́нїе
да́стсѧ на ѡ҆пꙋстѣ́нїе.

_____

* Є҆вр: Мессі́а.

р҃и

Figure 2. Tolstoy's notations concerning number seventy-seven in the Book of Daniel. Courtesy of the Tolstoy Museum Estate at Yasnaya Polyana (Muzei-usad'ba L. N. Tolstogo Yasnaya Polyana-Музей-усадьба Л. Н. Толстого «Ясная Поляна»), 2021.

Commentary to Figure 2

Quote occurs on page 441 in the edition cited below:

> *Biblia ili knigi Sviashchennogo Pisaniia Vetkhogo i Novogo Zaveta.*
> Biblia sirech knigi Sviashchennogo Pisaniia, Vetkhogo Zaveta,
> Grecheskomu Bogomudrykh sedmidesiati dvoikh tolkovnikov
> prevodu, Novogo zhe, samonachalnomu sviatykh Apostol pis-
> meni, tshchatel'nee i vernee ot prezhdepechatannoi (1663)
> goda v tsarstvuiushchem grade Moskve, na Slavianskom iazyke
> vo vsem soglashennaia, i v chem potreba be, ispravlennaia:
> nyne napechatasia v Bogospasaemom tsarstvuiushchem grade
> Sviatogo Petra, v leto ot sozdaniia mira 7370, ot Rozhdestva zhe
> vo ploti Boga Slova 1862, Indikta 5, mesiatsa Septemvriia, 639
> str. + 3 l.

[*The Bible or the Books of Holy Scripture of the Old and New Testament.* The Bible
or the Holy Scripture of the Old Testament, translation of the Greek Septuagint
by seventy-two textual scholars learned in God. The New Testament based on
the original texts by the saint apostles. The verified and corrected edition of the
earlier version published in 1663 in Moscow, the seat of the czars, written in, and
abiding to the Slavic tongue. Corrected where necessary, now being published
in the reigning City of Saint Peter, in the Savior's protectorate, in the year 7370
since the beginning of time, on the fifth of September in the year 1862 since the
incarnation of God through the birth of the Word in the flesh. 639 pp + 3 leaves].

The description of this edition in Tolstoy's personal library can be found in
Bulgakov, V. F. et al. *Biblioteka L. N. Tolstogo v Iasnoi Poliane. Bibliograficheskoe
Opisanie* [The Library of L. N. Tolstoy at Yasnaya Polyana: A Bibliographic
Description], parts 1, 2, and 3 (Moscow: Kniga, 1972–2000), 96. The text
underlined by Tolstoy is this:

> Sedmdesiat sedmin sokratishesia v liudekh tvoikh, i v grade
> tvoem s/via/tem, tako da o/b/vetshaet sogreshenie, i skon-
> chaetsia grekh, i zapechatleiutsia grekhi, izgladiatsia nepravdy,
> i ochistiatsia bezzakoniia, i privedetsia pravda vechnaia: i zape-
> chataetsia videnie i prorok, i pomazhetsia S/via/tyi s/via/tykh.
> I ub/o/esi i urazumeishi: u iskhoda slovese, iezhe obeshchati, i
> ezhe sograditi Ierusalim, dazhe do Kh/ri/sta Stareishiny sedmin
> sedm', i sedmin shest'desiat dve: /i vozvratitsia, i sograditsia
> stogna, i zabrala, i istoshchatsia leta/. (*Biblia* 1862, 441).

There is a footnote in this copy of the Bible at the bottom of the page that points to the translated choice of "Christ" in place of the "Hebrew: Messiah" (ibid.).

The Modern Russian version of the book of Daniel (9:24-25):

> 9:24. Sem'desiat sed'min opredeleny dlia naroda tvoego i sviatogo goroda tvoego, chtoby pokryto bylo prestuplenie, zapechatany byli grekhi i zaglazheny bezzakoniia, i chtoby privedena byla pravda vechnaia i zapechatany byli videnie i prorok, i pomazan byl Sviatyi sviatykh. 25. Itak znai i razumei: s togo vremeni, kak vyidet povelenie o vosstanovlenii Ierusalima, do Khrista Vladyki sem'sed'min i shest'desiat dve sed'miny; i vozvratitsia narod i obstroiatsia ulitsy i steny, no v trudnye vremena. ("Kniga proroka Daniila" (861-877), in *Biblia. Knigi Sviashchennogo Pisaniia Vetkhogo i Novogo Zaveta. Kanonicheskie* [Moscow: Izdatel'stvo Vsesoiuznogo Soveta Evangel'skikh Khristian-Baptistov, 1968], 874).

Minor prophets of the Tanakh (Kethuvim, the book of Daniel 9:24-25):

> Seventy weeks have been decreed for your people and your holy city until the measure of transgression is filled and that of sin complete, until iniquity is expiated, and eternal righteousness ushered in; and prophetic vision ratified, and the Holy of Holies anointed. You must know and understand: From the issuance of the word to restore and rebuild Jerusalem until the /time of the/ anointed leader in seven weeks; and for sixty-two weeks it will be rebuilt, square and moat, but in a time of distress. (*Tanakh, A New Translation of The Holy Scriptures According to the Traditional Hebrew Text* [Philadelphia and Jerusalem: The Jewish Publication Society, 1985], 1487).

Modern English translation (*The Oxford Bible*):

> 9:24. Seventy weeks are decreed for your people and your holy city: to finish the transgression, to put an end to sin, and to atone for iniquity, to bring in everlasting righteousness, to seal both vision and prophet, and to anoint a most holy place. 25. Know therefore and understand: from the time that the word went out to restore and rebuild Jerusalem until the time of the anointed

prince, there shall be seven weeks; and for sixty-two weeks it shall be built again with streets and moat, but in a troubled time." (Bruce M. Metzger and Ronald E. Murphy, eds., *Bible with the Apocryphal/Deuterocanonical Books* [New York: Oxford University Press, 1994], 1142-1143).

Metzger and Murphy explain that it is primarily about a place, not a prince, not a person: referring to Antiochus who with the help of Hellenizing Jews laid waste to the city and desecrated its temples, "the prince who is to come" is the admonition in some corrupt translations about the foretold desolations to Jerusalem (see footnote p. 1143). In the Hebrew Bible, one week usually means seven years, seven weeks is forty-nine years, sixty-two weeks is 434 years, etc. (*Oxford Bible*, OT, 1143).

FRAGMENTS, LETTERS, NOTES, REFLECTIONS, AND TALKS

PART 1

Tolstoy's Juvenilia (1835–50)

1. Childhood Fancies[1]
[1835]

First Division: Natural History

1. The Eagle: The eagle is the tsar of the birds. They say that once upon a time a boy started teasing him but that he grew angry and pecked the boy to death.
2. The Falcon: The falcon is a very useful bird which hunts for gazelle. The gazelle is an animal that runs so fast that dogs can't capture it; but the falcon descends and kills the gazelle.
3. The Owl: The owl is a very powerful bird. It cannot see when the sun is out. The eagle owl and the owl are the same. The eagle owl differs only thanks to its little horns.

---

1   **Part 1: Tolstoy's Juvenilia (1835–1850). Entry 1. "Childhood Fancies"** [*Detskie Zabavy*] (1835). From the journal *Childhood Fancies* [*Detskie Zabavy*], founded in 1834 by the young Tolstoy brothers. Tolstoy wrote the entries on nature describing the owl, the parrot, the peacock, the colibri, and the rooster. His elder brothers Nikolai, Dmitry, and Sergey wrote on a variety of other topics in their homework assignments. The fragments of the journal were first published in 1912, though the manuscript of this handwritten journal has not survived. A photograph of the cover of the original, which has survived, was signed as follows: "Written by Count Nikolai Nikolaevich Tolstoy, Sergey Nikolaevich Tolstoy, Dmitry Nik. Tolstoy; Lev Nikolaevich Tolstoy." Tolstoy's authorship is confirmed by an inscription on the obverse of the cover: "*The First Division: Natural History*. Written by C[ount] L[eo] Ni[kolaevich] To[lstoy]. 1835." (Pisano G L: Ni: To. 1835). Tolstoy was seven or eight years old at the time of writing. When writing his first entry, he must have been inspired by Prophet Isaiah, who had a similar vision of the tsar of the birds and was teased by other children. Tolstoy's propensity to challenge power and authority is already clear: the two-headed eagle is also the symbol of the Russian Empire. The first three entries ("The Eagle," "The Falcon," and "The Owl") appeared in volume 1 of *The Jubilee* in 1928 (1:213) and were edited by Aleksey Evgenievich Gruzinsky (1858–1928; henceforth, A. E. Gruzinsky or Gruzinsky), a veteran scholar from

4. The Parrot: The parrot is a very beautiful bird that has either a flat or a crooked nose, and people teach it how to talk.

5. The Peacock: The peacock is also beautiful; it has blue spots and its tail is larger than its body.

6. The Colibri: The colibri is a very small bird and it has a golden tuft of hair on its head ; its look can also be white.

7. The Rooster: The rooster is a beautiful bird; its motley tail has a bent tip, its throat is red and blue and of all colors, and its beard is red. When the Indian rooster sings, its tail fans open and its throat fills with air, all black and of all colors, but the beard is red just the same as with the rooster. The Indian rooster has a different tail than the rooster: the Indian rooster has its tail fanned open.

2. Love of the Fatherland [Amour de la Patrie]²

We should all love our fatherland because it is where life was given to us, where we saw the world for the first time, where we received our first maternal kiss,

---

the old literary guard. Gruzinsky, a staff librarian at the Rumiantsev Library in Moscow (which was known as the Lenin Library between 1925–1992), was invited by Alexandra Lvovna Tolstaya to join her team of manuscript readers during the preparatory stages of the creation of the complete edition of Tolstoy's œuvre, sometime during the first years following Tolstoy's death; he was tasked with editing Tolstoy's works written before 1880. The rest of the entries ("The Parrot," "The Peacock," "The Colibri," and "The Rooster") were joined with the original three entries that appeared in volume 1 and were published together almost three decades after Gruzinsky's death and Alexandra Lvovna's defection in 1929, in volume ninety of *The Jubilee* (1958), edited by V. S. Mishin (90:93-94). There was an interim publication of the journal of the brothers Tolstoy in the combined volumes 35-36 of *Literaturnoe nasledstvo* ([Moscow: Nauka, 1939], 268). Gruzinsky's commentary on Tolstoy's juvenilia ("Detskie uprazhneniia. Iz uchenicheskoi tetradi 1835 g" ["Childhood Exercises: From the Study Notebook for 1835"]), was published in volume 1 of *The Jubilee* as "Kommentarii k 'iunosheskim opytam'" ("Commentary on *The Juvenilia*") (1:338-44). *The Juvenilia* in volume 1 followed the text of Tolstoy's short novel *Childhood* (*Detstvo*), edited by M. A. Tsiavlovsky, in *The Jubilee* (1:3-101), and Tsiavlovsky's commentary (1:303-37). Mishin's commentary can be found in *The Jubilee* (90:385).

2   **Entry 2.** Love of the Fatherland [Amour de la Patrie]. This fragment, which was signed "Léon Tolstoi" and was dedicated to his "dear aunt" Tatiana Ergolskaya ("À ma chère Tante"), was likely written in 1837 and was published in *The Jubilee* (1:215). At eight or nine years of age, the future author of *War and Peace* gushed this patriotic effusion in the language of Russia's greatest defeated enemy, for French was his best written language at the time. The French line in the title, moreover, strongly echoes the sentiments in *La Marseillaise*. By a peculiar coincidence, the would-be French national anthem was originally a patriotic war song titled "*Chant de guerre pour l'Armée du Rhin*" ("War Song for the Army of the Rhine") and was

and where the first years of our childhood passed. The fatherland will always find its ardent defenders, ready to give their lives for its salvation. This love of the fatherland can never go out in our hearts. How many examples of this we have seen: how many agrarians, at the sound of a rallying call to save the fatherland, abandon their fields in the middle of ploughing and hurry to die to try to save it; how many fathers leave their children to the will of providence;[3] how many spouses are parted from each other for the welfare of the fatherland. We witness a fine example in Leonid: he had the courage to fight fifteen thousand men with three hundred brave men of his own, and he put up such valiant resistance that only one man remained alive to inform the Spartans about the death of the rest.[4] And so, our holy Russia has always had, in times of every calamity, defenders such as Minin,[5] Pozharsky,[6] Suvorov,[7] and Kutuzov.[8] During the

---

written by citizen Claude Joseph Rouget de Lisle in 1792, during the war of the revolutionary troops against the international coalition that was supporting the French Monarchy. In 1792, Lieutenant Colonel Napoleon Bonaparte was still in Corsica, his victory at Toulon still a year away. In fact, in July of 1792, Bonaparte was demoted to the rank of Captain, after service troubles in his garrison at Ajaccio.

3   Tolstoy capitalizes the word "Providence" in his French original.

4   Tolstoy is here referring to Herodotus's description of the heroism of King Leonidas of Sparta against the Persian army during the Battle of Thermopylae in 480 BCE.

5   Kuzma Minich Minin (Zakhar'ev-Sukhoruk), whose date of birth is unknown, died in 1616. Minin was in the service of the governorate of Nizhniy Novgorod when, upon election to the rank of Zemstvo Elder on September 1, 1611, he raised money, armed, and invited Prince Dmitry Ivanovich Pozharsky (1578–1642) to command regiments of volunteer corps during the Polish-Lithuanian invasion of Russia and the occupation of Moscow between 1610 and 1612. Minin and Pozharsky became popular faces of Russian heroism, instrumental in the country's expulsion of the Poles and its victorious reemergence from the long Time of Troubles. For his many contributions and personal heroism, Minin was awarded a noble rank and was made a Boyar. Prince Pozharsky became a Boyar in 1613 and served as Military Commander of Novgorod from 1628 to 1630. The iconic monument to Minin and Pozharsky in Moscow's Red Square is a work by the sculptor I. P. Martos, which was completed in 1818.

6   See the previous note.

7   Buried among the Emperors and the sainted at Saint Alexander Nevsky Monastery in St. Petersburg, Generalissimo Alexander Vasilievich Suvorov (1729/1730–1800), the Count of Râmnicu, the Prince of Italy, nicknamed the "Father to the Soldiers," is one of Russia's most beloved military leaders and was the teacher of Mikhail Illarionovich Kutuzov. Suvorov was made a generalissimo in 1799 after his surprise crossing through the narrow gorges of the St. Gotthard Pass in the Alps upset Napoleon's designs.

8   Otherwise known as the "Savior of Russia," General Field Marshal Mikhail Illarionovich Kutuzov (Golenishchev-Kutuzov-Smolensky) (1745–1813) is celebrated as one of Russia's most accomplished military leaders of all time. Although not without his detractors for his indulgence in court intrigue and after his ceding Moscow to the French in 1812, since 1813 Russia has venerated Kutuzov's brilliant strategic victory over Napoleon and the decisive role he played in the crushing defeat of the Grande Armée. The Order of Kutuzov is second

period when Russia had trouble breathing under Polish yoke, a simple butcher, Minin, inspired the burghers of Nizhniy Novgorod by his example: Minin sacrificed all of the few possessions he had for the benefit of his fatherland.—Yes, he said to the merchants of Nizhniy Novgorod: Let's leave our wives and children, sell our lots, so that we may, through our blood, blot out the stain inflicted on Russia by the Poles.

3. A Fragment on the Past, the Present, and the Future [end of the 1830s/the early 1840s]

The past is what has been, the future is what will be, and the present is what does not exist.—Therefore, the life of man consists in the future and the past, and the happiness that we desire to possess is only a chimera, just like the present.[9]

4. Notes on the Second Chapter of the "Caractères" of La Bruyère[10] [end of the 1830s/the early 1840s]

La Bruyère says: "Is there anyone who, when dying and leaving this world, is not struck by the consciousness of his uselessness, by the awareness that his loss will not be felt when there are so many other people who will replace him?" This thought is unclear. It suffers from exaggeration, and I dare to say that it is more untrue than true. Even if he doesn't realize it or wish to be useful, every person contributes his bit of good. Moreover, if he feels the demand to

---

only to the Order of Suvorov in the hierarchy of Russian military distinctions. The Kutuzov Prospect and the Arc of Triumph in Moscow are testaments to Kutuzov's undying national prestige and general popularity.

9 Entry 3. "A Fragment on the Past, the Present, and the Future" ["Le présent, le passé, et le future"]: *"Le passé est que fut, le future est qui sera, et le présent est ce qui n'est pas.—C'est pour cela que la vie de l'homme ne consiste que dans le future et le passé et l'est pour la même raison que le bonheur que nous voulons posséder n'est qu'une chimère de même que le présent."* Written in French at the end of the 1830s or in the very early 1840s, the maxim is signed in French: "Léon Tolstoi." It was published in 1928 in *The Jubilee* 1:217.

10 Entry 4. "Notes on the Second Chapter of the "Caractères" of La Bruyère." The original title is given in French as *"Notes sur le second chapitre des 'Caractères' de La Bruyère."* The text of the "Notes" is the last of the early texts written entirely in French, published in 1928 in *The Jubilee* (1:219-20). Based on the location of the Notes in the manuscripts, Gruzinsky dates this text to the 1840s, although he suggested that it was a later fragment than the previous one (*The Jubilee*, 1:338). On La Bruyère, see also entry 55.

be useful and pursues this aim, he shall attain it for certain; he shall then make sufficient contributions to the common good. Without a doubt, a dying man will sense his insignificance, the nothingness of the good he has made in comparison with the *summum bonum* of happiness. With quite a number of people, just their name carries some value… [11]

This thought is quite just. Indeed, while reading the works of some writer who only has wit and style, we form an opinion of him that infinitely surpasses his real value and do not suppose him to have certain shortcomings. La Bruyère says that there have always been and will always be people of genius who are incapable of attaining glory. I do not agree with this because I understand genius quite differently than others do. What I call genius is a combination of three basic qualities of the soul at their summit of power and development, namely: a great mind, richness of feeling, and firm will. I am not inclined to name great artists "geniuses"; I call them "talents." And thus, should we understand genius as I understand it, the mind of the genius will grant him an awareness of superiority, his feeling will incite him to strive for the welfare of others, and his will shall vouchsafe the success of what he intends.

—Consequently, he shall attain renown.

"Self-love prevents us from marveling at the perfection of others." This thought is quite true.

"Modesty is for merits what shadows are for figures in a painting: it empowers and shapes them prominently." Indeed, nothing impels us to value merits as does modesty. Every human being has a greater or lesser tendency for originality or contradiction; when people observe that you are diminishing their merits, they tend to augment them over others.—

People who take credit for imitating simplicity are akin to someone of medium height who bends down while passing through a door jamb… [12]

—It is easier to ascend for free individuals (bachelors)[13] than it is for the married. The married for the most part remain at the level they have attained. People look at a married man as if he has already lived through the most important part of his life.

---

11 A whole line and a half of elliptical dots in the original might indicate a "secret" thought not sharable even with himself, a typical prank on the part of Tolstoy paying ironic tribute to the rules of the aphoristic genre, or it might indeed simply have been a placeholder for a forthcoming quote from La Bruyère. Gruzinsky suggests that the third of these possibilities is the most likely (see *The Jubilee*, 1:218).

12 Tolstoy's ellipsis.

13 Tolstoy uses *"les hommes libres"* (*célibataires)"* in French.

5. Philosophical Observations on the Discourses of J. J. Rousseau[14] [ca. 1847–52]

First Discourse

Has the restoration of the sciences and the arts contributed to the purification of mores?

It is known that Rousseau tried to prove a harmful influence of the sciences on the morals.

The first objection that I am going to pose to Rousseau consists in a question: Would he agree that an individual who enjoys freedom is capable of committing more good or more evil than an individual deprived of it? Would he agree that, in general, people who tear asunder the restrictive ties of ignorance are capable of committing more good and evil than people whose ignorance restricts their freedom? I am confident that every reasoning individual would agree that the less developed one's human faculties the more limited one's freedom, and vice versa. Hence, in order to answer this question, one should first answer the questions that our reason immediately raises. Are there inborn human inclinations? And if there are, are the inclinations toward good and evil of equal power or does one of them always prevail?

It is clear that in order to make a straightforward decision about the question regarding one of the first principles of reason posited by Rousseau, one must first solve these three questions.[15] If there are no inborn human inclinations, it is then clear that good and evil depend on upbringing. If good and evil depend on upbringing, it is clear that science in general and philosophy in particular—which is what Rousseau is attacking so hard—are not only not useless

---

14 **Entry 5. "Philosophical Observations on the Discourses of J. J. Rousseau."** Based on its location in the manuscripts among sixty-eight loose leaves tied together with thick thread into a handmade notebook, Gruzinsky dates Tolstoy's observations on Rousseau to 1847–52 (*The Jubilee* 1:338). The drafts on Rousseau occupy thirteen of the sixty-eight leaves. Gruzinsky refers to the quality of the notes as "remarks written in haste" ("*speshnye zapisi*") (*The Jubilee* 1:338). While the quality of Tolstoy's handwriting might be rushed, the quality of his thinking does not betray signs of hurry. Focusing his notes titled "First Discourse" on Rousseau's prize-winning *A Discourse on the Arts and Sciences* (1750) [*Discours sur les science et les arts*], Tolstoy in fact interrogates claims that were better developed in *A Discourse on the Origin of Inequality* (1755), *A Discourse on Political Economy* (1755), and *The Social Contract* (1762).

15 A footnote by Tolstoy here reads: "I shall endeavor to determine in another place which one of these three suppositions is just."

but are necessary, and not just for the Socrateses[16] but for all. If, however, the inclinations toward good and evil are of equal power in the soul of man, the less human freedom will prevail, the less his good or evil influence will be, and vice versa. Hence, should we suppose this to be true, the sciences and the arts can produce no difference in the ratio between good and evil.—If the element of good rules supreme in the soul of man, it will develop with the development of art, especially the fine arts. It is only insofar as the element of evil rules supreme in the soul of man that Rousseau's idea will justly apply. And I am confident that for all his eloquence, for all his art of persuasion, the great citizen of Geneva could never have brought himself to prove such a utopia—the inanity of which I shall hope to prove at some later point.—The thought now crosses my mind that all philosophical questions—the belaboring over which so many (useless) books have been written—can be reduced to very basic elements . . . We are more amused by the leaves on a tree than by its roots. One of the major errors committed by the majority of hard-thinking minds[17] is that, having become aware of their inability to derive the first principles of reason, they wish to resolve philosophical issues historically, oblivious to the fact that history is one of the most deficient sciences; it has lost its purpose.—Its most ardent partisans will never find a decent purpose for it.—History is a science of by-products. One can say this without proof. The mistake is precisely that it is studied as an independent science; it is not studied for the sake of philosophy (the only science that needs it) but rather for its own sake.—As a result, history will never reveal to us at any given time the relationship between the sciences and the arts and good mores, between good and evil, between religion and civility, yet it will inform us—incorrectly at that—whence the Huns emerged, where their habitats were, who was the founding force behind their might, and so on.

Part the First

Rousseau says the following when discussing the initial influence of the sciences and the arts: *Human beings began to feel the main advantage behind the influence*

---

16 The "plural" Socrates is Tolstoy's wishful exaggeration.

17 Tolstoy describes the owners of these minds as *dumateli*, a word he coined early in life and continually applied to those who do not think naturally. The people he calls *dumateli* are those who would strain their brains, though not simply through hard work: the *dumateli* were those with ponderous intellects, pundits with too much time and leisure on their hands throughout their vacuous, yet still "hard-thinking," careers.

of the muses, which rendered them more capable of living in social communion, inspiring in them a desire to be liked by one another thanks to producing works that deserved reciprocal approval. —All that we do, we do solely for ourselves; but when we find ourselves in society, everything we do becomes advantageous to ourselves only when our deeds are liked by others and when we receive their approval; hence, striving separately for his individual benefit, each human ends up contributing to the communal welfare. And because not all people found their individual benefit in the works of the sciences and the arts, one may not assume that a capacity for social communion stemmed only from the works of the sciences and the arts. Ibidem: *Furthermore, since government and the laws take care of human inviolability and welfare, the sciences and the arts, whilst not as despotic, are perhaps nevertheless mightier: they portray the heavy irons in which humans are enchained as floral garlands, muffling our sense of freedom, forcing us to love slavery, to forge society into a so-called "educated nation."*

—We shall find an obvious contradiction in these words of Rousseau's, a contradiction with the very idea that he is defending. *Necessity produced sovereignty, while the sciences and the arts reinforced the latter.* These words make it clear that the author is at least in agreement with the idea that the sciences and the arts supported the monarchy; insofar as they had not supported it, the monarchy would have tumbled. How many virtues would have come tumbling down with it? Into how many vices would have humankind instinctively fallen?—One cannot help but admit that the sciences did exert a bad influence on mores; likewise, one cannot help admitting that they saved the human race from still greater evils.—Rousseau further claims that even though human nature has not improved since the advent of society, mores used to be purer: *realizing how vulnerable to others' attacks they were, people found security by avoiding committing a great number of sins—a development the value of which we still feel today.* Since it seems to me that I have already proven that the reign of secrecy among us does not originate from the influence of the sciences and the arts alone, I do not deem it necessary to refute this perfectly correct thought, exempted from the first part of the deliberation.—

The majority of opponents who have attacked this Discourse have said, with regards to this thought, that had evil not been concealed, it would have been more infectious. I would say that though it is true that evil is not as infectious when concealed, the same is true of goodness. Moreover, were good and evil to have their effects made explicit, everyone would agree that goodness would enjoy a greater following.—Historical proofs begin here.

I have already cited my opinion about proofs concerning this, and objections from Gauthier[18] and the King of Poland[19] confirm my opinion that "History is too little known to us in the present sense such that we could rely upon it in solving philosophical questions."—They both refute quite substantially, and in an historically informed way, Rousseau's historical proofs.—

I shall only point out the places where Rousseau contradicts himself in a very obvious way.—Among the evils inflicted by the sciences, the chief one is the collapse of military discipline, effeminacy, and the absence of all military qualities in general. But why should virtuous people need military qualities, I ask? To protect the fatherland, you might say. Yet history itself, on which Rousseau relies so heavily, demonstrates that nations were defensive when the sciences and the arts were known, and that they were the conquerors at the time when those were not known.

---

18 Here, Tolstoy misspells the name of French historian Pierre Edmé Gautier de Sibert (1725–97), author of many works that were popular in the 1760s, which include objections to Rousseau's ahistorical view on the matter of the relation between statehood and political tradition. In his many works, de Sibert speaks about the real links that exist between the two in his considerations of variations of the levels of state power in antiquity and the French monarchy, and in the histories he wrote of charitable institutions in the religious orders of Saint-Lazare and Notre Dame. None of Gautier de Sibert's works are in Tolstoy's personal library at Yasnaya Polyana. Yet it seems that when he mentions de Sibert, Tolstoy was most likely referencing one of the following hefty tracts: *Variations de la monarchie françoise, dans son gouvernement politique, civil et militaire: avec l'examen des causes qui les ont produites: ou, Historie du gouvernement de France, depuis Clovis jusqu'à* la mort de Louis XIV, *divisée en neuf époques* (Paris: Saillant, 1765), *Vies des empereurs Tite-Antonin et Marc-Aurele* (Paris: Musier fils, 1769), or *Histoire des Ordres Royaux, Hospitaliers-Militaires de Notre-Dame du Mont-Carmel et de Saint-Lazare de Jérusalem* (Paris: Royale, 1772).

19 Here, Tolstoy must mean Stanisław August Poniatowski (1732–98), King of Poland, elected by the Polish Diet in September 1764. Poniatowski became the successor to the Polish throne following the death of King August and the deftly orchestrated intrigues of Catherine the Great. Rousseau speaks of him as an opportunistic contractarian rather than a hero in "Considerations on the Government of Poland and on its Proposed Reformation" ("*Considérations sur le Gouvernment de Pologne*") (1772). Because this work by Rousseau only came to be widely known much later than *The Social Contract*, and because no copy of this work was found among the editions of Rousseau that Tolstoy did possess, Tolstoy must have had in mind a briefer, passim discussion of the Polish government in several of the early-to-middle chapters of Book 3 of *The Social Contract*.

Part the Second

This is full of historical proofs that prove nothing.

He [Rousseau] says the following when addressing scholars: *Answer me, ye who have so inspired us with enormous chunks of knowledge: Had you never taught us any of this knowledge, would we have been fewer in number, harder to govern, less dangerous, less prosperous and more corrupt?* —

It follows from these words that the author identifies as equal the well-being of private individuals and the human race; whereas, the well-being of private individuals is for the most part in reverse ratio to the well-being of the State.—The author continues to discuss the harmful influence of luxury.—You can get everything with money, except good citizens and good mores.—(This thought is quite right and is superbly expressed).—I shall here analyze what luxury is. Whence its origin and what are its consequences?—The word luxury is perfectly conventional; when everyone goes around without clothes, the first one to put on some animal's hide became a person of luxury, while in our time an individual who forces thousands of human beings to toil for his serenity is considered only to be meeting his vital needs.—

The satisfaction of needs is a source of pride.—Needs grow over time. As needs grow, so too does the difficulty that every individual faces in satisfying all of his needs, such that the idea of the division of labor evinced itself with the increase in that difficulty.—Some were preoccupied with the satisfaction of more significant, others of less significant, needs. This is one of the reasons for human inequality. Those who were preoccupied with the satisfaction of non-major needs began to experience their dependence on others; this very dependence, and its evil abuse, produced luxury.—I call luxurious any individual who enjoys a greater good than he contributes to society.—It is clear that the pride of the powerful and the envy of the weak will be the consequence of luxury, the two vices precisely that serve as the source of the greater part of all evils.—And so, if luxury is one of the greatest evils, it doesn't follow from this that the sciences begat it, however, for only the science of governance is among the main human needs. If, and in accordance with Rousseau, the sciences and the arts support supreme power, they have contributed to the development of luxury but did not beget it.—

One cannot help noticing another error that the author makes when he speaks about the influence of one sex on the other. He says that the influence of women is predominantly beneficial and that all evil that results from this influence only depends on the incorrect upbringing of women.—Only what is beneficial for a man of society is what is good for him in his natural state. But the closer to his natural habitat that we observe man, the less of that harmful female influence do we observe, for its source is luxury and idleness.—Nature has placed women in a position of dependence to men due to their lesser capacity to satisfy vital needs, and in the execution of their assignment (the birth and rearing of children), the former completely depend on the latter.—Idleness was the inevitable consequence of luxury; and vices were the inevitable consequences of idleness, for the urge to express and make manifest all of these desires finds itself among all the other strivings of the human soul.

6. A Fragment without a Title I[20] [undated, 1840s]

First Variant

From as early as I can remember, I have always found a force of truth within myself, some striving that wasn't being satisfied, only contradictions and pettiness all around.

The more I lived, the more unbearable life became for me. [illegible]... could not be stopped. I started drafting plans on some topics for myself, which for a while I found to be of some use, though they would soon prove unsatisfactory. I would draft a different set, with the same result. At last, as I was looking at the rules, I found consonances among them and realized that all of them fall under the same principle or are derived from the same origin. But how to find this origin? Could it be deduced from particular cases? I tried to figure this out but in vain.[21]

Having made no progress along this route, I took another path: I started looking at the topics for which I was drafting rules—everything, that is. I identified an activity within myself whose cause was I and not I.[22] I became cognizant of causes within myself; one of them by means of consciousness—unclearly—, another one by means of feelings—clearly. And then I started looking at [illegible], to no avail ... The only method remaining is to look at both causes.

---

20 **Entry 6. Fragment without a title I.** Published in 1928 in *The Jubilee* 1:226, this untitled fragment and the untitled one that follows were written sparsely on four pages of six connected leaves according to Gruzinsky (*The Jubilee* 1:338).

21 Among several corrections, Tolstoy added the following curious remark to the margins: "I gave up on all prejudices, having found in them nothing that can be satisfactory." (*The Jubilee* 1:226).

22 Added in the margins: "Skepticism is I" (*The Jubilee* 1:226).

I am not delimited in the combinations with the non-I, but I am delimited by the combination as such. The synthesis of the conscious "I" with the sensual (to comprehend the sensual).

I am bipartite.

Only one I is spiritual.

7. A Fragment without a Title II[23]
[undated, 1840s]

Second Variant

From as early as I can remember, I have always found a force of truth within myself, some striving that wasn't being fully satisfied, even though I was aware, on some level, of its being satisfied.

I was aware of being finite among everything—and was nevertheless aware of infinity, and I even spotted this infinity within myself.

To harmonize this contradiction, I drafted rules,[24] which would make definite the manifestation of the infinite within the finite. Yet first I had to experience evil while drafting the rules, so that I might avoid it. Having found no satisfaction through this method, I came to understand that the striving that I found within myself was a result of the combination of the finite with the infinite, and so I had to know how I (the infinite) was supposed to coordinate with the finite. And to know this, it was necessary to know what's infinite and what's finite.

---

23 **Entry 7. Fragment without a title II.** This fragment was published in 1928 in *The Jubilee* (1:227-28) (see note 21). The extensive additions that Tolstoy planned for this note are discussed in my Introduction to this volume.

24 The rules of which Tolstoy speaks drew inspiration from Benjamin Franklin's ledgers and personal journal, and in their particularity and attention to detail they resemble what we might call a daily or weekly planner—except that the plans are, by and large, too grandiose to be fulfillable. If not exactly otherworldly and transcendent, Tolstoy's plans are intellectual, moral, and spiritual, for the most part, aiming to train physical strength in increments of weight lifting, with a view to subjugating this sensual and physical power and will to higher needs. Tolstoy was very active with the planner from January 27, 1847, through the undated entries up to May 1847. Then he slacked for three years, only resuming the practice on June 15, 1850. He continued on and off from 1850 through January 1854, at last giving up entirely at age twenty-five. The rules can be found in the autobiographical additions to his diary published in 1934 in volume 46 of *The Jubilee*, which was edited by Gruzinsky's younger colleague at the Lenin (Rumiantsev) Library, Alexey Sergeevich Petrovsky (1881–1958) (see *The Jubilee* 46:245-76).

I swept aside everything else, all the concepts that I had previously accepted as true, and I began seeking the principle that could be clear to me immediately, that would not stem from yet another concept, that is. And thus, the more mediate the concept, the vaguer it would be for me, for example, the concept of a tree became vaguer to me than the concept of the sense of smell or the sight of a specific tree.

I had two concepts that required no proof and were unconditional. These concepts I expressed thus: I am delimited and I am active. With these positive concepts of varying degree, I can represent to myself an infinitely small degree of both of these concepts, the one that we call negative: infinity and inactivity, that is. By synthesizing these concepts, I shall get 4 composite concepts: 1) limited activity, the activity that is quite comprehensible and that I find in myself; 2) unlimited activity; this concept can't be, for one contradicts the other; activity cannot be unlimited; 3) limited inactivity, the concept that cannot be, for there is nothing; and 4) unlimited inactivity.

8. On the Aim of Philosophy[25]
[undated, 1840s]

a) Man strives; man is active, that is. Where is this activity directed? How to render this activity free? This is the aim of philosophy in its true significance. In other words, philosophy is the science of life.

In order to define this science more precisely, one must define the striving that provides the concept for it.[26]

The striving found in all that exists and in a human being is the consciousness of life and the striving to preserve it and make it more powerful.

When I say to make it more powerful, I mean that human striving must have more impressions or attain what we call happiness, well-being.—To satisfy this striving for happiness, man must not try to seek happiness in the external world—in other words, not among the accidental pleasant impressions of the external world. Rather, one must seek to cultivate oneself formally so that any given impression affects one just as one wants.—A human being would otherwise resemble a madman who, instead of entering a house, would instead

---

25 **Entry 8. "On the Aim of Philosophy."** This piece was published in 1928 in *The Jubilee* 1:229-232. Gruzinsky calls this collection of notes on the aim of philosophy "disordered" (*The Jubilee* 1:338).

26 Here, Tolstoy means to refer to a scientific understanding of the concept.

wait for the house to move him into it.—And so, the aim of philosophy is to demonstrate in what form it is that man must form himself.—An individual is not alone, however; he lives in society. Hence, philosophy must determine an individual's relationship toward other humans.—If everyone pursued his own well-being, looking for it externally to his self, the interests of private individuals would conflict and disorder would follow. But if every individual instead strived for self-perfection, there would be no way that order could be violated, for everyone would do for others precisely what he desires that others do for him.

—For the sake of acquiring philosophical wisdom, to acquire the knowledge concerning in what way every individual ought to direct the natural striving for well-being with which each of us humans is endowed, that is, it is necessary to form and comprehend that capacity with which man can limit his natural striving, or will, and subsequently all of human capabilities, for the attainment of happiness (Psychology).

The method for the in-depth study of speculative philosophy consists in the study of psychology and the laws of nature, in the development of mental capabilities (mathematic), in the practice of expressing one's thoughts with ease, namely[27] in definitions.

The method for the study of practical philosophy consists in the analysis of all questions encountered in individual life, and in the strict fulfilment of the rules of morality, in the following laws of nature.—

b) The definition of a definition

The definition of a concept is: the substitution of the most basic concepts for a definite one of which it consists. This action is called analysis.—By means of analyzing any concept whatsoever, one can deduce from the most complex one the most abstract one, a concept that cannot be defined, that is. This kind of a concept is called consciousness. What is consciousness, then? Consciousness is the concept of the self—of an I, in other words.

c) On thoughts that concern the afterlife.

Everything that exists can't stop existing without a sufficient cause; and all that does not exist can't come into existence without a cause. The soul exists; therefore, it can't stop existing without a cause. But what is the soul in its essence?

---

27 Gruzinsky earmarks this word as illegible and adds a question mark after the word "namely." (*The Jubilee* 1:230).

The consciousness of *I*... —What is consciousness? It is the awareness of the *I* as existing at different stages of activity or motion.

What capability represents the *I* as it exists at different stages of motion? Memory. We see that memory depends completely on the body, and so a deformity in one part of the human body destroys this capacity; death should hence destroy it completely. And thus, what remains is only the consciousness of the *I* with which man is born into this world. As regards the hypotheses about any definitions of afterlife—allegedly swift in coming—they will always hang on hot air.

d) Method

The aim of philosophy is to say that the sole human striving must be that of formal self-cultivation. In order to form himself, one must first of all know what an I is, and what authentic education is. For this, a method is necessary, namely: 1) to subjugate all bodily demands to the will; 2) to subjugate the capacity for imitation to the will and to develop it in accordance with the following rules: to remember for a whole week every thought that you find good, then record it, and to repeat all of these thoughts every night.—Exercises: study Mathematics.—3) To subjugate reason—or the capacity for deduction—to the [power of] will and to develop it in accordance with the following rules: I) To define each concept, that is, to substitute two broad concepts for a narrow one that means the same, then to define both [of the broad] concepts, ultimately deriving concepts that can have no definitions but of which we are conscious, because they are nothing other than the necessary features of the I itself.— II) Regardless of the way the new thoughts are procured, to keep track of the train of thoughts and to observe the number and methods of thinking.— Exercises—Mathematics and debate.

With all that, to not lose sight of the true aim of philosophy and to remain preoccupied only with the study of those truths that are necessary for this aim, never letting go of any thought the truth of which you are convinced, so much so that you can put it into words. 4) The capacity of will; the development of which shall consist in the habit of maintaining dominion over all the capacities and their operation.

By the aim of philosophy in general one must also mean the method of expressing one's thoughts. The rules for this will be as follows: 1) To not write down on paper a sentence until you have found it quite formed within yourself in relation to its antecedent and to what follows.

Exercises: definitions and poetry

e)[28]

I assume that everything has two main elements—parts or primary principles—which I understand as complete opposites that we can identify for each thing, the joining together of which would result in zero. The concept of negation itself has its origin here, because each of these elements produces endlessly different effects: in other words, everything possesses an endless quantity of gradations, hence I can only imagine an infinitesimal degree of movement, which is negation. In essence, an infinitesimally small movement of either element is possible in their unity (infinite non-activity).

Having not rationally identified the truth, we can nevertheless anticipate it, and thus this is why I wish to define the rules of life.—These rules can be divided into two kinds—corporal and mental—the motor for both of which is the will.—1) to eat, drink, sleep, and...[29]—but it's necessary not to lose sight of the aim of everything, no matter what we are doing, not to steer away from commonly practiced rules, evading evil deeds.—

9. A Fragment without a Title III[30]
[undated, ca. 1847]

If man did not strive, there would be no man.[31] Desire is the cause of all activity. Desire is the driving force of activity. But, since the cause for any activity is dual—it either originates from desire or from another activity—then desire itself has a dual nature: mediate and immediate. Activity is the effect and the cause of desire. When activity is the cause, what then is its own cause? The cause of activity is the external world.

I desire to know the truth, desire to know what I am: why can I sense impressions? Could it be that there is no truth, there is no me, no impressions?

---

28 Section "e" has no subtitle in the original.

29 We will never find out what other guilty physiological pleasure the ellipsis hides until there is a chance to reexamine this part of the original manuscript. Gruzinsky comments on the expurgated word: "a word of three letters follows suit" (*The Jubilee*, 1:232). In the commentary section of volume 1 of *The Jubilee*, Gruzinsky goes to some further lengths with his explaining: "There is, toward the end of this fragment, a word of three letters that was omitted as unacceptable in print." (1:338).

30 **Entry 9. A Fragment Without a Title.** This is fragment No. III without a title among the Juvenilia.

31 Published in *The Jubilee* (1:233-36), Gruzinsky dates this fragment, which begins with a reflection on striving ("*Ezheli by chelovek ne zhelal*") to 1847, which marked the conclusion of the Kazan period of Tolstoy's life—by which I mean the period during which Tolstoy was a student at the University of Kazan, where he wrote this reflection (see *The Jubilee*, 1:339).

Might all of this be deceit? But why do I cogitate? Because I want to know the truth, because I desire not to be deceived. And so, I can refute everything except this: I desire, for were I not desiring, I wouldn't be refuting; hence, only one thing is true: that I desire, and [illegible] is needed consequently. What is the reason for desiring? (If desiring exists, so must its cause.) (The reason for desiring is activity; the reason for activity is the striving for independence, for satisfaction; all that influences me, or everything that exists, is desiring as such. The reason for my desiring is the existence of everything, including my desiring (and so, if it weren't for everything, there wouldn't be my desiring, wouldn't be me). Desiring is thus the cause and the effect. It follows from this that desiring acts differently: it self-defines and acts immediately or acts by way of impressions, and so the acts of desires are completely juxtaposed.

An Axiom: That which exists without cause is independent.

An Axiom: 1) All that exists has an existential cause unless the cause is the effect and the effect is the cause.

When looking at the cause of the faculty of desiring, I find that: a) desiring is an inward activity whose cause is nothing other than impressions; as regards the impressions, their cause is everything that exists. I can see from this judgment that desiring has a cause, and that desiring is not its own inward cause; the cause is the external world that exists, because there is a cause for that which exists. I should note that desiring has a joint effect on me along with the effect of impressions.

I deduce from all of the above that everything that is external exists— including my body—and that the cause of my existing or of desiring is the external world. And so, were it not for the existence of the external world, part of which is taken up by my body, I would not exist in the spiritual sense either, in the sense of desiring, that is. Because desiring is just the spiritual aspect of what exists within me solely, for spirit dies together with the body.

2) Yet, looking further at the causes of desiring, I find that its cause is the very same desire; hence, desiring has no cause and, moreover, it possesses within that toward which it is striving—independence, that is. And because that desiring is independent either of the body or of time, desire is hence independent, infinite, self-determining, self-satisfying, and immortal.

Thus, man consists of two different activities or capacities for desiring, one of which is finite and dependent and comes from the body and comprises all that we call human needs, and the second is the capacity for desiring or infinite will, self-determining and self-satisfying.

Now let us look at the relationship of these two principles in their essence and their manifestations. These capacities must either be of equal power or one of them must prevail. They cannot be of equal power because one of them cannot exist by itself but is the necessary consequence of something pre-existing; the other is the cause and effect of its existence and, various visions of its manifestations notwithstanding, it does not change its essence. This latter must prevail eternally. 2) In reality (I have proven this in tr[uth]), it is not only frequently but for the most part that needs prevail over the will; the summit of perfection that man can attain is the perfect predominance of the will, which can never be achieved but yet remains the constant aim of man's efforts.

And so, man consists of two opposite types of activity. Let us look at the first one: activity out of necessity. The beginning and cause of such activity is, as we have seen, in everything that exists; the nearest cause is in the individual himself. By means of bodily feelings, man perceives objects (feeling is not an activity; it is what we suffer); perceptions transition into bodily activity on their own; this activity is of the basest kind and can be found in all animals and even in the great majority of plants. 2)[32] (sic) Perceptions also transition into receptivity (which we call memory and imagination). I do not make a distinction between either of the two capabilities because I do not understand the capacity to reproduce without a capacity to retain; and vice versa, the capacity for reproduction has an effect on the lower capacity, and this is a capacity of secondary order that some animals also possess.

Everything that we call feelings or passions belongs to this latter activity. The capacity to reproduce transitions to the capacity to deduce, which affects the capabilities of the lower order and of necessity absorbs within it the impact of the capacity to reproduce. This capacity is the highest among the necessary types of human activity; it is exactly what we call mind, and it is to be found in the majority of animals.

And thus, corporal, sensual, and mental activities are interdependent and impact one another; and so, human striving for independence is not satisfied because this activity is passive [stradatel'naia].

Let us look at free activity now.

The will is not delimited; it is self-determining, and it expresses itself in the following way: I desire to desire. Why would it express itself in this manner and not otherwise? The essence of the will is independent, but its expression, direction, or form must depend on something, to wit: on another desire, on need,

---

32 The number "2)" here is how Tolstoy's itemized list of argumentative points appears in the original.

for example, the need of the body. And so, despite the will being unlimited, it is expressed in a certain form. The will cannot impact sensations because their cause is outside of its sphere, outside of man, that is. The will produces its effect on sentient receptivity in such a way that it represents the objects that it desires and not those that are manifested; the same capacity has an effect on the capacity to deduce, which, with the action of the will applied to it, deduces what it wills and becomes reason. The supreme necessary activity directs the will.

Now we confront the question of how a transition takes place through the mediation of the will from the state of the necessary to the state of the free. The will acts upon the capacity of supreme necessity and acts upon the body in accordance with this deduction. Free sensations transition to the capacity to perceive, defer more objects to the latter, to be made clearer, the capacity to perceive transitions to the capacity to deduce. This latter will be superior to the former deduction, but it can't satisfy the will either. The will takes it from there and accepts the third deduction which, by forcing imagination to accept this and not that, will be superior to the second and the first. Without a need to satisfy, the third deduction affects the will which affects the deductions itself, by forcing it to deduce this and not that. The fourth degree of deduction takes place—the free deduction, or, put differently, the deduction of rational will—which alone self-determines and finds within exactly what I accepted as an axiom at the beginning, namely: that I desire.[33]

Now, let's take a look at what these inborn human concepts—intuition—will be if not none other than the concept of space, line, point, size, quantity? Only his infinite will and its cause, also contained therein, is what constitutes the essence of man. Everything else has no original cause within itself, but has it only externally—i.e., not spiritually, for it has physical causes in the physical.[34] What we call intuition is nothing other than the necessary deduction whose cause is in sensual perception, whose cause is in the external world, and because we can see no cause for the world, there is none, therefore.

I said at the beginning that I identify two activities in everything as my driving cause. But what is "I"? The "I" is a combination of these two activities; activity is an unsatisfied striving or struggle. The former cannot be called action but rather is movement, because activity presupposes striving, but we see none here; all we see is movement or a part of the infinite activity. The second I understand as infinite but cannot represent it to myself otherwise than

---

33 In the original, Tolstoy wrote "I desire" [ia zhelaiu].
34 Tolstoy's original has it thus.

something that is manifested in a certain way; something that is not satisfied in its manifestation—something that is in struggle, that is.

10. A Fragment on Criminal Law[35]
[1847]

[. . .]ment[36] may not concern private law by the standard of present-day opinion. For in so doing, the correct vantage point from which to view the entire system of law would be completely lost.—One should not forget that, with some exceptions, the systems of criminal law in ancient Rome and in ancient Germany belonged entirely to private law. The current distribution of law is the product of our history and our current relations—not simply by default but rather because this distribution has been necessitated by all of these conditions. Although private law has been separated from criminal law, both agree that, irrespective of how a government defines criminal law, a plaintiff has the right to restitution from injury. The prerogative to judge this restitution falls to the courts—their duty, fittingly, being the imposition of punishment. Central to criminal law are the criminal trial, criminal politics, and criminal police. The first of these sciences embraces the norms that determine the application of statutes concerning punishment and the mode of action to rely upon. It is in this regard that it should be distinguished from the aggregates of statutes on punishment, although it doth stand closer to the latter than to civic court justice.—Having only recently received its special name and an independent place among the juridical sciences, criminal politics became absolutely necessary when people began to think about the contents of legal books on crime.—Criminal politics deals with exposing the political side of criminal law; its aim is to demonstrate how state interest and the requirements of justice may be harmonized in the positive right of a given state. Finally, criminal police constitute that part of the police force which provides for us the most expedient methods of crime

---

35 **Entry 10. "A Fragment on Criminal Law"** (1847). The beginning of this fragment, which was published in *The Jubilee* (1:237-40), has been lost. The available text begins with the suffix of a noun that may be "development." Gruzinsky dates this fragment to 1847, the Kazan period of Tolstoy's life. The writing of the fragment may have been prompted by a school assignment. I tend to disagree with Gruzinsky that this reflection on criminal law is a rewritten ("fair") copy of Tolstoy's lecture notes (see *The Jubilee* 1:339). The contents of the note and the turns of thought and phrase in it suggest a critique of a professor's lecture or of a course assignment or a critical commentary on an additional source (or sources) that Tolstoy may have read on the topic.

36 This is the beginning of the surviving leaves of this fragment.

prevention. Criminal law keeps all branches connected in the general narrative of its science. Contemporary writers have also invented another new science: criminal legislature. Insofar as this science is distinct from criminal politics and criminal law, it concerns the most purposeful elucidation of, and the best, most comprehensible, and most direct methods of expressing laws on crime, since these latter are the necessary conditions for improving both the issue of new laws as well as the revision of old criminal laws.

The Division within Criminal Law

One of the most important and beneficial consequences of the division of this science is its division into positive law and philosophical law (or general law, also known as natural law).—This division is almost universally accepted and is so strictly enforced by some that they go as far as giving each of its parts a separate title, namely: they call *Strafrechtswissenschaft* "natural criminal law," and they call *Strafgesetzkunde* "positive law." We shall not indulge in an argument about the content of natural criminal law given the unspoken equivocity of this word and the difference of opinion among its adepts. Besides, the question of whether natural criminal law does or does not exist coincides with studies of the supreme philosophical foundations of criminal law. This division has caused many errors, the following of which should be noted. Philosophy cannot be regarded as a source for the judge to rely upon in practical criminal law, even less so as being able to offer a rational deduction from the *a priori* first principle into the construction of a system of practical legislation, abstracted from all positive and historical data.

—An extraordinarily important and dangerous error that has led to most ruinous consequences is the attempt to interpolate positive law into these purely subjective systems with a view to postulating some semblance of a source of origin—or, otherwise, to encroach on positive law by interpolating into it the so-called philosophical system of criminal law (these systems being totally distinct). Very recently, the conviction has taken root that law that is rationally deduced or *a priori* discovered scholastically, which stands contrary to positive law, has absolutely nothing to do with reality, and that its significance rests only in the fact that it reflects an error of our time. The philosophy of law has as its aim to know and penetrate what is rational in its manifestation—that is, to combine subjective human reason with the objectively rational. Far from distancing itself from any historical foundations, the latter constitute the necessary substratum of the philosophy of law; they are the matter with which it should deal and systematize philosophically.—And thus, in case there is a desire to give the title of "philosophical criminal law" to philosophical preoccupations with criminal law especially, there is as much to be said against this title as about the thing itself. What should be abandoned above all, and completely, is the expression of "natural law," which has too many meanings and is, all too frequently, very poorly understood. For, historical law is also natural law, in a certain sense. The other division that originates from the sources of criminal law is the division into Germanic Law in general and, taken separately, the criminal law of individual Germanic states. We are faced with a question in this regard: Did Germanic Criminal Law in general come into existence following the 1806 partitioning of the German state[37] and following the formation of individual criminal legislatures that cover criminal law in its entirety or parts of it across the greater majority of new German lands? One can answer this question accurately by making a distinction between the different meanings of the term "general law." For, no binding state laws can exist with the cessation of state power. But if these laws obtain their active force in partitioned states that have retained ancient roots, these latter can be viewed as general law, provided they remain active.—

But for as long as each partitioned German land has its own criminal law or will soon get one, the general law of the land exists only where the common historical foundation and the ancient statute are meant. Though they have recently disappeared, specific new legislatures have been formed from them, many of which are similar, in which universal basic articles are echoed, for the most part.

The division of law into written and unwritten also depends on the sources, and the erstwhile division of criminal law into *jus poenale, publicum et privatum*,[38] above all (depending on whether it related directly to crimes committed by officers in the employ of the empire or not). This division is no longer in use since no criminal law exists to obtain in the Germanic alliance over its members. As regards the distribution of the subject matter that pertains to the sphere of law, the institutions of learning and legal manuals usually arrange it as follows: criminal courts are separate from criminal law. Criminal law is divided into general and particular parts. The former embraces not only philosophical law but also positive law, covering teachings related to all crimes and punishments.

---

37 Tolstoy focuses on the state of German law during the Napoleonic era and refers here to the fall of Berlin to Napoleon on October 27, 1806 in the aftermath of the fiasco which befell the Prussian troops during the Battle of Jena-Auerstedt. The French retreat from Germany would not be complete until 1813–14, following the serial defeats Napoleon suffered after his failed invasion of Russia in 1812. Until then, Napoleon's Continental System determined the law of occupied Germanic lands.

38 Penal code, public and private.

The latter includes teachings about individual crimes, their content, punishment, and other relevant peculiarities.

These divisions are unknown in both Roman legal sources, as well as the Carolina[39], although they are found in modern legal codes. We shall abide by this division in our current narration of criminal law. Let us note, however, that the generalization and stretching to apply universal laws to individual crimes must be assiduously eliminated from the presentation of the teaching in general.

11. Three Fragments on Music[40]
[1848–50]

First Fragment

Temporal Method for the Study of Music.
Music is the expression of the relation of sounds in space and time, which are given a certain force. The study aimed at knowing music consists therefore in comprehending the method of expressing sounds in space and time, and the expression of intervals between sounds in space and time, depending on force. For this, one needs to read many scores by good composers, making an effort

---

39 Tolstoy's abbreviation in the manuscript "C.C.C." can only mean Constitutio Criminalis Carolina—or Carolina for short—the corpus of civil law ratified with the blessing of the Holy Roman Emperor Charles V at the Diet of Regensburg in 1532.

40 **Entry 11. From "Three Fragments on Music"** (1848–50). The three fragments translated here were first published in volume 1 of *The Jubilee* (1:241-45). They are translated in full, except for the very few brief passages that are abbreviated by Tolstoy to such an extent as to render them meaningless in translation. These spots are indicated and explained in my editorial notes. Also excluded is *The Jubilee* editors' attempt at reconstructing in this volume, Tolstoy's drawing of a kind of a graphic guide for the study of music, which is barely legible and requires correction and a lengthy commentary in its own right (see *The Jubilee* 1:243). Gruzinsky confesses to having recomposed the graph of Tolstoy's original, which he calls "illegibly executed" ("*sdelannyi nerazborchivo*") (*The Jubilee* 1:339). This repaired fragment should be forthcoming in the revised transcription as part of the newest one hundred-volume edition of Tolstoy's complete works under the aegis of The Institute of World Literature in Moscow (L. N. Tolstoy. *Polnoe sobranie sochinenii*. 100 vols. ed. G. Ia. Galagan, A. V. Gulin, and L. D. Gromova et al. (Moscow: Nauka, 2000–in progress)). The fragments on music were most likely all composed after Tolstoy left Kazan, quitting the university setting for Yasnaya Polyana. The period from June to December of 1850 marks the peak of Tolstoy's study of music. Gruzinsky notes that the first of the fragments on music was written on leaf 66 of the 68-leaf-long handmade notebook, which also includes the rest of the philosophical juvenilia. The second fragment is found on a separate leaf of a large format. The third fragment was recorded in a thin notebook, which measures four by eight inches (see *The Jubilee* 1:339).

to memorize them, with the greatest and most immediate attention, and then to reproduce them—listening to them and trying to write them down.—But, for any given instrument, in order to reproduce certain sounds, one's fingers must be practiced, something that one acquires only through frequent repetition of difficult stretches of music. In order to express music, one needs a certain knowledge of composition, which consists in sequencing sounds in relation to time, space, and force.—Music can be expressed to us in three modes, namely: on paper, on an instrument, and aurally in our ear; hence, to know music, one must know these three modes of expression and know how to transmute what is expressed in one mode by means of another, without losing sight of space, time, and force. Here is how:

1. *Translate from a score to an instrument*: One's hands need to be practiced and to have a dexterity that is acquired thanks to frequent repetition of exercises and, in particular, difficult parts of a score;

2. *Hearing practice from reading scores*: This understanding is acquired as a result of reading scores without an instrument and then by verification.

3. *Take notation from hearing someone play an instrument*: This understanding is acquired through practicing the distinguishing of intervals and taking quick notation while listening.

4. *Listen to someone playing an instrument*: Anyone can do this.

5. *Play by ear*: This can be learned through patient identification of certain motifs on an instrument, by playing unknown scores twice, and then trying to play from memory.

6. *To write by ear*: For this, one needs the same skills as for point 5, only then one needs to be able to write the music instead of playing it.

Second Fragment[41]

Knowledge of music is subjective and objective. The theory of music—i.e., the theory of the basic foundations of music—is objective knowledge. Knowing the rules of music and knowing how to reproduce music are subjective knowledge. Music begins with the capacity to express some musical thought.

A musical thought is a combination of sounds comprising an integral whole, having a beginning and an end.—

---

41 Untitled in the original.

These thoughts are expressed on a particular instrument. For the sake of facilitation, the expression of musical thoughts on paper was invented, and while this is not music proper, it mediates the expression of music.

The capacity to put a musical thought together is called imagination; the capacity to understand this thought consists in having the correct ear for music, and in having what is called a sense for music.

We call a musical sense a capacity to perceive a musical thought in such a way that its harmony suffers no discord in the soul.

The capacity to transmit a musical thought depends on 1) musical memory and 2) musical training and learning, depending on whether the thought is transmitted through music directly or in writing.

And thus, the subjective study of music consists in 1) developing the capacity for imagination; 2) developing a musical mentality and sense; 3) developing [a] musical memory and [b] a capacity to play an instrument, sing, or to compose music.

3rd section

1st part: The development of musical memory.

2nd part: Expressing a thought on an instrument

(all instrumental schooling and singing). The school of piano forte.

2) Expressing thoughts in writing.[42]

(Basso grosso).

3) Developing the capacity to translate music from the mind to an instrument and into writing, i.e., an ability to commit music to memory and into a score. - - - -

And from a score to the instrument and back again....

1. Exercises - - - -

The relationship of sounds, with regards to force. - - - -

This relationship may be infinite. A different degree of force is applied for every sound. - - - -

Five degrees can be distinguished: *even, forceful, very forceful, soft, very soft.*[43] Just as a tuning fork is used to define simple pitch, and a metronome to define timing, a special instrument could be used to strike keys *evenly.*[44]

---

42 A whole line of elliptical dots follows here in the original.

43 Tolstoy was reluctant to use Italian terms and thus used the mundane substitutes from everyday discourse. We have respected his choice and translated his chosen Russian terms to their direct English equivalents.

44 The excluded graph for the study of music follows here in *The Jubilee* (1:243). Also omitted from this translation is an extremely elliptical series of remarks that simply repeat what Tolstoy already said in the first two fragments, many lines of which, moreover, are completely illegible. One novel thing here, though, is how Tolstoy attempted to count rhythm

Third Fragment

The Foundations of Music and Rules for Its Study.
June 14, 1850
The Definition of Music
Music is the sum total of sounds, in two aspects: 1) in relation to space; 2) in relation to time. What I call the space between two or more sounds is the degree of how fast air fluctuates after any kind of disturbance. The cause for the concept of space is movement; movement necessarily requires the concept of some points or moments. In musical space, these moments are the highest and lowest pitch, octaves, and so forth, from C to C and from D to D. Any individual can imagine space as infinite; an individual can therefore imagine an infinite number of octaves. This space is delimited differently in reality—partly thanks to the very structure of the human ear, and partly thanks to the structure of an instrument. The flute has five octaves, for example, whereas the violin and cello have from six to nine. Depending on the time of its construction, a pianoforte can have anywhere from four to seven octaves.

I call the time between two or more sounds "spatial measure." ... ...[45] Just as the concept of space requires the concept of movement from one moment to another, the concept of time requires conceptualizing these two moments.

In the musical sense, these two moments will be the beginning and end of a musical thought. Just as an individual can imagine infinite space, so, too, can he imagine infinite time. In reality, he is delimited by the quality of his imagination and the construction of an instrument.

For example, in both wind and bowed string instruments, the duration of a sound depends on the player. However, in instruments where the sound is extracted by means of touching the strings with a digit or some other device—

---

and beat—remarking that the infinite fragmentation of a single note cannot be reduced below 1/64th. The following sentence is also worth quoting: "To designate in writing sounds proper, it is best to adopt letter icons, using numbers to indicate the tempo, putting one number beneath each letter in the manner of the following fraction: ¾|; gliss/8 c/4|; d/4 f/4/|. To indicate force, one ought to use a line or underline for each of the notes for the 1ˢᵗ [illegible: "step" or "degree"]; two for the 2nd, and so forth; if above even pitch, one line or two overhead; if below even pitch, it should then be placed underneath" (*The Jubilee* 1:244). There must be a transcription error on the part of *The Jubilee* editors in "¾." Since Tolstoy speaks of motion in a melody, there is likely an "a" instead of a "3," since a letter would normally be required over a number. In "gliss" (as in "gliding" [*glissando*]), *The Jubilee* editors have made another transcription error ("ghis"), which I have corrected here.

45 There is a long elliptical break, about one third of a line worth of dots, in the original.

for example, the pianoforte, the gusli, the cymbals, and so on—the sound does not depend on the player but on the quality of the instrument.

The Definition of Music:
Music is the sum total of sounds that strike us aurally in three ways: 1) by way of space; 2) by way of time; 3) by way of force.
December 17
The word "music" has a triple meaning: 1) it has a factual meaning, the definition of which is given above; 2) it is the science and knowledge of the laws in accordance with which sounds connect in the triple sense outlined above; and 3) music is an art by means of which sounds connect in this triple sense. 4) There is a fourth definition of music—a poetic one. In this latter sense, music is a means to incite certain feelings through sounds and to transmit them.

Musical Analysis:
For the current study of music—after the study of the initial musical rules, i.e., notes and intervals, tempo and accentuation—I find it necessary for a student to analyze music, that is, to look at a musical composition in terms of musical rules, depending on how far along in the study of music the student is. For someone who has completed a full course of study of the science of music, they must analyze music as follows: 1) with regards to space: they must analyze each sound, i.e., what interval a tonal sound takes up; 2) with regards to time: they must analyze each sound in relation to an entire bar, i.e., what part of the entire bar a sound takes up; and 3) with regards to force: they must analyze the degree each sound has in relation to the force of the entire piece. This will constitute the base, grammatical meaning of music, so to speak.

There is a higher form of analysis, which consists in the following: 1) with regards to space, analyzing the sequence of sound concatenations—chords, that is—by following the rules and divisions acceptable for a chord;

With regards to time,[46] analyzing the temporal relation of sounds among themselves (for which no rules exist);

With regards to force,[47] analyzing the power relation of sounds among themselves (for which no rules exist).

---

46 The expected ordinal numeral 2) that coordinates with this part of Tolstoy's analysis is absent in the manuscript.
47 The expected ordinal numeral 3) is likewise absent from the original manuscript.

3)[48] The highest degree of analysis consists in analyzing transitions between tonal keys and between tempos, from one accentuation to another. For every brand of analysis, I have invented written signs rather than verbal ones to help students with translations. Here, it is necessary to understand what one would like to translate.—

---

48 Again, contrary to what we could expect, Tolstoy puts the number 3 in this spot of his fragment. The disorder in the numerical designations of these drafts speaks volumes about their still-underdeveloped state.

PART 2

Writings of the 1850s

12. Why People Write[1]
[1851]

1) Why do people write? Some write in order to procure money, others to attain fame, some others for money and fame. Yet there are a few who say that they write to teach people virtue. Why do people read? Why do they pay money for, and glorify, books? People want to be happy; this is the common cause of all actions. Our only means to be happy is to be virtuous; hence, it is only reasonable to read and offer fame and money only for those books that teach virtue. What are these books? They are dogmatic books, those based on the foundations of reason, which are also speculative—sound reason would not admit any others.

But aren't those books useful that, while exquisitely portraying virtue, conduct by way of example? Nearly everyone agrees that by virtue one is to understand the subjection of passions to reason. Poets and novelists, historians and natural scientists meanwhile, instead of inducing people toward reasonable actions by means of developing their reason, develop their passions and induce people toward unreasonable actions. They may say that natural sciences are necessary for the comforts of private life. But are the comforts of private life conducive to the development of virtue? Not in the least; on the contrary, they subdue us even more to the passions.—

Certainly, everything has its utility. It has been proven that the existence of a flea benefits man—whom it bites, we should add. But this utility is objective and should rather be called "necessary influence." There is, however, also a subjective utility. And it is to the latter that I have been referring to here. —

---

1   **Part 2: Writings of the 1850s. Entry 12. "Why People Write"** [*Dlia chego liudi pishut*] (1851). This fragment was most likely jotted down in 1851 and was first published in *The Jubilee* 1:246. The fragment is unfinished: there is no "category 2" following what was sketched as "category 1."

13. On Prayer[2]
[1852]

Only middle-aged family men who have no permanent connection with the secular youths of this century might not know that the majority of young people do not believe in anything. They might also be surprised that I subdivide this young generation into classes: excepting the aforementioned honorable personages, everyone will agree with me that disbelief has cast a deep root in the contemporary generation of the highest social circle and has become so widespread that it is frightful even to consider the fate awaiting our fatherland, assuming it is true that the higher class leads lower classes along the march toward enlightenment...

There are three foundations for disbelief: intellection, vanity, and weakness. According to this division, there are three classes of disbelievers: intellectuals, the vainglorious, and the weak.—Belonging to the first class are individuals endowed with a strong mind and big energy. They feel such an insurmountable need to subjugate everything to the implacable laws of reason that they can't help but refute the laws of religion based on faith and revelation.—Why are they given the opportunity to refute these laws intellectually? Why should they pass through a state of torturous doubt and uncertainty?—These are questions that it is not given to a human being to answer.

—All that they can say is that they are less guilty than they are unhappy—they can see it as against their will, more than that, unconsciously—watching in horror as that which was their firm foundation collapses; and *an unknowable, insurmountable force* draws them toward destruction.—This class of unbelievers has existed always and everywhere, mostly among those who are approaching old age; when the energy diminishes and the need to reflect decreases, they return to religion filled with repentance. Belonging to the third class are all those who—out of intellectual weakness and weakness of will—or out of imitation—submit to the opinion of the majority and stop fulfilling the dogmas of

---

2   **Entry 13. "On Prayer"** [*O molitve*] (1852). This text was published in *The Jubilee* (1:247-48). In his commentary, Gruzinsky notes that the manuscript of "On Prayer" [*O molitve*] (1:340) was executed with the calligraphic precision characteristic of the young Tolstoy's more meticulous hand. In his diary entry for April 1, 1852, Tolstoy described his state of mind when he was composing this note on prayer: "Have been writing a chapter on prayer. Was moving droopily . . . I kept writing and writing and then I started noticing that my reflection on prayer lays claims to logical consistency and intellectual depth but is inconsequential. Have made up my mind to finish it somehow, on the spot, and now burned half of it—I won't place it into my novella but will preserve it as a memorial" (*The Jubilee* 46:105).

the Christian religion and finally stop believing in it. The number of disbelievers of all classes is so great that they comprise the majority in young circles. How can a young lad withstand public opinion—in his heart of hearts, he is afraid, since he feels that he is not acting well—he would be glad to sign himself with a cross, but he is being watched, and he is threatened with . . . ridicule, the ill opinion of other people whom he has chosen as models for imitation and with whom he cannot help but interact constantly.

—The root of the trouble for these people is their youth, their weakness, and their vanity.—Should destiny thrust them into a circle of virtuous people, they would become virtuous—but they find themselves in a circle of disbelievers, and so they become the same.—

Belonging to the second class are those who, having found themselves enticed by intellectualism and philosophical theories (which novels have made accessible to everyone), have swapped Christian beliefs, instilled in them from childhood, for pantheist ideas, intricate suppositions of witty writers, or their own inventions.—Each of them puts together a special religion of his own, which has neither consequence nor foundation, but which is in keeping with the passions and weaknesses that suit it. They believe in what pleases them, refute what is difficult for them to believe, sacrifice their former beliefs in order to massage their egos—to impress others or themselves with a poetic fancy or witticism and on the wreckage of religion they erect a temple to their vanity and weakness. Depending on greater or lesser flexibility and the capacity . . .[3]

14. A Note on Farming[4]
[1856]

Farming is about letting agrarians own portions of land such that they are not left in the position of needing to seek means of sustenance.—When drawing up a contract, one side always enjoys more rights and power over the other side, and the latter is dependent on the former.—With regards to the contract for the

---

3   This fragment breaks off on this word.

4   **Entry 14. "A Note on Farming"** [*Zapiska o Fermerstve*] (1856) discusses the advantages and disadvantages of farmstead versus commune-based systems of agriculture. It survives in the original on a separate leaf. Its unhewn style regardless, the phrasing is precise and without corrections. Tolstoy wrote the fragment in the earlier days of his stay in St. Petersburg after his discharge from active military duty. It is likely related to the conversations in April 1856 with liberals Nikolai Miliutin and Konstantin Kavelin on the emancipation of peasants from serfdom. Published in 1935 in *The Jubilee* 5:241, this fragment was edited and commented on by N. M. Mendelson (5:339).

tilling of landed property, it is fairer for the working side to enjoy more power. This is the position in which to put peasants after having liberated them—for which it is necessary to secure a requisite amount of land and put them in charge of it. Having secured the fiat, the landowner will be dependent on the work of the peasants and will be forced to give away more to them when they produce a greater yield and less to them when they produce a paltrier yield. To whom shall the landowner give what? He will not distribute evenly but will give the most to the most capable.—It ends up being farming with property.—The nobleman cannot be the landowner because then he would be on the same level as the lower class—his enemy. Democracy is impossible because of the inequality in education. The nobleman will serve as the protector of the peasants because his land will be in their hands. The proletariat exists but is coerced into invisibility within the commune.

15. A Letter to Count Dmitry Bludov[5] [1856]

Your Highness Count Dmitry Nikolaevich![6]

On the eve of my departure from Petersburg it seems that I have had the honor of informing you about the purpose of my trip to the countryside. I wish to resolve for myself in particular the question about liberating my peasants, which has been preoccupying me more generally. I even submitted a report to the Vice-Minister of the Interior before my departure in which I listed the principles that I have concerning tilling farmers at large and bonded peasants on

---

5 **Entry 15. A Letter to Count Dmitry Bludov** (1856). Remaining unsent, the letter was a casual address of a high society acquaintance to an older and high-ranking friend, not intended to be an article. This letter was originally published in volume 5 (1935) of *The Jubilee* (5:255-57) and was edited by V. F. Savodnik and N. M. Mendelson as part of the drafts associated with *The Diary of the Landowner* (June 7, 1856).

6 Several generations older than Tolstoy, old enough to have served as Alexander Pushkin's doting literary guardian during the poet's libertarian youth, Count Dmitry Nikolaevich Bludov (1785–1864) was the holder of many important government posts throughout his long career: he was Minister of the Interior from 1832–1839; Head of the Imperial Chancellery from 1839–1862; and was named President of the Academy of Sciences on November 25, 1855, a new appointment that coincided with Tolstoy's loose military affiliation in St. Petersburg after the Sevastopol campaign. Bludov was part of Tolstoy's high society circle despite the disparity of their ranks: In 1856, Tolstoy signed his official papers "Count Tolstoy, lieutenant of the artillery, landowner of the Tula District." Tolstoy's diary in St. Petersburg records many amicable if slightly boring dinners with Bludov. In 1862, Bludov would become Head of the State Council. In fact, it was reading Pushkin's then newly published but soon to become bestselling biography by Petr Bartenev, *Materialy dlia biografii Pushkina* (*Materials for the Biography of Pushkin* [1855]), that prompted Tolstoy to write

whom I was going to exercise the deed—principles that do not quite square with the current laws.[7] Mr. Minister sent a word to me through his assistant that he was in favor of my plan, that he had looked at it and will try to approve a detailed proposal that I promised to send from the countryside[8].—I proposed to the peasants upon arriving to opt for a quitrent, half the amount of the going rate in nearby villages, in place of a corvée.[9] The commune responded that the quitrent was too high and that they would not be able to pay it. I proposed wages—obtaining no agreement. I proposed that they shift to bonded peasants with a three-day-a-week work requirement and land supplement so that after the elapse of 24 years (the term set for the payoff of the mortgage), the peasants will receive free status with full ownership of the land. To my surprise, they refused and even asked, as if mockingly, whether I will give away all of my land as well.—I did not despair and continued to converse with the commune at communal meetings and separately.[10] I have finally discovered the reason for their refusal, which had previously been incomprehensible to me. In keeping with their customary lying, deceit, and hypocrisy, inspired by management by

---

this letter to Bludov. Tolstoy wrote the following in his diary on June 9, 1856: "I am reading the biography of Pushkin with delight. It crossed my mind to write a letter to Bludov about serfs, which I drafted" (47:80; volume 47 of *The Jubilee* published in 1937 and edited by V. F. Savodnik, V. I. Sreznevsky; M. A. Tsiavslovsky). The letter to Bludov remained unsent, however. Here, I have translated the edited version of the letter later published in volume 60 of *The Jubilee* in 1949 (60:64-67).

7   Tolstoy's report to Vice-Minister of the Interior Alexey Iraklievich Levshin was published in volumes 5 and 60 of *The Jubilee* (5:247-48 and 60:463-65).

8   Tolstoy means Sergey Stepanovich Lanskoy (1787–1862) who was Minister of the Interior from 1855 to 1861. Tolstoy's report to the Minister was sent on April 25, 1856 (60:57-59). Lanskoy "sent word" to Tolstoy on May 10, 1856.

9   At the time of Tolstoy's application letters to government dignitaries, Yasnaya Polyana was mortgaged for debts to The Guardian Council, an institution founded in 1763 for financial guardianship of disorderly estates. Since 1808 it had been affiliated with bonds and loans offices, designed to beef up the protection of the estates against loss of value and impoverishment of the nobility, guaranteeing liquid and real estate possessions. The mortgaging of Yasnaya Polyana complicated Tolstoy's intention to liberate his peasants, as is clear from a number of explanations and letters of solicitation that he wrote to Ministers Lanskoy and Levshin. In July 1855, Tolstoy notes that paying down his debts was his primary task before he could liberate his peasants (47:50). In August of the same year, he was already working on *The Novel of the Russian Landowner* (which he never finished). But, as he pledged, he did eventually pay off the debts and bought back Yasnaya Polyana.

10 Tolstoy's befuddling negotiations with his peasants took place upon his arrival at Yasnaya Polyana on May 28, 1856. In his diary, he notes that the peasants were more open to negotiating when they saw him as a swindler. They trusted him more when they understood him to be seeking the customary landowner profit, yet suspecting worse trickery from the reform business (47:77). His own beloved aunt Tatiana Ergolskaya obstinately refused to ever condemn serfdom (see Tolstoy's diary for May 28; 47:77; June 9, 1856; 47:80).

proxy practiced by landowners for many years, behind my back the commune said that they were happy but only saw in my words and proposals a desire to cheat and rob them. To wit: they are all firmly convinced that all bonded serfs shall be granted freedom during the coronation, and they even vaguely fantasize that this might come with land, all the landowners' land, even. In my proposal, they see a desire to keep them beholden, even during times of freedom, through a signed contract that will remain valid.

I am writing all of this only in order to inform you about two facts, extraordinarily important and dangerous facts: 1) The conviction has become rooted in all common people, even in the remotest parts [of Russia], that universal liberation will follow the coronation; and, most importantly, 2) the question about who owns the land that ostensibly belongs to the landowners but is populated by the peasants is extraordinarily tangled, and is decided among the people in favor of peasants, for the most part, which, moreover, goes for all landowner holdings. We are yours, but the land is ours. Despotism always begets the despotism of slavery. The despotism of the king's rule begat the despotism of the mob. The despotism of landowners begat the despotism of peasants. When they told me at the commune assembly that I should give all my land to them and I responded that that would be giving them the shirt off my back, they had a laugh, for which they cannot be blamed: this was as it was supposed to be. The government is to blame, for it skirts the question any time this issue makes it to the top of the agenda. The government is losing its dignity and has given birth to the despotic talk that has now become so rooted in the people.

Inventories:[11] Let the government straightforwardly say to whom the land belongs. I am not saying that this decree be recognized for all landowner property; let it be recognized for peasant property in part or even entirely. The time is not right to think about historical justice and class interests; it is time to save the whole edifice from burning to the ground, from the fire that is about to envelop it, any minute. It is clear to me that landowners are faced with the following question: life or land? And, I have to confess, I have never understood why it is not possible to make the land the landowner's property and yet liberate the peasant without this land? The proletariat! But is the proletarian not worse off when he is hidden from view and is dying of famine on his own land that cannot feed him, when he has nothing to till it with, and has no opportunity to come into the square yelling and crying "give me bread and work?" All are rejoicing

---

11   "Inventories:" Here, Tolstoy refers to the law of "bonded" peasants from April 2, 1842, which restricted their freedom of movement between censuses and reaffirmed a strict regimen for their economic and personal obligations to their landlords.

for some reason, alleging that it has been proven that liberation without land is impossible, and that the entire history of Europe has demonstrated ruinous examples to us that we refuse to follow. But those historical phenomena that the proletariat produced through revolution and Napoleons have not spoken their last word; they cannot be adjudged to be finished. (Lord knows, might it not be a foundation for the renaissance of the world toward peace and freedom?) With the exception of Prussia, where the question was prepared, it was not possible to skirt the question in any other way in Europe. Here with us we must lament the general conviction, albeit quite a just one, that liberation with land is necessary. We must lament this conviction because liberation will never be resolved by means of land. Who will answer the following unavoidable questions: How much land should each peasant receive? What piece of the landowner's land? How is the landowner to be compensated? When? Who will compensate him? These questions have no resolution; or rather, to resolve them would take decades of field research across the entire expanse of Russia.—

Yet this issue cannot wait, because it has arrived historically, politically, and by accident. The beautiful, truthful words spoken by Sire[12] in Moscow flew across the state,[13] reaching all the estates, and everyone remembers them. First, this is because they were neither tidbits for a parade nor mere jigsaw pieces for a tableau vivant, but words about a cause that is dear to everyone's heart. Second, they're sincere-direct-true.—It is impossible to renege on them because, to repeat, they are true. To renege on these words would be tantamount to besmirching the *prestige*[14] of the throne by, as it were, dropping it in the mud; there is thus no delaying their fulfilment, because the suffering are waiting.[15]

Let them simply announce clearly and distinctly, through a law made public, to whom the land tilled by the bonded peasants belongs. Let them also

---

12 Alexander II speech in Moscow March 30, 1856. The official coronation of Alexander II took place on August 26, 1856. Tolstoy uses *Gosudar'/Gosudaria* for "Sire."

13 Tolstoy deliberately chose the word *gosudarstvo* to speak about the Russian Empire. Here, he is playing on the similarity of the words *gosudar'* and *gosudarstvo*—both in sound and writing—underscoring the relatedness of these words for the Russian people. Whether the idea of the Russian state is inextricable from the concept of the monarchy or rather that the two are independent as terms and historical developments was a traditional point of contention between those Russian intellectuals who identified as Slavophiles and those who identified as Westernizers. The former position was more characteristic of the Slavophiles, while the latter was more typical of the Westernizers. Uncharacteristically for his spelling habits, which frequently lacked all piety, Tolstoy capitalized both of these words. During a time of intensive conversations about the future of Russia with members of both of these intellectual groups, Tolstoy's spelling could hardly have been an accidental slip.

14 Here, Tolstoy writes the word in French.

15 The Russian original reads: "*ego dozhidaiut liudi stradaiushchie.*"

announce the liberation of all, conditional on six months of probation, and the extension of the peasants' current conditions,[16] under the supervision of specially appointed officers. Let them draft conditions[17] that would regulate and leave in place the relationships between peasants and landlords. Let them even stipulate unlimited resettling from the lands, allowing the local governorate to determine the *minimum*[18] necessary for this [resettlement]. There is no other way of resolving this issue, and resolution is necessary.—If the serfs are not freed within 6 months, everything will catch fire.[19] Everyone is waiting for the conflagration to be sparked, the incendiary hand of a traitor being all that is necessary to light the flame of revolt, and then fire will rage everywhere. We have said all along that this all requires a lot of work, that we must think things over, take our time. But no! The time is ripe. There are three ways out: First, money! But there is none. Second, a prorated payout. But there is no time. And third, liberation without land, which can be approbated later. But first of all an announcement must be made as a preliminary measure: there is nothing to hide, everyone is aware.—

16. On Military Criminal Law[20]
[1856]

A.

I would like to take a closer look at extant Russian military criminal law.— Military society cannot be viewed as civil society. The aim of a civil society or

---

16 Tolstoy repeats the words "*s usloviem; na prezhnikh usloviiakh.*"

17 Again, I have translated "*usloviia*" as "conditions" here.

18 This was written in Latin in the original.

19 The image of fire ("*pozhar*") is traditionally associated with political disorder, revolt, and revolution.

20 **Entry 16. "On Military Criminal Law"** [*O voenno-ugolovnom zakonodatel'stve*] (1856). This note was published for the first time in volume 5 of *The Jubilee* (5:237-40). From the fall of 1855 onward, Tolstoy was semi-retired from military life, on military leave in St. Petersburg as a noncommissioned officer although his resignation had not yet taken full effect. He still felt affiliated with the army. Non-coincidentally, one of the manuscript parts of the note is titled "From the Records of an Artillery Officer," which was subsequently crossed out (see the commentary of N. M. Mendelson in volume 5 of *The Jubilee*, 5:334-35). Manuscript B is a later and cleaner, if not an entirely fair, copy of manuscript A. Mendelson thought that Tolstoy's activities around the emancipation distracted him from finishing this project,

union is internal—carrying out the ideals of eternal truth, goodness, and general happiness—whereas the aim of military society is external. The military society is one of the instruments for carrying out contemporary justice, and its aim is murder. It is abnormal: what is criminal in civil society is not so in military society, and vice versa. The more abnormal the society, the more powerful is the connection between civil society and military society. What connects the two are laws. The aim of laws in civic society is justice, whereas the aim of military society is force. The power of the military society lies in the unity of all its members in one whole. Discipline—the unity of all in one—differs from the unity of all members in the civic society of a state in that it is rational in the latter and does not constrain arbitrary willing, whereas in the other case it is mechanical and preempts arbitrary personal willing.[21] The spirit of the military differs from the spirit of society in that it is only an effect of legislation, whereas it is the aim in the former, since the aim of military society is force and the consciousness of force is the first condition of power.[22] (Military affairs are decided by means of spirit and not by fire and sword.) The main method for achieving discipline through all preceding centuries—or at least mechanical obedience—was habit and the inviolability of criminal law (it wasn't fear, because the fear of death is greater than the fear of a rod. Whereas the former *might be* correct, the latter *is* just right).[23]

Russian martial law allows the following kinds of punishments for crimes: arrest, probation, transfer to the regular army, etc., demotion, transfer to penalty units, extension of service, running the gauntlet to death, a certain number of strikes with a rod, and punishment by whipping. The execution of a sentence on criminals is carried out differently in times of peace and times of war, depending on the offender's rank and his crime. In the majority of cases, a sentence depends on the arbitrary rule of the one nearest in command.

---

because the note on farming (see "A Note on Farming" in entry 15 above) is written on the obverse of manuscript C.

21   Tolstoy mistakenly uses the description "latter" for both types of social discipline that he is contrasting here.

22   Military: Tolstoy plays on the double meaning of the Russian word *sila*, which means "force" and "power."

23   Here, Tolstoy plays on the notion of "correct" as in correction by the means available to justice. The obedience to law was mechanical, not metaphysical. The fear of death (metaphysical fear) is greater than the fear of punishment (the rod). If the rod just "might" be correct, the fear of death is always "right," for it always prevails.

Let us look at some of these punishments and the methods of their administration.

I would like first of all to entertain some considerations regarding the peculiarity of military society—first, its difference from civic society and of the aim and impact of military laws as a result of this difference. The aim of civic criminal laws is general justice; the aim of military society is discipline, and moreover, the spirit of the troops. 1) Transfer to the army: The influence on discipline and the spirit. An example of aristocratic corruption of the army. 2) Demotion of the soldier, who is the predominant builder of the spirit of the troops. A view on him and for the duration. [Illegible: corruption, classes, cruel.] 3) Running the gauntlet: a) an impossibility that is accepted as a law. Henchmen—everyone. Corruption. Purposelessness. Horror only for spectators. Who decided that simply dying is not enough? 4) Punishment with a rod: Arbitrariness. Contrary to discipline. Aim not achieved. Judges are henchmen. The judge and the accused. Head of pretrial confinement.

Neither correction nor threats. What to put in its place, they'd say? Yes, go ahead, prove the necessity of this barbaric custom. The model is the French army, which is the best. There are examples in our army.

[the power of the military society is in the discipline and the fighting spirit].[24] Discipline is obedience and the awareness by each individual member of the force, both personal and general. The consciousness of power is affected thanks to the awareness of duty and one's independence from others.

B.

The following kinds of punishment exist, by the way, in the Russian military criminal law:

1. Transfers from the guards to the army, to front-line battalions and garrisons;
2. Demotion to the rank and file;
3. Extension of duty;
4. Discharge;
5. Running the gauntlet;
6. Punishment by rods.

---

24 This is one of the examples of the crossed-out text discussed in "A Note on the Text" at the beginning of this volume.

These punishments are awarded by a sentence, which is based on whether the crime was committed in times of peace or war, how grave the crime was, the rank and distinction of the criminal, the trial, and the arbitrary will of the superior.

When willing to investigate the justice and purposefulness of the five existing kinds of punishments, we see it necessary to provide a preliminary elucidation of the difference between criminal laws in the army and the general criminal laws of the state.

One may not regard military society as part of one whole, the state, nor can it be subsumed under general laws, because the rights and duties of the members of that society are completely different and frequently contrary to the rights and duties of members of civic society.

Murder is a crime if committed by a citizen based on the laws of general justice, whereas in many cases, it is the duty of a warrior. The cause for such a difference lies in the connection between one and the other society.—The aim of civic society is general justice and the welfare of all its citizens, which is embedded by default.

The nearer the laws of such a society approach the universal and eternal ideal, the more perfect they are. The aim of military society is murder, violence, or, in a word, force, which is external to society. The closer its laws approach the administration of power, the more perfect they are. (I consider it redundant to talk about the legality of the existence of military society, despite its injustice. No society carries out the general aims of eternal justice completely and directly, but by way of contemporary injustice they all move toward general and eternal truth.)

C.

What kinds of martial punishments exist in Russia? What kinds exist in Europe? In nation states? What is the general spirit of such laws? What is the general spirit of European laws? How is Russian military criminal law carried out in reality (incommensurability of reality with laws) (customary trespassing of laws, and the reasons for that—)?[25]

The aim of criminal law in general and of the military in particular—morality and spirit, aversion to threats, correction, retribution are the only applicable [. . .illegible in the manuscript].

---

25   The following was crossed out by Tolstoy: "it cannot transcend beyond murder for its ideal."

What should the spirit of military law be? The possibility of advancing toward ethics and loftiness of the spirit in the current form, and in this consists its difference from civic society. What aims does the Russian legislature and preemptive threat have? And how—to what degree? What is its spirit? Recognizing soldiers to be on the lowest of rungs. Comparison with the European (the historical view and the accidental, on this, and the other).

Is it possible to improve ethics and spirit in the Russian army with the current legislature?

What is defined as a crime? Not discipline, but a means to oppress.

A comparison:—How to define a crime and sentence a punishment. (Domestic correction).—What punishments? Their execution in real terms, the necessary and the accidental, the historical. (How are they administered?) The needs of a soldier. Incidental punishments: 1) inhumanity; 2) incomprehensibility; 3) aim not achieved; 4) injustice; 5) harmful influence on the punished and the punishing; 6) impossibility to respect laws as a result and fall (depression) of morale.

Related to everything—facts, incidents, personages, characters.

Is it possible to substitute: Penalty by fine? Defeat in rights? extension of the term?—No. Incarceration without pay for the service that the offender misses.—

Mock Punishment.—The morale of the troops with corporal punishments and without those. Impossibility of a comparison with criminal law in general, because, aside from morality, the aim of the military is spirit.

17. A Note on the Nobility[26]
[1858]

In his speech delivered in Moscow,[27] our Lord the Emperor[28] reproaches the noble class for being slow to express their consent to liberation and the committee for being slow to take action; and he lets it be felt that the tarrying may land the nobility in a precarious position.

In what does the cause of liberation consist?

It behooves our Lord the Emperor to liberate the peasants from their noble lords. He was persuaded—quite rightly—that the peasants cannot be liberated except with the land on which they reside. This land belongs to the landowners. It is therefore necessary, after having rescinded certain rights of the landowners to portions of the land, to transfer these rights to the peasants.—Four ways appeared plausible to carry out the transfer: 1) To buy the land from the landowners and give it to the peasants. 2) Taking state welfare into account, to remove the land from the landowners without compensation and hand it over to the peasants. 3) To ask the nobility to resort to self-sacrifice for the sake of the welfare of the state and give up their land to the peasants. 4) By making the state of its finances public, to rely on the cooperation of all estates, especially the most educated among the noble class, who might identify measures for bailing out the land expropriated from the landowners.

If the first choice were made, the nobility would have to please the Tsar by consenting to the purchase. If the second choice were made, the nobility would have to respond with submission and with silence to the expropriation

---

26 **Entry 17. "A Note on the Nobility"** [*Zapiska o Dvorianstve*] (1858). This text was first published in *The Jubilee* (5:267-70). According to a note in Tolstoy's diary, it was written around December 12, 1858, while he was in Moscow: "I have written a note on the question of the noble class and burnt it, without showing it to anyone" (48:19). N. M. Mendelson claimed that only one draft copy of this note survived (5:354).

27 Tolstoy must be again referring to the addresses of Alexander II to the Moscow Noble Assembly on March 30, 1856, in which he warned about the difficulty of the upcoming reform, made it clear that it must require several stages, was open about its unpostponable urgency, and famously averred that it would better be delivered from above than arrive from below. In 1857, the tsar formed a secret committee for the drafting of measures necessary for the implementation of the reform.

28 Tolstoy's increasingly caustic attitudes toward Alexander II's liberal pretensions is obvious even from his slightly modified tone of reference to Alexander's Imperial title, best rendered in English as a switch from a more cordial "our Sire" (such as in the letter to Bludov) to "Our Lord the Emperor," perhaps meant to keep clear the Tsar's status as the richest lord, landowner, and serf owner in the land. Tolstoy goes as far as to mock the Emperor's suggestion that the government would have achieved its goal with lesser losses were there greater input from the nobility.

without compensation. If it came down to self-sacrifice, the nobility could clearly inform the government of its expectations. If, having confessed to its dysfunctionality, the government resorted to the aid of noble assemblies, the educated estate could assist government efforts. But none of these manifestly possible measures was chosen by the government. A rescript appeared at the beginning of the current year in which the future conditions for the peasant estate were defined quite clearly, but conditions for the estate that was invited to undergo expropriation of half of its property were completely absent. Circulars from the minister, amendments to circulars, the speeches of our Lord the Emperor appeared, but—just as with the rescript—these are all silent about who will pay for the land expropriated from the landowners.

We should remember what took place in France and England, states where the level of education and therefore the degree of awareness concerning common welfare stands so immeasurably higher than with us: the government found it impossible to liberate slaves other than by paying money to the owners for their purchase. How could we have expected the nobility to greet a rescript that not only deprives them of a valuable right to own peasants as property without compensation, but also of a significant portion of the land, without defining any guarantee to compensation, other than by tasking landowners (without changing the disgraceful police system) to run up enormous sums to charge peasants for their own liberation from slavery as a ransom for the cost of the expropriated land?

In place of the universal indignation and embittered anger with which it was expected that the nobility would greet the rescript depriving it of half of their property while asking them to keep mum about the conditions of the sale (the rescript resembled the words with which a crafty kulak entices an inexperienced seller), the nobility met the rescript with unalloyed exultation. In case a murmur could be heard among the majority—and not on account of the expropriation of personal property without compensation but on account of a bailout without a guarantee, this murmur was muffled in literature, in society, and at noble electorates with the exaltation of the minority—the best educated and the most powerful, therefore.

This still underappreciated phenomenon, one of a kind in history, came into being because the rescript on liberation was a response to an ancient desire of the sole educated class in Russia, the nobility, which has found such an eloquent expression throughout the new history of Russia. Since the times of Catherine the Great,[29] only the nobility has treated this question—in literature,

---

29　Catherine the Great ruled from 1762 to 1796.

in secret and non-secret societies, in word, and in deed. It and it alone sent its martyrs to help bring this idea to fruition, at the price of exile and death by gallows in the years between 1825 and 1848, and throughout the whole of Nicholas's reign.[30] The noble class supported this idea in society and allowed it to become ripe to such an extent that the current weak government found it impossible to suppress it anymore.

Even if some were spurred to action by excessive exultation, while others thanks to substituting for the great cause a career in vile flattery, they succeeded in convincing our Lord the Emperor that he is Peter the Great the II and a great reformer of Russia, that he is making Russia new again and so forth. This is completely in vain, sire needs to hurry up and lose this enchantment, for he merely responded to the demand put forth by the nobility; it was not he, but the nobility, that raised, developed, and worked out the idea of liberation.

The exultation produced by the rescript in the minority—yet who became a major force thanks to their education and influence—was expressed so strongly that nobody noticed in the first minutes the injustice and impossibility of those elements in the rescript from which our Lord the Emperor would not retreat, as he stated in his speech. But everyone rushed into feverish action to bring their once-favorite idea into reality, even if it was on the inane conditions of the government. People showed up who began to adjust history to the yardstick of the government, proving the right of the peasants to land. The exultation cooled considerably once push came to shove. When invited to discuss the question and without insisting on the right of personal property of the peasant, the outnumbering noble majority—less independent in means, less educated—came across the gaping hole in the securities guaranteeing the land, and this slowed down the course of all progress.—"Who shall pay for the right to own—or perhaps the right to use—the land being requisitioned from us?" this majority asks. Peasants? Okay, let the government, which has more means than we do, get this money; we believe the government, but we do not see it possible to impose charges on peasants in their new situation and under the old state with the police. The quitrent levied, no matter how cheaply we may value the land, is four times higher than what the state peasants living next door are paying.—"And what will our income be after we are deprived of both our workforce and our land if all that we have now are bare necessities," others asked. "And what is so criminal about the way we have lived since 1858?"—Having

---

30 Nicholas I ruled from 1825 to 1855. Tolstoy here is referring to the martyrdom of the Decembrists (survivors amnestied in 1856), forced emigration of Alexander Herzen in 1847, and the arrest and sentence to hard labor of the members of the Petrashevsky Circle in April 1849.

encountered such questions, the educated majority felt that: 1) it was completely fair that—their convictions in the necessity of sacrificing one half of their property notwithstanding—it has no right to coerce the lesser educated majority which was deprived of living necessities; and 2) they are not yet aware of having been forced into the position of choosing between cutthroat death or dire poverty. The majority understood the understatement of the rescript clearly and started looking for alternative means for solving the question.

It naturally occurred to them that the nobility's sole means was a bailout or guarantee. Bailout proposals seeking to balance all interests came from all sides. The most ardent defenders of liberation at any cost understood the perfect justice of the bailout or the government guarantee on land.—Yet, and this is a strange matter, despite the fact that bailout is the sole solution for the current impasse, despite the fact that voices on all sides and from all estates are clamoring for a bailout, the government continues to cling obstinately to the clauses of the script and either keeps silent or rejects all proposals for bailout or guarantee by the state. This is the same government that has been constantly appropriating all kinds of property into the hands of the state: plants, forests, lands and so on, and it now obstinately refuses to assume guardianship of landowner peasants with their lands and to charge them the bailout that it agrees is just. The possibility of financial measures remains a mystery. It would seem that having met with such a premeditated or deliberate cunning, the nobility might have tried to halt the whole affair. Quite the contrary, left to its own devices, even as it gave up on the weak government that shielded itself behind its back, the nobility is trying to identify the means for finding, through strenuous work from the inside, a way out of the dead end.

Resounding all across Russia amid this difficult work are the words by the head of the state addressed to the nobility from Moscow: "Having given it a long thought and after praying to God, I began liberation. You cannot be thanked, but I wished I could thank you, for I was born in Moscow. Do try to justify my high trust in you or else I cannot stand by you, and so forth. But I shall not retreat from my principles." —What an insulting piece of comedy, which betrays a complete lack of comprehension about such an important matter! Whether it prays to God or not, it wasn't the government that raised the question, and it is not by its high trust and gratitude or with threats of massacre that it moves it forward. The government has for so long suppressed the question; it is the government also that erects insurmountable obstacles to its solution. It is the nobility that moved the issue forward and is solving and shall solve it despite all the governmental debacles. It is therefore not in good taste to incite it by the promise of gratitude and high trust; it is unfair to reproach it for being slow; and it is neither honest nor reasonable to threaten it with massacre, hinting that it might not be bad at all in a sense, on account of the weakness and inanity of the government. Having assumed of its free volition its own position on which to stand its ground, the nobility knew what it was doing. But does the government know, given its feint of oppressed guilelessness, about the misfortunes for which it is preparing Russia with its obstinacy and incapacity? Should the government lead us to the liberation from below, and not from above, we shall quote our Lord the Emperor's witticism: the destruction of the government would be the lesser of two evils.

18. A Talk Delivered at the Society of Lovers of Russian Literature[31] [1859]

Messieurs,

My election to Society Member is flattering to my self-esteem and makes me feel sincerely overjoyed. I attribute this flattering election not so much to my feeble attempts at literature as to the sympathy I have expressed toward the field of literature in those feeble attempts. In the past two years, the remarkably intelligent, honest, and talented proponents of political literature—and the literature of exposure, in particular—have drawn on the devices of fine art to ardently and resolutely answer every question relevant to their moment in time and respond to every momentary social wound. This kind of literature has absorbed all of the public's attention and has divested literary fiction of its importance entirely.

---

31 **Entry 18. "A Talk Delivered at the Society of Lovers of Russian Literature"** [*Rech' v obshchestve liubitelei rossiiskoi slovesnosti*] (1859). This is the first of three public statements or records of public appearances by Tolstoy included in this volume. In 1857–59, Tolstoy was veering away from social criticism-oriented artists and political satirists such as Nikolai Nekrasov and Mikhail Saltykov-Shchedrin, and instead forming closer ties with the Russian representatives of the pure art movement, such as Vasilii Botkin, Apollon Grigoriev, Alexander Druzhinin, and the poet Afanasy Fet. He always had affinity with the great Russian writer of drama Alexander Ostrovsky. In the years leading up to the emancipation of the serfs in 1861, he was sympathetic to the Slavophile writers and thinkers who were in support of the idea of the peasant commune: Alexey Khomiakov, Konstantin Aksakov, Ivan Aksakov, and the historian of Russian and Ukrainian religious folklore Mikhail Maksimovich. Founded in 1811 and incorporated with the University of Moscow after decades of inactivity during the reign of Tsar Nicholas I, in 1859 the Society of Lovers of Russian Literature resumed its work. On January 28, 1859, at the recommendation of Konstantin Aksakov, Tolstoy was elected to membership at age thirty, simultaneously with Ivan Turgenev who was ten years

The majority of the public began to think that the sole task of literature is to expose evil, through discussion and edification—in a word, that literature's only aim is the development of civic consciousness throughout society. I have happened to read and hear judgments that the time of the little fable and the verselet has irreversibly passed, that the time is coming when Pushkin will be forgotten and never again published. I have heard it said that pure art is impossible, that literature is just a tool for the civic progress of society, and so on. One can hear the voices of Fet, Turgenev, and Ostrovsky—muffled as they have been by political noise—and other voices, in fact, recapitulating the art for art's sake criticism, yet others arguing that society knows what literature's purpose is, and that it continues to be in sympathy with political literature alone and to consider it alone to be literature. This obsession was noble, necessary, and even provisionally justified. In order for our society to have been able to make the huge strides forward that it has made of late, it had to be one-dimensional, it had to have its aspirations run ahead of its aim; to achieve its aim, it had to fix its eyes on nothing else.

And in truth, is it possible to think about poetry when a canvas depicting the evil that surrounds us is unfurled before our eyes, one that shows us how we might rid the world of it? How can we think about the sublimely beautiful when it has come to feel so agonizing! It is not up to us who have exploited the fruits of this infatuation to raise reproaches against it. This noble infatuation has borne many fruits: not least, the unconscious demand for respect toward literature that is widespread in our society, the emergence of public opinion, and self-governance (I might even go further here and say that our political literature has substituted for a lack of self-governance). However noble and beneficial, this one-dimensional infatuation was, like any other, short-lived.

National literature is its own complete, multi-dimensional consciousness, which must reflect both the love of its people toward goodness and truth, as

---

his senior. Tolstoy spoke at the very next session following the election, on February 4, 1859. A lot of luminaries were present at the session that Khomiakov chaired, including the famous historian Sergey Solovyov, the aforementioned Pushkin biographer Bartenev, and several veterans from the Pushkin circle: Stepan Shevyrev, Mikhail Pogodin, and Alexander Veltman. The proceedings remained barred from publication by the Tsar's censors. *The Jubilee* published the text in volume 5 in 1935 (5:271-73) from the copyist's fair version corrected by Tolstoy, which originally appeared in V. S. Savodnik and A. E. Gruzinsky eds., *Neizdannye khudozhestvennye proizvedeniia L. N. Tolstogo* (Moscow: Federatsiia, 1928), 247-50. N. M. Mendelson provided the first detailed commentary in volume 5 of *The Jubilee* (5:355-58). For the other public presentations by Tolstoy in this anthology, see his defense at the court martial trial of soldier Vasilii Shibunin (1866) and "The Concept of Life," his presentation on March 14, 1887, to The Moscow Psychological Society.

well as the contemplation of beauty in every epoch of the nation's development. Now that the first flush of the fervor of this novel activity has passed, as has the triumph of success, now that the political torrent that was kept blocked for so long lest it swallow the whole of literature, emerged and spread out, though then calmed down and sleepily got back into bed, society has come to realize the one-dimensionality of its infatuation.

We have started to hear people say that dark pictures of evil have grown tedious, that to describe what we all already know is worthless, and so on. And society is right. This naively expressed displeasure signifies that society has come to an understanding through practice and through lived experience of the seemingly simple truth, rather than only through criticism, and is now conscious of the following state of affairs: however great the importance of political literature that reflects the interests of the society of the time, however necessary it is for national development, there is a literature of another kind that reflects the eternal interests of humanity, the dearest, most intimate states of awareness of national consciousness—this literature is accessible to every individual of every nation and every period, the kind of literature without which not a single people has developed who come to possess power and suppleness.

This newly emerged conviction is doubly joyous for me. It is joyous for me personally, as a one-dimensional lover of the *belles lettres*—I open-heartedly confess to self-identifying as such—and joyous more generally, providing new proof of the strength and maturity of our society and its literature. Our social consciousness has come to realize the necessity and importance of two separate types of literary genus, which itself serves as the best proof that the literary art of our nation is not a foreign transplant for mere childish amusement. Russia's literary art stands firm on its own grounds, responds to the multidimensional needs of its society, has said and still has much to say, and constitutes a serious consciousness of a serious nation.

Now that our literature is mature, one can feel even prouder to be included in the rank of contemporary Russian Writers, and indeed one can rejoice at the resumption of the Society of Lovers of Russian Literature. It is as such that I offer my sincere thanks for the honor of being elected to membership of this esteemed Society.

PART 3

Writings of the 1860s

19. On Violence[1]
[late 1850s–early 1860s]

At all times and in every locale of the globe, one and the same incomprehensible state of affairs comes to pass over and over again: power, the law, external force—and human force of its own—make people live against their desires and needs. What is this incomprehensible force to which people submit the way they submit to gravitational force without asking themselves about its origin, its beginning, or whether this strange force ever ends? This very question I pose to myself and will try to answer. This question may be answered in two ways: *abstractly*, by considering the concept of force and deducing its origin out of human nature; or *historically*, by regarding its manifestation, development or decay, the movement of this force in a given society.—What kind of concept is force (violence)?[2] It is subjugation of one person by another to be coerced into doing or enduring something that that other considers unjust. Violence can be done only by someone with more power, and it is suffered by someone who is weaker. One person may sometimes be stronger, but many individuals are always stronger than one. The former case is possible only outside of human society, because society creates a defense based on humans' sense of self-preservation. It obviously follows that in society violence is only done by

---

1   **Part 3: Writings of the 1860s. Entry 19. "On Violence"** [*O nasilii*] (late 1850s–early 1860s). First publication in 1936, in volume 7 of *The Jubilee* (7:121-24). Written on two full leaves in-folio, seven of the eight pages are fully covered with text; the eighth page is blank. Starting on the third page, the writing becomes sketchier, according to V. F. Savodnik, who was the editor of, and commentator on, the fragment in volume 7 (7:365).

2   By *sila*, Tolstoy here means "force," which he follows directly with *nasilie* meaning "violence," the latter word enclosed in parentheses, playing on the reversible connotation in the Russian original. "Violence," a derivative of the word "force," literally means "forcing" or "coercing" in Russian. Thus, everything that happens against the will or subjective volition toward the desirable or "just" is violence, the smallest restriction of freedom becomes violence.

many against one or by the majority against the minority. For many to do violence to one person or a small number of people, it is necessary for the multitude to have one and the same goal and be in unanimous agreement, because it is apparent that individuals are equal in power if each of them has different goals. Therefore, violence in society can be done only by the unanimous majority—either to one person or to the unanimous minority.

What is the unanimity or agreement of many persons under known circumstances? An identical view on the same circumstance is a shared idea. An identical view or shared idea is a view or thought that is relatively just for a certain majority. Therefore, violence may be produced only by a relatively just majority. But the concept of enduring violence presupposes enduring a deed that is relatively unjust for the minority or for one person. Hence, violence is the carrying out of a deed that is relatively just from the point of view of the majority and relatively unjust for the minority.[3]

Why are there two kinds of justice in every society whenever violence is done: justice of the minority and justice of the majority? And what general qualities does either form of justice have in all societies?

In order to answer these questions, it is necessary to accept as axiomatic the following two conditions that are provable but whose proof would require too much of a digression.—

1) There is a concept of abstract justice, common to all people at all times—the idea of justice that embraces ideas of equality and freedom.

   Because of the kind of human confrontation that violates these ideas of equality and freedom that are absolutely mutual, there is another idea: relative justice, relative equality, and freedom.<The idea of absolute justice and the need to convert relative justice into absolute lies in human nature.>

2) Human nature tends to convert itself from a particular idea to a higher idea and never vice versa.

3) <In the course of history, the human idea of relative justice, by changing itself constantly, approaches the idea of absolute justice.>

4) The idea is conveyed by violence and by word.

---

3   On the "relativity" of justice and on a "somewhat just" justice, see my comments in the "Editor's Introduction."

Having adopted these postulates, it becomes clear why there is always the justice of the majority and the justice of the minority. Why do the minority or the one person upon whom violence is inflicted consider the justice of the majority unjust? All people <at the lowest stage of development> must agree with each other and have identical needs. If there appeared those who disagreed, that was only because the justice of the majority was injustice to them; they had another justice, that is, a superior one. As soon as they stopped sharing the idea of justice entertained by the majority, the majority used violence against them. But the idea of violence is contrary to the idea of general justice—of freedom and equality; hence, the minority that suffered violence could not comprehend the idea of relative justice of the majority and found it unjust. In other words, the minority constructed for itself a different idea of justice, a more general one, one that is closer to the idea of absolute justice and therefore excludes the former idea of justice. But there is this idea of not being destroyed by anything but by a more general and embracive idea. Therefore, a more general idea of the minority remained, and the majority started sharing it, and, finally, the new idea became the idea of the majority, which used violence and was rendered less just; the old idea, meanwhile, became the idea of the minority and suffered violence, and this gave rise to a more general idea, and so on and so forth.

Violence henceforth appears only as a result of a more general idea, and a more general idea arrives as a result of violence.—Only in this way does a more or less general idea of justice develop in all humankind, approximating the unattainable eternal idea of justice.

Violence always remains but is always lesser in the sphere of a more general idea than in the sphere of a more specific idea, because the most general idea of justice comprises the ideas of general freedom and equality and the absence of violence, while the most specific idea of justice comprises only the ideas of partial freedom, equality, and the right to violence.

The achievement of the general idea of justice and complete destruction of violence would henceforth be possible only if the whole of humankind had the same idea at the same time. The state of humanity that is furthest removed from the general idea of justice and the one most replete with violence would exist when every person had his own idea of justice. (It is evident that in the former case, the life of humankind would come to a halt because of the inability to meet vital needs, while in the latter case, because of the infinity of contradictory needs. In the former case, the point of activity is destroyed, and in the latter case, one activity precludes the other.—) The eternal movement from the lower spheres of the idea of justice to the higher is the eternal aim of humanity. The closer to the former and the general, the higher it stands on the path of development; it is higher because it can't go back; the closer to the latter, the lower it stands. (Its goal is to get rid of violence by means of violence.)

Therefore, in answering the questions that I have posed to myself at the beginning, I would say this: As a force that people abide against their will and call despotism, violence is the idea that is relatively less just, which purports to subjugate the idea that is more just.—

The reason for this force is a plurality of thinking in men, and its end is unanimity of thinking.—

What is the difference in, and agreement of, thinking?—What is the cause of either? And how to achieve unanimity?

1) The more unanimity, the fewer people there would be to suffer from violence.
2) The higher the sphere of the idea in which the people are unanimous, the less cruel this violence is, because violence itself is unjust. But violence has already worked out the tool for thought.

What brings about unanimity?—Thought.—How is it transferred?

1) Identical conditions of life (nationality, state).
2) Proximity, convenience of communication.
3) Coincidence of interests in one circumstance.
4) Convenience in conveying thoughts that comprise the very convenience of communication (book-printing) and the convenience of reception (education).—

(The latter comprises all of the other conditions, because if thoughts could be transferred instantly, there would be no separate states, would not be…).

Depending on the degree of unanimity of thought in humanity, there exist various means of transferring it: 1) war, religion, trade, and, finally, book-printing.—

Power and thought. But power—or violence—was in control of thought, used it—and had its means: 1) national spirit; 2) war; 3) trade. Thought had its tools: The sermon, the election, the book. The more general, the weaker the tools of power, and the more powerful the tools of thought.

Now is the time to become conscious of this power.

20. On the Tasks of Pedagogy[4]
[1860]

Education is beneficial.[5] Education is provided by life. Teaching and learning must be a part of life and as immediately and unconsciously perceived as each vital function. Natural striving is the single best guidance for measure and timing, which are the conditions for satisfying needs.

The history of pedagogy is twofold: A human being undergoes his own development under the unconscious influence of other people and of everything that exists; and he also develops under the conscious influence of other people, too. It is only the latter that is typically covered by the history of pedagogy. However, the former, which is typically absent from the history of pedagogy, would be more instructive: the more immediate that which a human being learns from life, the more instructive life becomes. As education has progressed independently of conscious pedagogy—sometimes under its influence, sometimes counter to it, sometimes completely independently—the more distinct education has become, with faster communication, the development of book printing, the change in state and Church governance, the more instructive human beings have become; new means of instruction have appeared where unconscious pedagogy is concerned.[6] This new history of pedagogy must be written and must become the foundation for all pedagogy. This science must demonstrate how a human being learned how to speak one thousand years ago and how he is learning this now, how he learned how to give names to things, how he learned various languages,

---

4 **Entry 20. "On the Tasks of Pedagogy"** [*O zadachakh pedagogii*] (1860). Written sometime in the spring of 1860, shortly before Tolstoy's trip abroad where he intended to study the latest of the progressive European educational models, this text was first published in 1936, in a section of volume 8 of *The Jubilee*, which contains pedagogical works (8:382-85). V. F. Savodnik limited his commentary to a barebones description of the manuscript, which was written on two double-sided sheets of paper of poor quality, on the obverse of another document (8:604). There are no substantive annotations to the text nor to the historical personages and titles in *The Jubilee* except for a general statement about the relation of this fragment to Tolstoy's famous pedagogical experiments in the 1860s. On these, see my notes that follow below. Savodnik mistakenly writes *"pedagogika"* in transcribing Tolstoy's title (8:604). There is no "k" in Tolstoy's suffix. Rather than referencing the German "Pedagogik," which stems from the ancient Greek, Tolstoy relies on the Greek original, *paidagōgia*, which meant "leading" or "conducting" a child.
5 To describe the benefits of pedagogy, Tolstoy uses his favorite word, the adjectival noun *blàgo*, meaning what is beneficial, felicitous, good (See "Editor's Introduction").
6 This strange wording ("instructive human beings") is deliberate. Tolstoy means that human beings have become more susceptible to learning and have become transmitters of specific models of learning.

how he learned crafts, how he learned ethics, how he learned the differences among people from different estates and how to socialize with them, and how he learned how to think and express his thoughts.

I shall attempt to write a brief historical survey of the history of pedagogy of a Russian peasant. The greatest abstract philosopher will not provide one thousandth of those foundations that I shall find in the methods of grandfathers, fathers, mothers, elder sisters, brothers, neighbors. I shall find these foundations among the peasants [*moujiks*] and not from a philosopher, not because a peasant is smarter than a philosopher but because the relationships of a child toward pedagogical activity are completely unbiased. Out of the countless multitude of life activities, only those that are akin to a child's perception acquire a pedagogical character, and the actions and methods of these have been for centuries irresistibly effective in their equal impact on generations; their impact is as multilateral as life itself. This pedagogy concentrates its focus differently than does conscious pedagogy, which focuses on methods alone, deeming support just as important: dwelling, income, food, types of work, domestic animals, and so on. In the pedagogical sense, it is no accident that a tsar is raised in the palace, always surrounded by other people, but a peasant is often alone in a hut when his parents are out in the field working. The best of the tsars cannot be raised otherwise than among the crowd, the best of the peasants not otherwise than alone and in a hut with a chimney without a vent, which makes his love for the open field even stronger. There is pedagogical purposefulness in every living condition, and it is the task of this type of pedagogy to identify it. Such a history of pedagogy would explicate many of the apparent difficulties of educating peasants.

They say that the main difficulty for the education of the peasant estate is the necessity of child labor. The history of pedagogy would prove that child labor is, on the contrary, the first condition for the education of a child. Only the history of pedagogy can provide positive data for the science of pedagogy itself. As regards the history of pedagogy in the narrow sense, as it has been understood up until now, it can provide only negative foundations. This history of pedagogy, which I would rather call the history of education theories of upbringing, is the history of the striving of the human mind from the idea of the formation of an ideal human being to the formation of a certain kind of human being. This course may be traced from the times of the renaissance of the sciences through Luther, Bacon(?),[7] Rousseau, Comenius,[8] Pestalozzi[9] up through the newest era. After classical education based on memorialization methods, certain religious education is necessary, for which thinking becomes a tool; following religious education, national and real education are necessary, for which the imagination is becoming an exclusive tool.

An implementation of education by force gives way to free choice of vocation. But pedagogy remains loyal to its history and continues to wish to be an independent science, the system of education applicable everywhere and always, an abstract philosophical science, rather than a historical and experiential science. Pedagogy still wishes to be theory, still wishes to form an individual,[10] still dotes on ideals, is still reluctant to descend or ascend to the level of experiential science, which acquires the knowledge about harmful or useful conditions for the education of its object only through the study of its own laws. The task of pedagogy used to be the formation of the best individual possible and the satisfaction of his educational needs based on his knowledge. It is not the education of a human being in general that must be the task of pedagogy. The task must be, for example, the best possible education for the Prince of Prussia in the year 1860 whose uncle is a wretch, whose father is such-and-such, and who is located in Prussia under the present condition of its development, or the education of a Negro in such-and-such State whose owner is wicked, and who has a blind mother and three sisters.[11] All these are legitimate and pedagogically

---

7 It appears that the editors of volume 8 chose a random and non-existent French-sounding spelling of this name, which must simply be Tolstoy's peculiar transcription of the name Francis Bacon. I thank Joel Thomas Paxton de Lara for this suggestion. In later years, Tolstoy treated Bacon's materialism with skepticism, mentioning him alongside other "insignificant thinkers" like Aristotle, Comte, Spencer, and Helmholtz in chapter 3 of his longer work *On Life* (1887).

8 Here, Tolstoy references the Czech (Moravian) theologian and pedagogue Jan Amos Komenský (latinized last name Comenius) (1592–1670), who was active throughout Central and Northern Europe and is considered among the founding fathers of modern educational philosophy and practice.

9 Johann Heinrich Pestalozzi (1746–1827) was a great Swiss innovator, the inventor of a democratic method of teaching through demonstration.

10 To educate is to complete one's image (*obraz*). The concept of completing form or formation as well as to educate is conveniently rendered in Russian by one and the same verb *obrazovat'*. Tolstoy uses this verb to great effect, showing the intrinsic affinity within Russian to the notions of Greek *paideia* and *paedagogia*, the Latin-derived notion of "education," and the German concept of *Bildung*. In addition, the word *obraz* conveys a religious connotation of the sacred and is synonymous with "icon."

11 There were no strict rules about the designation of races in Tolstoy's time and Russian is traditionally more lax in this regard. In nineteenth century Russia, the word "negro" was by no means pejorative, although its use did prove to be racially insensitive. Starting in the early

purposeful conditions; they are not only not to be ignored, but it is on them that all education is unconsciously built. This task is impossible without the aid of the freedom of expression of pedagogical need. Freedom, for its part, points without doubt to the conditions that must be eliminated, and to the needs that must find satisfaction. The delivery of instruments for the greatest range of activity in life, whatever this sphere may be, is the sole purpose of pedagogy.

Pedagogy is experience. Pedagogy must not destroy the links with the vital sphere. Every environment is legitimate. The influence of unconscious pedagogy is invariable and should therefore be non-disruptive.

The teaching of religion: By destroying superstition, you are destroying religion. Wait for questions.

In the case of weak memory, it requires its naturally free development. The wider sphere of the mind calls forth memory. The wider sphere of memory calls forth the capacity to coordinate ideas.[12]

Abstract pedagogy purports to deconstruct the human capacity to know and learn into imagined quantities, which it takes for guidance. Empirical pedagogy takes this knowledge for a fact, studies each variation, identifies issues for every variation and responds to them. Pestalozzi's idea and that of others to *mecaniser l'instruction* (to mechanize instruction) stems from this. The framework for education is old but the demands are new because of this.

---

decades of the nineteenth century, a link was made by those within the liberal circles of the Russian intelligentsia between Russian serfdom and American slavery. The emancipation of Russian serfs would occur only several months after Tolstoy wrote this, during his tour of the educational institutions of Europe. In Tolstoy's usage, we see that he subscribes to the traditional description of the plight of North American slaves. On the "savage's" vision of the soul, see also Tolstoy's controversial thoughts in entry 29. Revealing a racialized tendency, Tolstoy consistently places a "Negro" (or, alternatively, "a savage")—who is never a concrete individual and who is standing on the "lower rung of knowledge" alongside children, old people, and incapacitated people, in contrast to "the greatest scientist." In Tolstoy's scheme and system of values, the professional intellectual is a staple negative character. Tolstoy's point is to show the destitute results of the blind faith of scientists within western civilization and its so-called world historical, dominant nations at the forefront of progress. Nevertheless, his linguistic choices to express this critique betray a racialized bias. We can also blame Tolstoy's culture, and blame it he does. See entries 59-62 for Tolstoy's negative references to himself as the product of this culture of educated elites. For Tolstoy's later commentary specifically on slavery, see especially entry 52, his 1903 introduction to the biography of William Lloyd Garrison in this volume.

12 To think, to coordinate ideas, is to make connections between forms. In the Russian verb *soobraz̄hàt'* that is used here by Tolstoy we again encounter the root form of *obraz*. To think as an educated person, one ought to think "holily."

Riehl says: the hierarchy of domestic order (*Zucht*) was transferred to schools in the sixteenth century, and this was good.[13]

He circles around the idea that the domestic educational order should be transferred to schools.

By way of introduction—moral physiology of society—nobody believes in this. Movement became its own goal. A special chapter—equality—evenly distributed education. Why is a scholar self-conceited, one-sided, exceptional?

Chapter 1. The influence of education on the political and social state of society. The new meaning of pedagogy. Russia will now provide this direction. The state being governed by the people, not by rulers. This has always been, but is now palpable, fast with transportation networks and steam power.

Chapter 2. Nobody believes in anything.[14] One should negate everything right away. The new generation—the only hope.

Chapter 3. Freedom of education.

Chapter 4. It is impossible or should be made enticing from the lowest rungs.

Chapter 5. Pedagogy is experiential science.

Chapter 6. What have we got out there now?

Chapter 7. How to achieve the goal?

Napoleon III could be a despot were it not for freedom of the press.[15]

The necessity of education:

from Proudhon.[16] economics;

from Fourier.[17] politics;

13　Wilhelm Heinrich Riehl (1823–97) was an antiquities curator and the author of *Land und Leute* [*Land and People*] (1857–63), the work that best captures Tolstoy's description of his views on community, national culture, and folklore, and stresses the advantages of pre-capitalist models of home schooling.

14　Tolstoy uses triple negation in this short phrase, which is perfectly admissible in Russian grammar, his choice making his statement even more effective: "*nikto ne* verit *ni* vo chto."

15　Charles-Louis Napoleon Bonaparte (1808–73) was a nephew of Napoleon I, President of the Second Republic (1848–52), and was France's last monarch before the dissolution of the Empire (1852–70) following the fall of Paris during the Franco-Russian War and before the commencement of the Paris Commune.

16　Pierre-Joseph Proudhon (1809–65) remained an important thinker for Tolstoy. In addition to *Qu'est ce que la propriété?* [What is Property?] (1840), Proudhon's theory of individualism, which was built on revulsion to the idea of being governed, was practically a lifelong inspiration for Tolstoy. See also my comments to entry 27, "The Society of Independents."

17　One can see rather easily how Charles Fourier's (1772–1837) "grand hotel" communes and "familisteries" might fit the bill as political and social "phalanxes" that liberate passions and creativity of the imitative child learner.

St. Simon.[18] religion.
Dupanloup[19]

21. On the Character of Thinking in Youth and in Old Age[20]
[1862–63]

When we are young and are not aware of all the myriad sides of life, we think a lot—without encountering obstacles and refutations from life itself, for life we do not know. We make complicated inferences and go far by way of thinking; we are clever and we know it—and this may well even be true. But as the years go by (assuming we are not lazy in spirit), we discover many new sides to life, many various views, and we encounter a countless number of rebuttals along the path of thinking; at every step, we stumble against the incomprehensible, insoluble, and boundless. We think little and contemplate much.

They say you get stupider with years.

Logically speaking, youthful lucubration is conclusive in its verbal expression, whereas thoughts in old age are loftier and therefore stand above the verbal. During our youth, plans to reconstruct humankind are only potentially possible—by means of education, thanks to new types of political or civil organization of society; in old age, man feels above himself that same implacable law of nature that also reigns over plants and animal life, and he contemplates it. His whole life's labor has brought him to this. Is he stupider or smarter than when he was young? He is stupider because he has come closer to the animal

---

18 Tolstoy is referencing Henri de Saint-Simon (1760–1825), a great political economist and sociologist, whose proto-socialist ideas fed Marxism. Specifically, Tolstoy must mean the ideas in St. Simon's *Nouveau Christianisme* (1825), which acknowledges only the society with a moral end for achieving prosperity and the spiritual rights of the industrial and working class united by a religion cleansed of church dogmas.

19 Félix Antoine Philibert Dupanloup (1802–78), ordained 1825, was a celebrated advocate of religious education, a member of l'Académie Française, and the author of *De la pacification religieuse* (1845) and *De l'éducation* (1861). A popular Catholic college in Boulogne bears his name.

20 **Entry 21. "On the Character of Thinking in Youth and in Old Age"** [*O kharaktere myshleniia v molodosti i v starosti*] (1862–63). This text was first published in 1936, in volume 7 of *The Jubilee* (7:120). The text occupies half a leaf, according to V. F. Savodnik, in handwriting that resembles other specimens from the early 1860s—for example, the manuscripts of *The Cossacks*. A phrase in Sophia Andreevna's hand on the top indicates that this was the article written at Yasnaya Polyana. For Savodnik's commentary, see 7:364.

and the plant, but wiser because he has now become a conscious animal and a conscious plant.

He who has ears, let him hear![21] This formula[22] is pronounced by Christ the enthusiast[23] every time he elevates himself to that altitude of thought when one needs not think, nor argue, nor criticize, nor object, that is, but instead seek after truth and absorb it with his whole soul, however unclearly it is expressed, since this truth is so high that it is awkward for it to fit within the frame of human words.

22. On Religion[24]
[1865]

Most curious would be a book that collected all proofs for the existence of a living, free God since the beginning of the human race. This would be the most godless of books. There is a great variety of methods to prove the existence of God. One of the latest means of proving this seems the most powerful to me because (they say) he takes human nature for his foundation; therein is his power and his weakness.

They say that in all ages and everywhere man has posed the following questions: What am I? Why do I live? What will become of me after death? Did I come here by myself and thus live? Or did somebody else make me who governs me? Is it contingency that rules over events? Or do events contain the thought and power of a higher order? And is there a connection between me

---

21 Tolstoy does not use quotation marks or provide a reference, but he is quoting from Matthew 11:15.

22 Sic; Tolstoy's use.

23 "Christ the enthusiast" is Tolstoy's exact phrase.

24 **Entry 22. "On Religion"** [*O Religii*] (1865). First published in volume 7 of *The Jubilee* in 1936 (7:125-27), the initial title of the fragment was supposed to be "Could Religion Be Proven?" Tolstoy then opted for yet another title at the end: "On the Liberalism of the Century and on the Constitution." V. F. Savodnik describes small typos, corrections, and insertions in the text of the three handwritten pages on an in-folio leaf without watermarks (6:366). Tolstoy mentions in his diary on October 16, 1865 (48:65), reading on this day the works on religion by Henrietta Guizot-Witte, daughter of historian François Guizot, as well as essays by Montaigne in relation to his writing this note. Guizot-Witte's books that could have been used by Tolstoy include *Petites méditations chrétiennes à l'usage du culte domes-tique* (1862), *Nouvelles petites méditations chrétiennes* (1864), and *Histoire sainte racontée aux enfants* (1865). V. F. Savodnik notes in his commentary that during the writing of this frag-ment Tolstoy also used Montaigne's *Essais*, especially book 2, chapter 12 of "Apologie de Raimond Sebonde" (7:366).

and that higher power that I can plead to—through prayer? There are other questions like this—all of which people call tasks of the natural order. Always and everywhere humanity has tried to solve these questions. It must be that their existence—and attempts to solve these questions—are the eternal qualities of human nature.

Only science and faith can provide answers. But science is powerless, faith—or religion—alone provides the answers. This judgment is indubitable. But what should a person do who asks himself, Why do I live?, Is there a God?, and so on, but isn't satisfied with the answer that there is a personal God, and that this person lives for a future life? It is not out of obstinacy that he is not satisfied with these answers but due to a thousand reasons and arguments, which—no matter how passionate his desire to receive an answer—would not allow him to accept answers about religion, due, as they say, perhaps, to the irregular constitution of his mind. But what is he to do? What is a man to do when he is pressed by a passionate desire to pray and who remembers suddenly—with bitterness—*that he has no one to pray to*, that there is nothing up there? And there are many people like him, as many as there are of those who are appeased by their belief in a future life and prayer. The aforementioned reasoning will hardly convince them. On the contrary, realizing that they are human creatures and that the qualities of human nature found in them did not lead them to religion—as they should in fact have done—they will doubt the very reasoning. And that's not all, they will straightaway find it to be erroneous, despite its logic—just as a sick man ("~~sated~~")[25] will find erroneous all arguments that force him to eat when he does not feel like it and cannot ingest any food.

The mistake of this reasoning consists in the following: the whole of humanity always poses natural tasks for itself and attempts to solve them. This is untrue, as is everything that refers to the whole of humanity in space and time. Humankind and its life through the ages is not a concept but is simply a word purporting to hint at the boundless linkage of events and thoughts that are quite incomprehensible. (Therefore, all inferences made by historians who speak of the progress of humanity is verbiage, a nebulous cerebral game having no meaning; but more on this later.) Humanity is one of those concepts that we can only imagine but that we cannot have mastery over; humanity is nothing and therefore as soon as we introduce the concept of humankind into our mental formulas—similarly to when, in mathematics we introduce the infinitesimal and the infinite—, we arrive at arbitrary and false conclusions.

---

25 The word "sated" is crossed out in the original.

Humanity does not pose to itself, and is not attempting to solve, any questions. As far as I know, at certain periods of their lives—though not always—people have posed questions to themselves and have looked for answers, and moreover—which is key—I myself have posed questions to myself and have attempted to find answers. This is what ought to be said instead of "humanity," and this is why such reasoning led non-believers to this desperate condition. By saying, however, that certain people known to me—and myself, at certain points in my life—have tended to pose natural questions for themselves and to look for answers, by saying this I infer only that this tendency is common to all people, that many people live their lives quite satisfied by the answers provided by religion, but many are satisfied by the questions alone—without answers. Not being satisfied by the answers provided by religion, they remain without an answer, and this does not prove to be a misfortune for them, because these questions do not confront them permanently but only temporarily, and because these questions are satisfied by passion, infatuation, through work, and through the habit to exile these questions. There are also people—indeed, many people—who die without ever having had such thoughts. In addition, I can conclude from observation that the destination of the former and the latter is equal. For the believers, there is in the very fact of the need of faith a secret feeling of distrust; for the non-believers, in their substitution for the calming answers there is a proud consciousness of the fact that man never deludes himself.

I will also deduce that religion itself is not the truth, because there are many religions, have been and will be; religion is only a creation of the human mind that responds to a known tendency of the mind (consider fortune-telling, songs, and so on). We are told: religion has explained everything; by admitting once to the existence of God, you know everything: how did the world begin? Man? Why are there different tongues? Why does the rainbow exist? What will there be after death? And so on. This is true. All is clear (except for religion itself, which becomes more opaque the clearer everything else becomes). There are many religions, and they all solicit a belief in and condescension to an unreasonable foundation, and the rest is clear. (I know one insane priest who claims that he is the God Deir, that his mother Gargara divided the globe into two hemispheres—that he rules over one, while a Kartograi rules over another, and so on. His mythology is complex and entangled, and it explains the origin of all things, and he gets angry when you inquire about the original cause, but in simple life matters he would show you with a smile that all living phenomena confirm these original causes and how clear they are.) For those people who are not satisfied by religious answers, all living phenomena are not clear, but at the same time there is no one phenomenon that is more unclear than the next. Why does the plant grow? What force restrains atoms? These things are as unclear as what will become of us after death, and where the first man came from.—

The circle of human knowledge is a choker with empty intervals between the beads. The beads are our knowledge and they are a delight to look at, and we finger through them with pride; it is the black thread—the chaos of thought—this unknowable that is frightful. In its primitive way, religion will shake the beads up and bring all the beads together, only it will keep in its hands the longer portion of the black thread at which we are not supposed to look. But as for the beads, pressed together—what love, what symmetry; no gaps or doubts. Nonbelievers divide the beads at equal intervals, with more art or less, in order to cover up the thread, but it shows in between every two beads. If we narrow the interval right before our eyes, the more remains at the other side of the circle.

23. A Speech in Defense of Soldier Vasilii Shibunin[26] [1866]

Soldier Vasilii Shibunin, the defendant accused of the premeditated and conscious striking of his company commander in the face, has chosen me to serve

---

26 **Entry 23. "A Speech in Defense of Soldier Vasilii Shibunin"** [*Rech' [L. N. Tolstogo] v zashchitu riadovogo Vasiliia Shibunina*] (1866). Published in 1956, in volume 37 of *The Jubilee* (37:473-477), this is Tolstoy's second public statement to appear in this volume. See also 18: "A Talk Delivered at the Society of Lovers of Russian Literature" (1859) and 42: "The Concept of Life" (1887). After taking his bar exams and passing them externally, Tolstoy was able to practice law. Instead, he exercised his civic function, serving as a justice of the peace in the newly reformed administration of the Tula Province. In 1866, he delivered a speech defending the infantryman Shibunin of the 65th Moskovsky Regiment, who was indicted for striking his commander in the face. Shibunin had chosen Tolstoy to represent him in court, but Tolstoy's presentation of Shibunin as a half-witted drunkard did not succeed in mitigating the soldier's punishment. Tolstoy appealed for the Tsar's mercy through his family connections at the imperial court, but Shibunin was executed nonetheless. See also 58: "Reminiscences about the Court-Martial of a Soldier" (1908) in this volume and Inessa Medzhibovskaya, *Tolstoy and the Religious Culture of His Time. A Biography of a Long Conversion, 1845-1887* (Lanham: Lexington Books, 2008), 143-44, 156. Russian military law was one of the most deficient among the codices of the Russian Empire. It was revised five times between January 1, 1859, and 1866. The more progressive collection of military laws went into effect in 1869 and then in 1872, until a new government body took over the process of its modernization in 1887. Shibunin fell victim not only to the cruelty of the bureaucracy but also to the obsolete character of the military codex itself. On Tolstoy's lifelong attempts to change the situation, see also text 17: "On Military Criminal Law" (1856) in this volume.

as his defense attorney. I have assumed this duty despite the fact that the crime with which Shibunin is charged is a violation of military discipline that cannot be looked at from the point of view of commensurability of guilt with punishment and must always be punished. I have also assumed this duty despite the fact that the accused wrote a confession asseverating his guilt, which cannot be overturned, and despite the fact that article 604 of the criminal military law that he is subject to has only one punishment foreseen for the crime committed by Shibunin.[27]

This punishment is death and it would therefore seem that his lot cannot be eased. Yet I have assumed his defense because our law is written in the spirit of preferring to pardon 10 who are guilty rather than punish one who is not guilty, because it foresees erring on the side of mercy and declares—ensuring this is not just *pro forma*—that none of the accused should enter a courtroom without their defendant and, hence, should never enter without an opportunity of, if not an acquittal, then of a commuted sentence. Assured of this formal stipulation, I hereby commence my defense. It is my conviction that the defendant is subject to articles 109 and 116 that stipulate the commuting of the sentence upon proof of the criminal's mind-numbing stupor, his being non-liable on account of proven derangement.[28]

Shibunin is not given to a kind of chronic insanity that is certifiable during a medical examination, but his mental state is abnormal: He is mentally ill, insofar as he is deprived of one of the key human capabilities, the capacity to consider the consequence of his actions. In case the science of mental illness has not approved this psychic condition as a disease, I suppose that prior to pronouncing a death sentence, we must look at this phenomenon more closely to make sure that what I say is not a lame excuse but is rather a real, indubitable

---

27 Tolstoy must be referring to books 22, 23, and 24 of part 6 of the Russian military-criminal code [*Svod voennykh postanovlenii*] (or S.V.P. for short) that came into effect on January 1, 1840. In the many versions and articles that came and went during its revisions from 1859 through 1866, this code covered punishments, disciplinary measures, and court-martial rules in the army.

28 Apart from article 604, which relates to the military criminal code and which Tolstoy does all he can to skirt in his deposition, here and throughout, Tolstoy accurately summarizes the statutes and provisions described in the latest edition of *The Harmony of the Laws of the Russian Land*, which was reissued in 1857 by the Imperial Chancellery. See *Svod zakonov Rossiiskoi Imperii*. (St. Petersburg: Tipografiia Vtorogo Otdeleniia Ego Imperatorskogo Velichestva Kantseliarii, 1857), especially volume 1 (*Fundamental Laws of the State* [*Osnovnye gosudarstvennye zakony*]); volumes 11 and 12 (*State Organization Statutes* [*Ustavy Gosudartsvennogo Blagoustroistva*]); 13 and 14 (*Police Laws* [*Ustavy Blagochiniia*]); and volume 15 (*Criminal Laws* [*Zakony ugolovnye*]). Volume 15 must have been Tolstoy's main source in building his defense.

fact. The condition of the accused is extreme stupidity, simplicity, and dullness of wit, foreseen in article 109 as a mitigating circumstance. At certain minutes and under the influence of wine that incites activity, on the other hand, we have the state of derangement as foreseen by article 116. Here he stands in front of you awaiting his death sentence, the pupils of his eyes sunk, his face indifferent, calm and numb, not a single facial muscle will twitch either during his cross-examinations or my defense, just as it won't twitch during the pronouncement of his death sentence or even at the minute of his execution. His face is immobile not as a result of his effort to control himself, but rather by dint of the complete absence of spiritual life in this unfortunate man. He is spiritually asleep now, as he has been asleep throughout his entire life; he understands neither the meaning of the crime he has committed nor the consequences awaiting him.

Shibunin is of a mixed, third-estate stock. The son of wealthy parents, considering their stratum, he was sent to study with "a German," as he puts it, "an artisan," and to a draftsman studio afterwards. We do not know whether he was able to learn anything, but one can surmise that he studied poorly, because his studies brought him no means to bail himself out of the military draft. He came into service in 1855 and soon defected, as his record shows: he went on the run to nowhere, for what purpose he didn't know, soon returning from his flight just as unwittingly. He got promoted to the position of subaltern warrant officer a few years later, solely because of his ability to write, one is to suppose, and got assignments around the chancelleries throughout the rest of his service. Soon after his promotion to subaltern and for no apparent reason, Shibunin forfeited all the gains of his position in the military following an inexplicable act: He stole things from his fellow soldier—not money or anything of value, not even something that is easy to conceal, but rather a state uniform and a hatchet, then sold them for alcohol and drank up the money. I do not suppose that the actions that we learn about from Shibunin's service record indicate that the defendant has a normal mental state. The defendant has no taste for anything; no hobbies; nothing interests him. As soon as he has a little time and money, he drinks wine, not in the company of friends, but all alone, as we can well see from his indictment. He developed his drinking habit in the second year of his service, imbibing in such a way that two carafes of vodka a day would not make him merrier or more enlivened than usual, but instead leave him as you now witness him. What he needed was something more resolute and enterprising that required an even lesser capacity for reasoning. Two months ago, Shibunin was transferred to the Moskovsky Regiment and put in the position of a copyist in the second company. His mental ailment became worse by the day and drove him to his present condition. He degenerated into complete idiocy: He only appears human in form; he possesses no human qualities or interests. This sanguine and physically healthy creature sits for days on end without stepping out once from a stuffy hut heated to 90 degrees plus, writing ceaselessly one or two reports a day which he then rewrites. All of Shibunin's interests are concentrated on the language in the reports and on the demands of his company commanders. These long, drawn-out, meaningless days would sometimes not allow him to eat lunch or have a good sleep; this work did not oppress him so much as it dumbed down his mental state further and further. Yet he was pleased with his position and he told his comrades that it felt easier and better serving here than in the Life Guards Ekaterinoslav Grenadier Regiment from which he was transferred. He likewise had no reason to raise a complaint against his company commander, who more than once told him (in Shibunin's own words to me): "If you are running out of time, assign one or two more copyists to help." His days have passed either in the chancellery, in his company commander's foreroom where he was often kept waiting a long time, or in lonely drinking. He would write and drink, and his mental state reached extreme derangement. It was at this time that a solitary thought related to the narrow sphere of his activity was born in his foggy head, becoming emboldened and acquiring the resoluteness of a fixation. A thought suddenly crossed his mind that his company commander knew nothing either about this business or about the art of report writing, which is a point of pride of every copyist—that he knew better how to write these reports, that he wrote well and will write still better, and the company commander, who knew squat about all this, forced him to correct and rewrite, and would foul up the whole process by adding work that sometimes did not allow him time to take a nap or have lunch. This solitary thought fell into the fertile ground of a mind deranged by wine. But this thought made this dumb mind react, under the influence of the frustration of insulted self-esteem, through constant repetitions of the same demands on the part of the company commander with whom the defendant remained in constant close contact; the thought bred enraged anger and acquired the power of a passionate, insane fixation in the sick soul of the defendant.

Ask him why he committed his deed. He will tell you (the only point about which he, the man condemned to death, speaks with passion and ardor) just what he has written in his deposition: that the inciting causes of his deed were the frequent demands of his company commander to redo papers in which he, the commander, had made less sense than Shibunin himself had, allegedly. Or he will respond by telling you what he said to me in response to the question I asked him as to why he had committed this crime: "I made up my mind accordancing my sane common sense, 'cause they don't know nothing about these businesses and they make demands, and it seemed hurtful to myself."

In sum, dear Sirs!, the sole cause of the crime committed that is punishable by death was that it seemed hurtful and insulting to the defendant to redo copies he had composed at the orders of the commandment who supposedly knew less about the business than Shibunin himself. Neither the investigation, nor the trial, nor Sh.[ibunin's] own naive statement could reveal other incentives. Is it possible, then, to suppose that a person in command of his mental powers could risk committing such a terrible act, both in terms of its essence and its consequences, simply because it seemed hurtful to him to keep rewriting the reports? Only a person possessed by mental illness could commit such an act on such grounds, and such is the defendant. Should medical examination not certify him as such, this could only be because medicine has not yet defined this state of stupor in combination with the frustration produced by wine. Could a person facing trial and expecting a death sentence be considered sane when all he talks about is the wounded pride of a copyist insulted by his company commander who knows nothing about what he nevertheless demands to be rewritten? Could a person who is literate and who, knowing the law, have denounced himself in the confession he wrote on the 6th and 7th of the month, which we just heard, be considered sane? In this confession, he wittingly and irrevocably hands himself over to death! This confession is obviously taken from the dictation of what the inspectors put into his mind and what he copied down, which can be ascertained in his words-—"exactly so," "yes, Sir"—that he senselessly and unconsciously uses to affirm anything proffered to him. Search and you shall not find a single copyist, nay, a single literate peasant across the Russian Empire who would denounce himself thus, the day after his crime.

What could induce a literate person to submit this deposition? If he were not an idiot, he would understand that his confession cannot commute his punishment. Repentance could not be the cause of his confession either, since his crime is of a kind that was not able to produce grave torments within his conscience that would seek a wholehearted confession for its outlet. Only a person quite deprived of a capacity to reason out the consequences of his deeds could make such a confession—a mentally ill person, that is. The confession made by Sh.[ibunin] serves as the best proof of the sick state of his soul. Could anyone be of sane mind if he committed his crime under the same circumstances as did Sh.[ibunin]? As a copyist, he knows that, according to the law, raising a hand against one's commanders is punishable by death, not least because a few days before committing his crime he copied in his own hand an order issued to the regimental corps about execution by firing squad an infantryman who had raised his hand against his officer. And, despite all this, Shibunin committed his crime in the presence of the chief sergeant, soldiers, and strangers. No premeditation and nothing conscious are in evidence in the deed of the defendant; it is obvious, on the contrary, that he committed it in the absence of psychic abilities, in a fit of anger or insanity. Constantly preoccupied with the same task of copying that is linked with a thought about a powerful insult and lack of knowledge about ruling orders on the part of his company commander, there he was, sitting alone in the chancellery after a sleepless night of drinking wine, dozing off over a heap of papers with a thought that wouldn't exit his mind, amounting to the point of insane fixation, about the insulting demands and incompetence of his company commander. And lo, the company commander walked in, the very person proximate to this point of fixation, the person against whom his enraged anger amplified by the wine he had consumed—all by himself—is directed. And then this person gave him new reproaches and subjected him to a penalty. Shibunin rose to his feet and, not having fully awoken from his nap, not realizing where and what he was, he committed the deed for which he can account only quite later after it was committed.

Shibunin's past, his appearance, and his conversation prove the utmost degree of his mental stupor, aggravated by constant wine consumption; his confession seems to wittingly increase his guilt; but, his crime itself, above all, committed in the face of witnesses and accompanied by nonsensical gibberish, all prove that the general state of his idiocy became lately joined by a state of psychic derangement. If the latter is not subject to a doctor's certification to qualify for insanity, it could not but qualify as a mitigating circumstance, nonetheless.

In accordance with article 109, Shibunin qualifies for a reduced sentence as a consequence of his obvious idiocy.[29]

Additionally, even though he is not strictly eligible for the qualifications in article 126,[30] as a result of his exceptionally deranged psychic condition, Shibunin qualifies for a commuted sentence thanks to the general meaning of this article. And yet, article 604 defines but one punishment for the crime committed by Shibunin: death.[31] And thus, the court faces the following dilemma: either unconditionally apply article 604 to this case, thereby deviating from the meaning of articles 109 and 116 that presuppose the mitigation of punishment when the criminal is found to be in abnormal psychic states,[32] such as which Shibunin has been found to be in; or, apply articles 109 and 116 that

---

29 This is a very accurate summary by Tolstoy of the content of "Article 109" (see *Svod zakonov* 15:25).

30 See "Article 26" (*Svod zakonov* 15:28).

31 In the 1857 code, article 604 relates to crimes against state property that are not punishable by death (*Svod zakonov* 15:171). Article 20 alone refers to the sentence of capital punishment that is reached through trial (*Svod zakonov*, 15:4).

32 See "Article 109" and "Article 116" in *Svod zakonov* 15:25, 26.

mitigate punishment, thereby also changing the meaning of article 604. I consider the latter resolution of this difficulty to be more just and legal, based on the fact that the mitigation of punishment in cases as defined in article 109 refer to all subsequent articles, and to article 604 consequently, for nothing is said to stipulate its exception.

Given the contradiction in the present case between article 109 mitigating punishment and article 604 that foresees only one kind of punishment, the court has two options: to deviate from the letter of article 108[33] or from article 604.

For the resolution in this choice, the court can take only the spirit of our legal code as its guidance, which tips the scales of justice toward clemency, and in the spirit of the substance of article 81, which states that the court should manifest its clemency rather than cruelty bearing in mind that the judge is a human being also.

With this lofty and stern reminder on behalf of the law, the accused commits his lot to the decision of the just trial.

24. **Progress**[34]
[1868]

(November 2 and 9, 1868)
How to decrease populations by various means: 1) Human sacrifice; 2) Roman circuses; 3) Wars; 4) Parisian debauchery. Polygamy in Turkey—decrease; polygamy of the Mormons—increase. Prescott says that Peruvians did not know man's main incentive: a personal interest in enrichment.[35]—They lived

---

33 Tolstoy refers to crimes committed in a state of frenzy with a temporary loss of capacity to judge or act rationally, as described in "Article 108" (see *Svod zakonov* 15:25).

34 **Entry 24. "Progress"** [*Progres*] (1868). Published for the first time in 1936, in volume 7 of *The Jubilee* (7:130-31), this note is written in a sprawling style with highlights, on a fourth of a leaf on paper of low quality, according to V. F. Savodnink (7:368-69).

35 Tolstoy refers to William Prescott's influential study *A History of the Conquest of Peru* (1847). Tolstoy owned two books by this distinguished American Hispanist, including the even more famous *The History of the Conquest of Mexico* (1843). Tolstoy read both of these two-volume studies in the German translation published by Brockhaus in Leipzig: William Hickling Prescott, *Geschichte der Eroberung von Mexico*. 2 vols. Leipzig: Brockhaus, 1845, and *Geschichte der Eroberung von Peru*. 2 vols. Leipzig: Brockhaus, 1848. See Bulgakov, V. F. et al. *Biblioteka L. N. Tolstogo v Iasnoi Poliane. Bibliograficheskoe Opisanie.* [The Library of L. N. Tolstoy at Yasnaya Polyana: A Bibliographic Description], parts 1, 2, and 3 (Moscow: Kniga, 1972–2000), vol. 3, part 2, 210-11]. Henceforth, this edition will be cited as follows: *Biblioteka Tolstogo*, 3 [2], 210-11 where the first Arabic number indicates a volume, the number in square brackets indicates a part, followed by page or pages after a comma.

and died for others, ran around like a squirrel in a cage—none richer nor poorer than any other.—Yes, the reward of labor is labor and not wealth. And labor for others with the certitude of permanence is the best incentive. They were ahead of the United States.

The best minds of Europe are hellbent on creating weapons of death and means of communication.—Both are the tools of destruction.—

Power and freedom

The main argument against dreams about progress is this: When has it ever been the case that we have seen progress approaching a state of perfection? We move along (as an individual tends to think) to satisfy our whims—and we think that we move toward absolute welfare.

(Power and freedom of citizens—two incompatible forces.) What they call freedom is only power that delegates by branching out. For the success of the human race, the same obstacle is as much in despotism as it is in so-called freedom, that branching out of power (property is power).

True freedom is unalienable: The attack of Alvarado on the Mexicans and their betrayal is a zoological feature and the retrofitted cause for it (to explain the event retroactively).—

9 November, 1869—"Why civil freedom, credit, and the railway network are good one could not comprehend if the ideal of progress is missing.

The true ideal is life—being busy, activities, the continuation of one's species, the making of more art, and the increase of the human population, of knowledge, of labor.

Progress: communication, the issuance of credit, and freedom of exploitation.—Insurance companies—banks—courts—parliaments. Publishing—non-productive labor. Manuscripts are quite sufficient for knowledge, not a shred of what is truly good is supplied by [printed books].

They take distilled rye spirits from the Kharkov Governorate to Moscow. Alcohol spirits in Moscow, preserves and decorations in Kharkov—the demand. Come to Kharkov and imbibe spirits.

Progress: is the exploitation of the poor and those who will follow suit.—We regard general welfare in progress on the ground that an individual observes in it and reasonably proves the benefit of the District Court or of anything that is profitable for himself.—

Former ideals of history: the menacing grandeur of Rome.—Jerusalem, Christianity. Nowadays it is—civilization.

25. On Marriage and On Woman's Vocation[36] [ca. September–December 1868]

The whole unsolvable complexity of the mysterious question about marriage that Mr. Auerbach is working on[37] along with other Europeans and, according to Mr. Turgenev's assurance, Russian thinkers, is concentrated on the same complexity of the question about the nutrition of man who wishes to eat two or even ten lunches during one meal. Someone who wishes to eat two lunches in one go will get nourishment from neither one nor the other. He will upset his stomach and the aim of getting nourishment—as a result of nutrition—will not be achieved. Someone who wishes to marry two or three people will not have even a single family. The results of marriage are children. Just as they need air and warmth in the physical world, so too in the moral world do children need the influence of the father and mother who live according to the compact of familial unity. There can be no familial agreement and unity in the presence of two or three mothers and fathers. All supernumerary mammals—male and

---

36 **Entry 25. "On Marriage and On Woman's Vocation"** [*O brake i prizvanii zhenshchiny*] (1868). Published for the first time in 1936, in volume 7 of *The Jubilee* (7:133-35), this text occupies one in-folio leaf, except for entry 26, "A Philosophical Fragment. 6 Dec, 1868. Not *cogito ergo sum*," which is written on the obverse. See the description of the manuscript by V. F. Savodnik (7:370).

37 Berthold Auerbach (1812–82) was an author whom Tolstoy much liked, having read him even prior to his first trip to Germany (see Tolstoy's diary 47:104, 234). Tolstoy enjoyed Auerbach's short story collections and novels written in the Auerbach-invented style "with a tendency." Auerbach is mentioned in Tolstoy's diary *passim* on a few dates in 1857 during his stay in Germany (48:24, 27, 35), but the two most important meetings took place during Tolstoy's second visit in Germany in 1861. The reference in the 1868 note is primarily to *Das Landhaus am Rhein* [*The Dacha on the River Rhine*] (1869). This long novel in three volumes must have been known to Tolstoy before its formal release, either through Auerbach or through Turgenev. Turgenev's introduction to a portion from the novel in the Russian translation was published in the journal *Vestnik Evropy* [*The Messenger of Europe*] in September 1868. Two novels by Auerbach are preserved in Tolstoy's personal library: *Barfüssele* (1857) and *Das Landhaus am Rhein*. All three volumes of the latter novel show signs of careful reading, with underlining and bookmarks (see *Biblioteka Tolstogo*, 3 [1], 63-64). In his future writings on art, Tolstoy would mention Auerbach's art with approval, as a positive model for both the correct type of didacticism and assimilation with cultural dignity (Auerbach was Jewish). See also entries 74-76 from part 8 in this volume for Tolstoy's own adaptations of parables from world folklore that came to him mainly through the medium of German translations.

female—fight and annihilate one another. For a human being, this is impossible save for despotism (in the way they torture stallions by assiduously locking them up apart from each other or as they hold wives captive in the Orient). The one who has marriage with children—its inevitable consequences, its aim—in mind cannot see marriage outside of its unity. The one who has only the sexual act of coupling in mind without thinking about the consequences must find complete satisfaction in the depraved institutions of our society.

"But why"—say those sweet ladies who deign to read my book as if gracing me with a reward, with a reservedly mocking but caressing smile, showing that they could have, but chose not to strike me too cruelly—"why, dear Count, should not a good mother be willing to coif her hair or get washed?—*Une femme doit être toujours soigneuse d'elle même* ["a lady must always take care of herself"]. Why do we then see mothers who go out and move in society, engage in charity work, even for potlatch migrants and famine victims, and who bring up their children EXCELLENTLY[38] at the same time?" "As an artist would, our author follows his special logic and always utters stupid things when intervening in our sphere of thinking." "He seems to be assuming that the vocation of women consists only in giving birth and raising children. In his ignorance, he hasn't heard about the newest breakthroughs worked out by social science with regards to woman's vocation, and he ignores the methodology for solving the unsolvable marriage question, and so on," the feuilleton critic will say.—I can answer both of these objections at the same time. Despite my disgust for polemic for the sake of proving something, I cannot hold back from stating out loud the reasons for my not sharing the general opinion regarding the vocation of women, which is contrary to mine.

Human dignity is not about possessing any kinds of qualities or knowledge but in fulfilling one's vocation. The vocation of man is to be the worker bee in the beehive of human society, which varies infinitely, but the vocation of the mother queen bee without whom reproduction of the species is impossible—this is her sole indubitable vocation.[39] And despite this fact, a woman does not see this vocation and chooses other, fake ones. A woman's dignity consists in understanding her vocation. The woman who has understood her vocation cannot limit herself to depositing her eggs. The more that she heeds her vocation, the more this vocation engulfs her entire being and appears infinite to

---

38 Tolstoy's emphasis.
39 See also entry 73, "Two Different Versions of the History of a Beehive" (1888/1900) in this volume.

her. The importance and infinity of this vocation and the fact that it cannot be fulfilled other than in the unitary form of husband and wife (the family, as it has been understood by all people previously as well as those who are living now). This is unclear only to someone who is lacking eyes with which to see. And the more of her personal aspirations she has tossed aside to establish herself in her maternal vocation, the better the woman.

"But why, dear Count, do we see such splendidly raised children of mothers who are the delight of society? Why do thinking and accomplished women raise their children as well as do those women who give up the sciences and arts to contemplate diapers?"—Yes, we can see that the children of those mothers who expose their bared backs for all to see and who write articles are as cleanly washed, coifed, and dressed up physically and morally as are the children of the mothers who have no time to style their hair. But we cannot see the children who did not survive, and, among the surviving children, we cannot compare those powers of the soul that defy measure by Greek grammar, the knowledge of languages, and the ability to dance.

And these powers of the soul are always on the side of the children raised by their mothers who had no time for potlatch canteens, political economy, or for powdering their bare décolleté.

"But why, dear Count, in the end?"

This is the sort of confused mess that visits the heads of those artists who meddle with something that's none of their business. Why? Because if the vocation of women (the highest of all, I am convinced) has the quality of all serious human vocations, it will reveal itself as more infinitely difficult the deeper one delves into it and will be almost impossible to fulfill given humans' weakness—like the arts and science in the eyes of men. If, as all agree, the maternal instinct has a supreme power over reason in terms of its influence, one cannot surmise that the greatest of the targeted efforts produced lesser or worse results than the smallest ones. If I can see two ploughing peasants from my window one of whom ploughs without break, while the other one smokes his pipe, sings beautiful songs, chats with passersby and does picturesque posturing, I can say with boldness that the one who was ploughing without a break will have plowed more and better despite breaking into a sweat and becoming tired.

The more his mother loved it, with an active love, the better the child.—

I do not know an example from a biography of a great individual any great individual who hasn't been his mother's favorite.

26. A Philosophical Fragment[40]
[1868]

6 Dec. 1868. Not "cogito ergo sum"; space and time are not innate but *all moves*. The word that expresses anything beyond movement = 0. Geometry is a science because it admits to infinite movement without asking what it is and where it finishes; it only studies the trajectories of the moving dots—and lines. Mathematics does not ask about a cause—what causes what—, and therefore arrives at results. *The aim of philosophy is to discover general laws, and for this you need to surrender personality. An individual person is a coordinate of meeting lines, and their combination [may be obtained] only when individuality moves.*

From this point of view: what do people do? What is their goal? Application of their abilities—movement in the direction given by Christ.—This movement provides the line, their combination, and laws.

The philosophy of Wundt[41] and Hegel—concepts. The refutation of concepts is thoughts. What is his refutation of materialism?

---

40   **Entry 26. "A Philosophical Fragment. 6 Dec, 1868. Not *cogito ergo sum*."** [Filosofskii Otryvok Ne *cogito ergo sum* 6 dek. 1868]. First published in 1936 in volume 7 of *The Jubilee* (7:132), this fragment was written on the obverse of the manuscript of "On Marriage and On Woman's Vocation" of the same year (see entry 25 above).

41   Tolstoy displayed steady animosity—comparable only to his similarly steady animosity to Hegel—toward the science and philosophy of Wilhelm Wundt (1832–1920). When Tolstoy wrote the fragment in 1868, Wundt's book of lectures in two volumes on the soul of men and animals had already been published as *Vorlesungen über die menschen- und Tierseele* (1863–64).

27. The Society of Independents[42]
[1868–69]

The aim of the Society:

1. To establish closer unions between independent people;
2. To provide mutual aid with the aim of maintaining independence; and
3. To provide aid to all Russian people for their liberation from dependence.

Any Russian who has received no titles, no cross decorations, and no money from the government can become a member of the Society, if he so desires.

Any member of the Society who has been the recipient of cross decorations, titles, or money from the government shall be excluded from Society membership.

Member activities:

1. Unless for special circumstances, members shall live in their place of birth or where they own property;
2. Excepting military service at the front, members shall engage in business that is not compensated by the government;
3. Members shall resist luxury and will exemplify a simple lifestyle;
4. Members shall not refuse any possible aid to another member;

---

42 **Entry 27. "The Society of Independents'** [*Obshchestvo nezavisimykh*] (1868–69). Published in 1958 in volume 90 of *The Jubilee* (90:122), this draft of the regulations for this planned society was discovered for the first time among Tolstoy's manuscripts by his former secretary Nikolai Gusev during his editorial work on the annals of the State Tolstoy Museum in Moscow (N. N. Gusev, *Zhizn' L. N. Tolstogo. L. Tolstoy v rastsvete khudozhestvennogo geniia* [*1862–77*], vol. 2 [Moscow: Izdatel'stvo Tolstovskogo muzeiia, 1927], 79-80). Based on the location of the document in Tolstoy's manuscripts, it must have been inspired by Proudhon and written after June 2, 1868: the draft appears on the blank third page of a letter to Tolstoy from the Head of the Nobility of the Krapivna District of the Tula Governorate. Russian has two second-person pronouns: the familiar "*ty*" (the second-person singular), reserved for family members, friends, children, and younger teenagers, or for people much younger or of a much lower social rank than the speaker, provided the situation is informal enough, and the second-person plural spelled with a capital letter ("*Vy*"), which is reserved for showing very high regard and is extremely formal, for use in official communications and correspondence (the more current "*vy*" is reserved for casual formal settings and official correspondence). See also a brief commentary in volume 90 of *The Jubilee* by V. S. Mishin that describes the manuscript (90:399).

5. Members shall observe purity of behavior (lechers and drunkards cannot be members);
6. Members must make an effort to increase membership;
7. Members must donate money solely for the purposes of the Society and nowhere and to nobody else;
8. Members must not assemble more than 10 members, be it for meetings, demonstrations, or dinners;
9. Members must not donate money to the Society for aims other than the support and proliferation of independents;
10. Any implementation of any political aim in the activity of the Society is forbidden; and pursuit of any action against the government by the Society members entails their automatic expulsion.
11. All Society members are made aware of each other's membership from the list of members available to each of them.
12. All Society members treat each other as equals and address one another with "you" ("ty"), in the second-person singular.

PART 4

Writings of the 1870s

28. On the Afterlife outside of Time and Space[1]
[1875]

(November 17, 1875. For the forthcoming)[2]
Those who might understand clearly what we mean by "the afterlife" are very few in number—among both believers and nonbelievers alike, those who admit to its existence and those who deny it.[3]

    1. For the materialist: The organ for the cognition of time (thought), and the organ for the cognition of space (the eye, feeling, and sense,[4] in general) are destroyed when the individual dies. To speak about an afterlife in time and space is therefore out of the question. But does our consciousness of time and space make up the whole of what we call life? Without a doubt, no.

    2. For idealists:[5] The afterlife cannot be a conscious continuation of this one. Consciousness and memory—as the products of activity within space and

---

1   **Part 4: Writings of the 1870s. Entry 28. "On the Afterlife outside of Time and Space"** [*O budushchei zhizni vne vremeni i prostranstva*] (1875). Published in 1936 in *The Jubilee* 17:338-39, this manuscript is described by V. F. Savodnik in the same volume (17:715-17). For a more detailed commentary, see Medzhibovskaya, *Tolstoy and the Religious Culture of His Time*, 166.

2   This cryptic phrase might mean a preparation for a longer work. Tolstoy refers to this fragment in his letter to N. N. Strakhov on November 30, 1875 (see entry 30 in this volume). Most of the writings in this part of the current anthology are such "preparations for the future." They were mostly written by Tolstoy for his eyes only and rarely addressed to close friends in letters, as in entry 30, the aforementioned letter to Strakhov.

3   In this draft, Tolstoy does not observe strict parallelism and mentions the denial of religion first instead of admittance to a future life, as would be necessitated by the rule of syntactic parallelism in English.

4   Tolstoy has this word written in French, *sens*.

5   Tolstoy has the plural here, unlike the singular in 1 (see above).

time—are destroyed at death; but life itself, that which is life—which is not thought, consciousness, or memory—might continue.

3. For believers: The afterlife holds the promise that our souls shall return to the patriarchs. What holds true in the afterlife is that our souls will repose where they used to reside, but one ought to understand how. Time is destroyed with life, but the soul will be both before and after time—the soul will repose[6] after death with Abraham, and Jacob, with all times, because outside of space it shall be everywhere and nowhere.

—One cannot repeat this thought process too many times, because it is rather difficult to reach it. Having reached thus far, everything heretofore inexplicable in the question of this life and the afterlife acquires explanation.

—The question about when and where the afterlife begins has no meaning because by using the words "an afterlife beyond the grave" we express temporally and spatially what is essentially not temporal and not spatial.

—The question is: Is there life for us beyond the form in which we understand it? Is there in our life something that is not subject to space and time? If there is, then it simply is, and "is" in this sense also means "always will be."

—The very concepts of time and space are self-annihilating.

—If there is infinite time, then my life is an infinitely small moment of time. And my whole life here is but a moment (in the mathematical sense); and, conversely, life is infinity, composed of moments on an infinite continuum. If there is an infinitely small space, my body embraces an infinitely great space and (mathematically) any point of it comprises me. And vice versa: I am a point comprised (mathematically) within infinity.

—The metaphysical explication of life is the explication of the limits of life within space and time.

---

6   Tolstoy uses the old Slavic word *vitat'* here, which can mean reposing in levitation, dreaming, or greeting and welcoming (the latter correlates with the Polish verb and noun *witać/witanie*).

29. On the Soul and Its Life beyond the Life Known and Comprehensible to Us[7]
[1875]

When I look at the world from the simplest, materialist point of view, I see an infinite plenitude.[8] We can all—the greatest sage and the most primitive child alike—also see a very sharp boundary dividing this plenitude of phenomena: between the animate and the inanimate (the organic and the inorganic). Due to a lack of experience, I might mistake a dummy for a living creature, or a living creature for a dead one, but this only requires us to perceive deeper to correct the mistake, and thenceforth no mistake will be made. In all that is inanimate, I search for and discover the laws that everything inanimate obeys. For a primitive human, this law is gravity, and that which affects the feelings; for a scientist, this is the indestructibility of matter and the law of the conservation of forces.— In everything animate I can also observe laws: while a primitive human recognizes them with difficulty in the living world, science demonstrates and proves that it has discovered the activity of the same laws in everything animate (or is on its way to discovering this if it hasn't already yet), i.e., through organic chemistry, physiology. We might even allow—and this is an enormous allowance—that science has discovered everything it has been looking for, i.e., proofs (based on the most rigorous experiments) that everything animate obeys the general laws of the inanimate world, and that an organism is only the result of a complex effect of forces on each other—a force or the phenomenon of the very organism. Yet, a phenomenon or the power of all the impacts of these forces combined will forever leave a sharp distinction between the animate and the inanimate (the organic and the inorganic). This, moreover, will not suffice— however complete the proof that any manifestation of life is an effect of the impact of laws that are universal for everything inanimate. We should apply such methods in the experiments purported to prove this that presuppose [an

---

7   **Entry 29. "On the Soul and Its Life beyond the Life Known and Comprehensible to Us"** [*O dushe i zhizni vne izvestnoi i poniatnoi nam zhizni*] (1875) First published in 1936 in *The Jubilee* 17:340-52, this manuscript is described by V. F. Savodnik in the same volume (17:718-22). For a substantive commentary, see Medzhibovskaya, *Tolstoy and the Religious Culture of His Time*, 166-67.

8   This unfinished work by Tolstoy is riddled with deletions and exclusions. Only the most essential deletions have been translated. Retained in the text is the bracketed language that Tolstoy used in the corpus of his draft. All other translated deletions appear in the Notes. Crossed out from the very first sentence is this phrase: "I exist. My existence is composed of me and of the infinite variety of the world already known and in the process of becoming known."

ability to make a] a clear distinction within us between the animate and the inanimate.

When we condemn a frog to scalding by red-hot wire, we witness the impact of this touch on the frog alone—and not on the table where it is sitting. When dousing a stalk of a plant with acid, we witness no changes in the soil around the root but only on the root and its thinnest fibers. Both a natural scientist and a primitive child know equally well and without doubt that a clump of moist earth forms no part of a plant but that the thinnest fibers of the root are part of it. They know equally well not just the phenomenon of integration but also its limit (not the limit between individual animate creatures about which one might be mistaken, but the more general boundary between the animate and the inanimate). Thus, for the greatest natural scientist of the thirtieth century as well as for the Negro, the division of the world into the inanimate and the animate and integrated will always remain the same, because this is a given and comes before all experience and study.[9]

This boundary may shift to different places for different people as study continues. The savage will mistake a dummy for a living creature and yeast for dead matter; but the boundary exists, and no knowledge is thinkable without it.

Knowledge is prediction, i.e., searching for the general laws that everything that exists obeys. Albeit to a different degree, the greatest scientist and the savage learn these laws in the course of their lives and get to know them in just the same way in the two different spheres of that which exists; neither ever mistake one for another—the animate for the inanimate, the organic for the inorganic world. This division is always common to man—at the lower rung of knowledge (for the savage) and at the highest one (for the scientist). It is not possible to think without this distinction.

By the way, we can frequently see in certain individuals and groups of people a desire to break out of the inevitability of the law of this division between everything that exists. We have seen and continue to see individuals with a presumptuous—both false and arbitrary— idea of life who animate inanimate nature (e.g., in thunderstorms, tempests, the sea), and who endeavor to subject the inanimate to the laws of the animate, and vice versa; we can see individuals who endeavor to subjugate the animate to the law of the inanimate.[10]

---

9 For Tolstoy's treatment of the racial divides, see "Editor's Introduction" and my editorial commentary in note 11 to entry 20.

10 "The law of the inanimate [sic]." There are many corrections in this part of the manuscript. Among the most interesting are the following lines crossed out by Tolstoy: "<the laws of the inanimate world have no impact on the world of the animate; and they will be frequently unable to distinguish individual animate creatures clearly from one another and from the world of the inanimate>."

Savage peoples find themselves in the former position: constantly collid-
ing with inert forces, they have animated the sea, the thunderstorm, and the
idols—to achieve the integrity of their comprehension as a result. The natural scientists of our times find themselves in the latter position: to achieve the
integrity of their comprehension, they deny the division between the animate
and the inanimate and attempt to explicate all that is alive based on the laws of
dead, inorganic matter.

The difference between the scientist and the savage consists simply in this:
without knowing the general laws governing the inanimate world, but knowing the laws governing the animate one, the savage assumes that the forces of
animate creatures are manifested in all the phenomena of the world. And the
scientist—who knows the laws of the inanimate world, but knows nothing or is
willing to know nothing of the laws of the animate world—[11] assumes that any
phenomenon in the animate world is only the consequence of the general laws
of the inanimate. To put this more precisely, every living creature is only a result
of the impact on it of the laws of the inanimate. And yet, the phenomenon of
integration shall be, for him, the same as for the savage: the indubitable given,
something inexplicable.

I know very well that the new school of thinkers does not acknowledge this
shortcoming of theirs.—[12]
They will say: we fully recognize the differences between the organic and the
inorganic world. But we can see that the same laws act without the slightest
alteration in the organic world as in the inorganic one; and we see no cause,
therefore, for ascribing meaning to the concept of life that is inexplicable reasonably.[13] On the one hand, if anything remains unclear in the concept of the
organism as such, we hope for clarification of everything still unclear, convinced
by the rapid strides made by the sciences. On the other hand, by allowing for
the division between the organic and the inorganic, we search for the laws of
the development of organisms, their origin, etc., and we hope, staying on this
course, to bring everything into conformed unity.[14]

---

11 Crossed out are these words: "the scientist . . . will see clearly and shall be able to prove . . ."

12 Crossed out after "the new school of thinkers": "would not be given pause by begging this
    question, but would consider the integration of the animate (the organic) as something
    requiring no additional substantiation besides searching in the animate world for laws that
    govern the animate."

13 Note Tolstoy's reference to the concept of life in this paragraph, to be continued in his
    work in the 1880s, more specifically, in the talk "The Concept of Life" (see entry 43 in this
    volume).

14 For the sake of ironic understatement, Tolstoy crosses out his objection to the proofs and pre-
    cision as foolproof; he finds them far from objectively proven, if not altogether far-fetched:

This answer is extraordinarily powerful, in general, especially for those who have partaken of the tempting charms of studying the natural sciences, wherein the commonality and certainty for the application of open laws for everything that exists is being proven so precisely, clearly, and irresistibly, by way of experiments and through observations.—

It appears so natural and insignificant to accept the division of the world into the organic and the inorganic—for scientific purposes and only provisionally and hypothetically. Yet, the majority do not notice that the division destroys the very foundations of all thinking.

These foreign words, the organic and the inorganic, have an important significance for me.[15] I have noticed that whenever there is a dodgy argument, where a train of thought leads to contradiction, where it becomes necessary to purloin an idea, a foreign word tends to be introduced.[16] And here this word is "organic."

No matter what laws governing the world of the inorganic and the organic are discovered, they carry no significance for a thinker unless this essential difference has been defined, for this is the whole question.

These laws might be of use for a particular science—for physics, chemistry, botany, or zoology—but they can have no significance for philosophy, because, in essence, there is only one philosophical question: What is life and what is death? (Only the wording of the question might differ.) And they are willing to answer this question to me by allowing, as a given, the division between the living and the dead.

It is quite possible that the laws for the modification of everything inanimate and everything living have been correctly identified and defined in the theories of the newest researchers. But even assuming that these laws have been proven beyond doubt, if science were to continue for one hundred centuries in the same direction, the question about what it is that constitutes the difference between the animate and the inanimate would still remain unresolved. This is because it is accepted as a given and is not an object of study. Having accomplished everything on its path, science will nonetheless arrive at the postulate that the world is an integration of inanimate phenomena whose laws are

---

"With philosophical aims in mind, I cannot acknowledge that these laws have even the slightest significance," finding the automatic application of the laws of the inorganic world to the organic world unjustified.

15 "These foreign words": in the original Russian. Tolstoy uses the singular *eto inostrannoe slovo* for the organic and the inorganic, treating both terms as describing one complex essence and therefore requiring one word for their description.

16 For fun, Tolstoy uses *escamoter*, a preferred word of Russian aristocrats to describe artistic thievery as creative conjuring.

unknown to us, but that there are organic ones among the aforementioned phenomenal series, and despite their total obedience to inorganic laws, the [nature of] their distinct status is still unknown to us.[17]

And it is only in the definition of this difference that the question of philosophy consists.

Only if one keeps in mind their infatuation with discovering particular laws, in combination with the polemical ardor that they direct at teachings that focus otherwise (which, unfortunately, is very much to the detriment of philosophical thinking in society today), can one wrap one's mind around the strange delusion that modern people suffer: They suppose that after proving the obedience of the entire living world to the general laws that govern the inorganic world, on the one hand, and uncovering the development of the laws of the animate world, on the other hand, that they will have solved the philosophical question! If they are not capable of such proofs, they suppose that in so doing, they will render this question redundant: they will show that it is impossible for philosophy in its current state to answer its own questions posited from the beginning of time, namely, what is life and what is death?—Having come to the inevitable necessity of acknowledging the division between the animate and the inanimate, a necessary condition for all thinking, but having couched this division in vague nomenclature, the new direction of modern thinking clearly supposes that it has resolved the philosophical question and consoles itself with a familiar, all-too-human argument about having no use for that which it lacks or about the poor quality of that which it lacks. With astonishing naïveté, positivists and the majority of moderns say that these questions do not exist, or that they do not require answers, that they are useless, and that this is all idle metaphysics.

All these questions are useless, idle, and inessential for a living human being! Really? These are questions about what life is, and what death is, about what happens to each of us when we experience our life, when we think, desire, rejoice, suffer, and about what awaits us beyond this life, where all of us are headed and for where people who are for us our entire joy, the entire meaning of our life, depart in front of our eyes. Of course, these must be idle, useless questions, holdovers of old superstitions, but otherwise uncharacteristic of human beings! Thanks to their polemical infatuation and their preoccupation with making discoveries in this science of theirs, as well as their obtuse

---

17 In crossed-out asides, Tolstoy expresses disbelief concerning definitions about the inert forces and the origin of all organisms, claiming that science will stumble upon the impossibility of resolving the main question: "what is the animate (the integrated) [*chto est' zhivoe, t.e. ob'edinenie*]?" and "what is the inanimate [*chto est' mertvoe*]?" (17:343).

thinking, the philosophers of the new school have failed to see that the questions at stake are far from idle—that these are the only fundamental questions that a human being has ever asked of himself; that all of the enormous merits of the scientific discoveries in the spheres of chemistry, physics, biology, physiology, and zoology made by the very people who think these thoughts owe their significance only to the fact that they posit these questions more clearly. It has slipped the mind of these philosophers that having been brought—thanks to the limits characteristic of each branch of the sciences—to the inevitability of allowing as given a distinction between the animate and the inanimate, without nary a definition nor a proof thereof, these sciences have only been instrumental in the clarification of the core question, the question that presents itself ever more powerfully in relation to the protoplasm and the speck of the particle than had the difference appeared to the savage between a living and a felled tree. The merit of the natural sciences—although not of the materialists—consists in their having demonstrated the futility of thinking that the animate does not obey the laws of the inanimate. But it would be just as futile to base the difference between the animate and the inanimate on the idea that the animate is outside of the laws of the inanimate. The difference does not lie in any lack in the animate, in any of the forces of the inanimate, nor in their both being juxtaposed to yet some other force: what has now become even more apparent is that, while they do obey the inanimate forces, the forces of the animate world are still distinct.

Everything that exists obeys the same laws, but in everything that exists there is still the distinction between the animate and the inanimate. In addition to the general inorganic laws, the animate obeys the laws common only to the world of the animate. (What in fact is this difference between the animate and the inanimate? This difference becomes known immediately to man, because he experiences himself to be integral[18] and alive.)

What, then, is this force of integration or life? Does the animate originate in accordance with the laws of the inanimate? No (Manet).[19] Does it hold together as a consequence of the laws of the inanimate? No. Does it vanish as a consequence of the laws of the inanimate (suicide)? No. But is there in this force or in this phenomenon anything that deviates from inorganic laws, assuming that science may have discovered everything for which it has been striving? No. Hence, life is not a force in the sense of inorganic forces, because if it were

---

18 The word for "integral" here is *ob'edinennyi*, which, more literally, translates as "united." See Richard Gustafson's book *Leo Tolstoy. Resident and Stranger* (1986) listed in Further Reading for a helpful explanation of this concept in Tolstoy.

19 As opposed to "exeunt" [exits], "manet" is Latin for "[that what, he, she, it] remains."

then, based on the law of conservation, it would not disappear. Life is not an effect of the forces either, for if it were then we could identify its causes in the inorganic forces, but inorganic forces cannot be recognized as the causes of life.

Everything that exists is given to me in two ways: 1) as something inanimate that obeys only the unchangeable laws of the conservation of matter and the forces in their interaction; or 2) as something that is alive, that acts in accordance with the same laws, but which is given to me as something living, which has its significance and meaning in accordance with some other laws, not accessible to my reason.—

The former is the relationship of the animate to the inanimate, which is comprehensible by reason. The latter is the relationship of the animate to the animate, which is incomprehension by reason, but of which we have complete knowledge from within, immediately, through knowledge of the self.—

Inorganic laws relate only to the inanimate; the animate is beyond these laws and has its own laws that are inaccessible to reason.—

What is real: the inorganic or the organic?

The materialists say that only the inorganic is real; what they know rationally seems real to them. Yet they forget that reason is the result of the life of vital organs, and that this knowledge is only relative, therefore. They claim that the concept of the soul is not real. But the concept of the soul is the concept of the life of the organism that we do not get to know mediately by means of perception, the organs, and reason, but immediately by means of knowing life.—

Without consciousness of life and the integral unity of the organism, we would not only fail to understand anything that is living but also anything that is dead. Matter, space, density, quantity—all of these are generated from integral unification.

Therefore, what is real is only the self-consciousness of being an integral living organism, hence the comprehension of the whole infinite number of integral creatures, as opposed to those not yet unitarily integral.
(What, then, is the consciousness of unitary integration?—Intellect, will, and love.)...[20]

—

It turns out that we know and can know fully—not rationally—only the living. By way of rationally abstracting from our knowledge of the living we discover the laws of the non-living.[21]

---

20 Tolstoy's ellipsis.
21 At this point, Tolstoy converts the terms "animate" and "inanimate" into "the living" and "the non-living," respectively.

Now, the materialists commit the opposite error: when wishing to define everything rationally, they set aside the immediate, the non-reasoned knowledge of the living and accept only the abstraction of this knowledge as applicable to the inanimate. With this instrument they approach their (living) source, for they desire to explicate it, and they stumble against the impossible. It is first of all impossible because, although there is in everything animate the affirmation of all the laws of the inanimate, the essence of life is evidently to be found beyond these laws. It is as if someone were trying to explicate chemical phenomena via appeal to the law of gravity. Gravitation effects every atom during attraction, that's for sure; but chemical integration is a distinct process, beyond gravitational attraction.

Second, it is impossible because the laws foregrounding the explication of a phenomenon from the realm of the animate are countless and infinitely variegated. Although fully and clearly comprehended by us, they cannot be subsumed under laws.—

Think, for a moment, about the phenomena of the organic world: the constant flow of particles for the maintenance of a single species, the development of particles, the development of the organism, sexual coupling, death. It is striking that these phenomena are more difficult to explain the simpler they appear to any plain mind. Fell in love, had sex, new birth, grew up, grew old, died: These are the simplest of words, the most important phenomena for man, and yet the most inexplicable by appeal to inorganic phenomena and reason.

Falling back on the source of my knowledge to answer this question, we involuntarily come across yet another, foregrounding and fundamental division, which serves as a source. Everything that we know, we know in two ways: as the self and as the non-self. We know the former immediately and without any experience: (painful, fun). We know the latter mediately, as a result of experience and reason. The world is divided into two parts for all of us: The one part that is "we," and the other part that is "not we." What we call "we" is the part of the world that is integrated within us and that is separated from everything else. Everything else is located outside of this integration.

What is integrated by us immediately becomes known through perception but without the participation of reason. What is not integrated by us becomes known to us mediately, through the organs and perception, and through reason. We call this our life, the core of existence, that which becomes known immediately. We call the world that which becomes known mediately.

In the world, we divide all creatures into animate and inanimate. We call "animate" every creature that is integrated the same way as we are. We call "inanimate" any disintegrated being or any being whose integrity we do not see.

In the world, whose integrity we do not see, we locate the presence of laws corresponding to our reason. In the integral world, we also locate laws, but these laws are not rational in the same way. The division of the world stems from the fact of our integration, embodiment, and the recognition of the self as part of the world through one's body.

In sum, not only is the materialists' aspiration to explicate the animate by means of the laws of the inanimate impossible, it is also incorrect: for all that we know derives only from the immediate knowing of the animate. Our knowledge of the laws of the inanimate is not only limited but only derives from our lack of knowledge of the animate, of which what appears as inanimate to us is but a part. We know for sure and immediately only that which is living. We call inanimate or dead only that whose life or existence we do not comprehend.

Just like the stone and the stars, the tiny cells of my body appear dead as a stone to a microscopic parasite residing in my body, while the tiny droplets of my blood will look like stars to it.

The organs that provide the conditions for integration also provide the opportunity for comprehending similar integrations that occur with the help of similar organs. Integrations without seemingly similar organs are concealed from plain view, however. We call "inorganic" that whose integration we do not comprehend, and we take a multitude for one thing (the stone) or one thing for a multitude (the stars). And science is not able to fix this.

Embodiment and integration have provided the boundaries for human comprehension. The limits of integration cannot be expanded.

There are three kinds of knowledge at our disposal: 1) the knowledge of self, of that part of the world that is integrated through me; this knowledge is certain, immediate, non-rational, and complete; 2) the knowledge of those parts of the world whose integrations are like mine and are comprehensible to me; I can comprehend them because, on receiving their impressions, I can put myself in their place and imagine their immediate knowledge of themselves; this knowledge is in part immediate and in part rational (based on analogy); and 3) the knowledge of everything that produces an impression on me but for which I cannot self-substitute; I cannot imagine how such a thing can immediately know itself.

—

You arrive at a strange perplexity when looking at the world from the standpoint of the materialists. When we study the phenomena of the inorganic world—their essence completely incomprehensible, the definition of the latter being impossible to understand and a constant contradiction (matter, force, atoms)—we find absolutely precise and reasonable laws that govern all the modifications of this incomprehensible essence (astronomy, physics, chemistry).

Yet, as soon as we turn to the other kind of phenomena (those of the organic world), these reasonable laws governing the material world appear insufficient; the phenomena of the organic world are inexplicable in terms of the laws of physics, astronomy, and chemistry.[22] The necessity evinces itself to divide everything that exists into the organic and the inorganic. And this division is not made on the basis of data supplied by reason but is based on a correct conviction that the division is unmistakably felt by everyone. What is left aside is the very essential difference between the organic and the inorganic, a difference that is taken for granted. The laws governing the organic world are sought and found. These laws are more shaky and less precise than the inorganic laws. Yet the essence of what these laws define is better understood and does not present the same contradictions as do those that appear in the essence of the inorganic world. Transitioning still further on from the phenomena of the organic world in general to the phenomena of human life, the laws of the inorganic become even more inapplicable: the phenomena of human life are even less explicable through physics, chemistry, and astronomy.

Again, the difference between a human being and an animal is taken for granted as something indubitable, non-deducible from the laws of the organic world. Left aside is the very essential difference, which is taken for granted, and new laws governing the phenomena of human life are searched for and discovered. These newly invented laws are even more arbitrary, shaky, and riddled with contradictions. However, the essence of what these laws define is not only clear and presents no contradictions but is the sole indubitable essence (and the sole source of any knowledge).

What a strange phenomenon! A certain method of study is directed at a subject whose essence is completely unknown to us (the inorganic world), which leads us to knowledge of a subject where rational laws well apply yet whose essence is completely incomprehensible. When applied to another subject (the organic world), which is better known by us, the same method leads us into doubt, rendering shaky the rational laws we apply, yet we have greater knowledge of the essence of this subject. When turned onto human life, the same method leads us to a total impossibility: applying rational laws to the sole thing we know for certain. The same thing happens as when a spyglass is turned onto distant objects, objects up close, and one's very self.

The error originates from the very understandable desire of turning the simplest instrument that had proved itself useful for the discovery of simple

---

22 Here, Tolstoy crossed out the beginning of the phrase "New laws are being invented for the organic world . . ."

laws within a known kind of phenomenon onto the laws of another kind of phenomenon. This instrument is logical in this case, based on experiment, and inductive thinking.—The materialists wish to subsume under the laws of this inductive thinking that which we know by means other than inductive thinking, namely—by life itself.

By way of experiment, materialism aspires to get to know the soul, the essence of the life of individual creatures.

The experiment is certain during observation by means of the instruments of perception (vision, hearing) of the movements of other animals and myself.

But no experiment should be conducted on the emotions by means of sense perception.

The internal experiment is *contradictio in adjecto*.

The external experiment convinces, through an infinite number of repetitions, that the sun shines at 2 pm. But now I watch the sun and it is not shining (during an eclipse), and the sensation of darkness destroys all the data of the experiment. There can be no experiment for inward knowing.

Hence, sensation[23] is an instrument of cognition completely contrary to experiment.

This instrument of cognition—which needs to be defined—is the human soul. Also, it is indubitable that the phenomena of sensation occur in parallel with physical phenomena.

But this is far from proving that physical and psychic phenomena are one and the same. On the contrary, this proves that what we call physical phenomena is based only on knowledge that we derive from perception. The parallelism of physical and psychic phenomena far from proves therefore that there are only physical phenomena; instead, it proves that there are only psychic phenomena, and that physical phenomena and all knowledge acquired through experience is only a result of sensations, i.e., of psychic phenomena. It is thus psychic phenomena that should be explained.[24]

Here is a question: Why does the whole world fall into two halves? The world accessible to me through experience and the other world that is I, which is available to me through perception.

---

23 "Sensation" here is a translation of *oshchushchenie*.
24 In Tolstoy's terminology, "psychic phenomena" refer to inner experience or perception. He also begins talking about the materialist scientists' experiments, but conflates experiments and experience, ending up speaking about that latter. The Russian word *opyt* can be used to refer to either. *Eksperiment*, a borrowed term, means "experiment" only. Similarly, *oshchush-chenie* translates as "feeling," "sensation," or "perception." The difference is delicate, and the nuance is best caught in context.

This partitioning is the task of defining the soul, all the while materialism thinks it can explicate the difference by appeal to forces.[25]

Even before any reflection, we know that we are alive, that we comprise an integral part of the world that we perceive as the self —that which we know differently from everything else, neither mentally nor experientially but which we know for sure. I don't know to what extent Descartes's expression is correct: "I think and therefore I am alive";[26] but I know that if I say: "I know (one thing indubitably) and before all else: that I live," this cannot fail to be exact.

Our first knowledge is the consciousness of one's integration, apart from the rest of the world.[27] We call this integration "life." The subsequent knowledge of the rest of the integrated and living world stems from this former fundamental knowledge. When we say that this dog is alive, or the tree lives, we are only saying: the dog and the tree are integrated just like I and have the same common characteristics that the primitive savage calls "life" and the scientist calls "an organism," yet neither can do anything to define it. The fact that consciousness results from a process of development, according to Wundt, says nothing to counter this. How do I know that I am one and not two?—The organic is all that we know thanks to the capacity to imagine other creatures to be integral in just the same way as we know ourselves to be. The source of this knowledge is our integration, nonetheless. The inorganic is all that we know thanks to our capacity to analyze and to deduce various elements of our integration and to distinguish them from one another.

The source, once again, is our being integral.

Concepts of matter, force, space, time, cause, effect, number, sphere are only concepts abstracted from one's consciousness of one's integral being. Matter is I without life; force is I without matter; space is I without matter and force; time is I without space and matter; cause is my desire; effect is the accomplishment of desire; number is the single I, in contradistinction to the miscellaneous multitude; sphere are the boundaries of my vision, and so on.

These concepts are fully known to me within myself, but their essence is meaningless in abstraction. Their laws are reasonable only because the very

---

25 This place in Tolstoy's manuscript is abbreviated. The version that I suggest appears to best fit the context of his argument.

26 This is how Tolstoy rewrites Descartes's phrase *cogito, ergo sum*: "I think and therefore I am alive" ["*ia mysliu, potomu ia zhivu*"].

27 "Unification apart from" [*ob'edinenie ot*] the rest of the world is one of Tolstoy's more paradoxical postulates.

abstraction of these concepts is performed by reason for certain reasonable purposes and therefore cannot be unreasonable.—
The philosophy of the materialists is founded on the following:

1. Man lives and dies; I live and I know from experience that I, too, shall die.
2. When I die, my immediate and mediate knowledge come to a stop, because the instrument of knowing is destroyed.
3. Only inanimate inorganic matter, which I know from experience, will not be destroyed.
4. Matter is indestructible.
5. From this, I conclude that only dead matter exists indubitably.
6. From the remaining dead matter alone, I conclude that only dead matter exists really, indubitably, and always.
7. From the conclusion that only matter exists eternally, I conclude that my consciousness of my personal life is only a result of a certain complex state of matter; my consciousness is an illusion, consisting only of mundane architecture. Plotinus. Having reached this final conclusion, this logical inference sits inconsistently with the inner human sense, with the arbitrariness of its conclusion that life is a consequence of a certain condition of matter—something that has never been proven and shows up only because we cannot see another result. The main error of this inference, however, is that premise 5—that there remains nothing but inanimate matter after death—is wrong. The untruth of this premise consists in my usage of the words "only dead matter exists," which are meaningless and contain an inner contradiction.[28]

Abstract matter that is objective has no meaning; it is only an abstraction of my consciousness of my existence. "Dead matter" only means the life of the matter whose life I don't know. And without knowing its life, I can make no assertions about its existence. It is only as life that I know and can know existence.—

Premise number 5 should therefore be substituted thus: when life is destroyed, what remains for me as an observer is only the abstraction of life—dead matter, that is—or such matter whose life I do not comprehend.

---

28 Tolstoy hilariously twists "state of the matter" from which a definite article is missing, making this stepping-stone of materialism an iffy foundation. Mundane architecture (*stroi mira*) is a pregnant philosophical term, alluding to the Kantian rational architecture—the building of the correct foundation for thinking, the building of world order. Materialists only see the external, material overlay of this construction.

I cannot say that everything gets destroyed, for what remains is: 1) the abstraction of life, matter (corpus); (2) the second abstraction of life—progeny; and (3) the trace of impact on other people. All this is not in unitary integration and is incomprehensible to me. (To find the possible ...)

30. A Letter to N. N. Strakhov[29] [November 30, 1875]

Your letter has produced such a strong impression on me, dear Nikolai Nikolaevich, that I felt nasal pinches and tears come to my eyes. It is the expression of everything real, *das Echte*,[30] so infrequently encountered, that has left this impression on me. It struck me also because your letter asked the very questions that have absorbed me—or at least you raise questions in the same sphere—about which I have been preoccupied trying to write answers of my own.

I am sending what I have written as a kind of a preface to a philosophical work that I have conceived. You will see that out of Kant's three questions, only one preoccupies me (in this our characters differ) and has since childhood— the last one: What can we hope for?[31]

---

29 **Entry 30. A Letter to N. N. Strakhov (November 30, 1875).** The former "man of the soil," intellectual, lifelong enemy of Western-inbred nihilism, historian of science, and literary critic, Nikolai Strakhov (1828–96) was one of Tolstoy's most loyal correspondents, as well as his editor, a tireless supplier of materials from The Imperial Public Library in St. Petersburg where for many years he served as a modest librarian, and was the only Hegelian whose company and wisdom Tolstoy not only tolerated but very gently enjoyed. From March 1870 until January 1896, Tolstoy and Strakhov exchanged a total of 466 letters. In their sum, they are indispensable for understanding Tolstoy's mind and for providing a snapshot of the state of the Russian intellectual milieu during the last thirty years of the nineteenth century. I translated this letter from November 30, 1875, from the most reliable version of the original Russian, which was published in *Leo Tolstoy and Nikolai Strakhov: Complete Correspondence*. 2 vols. eds. Andrew Donskov, Lydia Gromova, and Tatiana Nikiforova (Moscow: The State Museum of L. N. Tolstoy and the University of Ottawa, 2003), 1:230-39. For a substantive commentary, see Medzhibovskaya (2008, 161-65).

30 The German word here means "the real thing."

31 Kant's three questions are found in the section "The Ideal of the Highest Good" of *The Critique of Pure Reason* (A 805-6/B 833-34). We can readily see that Tolstoy had, indeed, been reflecting on these questions "since childhood:" not only is this made apparent in the Juvenilia fragments but also in a copy found in Tolstoy's personal library of a French translation of Kant's first *Critique*, which the editor of this volume was able to study. In the latter, we can see that Tolstoy drew an ecstatic circle around these questions from A 805/B833, concerning how we can "fulfill our vocation in this present world ... to adapt ourselves to the system of all ends:" "(1) *Que puis-je savoir?* ['What can I know?']; (2) *Que dois-je faire?*

The difference between you and me is only superficial. For a thinking person, all of Kant's three questions are inextricably tied into one: What is my life—what am I? To every individual, the instinct of prescience or—if you prefer—the experience of the mind indicates which of the three locks it is easier to pick to open these doors. For which lock is there a key? Or, perhaps, which of these doors is the individual pressed against by life? What is certain is that opening and entering one of the doors will reveal what is hidden behind them all. I have understood quite well what you have said, and although I would rather wait to receive elucidation and your distinction between the passive and active activities, I cannot hold back my desire to lay down my response to the second of these questions: What should I do?

I know that this is very insolent of me and may seem strange and supercilious to try to answer this question on two small sheets of postal paper, but I have reasons to consider not only that I can but that I must do so. And I would do so were I to write a letter not to you, the human being close to me, but were I to write my *profession de foi*,[32] knowing that all of humankind was listening to me.

These are my reasons:
(Please, do listen to me attentively, don't get angry at this digression and correct what's imprecise, clarify what's unclear, and refute what is not right. This digression is in essence what they call the discourse on method.)

When it comes to a scientific discourse, it is supposed that the discourse is about something unknown to the listener or reader. If it is about something known, the author of the discourse demands that the reader forget what he knows, and the author begins by providing his own definitions of each of the phenomena familiar to the listener, in accordance with the aims he has for science.

I suppose that, upon reading this, you will have in mind your own example from the mathematical, natural, or political sciences, in support of the fact that this indeed is the method and course for the exposition of all the sciences.

This method is natural and necessary in all the sciences, because the results of knowledge—in whatever branch of science—may not be known to the listener: he cannot understand them or believe in their reality if his former conceptions of the phenomena in the sphere of knowledge known to him have not

---

['What ought I to do?']; (3) *Que m'est-il permis d'espérer* ['What can I hope for?']" (Immanuel Kant, *Critique de la raison pure. Traduite de l'allemand par C. J. Tissot*, 2 vols. [Paris: Ladrange, 1835–36]). See also Medzhibovskaya 2008, 36-37; 51-52; 161-65; 340; and 355. Tolstoy's notations to Kant's three questions can be found on page 414 of the French edition.
32 Tolstoy uses the French term here for "profession of faith."

been corrected and if he hasn't been brought up to speed, step by step, with the explications of these phenomena.

Man cannot get to know the weight of the sun or believe in the truth of the calculation if it has not been demonstrated to him that the sun does not rotate; he cannot believe in the Darwinian system if the concepts of horse and fish have not been substituted in him by the concept of an organism and its functions.

It must be noted as well that in the exposition of all the sciences, the method of discourse, the corrections that are made in the concepts of the listener, the method for defining the simplest scientific phenomena, that is, is not done in accordance with one and the same general law, but only and always in correspondence with the latest results that a science has reached (although familiar to the author of the discourse, they are unfamiliar to the listener). And so, the definition of the simplest phenomenon appears to be arbitrary—and is as much—or is dependent on the stage of development achieved by science. What they called in ancient times the "element of fire," they called in Newton's times "corpuscular rays," and they now call "ethereal circulation." All the sciences are bound to behave thus, for there are always results in science that are known to the discoursing author but are unknown to the listener, and they must be presented to the listener so that he is persuaded of their truth.—

Only philosophy (real philosophy, which holds for its task responding to Kant's three questions, i.e., explaining the meaning of life) does not possess this quality of the other sciences: Philosophy does not consist in correcting the primordial, most basic concepts of the listener and providing new definitions so as to bring the listener to the latest results reached by science which are known by the exponent and not by the listener. Philosophy (or at least, real philosophy), I am saying, does not have this quality. Indeed, all it would take to see what is alien to philosophy is to read precisely all the books that bear the word "philosophy" on their spines.

This happens because many of these books are far from philosophical, such as all the positivistic writings in which the scientific method is used and allowed to be used with all its rigor, while other truly philosophical books (e.g., those of Descartes, Spinoza, Kant, Schelling, Fichte, Hegel, Schopenhauer) have adopted an uncharacteristic method for the exposition of their subject. (Plato stands out sharply from the rest thanks to the correctness of his method, in my opinion. And Schopenhauer is the closest of all to him.) From this point of view, all works of philosophy can be grouped into three different categories:

1. Materialists, positivists: they place the bar low for philosophy and misconstrue its aim, applying the general scientific method with full

rigor in philosophy. In so doing, they achieve their own aim, but one that is, in essence, beyond philosophy.

2. Idealists, spiritualists: they posit the aim of philosophy in its totality, but they adopt general scientific methods of discourse, from which they stray more or less depending on the might and depth of their thinking (Hegel never strays; Schopenhauer strays all the time).

3. Plato, Schopenhauer, and the religious teachings: they posit the real aim for philosophy and they do not adhere to the scientific methods of discourse. In other words, they do not correct the primeval and simplest concepts of their listeners but search for the meaning of life without the vivisection of those essential substances of which life is composed for every human being.—

You might wish to ask what right I have to subdivide all philosophical teachings on the basis of the different condition of their method of philosophy and of all the other sciences, when the necessity of such a distinction has not yet been proven.—

The necessity of this distinction is proven in the following:

1) If it is just that the scientific method of discourse consists in correcting the concepts about known subjects in the listener and replacing them with known precise definitions, with the aim of letting the listener in on these definitions in this way to the cognition of general laws, it is obvious that this method is inapplicable in philosophy, because none of the foundational concepts of which philosophical knowledge is composed can be altered, differently comprehended, or differently defined at the highest steps of philosophical knowledge. In physics, the concept of a low-sunk and moving winter sun is replaced by an altogether different concept—the changed position of the earth on the sun's orbit. And in chemistry, the notion of the flame of an icon-lamp is replaced by the concept of a chemical compound. But the main concepts of philosophy, the elements out which philosophy is composed, can never be changed: they haven't changed since the dawn of humankind—neither with the savage nor with the sage. My body, my soul, my life, my death, my desire, my thought, that I feel pain, that I feel faint, that I feel good, that I feel joy: these are always the same and can never be either clearer or more vague, neither with the savage nor with the sage.—Hence in philosophy, that sphere of knowledge that has the soul, life, thought, joy, and so on for its object, the scientific method—which consists in making corrections and changing the definitions of such concepts—is inapplicable.

2) I base my proof that the scientific method is inapplicable to philosophy on the fact that every science begins by separating that aspect of a phenomenon which is its subject, while sharply rejecting as beyond its purview all the other aspects of the phenomenon. Having passed its entire course, each science generalizes about only one aspect of a phenomenon, not only caring nothing about the agreement of the phenomenon's other aspects with the data it has drawn for its conclusions but frequently celebrating its triumph over the disagreement, for it proves scientific success. As per its own aim, philosophy cannot relegate as beyond its purview any of the aspects of the phenomena that interest it. The very subjects of philosophy: life, the soul, will, reason cannot be vivisected for the removal of their known parts. The phenomena that comprise the subject for the sciences are the phenomena that we cognize mediately in the external world. The phenomena that comprise the subject matter of philosophy, meanwhile, get cognized immediately in our internal world, and we can only observe them in the external world because we know them from the world within; and these phenomena can only then comprise the subject matter of philosophy when they are taken in their integrity and as such as we recognize them immediately. Take life, will, and reason, for example: As the activity of an organism, life can be a subject for physiology; as a phenomenon pertaining to the state, [it can be a subject] for history; as a series of chemical processes, [it can be a subject] for chemistry; as a series of physical phenomena, [it can be a subject] for physics. But as the subject of philosophy, life must be taken in its integrity—in the entirety of what that which is alive knows about itself. And so, if it is necessary to extract one aspect of a phenomenon and to neglect everything else for the exposition of the sciences, this method is inapplicable to philosophy, thanks to the essence of its very subject.

3) The persuasiveness of the principles advanced by every science consists, according to Schopenhauer, in their logical, physical, mathematical, or moral necessity. Thanks to setting aside certain aspects of things and describing only one aspect of them, and through drawing a series of conclusions about that aspect, the exponent of science guides his listeners toward becoming persuaded in the general laws which are derived from these aspects of phenomena. The listener is formally and quite irrefutably convinced as a rule in the data communicated to him in this way. But internally, he remains quite free from the accepted convictions.—

Something altogether different takes place during the exposition of philosophy. It is impossible to redefine the concepts out of which philosophical knowledge consists during its exposition, impossible to reduce them; one must leave them in their complete integrity: these concepts are acquired immediately and it is not possible to construct a chain of whatever necessity out of them in consequence. The persuasiveness of a philosophical teaching is never achieved by means of logical conclusions; it is achieved only by a harmonious unification into one whole of all these non-logical concepts. In other words, philosophical persuasion is achieved momentarily, without conclusions and proofs, and it has only one method of proof—that any unity except this one is meaningless. Therefore, by harmonious unification, I understand only the best of all unifications. As a way to substantiate this position, I ask you to recall the invalidity of scientific philosophical theories and the validity and power of religions—not only in their impact on crude and illiterate minds.

The other confirmation for this position is that philosophy is that kind of knowledge on which an entire view of the world rests (with all the branches of knowledge), that in philosophy all branches of knowledge interlock.

If branches of knowledge with their infinite progress are like the walls of a cylinder, then there could be no philosophy. But if the branches of knowledge are like the walls of a conus, then the tip of the conus cannot be built in the same way as the walls are. And thus, the third proof that the scientific method is inapplicable to philosophy is that the persuasiveness of the sciences rests on logic, on conclusion, whereas the persuasiveness of philosophy rests on harmony.

Speaking about the difference between the method of philosophy and science, I have almost made an unwitting definition of what I mean by philosophy. I am glad to have done so, and shall now attempt to make this definition even more definite and precise. Because it is very frequent that we, the lovers of philosophy, are poorly understood and do not understand others. They demand either too much or too little from philosophy. A positivist says: You cannot prove the justice of your view logically; it is therefore not scientific and is not needed. A believer says: you cannot substantiate the justice of your view with anything; it is therefore arbitrary. As such, it seems to me, we need to define clearly what we mean by philosophy, lest we be told that it is not needed, lest demands be placed on it to provide what it cannot provide, and at the same time so that it be acknowledged that philosophy is not something arbitrary.—

In the subjective sense, philosophy is the knowledge that provides the best possible answers to questions about the meaning of human life and death.

In the general sense, philosophy is unification into one harmonious whole of all those foundations of human knowledge which cannot receive logical explanations.

I can see a chasm of innuendos, ambiguities, repetitions, and an obnoxious doctoral tone in everything that I have written, but I stand by the main thought about the method of philosophy, which, I hope, you can make out in this confusion. This thought is necessary for me to begin the narration of those questions that preoccupy me. My main thought is that any philosophical view borne out of life (and mine therefore as well) is a circle or a sphere.[33] As such, it has neither end, middle, nor beginning, neither anything most important nor unimportant; all is the beginning, all is the middle, all is equally important and necessary. The persuasiveness and truth of a philosophical view depend on its inner accord, its harmoniousness; in wishing to express this view, it is the same whether I begin by answering that very second question of Kant's about what I must do, which is preoccupying you. In my plan, however, this question of ethics seems to me to be one of the last.—You are saying: What must I do? A suckling infant does not ask what it must do; it sucks, wants to live—loves itself. And similarly, a person dying of illness or old age does not ask about this: He wants not to suffer, wants to die; he loves not the self but loves the non-self.[34] And so why are we asking ourselves what to do? Only because we both want to live and to die together. Yet we do not live from old age toward childhood but from childhood toward old age. One should follow the current in order to feel calm, firmness, inner satisfaction; one must want to die.

What does it mean to want to live? It means to love oneself. To want to die is not to love one's self, to love [that which is] not one's self—that which is the same.

If it were clear to you as it is clear to me that to love, to desire, and to live are one and the same thing, then I would say directly that during childhood one desires for oneself, lives for engulfing within oneself, loves one's self, whereas during old age, we do not live for ourselves, we desire beyond ourselves,[35] and love [what's] not ourselves. I would say that life is only a transition from love of one's self—that is, from personal life, this one—to love of [what's] not myself—that is, universal life (in common), which is not this one. In other words, I would resolve every moment of doubt by choosing to satisfy what is not the love of the self.[36]

---

33 See also entry 58, Tolstoy's note on upbringing (1909) and entry 61, his reminiscences on N. Ia. Grot (1910) in this anthology.

34 "He loves not the self [*sebia ne liubit*] but loves the non-self [*liubit ne sebia*]."

35 "Lives for engulfing within oneself [*v sebia*], loves one's self, whereas during old age, we do not live for ourselves, we desire beyond ourselves [*vne sebia*]."

36 This is the end of the text written by Tolstoy. What follows is in his copyist's hand, although not to the end of the letter, as Tolstoy would indicate to Strakhov.

WHAT DO I WRITE FOR?[37]

I am 47. Whether because I have lived too passionately or because it is normal, I feel that old age has arrived for me.

I call "old age" that inner state of the soul when all external world phenomena have lost their interest for one. It seems to me that I know everything that people of our time do. If I don't know such-and-such, it seems to me that were I to discover this unknown knowledge, it would not be captivating for me, would not open up to me anything new—the kind of new that I would like to know. I do not desire anything from the external phenomena of the world. If a fairy came and asked me what I desired, I would not be able to express a single such desire. If I still have any desires—for example, as I have dreamt about, a desire to breed horses of a certain breed, or to hunt down ten foxes on one field, or for enormous success for my book, or to become a millionaire, or to learn Arabic and Mongolian, and so on—these I know to be inauthentic and transitory desires, holdovers of previous desires that show up during bad moments in my spiritual condition. In those moments when I have these desires, an inner voice already tells me that they will fail to satisfy me.

This is how I have lived up to old age, to that inner state of the soul when nothing from the external world represents any interest for me, in which there are no desires and one sees nothing but death ahead.

I have lived through that period of childhood, youth, and young adulthood when I ascended the magic mountain of life, getting higher and higher, hoping to find at its apex a result worthy of the labors I had invested. I have lived through that period of maturity during which, on my ascent to the top of the mountain, I took a leisurely, measured, restful, and unhurried stroll, looking around for the fruits of life that I had reaped. I have lived through that bewildered phase during which, little by little, the thought repeatedly invaded me that I might have erred when ascribing such significance to the fruits that I have reaped or, alternatively, that maybe the lack of correspondence between the fruits and the desire to reap them is the common lot of all people. I have lived also through the conviction that there was nothing whatsoever on the apex of the mountain, nothing that I had expected, and hence that one choice remains open to me: that, like it or not, I must start the descent on the other side, down from whence I had traveled. And I have commenced this descent. Not only have the desires that so inconspicuously carried me all the way to the top of the mountain disappeared, but I now have the opposite and undignified desire to stop and hold on to

---

37 Tolstoy adds emphasis to this question by writing it in all capitals: WHAT DO I WRITE FOR? (*DLIA CHEGO IA PISHU?*). Compare this question with the one that the very young Tolstoy asked in "Why Do People Write?" (1851) (see entry 12 in this volume).

something. There is momentary terror (even more undignified) about what is awaiting me. And I am walking downward with circumspection and remembering the path I covered, analyzing the present course, and attempting to penetrate the mystery of what is expecting me on the other side, in that place where I am involuntarily headed.

I call this state old age and I have lived up to this state at the present minute.

As I said, the first feeling I experienced upon my entrance into old age was bewilderment, then horror, then the heavy feeling of despair that the poet's cavalier phrase—that life is really just an empty and silly joke which somebody plays on us—is not just a phrase.[38] But the consciousness that my life cannot be a joke, that same consciousness thanks to which Descartes arrived at the proof of the existence of God, which he expressed by way of a conviction that God could not have played such a joke on us, this consciousness triggered resistance within me as it would in any man forced into acknowledging the meaninglessness of the life of a reasonable creature. This consciousness forced me to cast doubt over whether I have understood the meaning of life correctly. And in fact, if it appears at a certain age that the life that has passed is nonsense, the disagreement of this conviction with a demand of the reasonableness of human nature may be resolved in two ways, by concluding either:

1) that the whole of human life really is meaningless and leads to despair in old age; or

2) that the meaning that I ascribe to life is incorrect and that this incorrectness becomes obvious at a certain age, just as the deviation of a line from parallel becomes apparent only from a distance.

Putting aside the inner consciousness that always stubbornly resists concluding that life is a stupid joke, the second supposition—namely, that the meaning of life has been understood by me incorrectly—is also confirmed by the fact that, having made the first allowance, it is necessary that those who have reached old age encounter a feeling of despair. My observations, however, suggest the contrary: far from arriving at despair, old people—with very rare exceptions in our time and in all times—enjoy old age as the most tranquil and quiet period of their lives, and have the most lucid and calm view of life and their forthcoming death.

---

38 Tolstoy means Mikhail Lermontov's poem "*I skuchno i grustno...*" [Feeling bored and sad..] (1840). He loved the lines so much that he quoted them again, for example in Chapter 23 of his later work *On Life* (1886–87).

And so, after having become convinced that my despair was caused not by the qualities of life itself but by my view on it, I started looking for that view on life through which the seeming meaninglessness of life would be destroyed. To tell the story about how I had transitioned from a state of hopelessness to making the meaning of life—which pierces through my past life and its source, the remaining part, and the end of it—clearer for myself comprises the aim and the content of what I am writing.

I could not have had the whole of it copied.

What follows would have led the copyist into temptation. If I finish writing it, God willing, I will, of course, send it to you.

What follows is a discussion about how religions satisfy these questions but how it is impossible for those of us with our knowledge to believe in religious postulates. I then discuss in what manner European people live without religion when religion is the necessary condition of life. And then I locate religion in the view of the materialists, positivists, and progressists—though as incomplete religions, religions of life but not of death.[39] Then I would like to clarify that it is completely in vain that Max Müller and Burnouf—whom I have just been reading—and that modern people in general juxtapose religion and science.[40] The concord[41] of the data of our time is the religion of our time. When Christians used to study religion in olden times, they did not juxtapose it to science; religion was the science of science—truth, in the same way as what they now call positive science. And then I would like to lay out the whole religious concord of views of the science of our time and to point out its gaps,[42] and—forgive my audacity—to fill in these gaps without rebuffing anything. This is my audacious plan. I ask for your help, chiefly in critiquing my positions by providing the most severe censure; and I also ask for your help directing me to materials. For example, I now stand in need of a book or books or your rendition of a general complete view of the materialists and the positivists on the world created by God[43] (religious in my word, and scientific in theirs). And then I need to know how people of authority are defining science, religion, and philosophy.

In my view, science in the general sense, philosophy, and religion are one and the same.

---

39 The original Russian reads "*no religiiu nepolnuiu, religiu zhizni, no ne religiiu smerti.*"
40 At this time, Tolstoy was reading Max Müller's *Essais sur l'histoire des religions* (1872) and taking copious notes in his notebooks. Here, he most likely meant to also reference Émile Burnouf's *La science des religions* (1872).
41 The Russian word here is *svod.*
42 The Russian word here is "*probely.*"
43 The Russian phrase here is "*na mir Bozhii.*"

Science is the assembly of all human knowledge, compartmentalized.

Philosophy is a harmony, and the result of, all knowledge—without its compartmentalization—and the refutation of all the other harmonies of knowledge.

Religion is the harmony, and the result of, all knowledge—without its compartmentalization—and without the refutation of all the other harmonies.

Science is a false concept when it is taken as a complete whole. In terms of its qualities, science is a series of subdivisions. Philosophy and religion differ only in that philosophy is polemical, whereas this is alien to religion.

And now I will add a few clarifications to the answer that I am providing to the question "what to do?" I am saying that to love, to want (desire, will)[44] to live is one and the same, though not the same at the same time. This is one of the applications of the philosophical method, which does not employ logical conclusions but convinces by the correctness of joining concepts,[45] also linking, joining, ordering, concatenating of what is here not a concord but a harmonization.[46]

Speaking in philosophical lingo, which has only a polemical aim, I would say: to desire is the concept of time, because one can desire only what will be. To live is the concept of space. When we say "lives," "life," we are thinking only about space encompassed by life. To love is a causal concept, because you can desire only what you love and love only because you love. But I do not posit persuasiveness here—in the harmonic collation of not just these but of all other philosophical concepts.

I am looking forward to continuing this discussion with you, to your responses and objections, so as to demonstrate this harmoniousness to you and to myself, and the legitimacy of collating the concepts of my religious (philosophical)[47] view.

Your L. Tolstoy 1875, 30 November

---

44   These are Tolstoy's brackets and synonyms.
45   The Russian phrase here is *"ubezhdaet pravilnost'iu soedinenii poniatii."*
46   The Russian phrase here is *"ne svod, a soedinenie."*
47   Tolstoy's synonym is provided in brackets.

31. On the Significance of Christian Religion[48]
[1875–76]

3).[49]

When considering the significance of Christian religions, albeit only within the kind of society best known to me—European, and specifically Russian society—I have arrived at the conclusion that all thinking individuals must have reached: it has been a long time since we stopped being Christian. Suffice it to look soberly at the significance of religion in our society and in European societies and one can't help but arrive at this negative conclusion. Whether we like it or not, the significance of religion in our time appears as a link that used to be the main force behind social solidarity but that has now rotted through and gathered rust. Some of the things held together by religion are still joined and show remnants of religion, but the link itself is gone. One can see that what used to be fitted together is falling away with every movement, freely and undeterred.

Let us take a look at state laws and state power, shall we? The holder of the power used to be the divinely anointed sovereign, and this was the main and sole title (*titre*) of his power.[50] Nobody can believe in this in our time. To solidify his power, Napoleon III seeks *suffrage universel* instead of anointment. It is evident that the religious connection does not obtain the same power as it did for his uncle. Without wasting his time on philosophizing, this practical man does not beat about the bush and chooses a link other than religion to achieve his aim.—

Similarly, everyone can feel that the pledge of allegiance that remains in use is only an empty, non-binding formality, implying no outstanding duty for anyone. The constant and apparently conscious abuse of oaths that are still practiced at the courts clearly prove that the erstwhile religious connection borne by oaths has none of its former strength. Religious tolerance, so much touted where the treatment of the Jews is concerned, is, in essence, only the most vivid proof of the absence of religion in society and the state. The religious

---

48 **Entry 31. "On the Significance of Christian Religion"** [*O znachenii khristianskoi religii*] (1875–76). Published in 1936 in *The Jubilee* 17:353-56, the manuscript is described by V. F. Savodnik in the same volume (17:723-25). For a detailed commentary, see Medzhibovskaya 2008, 173. Tolstoy's reading of the journal *Revue des deux Mondes* most likely prompted this fragmentary reflection. Toward the end of his fragment, Tolstoy mentions the liberal theologian Albert Reville (1826 – 1906) and the famous historian of religion Ernest Renan (1823 – 92), both of whom frequently contributed to the journal.

49 This fragment begins with "3)."

50 The Russian term *pomazannik Bozhii* for "sovereign" provides a more immediate sense of divine appointment, the title crown of governance being received from heaven. Anointment to Tsardom is one of the main sacraments of the Russian Orthodox Church.

state that punishes blasphemy and the maligning of faith cannot tolerate the professing of Judaism, which is, in its essence, the denial of the Christian belief, and the acceptance that the Son of God was an imposter.

The struggle of the supporters of religion with their opponents provides yet more proof of the absence of religion in society. For, thanks to its very basis, religion and its servants cannot deign to struggle against secular power.—

The absence of religion in the family is made most manifest in the main familial act of marriage, which used to be intrinsically religious. Leaving aside the fact that the majority of the educated circles about whom I am talking are copulating without any religious restrictions—which they regard as a nuisance—and bypassing the religious rites, let me focus on the practically minded, the so-called Christians, among the majority of the Europeans. For the purpose of replacing the dilapidated religious link, they arrived at the necessity of civic marriages. Religion itself caved to the demands of the masses and condescended to allow divorces. It thus became involved in the destruction of its own bonds, letting loose what was already slack, lest it be simply torn apart.

The absence of religion is most noticeable where it used to occupy the primary place in governing everything—in education. It is only natural that in raising the young generation and in their love for it, fathers, and grownups in general, strove to transmit the one main thing that children need to know, the explication of the meaning of life and death, above all—and not a collection of information about the world, not studies of nature, not the collection of practical and useful knowledge acquired by humankind. Religion used to provide that explanation and it therefore occupied and continues to occupy its prime place among the uneducated masses who are possessed of the correct instinct of love for their children.

This place is now empty and vacant, and we witness all the anxious, complicated, contentless, and unfounded arguments in ongoing discussions about what the main subject matter and the aim of upbringing should be.

Some demand a classical upbringing for children, observing the practical results of studying the ancients that were achieved after the restoration of the sciences and the arts; others notice the progress in the natural sciences in recent times, demanding that these sciences be given central place; a third group demand that practical knowledge be given pride of place; meanwhile, a fourth say flaccidly and without faith in their own words that religion—the selfsame religion in which they do not believe—should continue to serve as the cornerstone of children's upbringing, just as previously.

None of these groups can be right. They all speak only from their respective vantage point about optimizing the utility of the leisure allowed by the age of the learner, but nobody speaks about what should replace religion—which can no longer be the core and main subject of learning; nobody speaks about the one basic thing needed. These four groups remind me of folks who run out of foodstuffs and who conjure recipes for filling the stomach of an animal. But neither classicism, a good dressing up of the old, nor realism, a useful utensil on which to put your food, nor religion without faith, leftovers from a meal that used to be good, will provide nourishment to a famished animal.

The Mohammedans have their faith and their solid educational system, albeit located at the lowest degree of progress. But the Christians have no system of education at the present time, and this happens because there is no religion.

About the different attitudes toward religion of people from the educated classes.

1. <By observing people around me, I have discovered that—just like me—the majority of educated and thinking individuals do not accept religious arguments and do not believe in religion. But there is also a variety of attitudes toward religion, and there are questions left unsolved by religion.>

Let us look around at particular individuals, men and women. I live in an educated environment where religious beliefs have been preserved better than elsewhere. I openly asked both my close and not-so-close acquaintances about their beliefs, and, with rare exception, I received the same answer from the hundred people I asked: "we do not require Christianity; we are non-believers."

During my observations, I have discovered three different approaches of people toward religious questions. Having stumbled against the impossibility of faith, yet with nothing to replace it, the first group try to pretend to be believers and to persuade others, because they regard the status quo with religion in place to be profitable for them. Having not yet come face to face with the questions of life and death, a second group cast off their faith, thinking it redundant. These people act rashly but truthfully, whereas the former act with cunning premeditation. Having cast off religion, a third group—very small in number—have stumbled upon the unsolvable questions and are attempting to solve them by means of rational thought.

<About the significance of the religion of life and the religion of death>
<In order to delineate clearly the character of these relationships of an individual toward religion, it is necessary to clarify the concept of religion satisfactorily

in its full unity, and not just the one that prepares for death, but the one that is as essential for moral life as air is for physical life.>

Women either tend to be non-believers or they merely observe the rites: they go to confession or bake blinis for Lent, attend Mass, and paint Easter eggs red. In government and society, one can moreover feel that all sovereign power of religion is lost. Articles about the death of St. Paul are banned in *Revue des deux Mondes*, while articles by Reville and Renan publish exposés—calm writings for the general public and without bile—about Joseph being a fable, Psalter a songbook put together by later collectors, and so on.

Attempts have been made to give the priesthood more dignity, but there are no takers to join the clergy. In Europe, in republican France, and in the Swiss Republic, any sermon is permitted—only not the Christian one. Yes, happy are those who do not see this and who hope to resurrect Christianity.

I do not argue and shall not argue with them.

32. A Conversation about Science[51]
[1875–76]

June 4: Nikolai Nikolaevich was invited to visit his neighbor. Iv. P. B., the neighbor, esteemed Nikolai Nikolaevich as an intelligent and learned man. He coveted the visit of my principal since he was apparently going to introduce him to a history professor, who was visiting from Moscow. Iv. P. begged Nikolai Nikolaevich not to deny the invitation. As it goes with all insignificant people who are only half smart, Iv. P. enjoyed listening to conversations of the intelligent set, even though he understood them only poorly. So, we went to the neighbor's house. The bearded professor was given a seat next to Nikolai Nikolaevich and our hosts played the role of matchmakers without disguise. Being of a kind-hearted temper, Nikolai Nikolaevich was averse to running afoul of his hosts' expectations. Although he could very well see the funny side of such "spectator tournaments," as he likes to call them, he was ready to enter the fray and nagged the professor to instigate an argument. He also happened to have a knack for arguing around dinnertime. And yet the Professor kept silent—contemptuously so, it seemed to me. The Professor was one of those young scholars who

---

51 **Entry 32. "A Conversation about Science"** [*Razgovor o nauke*] (1875–76). Published in 1936 in *The Jubilee* 17:139-41, this manuscript is described by V. F. Savodnik later in the same volume (17:619). For a detailed commentary, see Medzhibovskaya 2008, 167-68; 176; 192. The "Nikolai Nikolaevich" in this dialogue is a transparently fictionalized Strakhov. Other encoded meanings are possible and discussed in the aforementioned sources.

talked with gusto: he had nothing to do, was a well-versed lord living an easy life, an honest gentleman, and so on. But he had an intelligent, firm, and calm face. He seemed to be *ferré à glace* [*well-heeled, ed.*] —about his subject matter, in particular. And so, after dinner, an argument about history and the law of progress broke out.

Nikolai Nikolaevich said that, as the single guiding thread of history, the law of progress hasn't been proven by anyone, and is more than a little dubious.

—He repeated the same thought a few times: How is that the law of progress applies to world history, but why do 9/10ths of the human race—from China, Asia, Africa—proceed in accordance with the reverse law?—

The professor said in response that the law of progress is visible in all historical peoples, and that science has no dealings with non-historical peoples.

Nikolai Nikolaevich stumbled and became embarrassed.

—"You don't want to know anything about these nations?"

Professor: "They are outside of the sphere of science."—

Nikolai Nikolaevich fell silent.

We were on our way home and the *esprit de l'escalier* [*smarts on the staircase, ed.*] of Nikolai Nikolaevich was on a marked upswing (this is how he refers to his judgments about the impressions of the day). I memorized and jotted down his "smarts on the staircase," because his expressions seemed remarkable to me.

—"Does not belong in science, is not in the sphere of science," he said, repeating to me the words of the professor. "Did you hear our dispute?"

—"Yes, in part."—

—"Kindly observe that this is what's so amusing," he told me with that meek and intelligent smile of his.—"It is amusing that it is only the philosophical idea of history that's interesting about history. That is, the law according to which history unfolds, which they have identified within history. What do I care about the people that Hannibal conquered or what the mistresses of Louis Quatorze were like? I am interested in the law, in terms of what follows from it. Yet it's 'the law of progress,' he says. And when I wish to put this law to the test, he tells me this: 'run your test only according to our science, which is founded on this law.' It's like I am arguing that this *desiatina* is 40 *sazhens* short, and he is saying: 'don't use your *sazhens* to measure; use mine: they make 40 *sazhens* exactly.'[52] I checked the measure. Before asking whether science is any good, they say: 'have faith in science; study it, just like religious missionaries. Study it, work on it, dedicate a dozen years of your life to it, let yourself grow bald from it,

---

52 An old Russian land measure, *desiatina* is equal to 1.09 hectares or 2,400 square *sazhens*. A *sazhen* is an old Russian land measure equal to 2.13 meters.

then you'll split no hairs doubting. And truly, you won't doubt, so sorry will you feel for the labors and the years that you've spent on it.' He can now agree with me no more. For then he'd need to renounce 10 years' worth of labor. God forbid!—

But the main thing is that this method is nothing like objecting; it is more like closing down a discussion—a recent and very nifty invention in the sciences. My main interest in it is its precise philosophical meaning. In other words, I'd like to know what truths history proves? What follows from that is the fact that the Punic Wars took place or that there used to be certain legal codes? I'd like to know what follows from a nerve having a reverse reaction, or the liver producing sugar, or that there are such-and-such theories of criminal law.

I ask: Is humankind becoming more perfect? Is the soul immortal? Is capital punishment just? And so on. And they tell me: 'vous êtes hors la question, cela n'est pas du domaine de la science' ['you are beside the question; this is not within the domain of science']. It is as if there were a discussion in the public session of a society about when to give dinner, and a clueless member asks an awkward question about what the society has accomplished: 'You are beside the question; you are not within the domain of science.'—

It used to be that none of the sciences steered themselves clear of the philosophical questions aligned with it. And today history states point blank that questions about the vocation of humankind and the laws of its development are of no interest to science. Physiology states that it knows the course of nervous activity, but that questions about freedom of the will or of human bondage are outside of its sphere. Jurisprudence states that it knows the history of such and such decrees, but that the question about the extent to which these decrees respond to our ideal of justice is outside of its sphere, and so forth. Still worse is when medicine says that this disease of yours has nothing to do with science. What the hell do I need your sciences for? I would rather play chess! The sole justification of these pursuits is that they respond to my questions. Without doing so, these are the kinds of study that one pursues for fun, knowing full well that one will learn nothing from them."

—"What to do then?" I asked.

—"Yes, sure: Nobody is guilty of anything. This is the powerlessness of knowledge, this is prohibiting man from eating from the tree of good and evil, something that mankind invariably seeks which is the invariable quality of mankind. Then just say so. And don't be proud. Why should I be proud to know the meaning of every hieroglyph down to the tiniest detail, but still be unable to make out the meaning of a hieroglyphic inscription?"

—"They hope to comprehend it," said I.

—"They hope. It's time to comprehend that this hope has been alive for 3000 prehistoric years and that we are not a hair's width closer to knowing what justice is, what freedom is, what the meaning of human life is. But it is a pleasant occupation, playing chess—only nothing to be proud of, still less is it something to despise people for who do not know how to play the game.

33. The Definition of Religion-Faith[53]
[1875–76]

The term religion-faith is comprehensible and certain for all believers. To avoid any misunderstanding, the term requires an exact definition for non-believers, those who have no religion or who suppose that they don't have any. Like the majority of other abstract terms (I shall call such terms metaphysical—for example, life, force, death, desire, and so forth), this term has two meanings: a personal (or subjective) meaning and the common (objective) meaning. The personal significance of the term is always clear and is the same in all individuals, but the common significance is quite variable depending on its implied meaning. It is thus that I consider it necessary to explain what I understand by the word religion.

Religion is a harmonization into integral agreement of all explications and answers to the inevitable questions concerning life and death. These questions are the only ones of interest during life, and reason provides only a particular answer to these questions to me—the most harmonious one among those known to me and in which I believe as a consequence—by which I am guided in every act in life.

In accordance with this definition, there is no way that religion can contradict the data given by reason or by life, but every knowledge and every act in life is based solely on the religious view.—

This definition is the <*Tolstoy tore off one word, ed.*> (subjective) definition of what I call faith.[54] The objective definition will be the same also concerning another person; but it is evident that the harmonization of objectives that a

---

53 **Entry 33. "The Definition of Religion-Faith"** [*Opredelenie religii-very*] (1875–76). Published in 1936 in *The Jubilee* 17:357-58, this manuscript is described by V. F. Savodnik later in the same volume (17:731). For a detailed commentary, see Medzhibovskaya 2008, 173.

54 The Russian term here is *vera*.

Christian poses for himself and that satisfy his reason might not be satisfactory all around, and this I call a belief.[55]

And so, a belief may seem false to me, but faith, as I define it, is always beyond doubt.

But for our ... \<the fragment breaks off>

34. The Psychology of Everyday[56]
[1875–76]

Section I: The superstition of corporal punishment. Literature.

Section II: Family life—to guarantee the happiness of one's husband, the wife—to love...

Section III: Characters—kindness, anger. All difference is consequential.

Section IV: Upbringing—loving by means of love.

Section V: Economy: The main engine of a nation. It has its physiological peculiarities, just like cows: it should be fed according to its capacity; not to mention using its bones for fertilizer; they don't know how to plant clover. It is good to introduce where you do your work on your own, but here, you must adopt this engine.—

Psychology is based on observing the *I*. Human peculiarities and powers by deduction from the self. Zoological psychology—conclusions drawn from centuries-old results of manifest human qualities.

For the 1st (section)—love, will, kindness, and so on.

For the 2nd —The times of kindness, thoughts, reminiscences, and so on.

35. A Christian Catechism[57]
[1877]

"I believe in a single true and holy Church that is alive in the hearts of all people of the entire earth; that is expressed in my knowledge of that which is good in

---

55 The Russian term here is *verovanie*.

56 **Entry 34. "The Psychology of Everyday"** [*Psikhologiia obydennoi zhizni*] (1875–76). Published in 1936 in *The Jubilee* 17:359, the manuscript is described by V. F. Savodnik later in the same volume (17:726). Even in this sketchy form, it is priceless to see Tolstoy's interest, despite his antagonism to physiology, materialism, progress, and all the shadings of the positivist outlooks, in that which comprises the everyday.

57 **Entry 35. "A Christian Catechism"** [*Khristianskii Katekhizis*] (1877). Published in 1936 in *The Jubilee* 17:363-68, this manuscript is described by V. F. Savodnik later in the same

the knowledge and life of all people. I express this faith in the Christian teaching of the Russian Orthodox Church, and I therefore believe in one God the Father, and so on."

This is the symbol of my faith and what follows is a statement of my catechism, with an introduction:

On Faith

Q. What is Orthodox catechism?

A. Orthodox catechism is an instruction of true faith to be shared with each individual, in general, and with Orthodox Christians, in particular, for the salvation of the soul—or life—the life that corresponds to the demands of the soul also, for the soul to have its complete satisfaction in correspondence to its demands, and not the demands of the body alone.

Q. How do the demands of the body and the demands of the soul differ? Are they not merged into one? Are not what we call the demands of the soul simply more complex forms of the demands of the body?

A. The demands of the body have individual happiness as their aim. The demands of the soul have general happiness as their aim, which is almost always—not only frequently—contrary to individual happiness. And, therefore, the demands of the soul cannot be more complex than the demands of the body.

(*Note*) The philosophy of today—materialism, especially—asserts that what used to be called the demands of the soul is nothing other than more complex overlays of the consequences of satisfying material demands. Frequently, they are expressed in the denial of direct material demands that have not undergone cerebral processing. This assertion is unfounded, because the materialists accept the impossibility of keeping track of this process and can scarcely hint at the way in which this process might be explicated.—Even if it were possible to lay bare this process, the juxtaposition of the psychic and bodily demands would still remain fully possible. Likewise, having as their aim happiness in

---

volume (17:730). For a detailed commentary, see Medzhibovskaya 2008, 174-75. Although couched in the traditional catechistic form, Tolstoy's dialogue between Question (*Vopros*) and Answer (*Otvet*) or Faith (*Vera*) and Revelation (*Otkrovenie*) in the catechism is all but un-Orthodox.

general that is contrary to individual happiness, the demands of the soul would be for sure based only in faith in this happiness.

Q. What is necessary for the salvation of the soul—that is, what is necessary for knowing the demands of the soul?

A. A clear definition of what we believe in, and living in keeping with what we believe in.

Q. What is faith?

A. According to St. Paul,[58] it is the annunciation to the thirsting ones, the revelation to them of things unknown. "[Faith] is the assurance of things hoped for, the conviction in things not seen."[59] Faith is knowing without doubt those things that are incomprehensible to reason.

Q. What is the difference between knowing through faith and knowing through reason?

A. All knowing through reason is based on previous knowledge. Knowledge through faith has a foundation of its own.—

Q. Is knowledge through reason possible without knowledge through faith?

A. This is impossible, because all rational knowledge is based on previous knowledge; this previous knowledge, in turn, must also depend on further previous knowledge, etc. The very means of knowing reasonably that is based on knowing previously precludes the possibility of knowing anything without having known something that is not based on rational knowledge.

Q. What kind of knowledge is this?

A. Knowledge through faith.

Q. What is knowledge through faith? And where can we encounter it?

A. Knowledge through faith is that indubitable knowledge of the meaning of the phenomena surrounding us, guiding us in every moment of life ... [and that ...]

---

58 The Russian term is "Paul the Apostle" or "The Apostle Paul."
59 Tolstoy is quoting freely and then more exactly from The Symbol of Faith in Hebrews 11.1.

Q. In what life situations are we guided by knowledge through faith that is not based on rational knowledge?

A. When we count on tomorrow, we believe that the sun will rise and we shall continue living; when we take pity on someone and give him food, we believe that he is hungry, that he is in pain; when we travel to another place, we believe that we will encounter people there. Not a single of the simplest actions that make up our life do we base on reason but on faith.

Q. Where can knowledge through faith be seen in the sciences, if they are based on it?

A. In astronomy, we used to take on faith the existence of celestial bodies and immeasurable celestial space, but only later were the movements of these bodies and the scale of that space measured. We believe in infinite divisibility in physics and chemistry, in the impact of forces, but we make the calculations later. In the political sciences, we presuppose from the beginning our faith in the meaning of life for humankind (progress), and we study the phenomena of this life after that.

Q. Is knowledge through faith possible without rational knowledge?

A. It is possible, for it does not require any kind of foundation.

Q. In what will the guidance for true faith consist of if rational knowledge is not required for rational knowledge?

A. In demonstrating the limits of rational knowledge, the point at which reasoned knowledge comes to a stop and arrives at the very foundations on which it stands.

On revelation.

Q. From where is the reasonable expression of knowledge through faith drawn?

A. Knowledge through faith has a foundation in the human soul, but the expression of this knowledge is communicated from person to person.

Q. From where does a human being receive this knowledge?

A. From the source of everything—from God.

Q. If it is communicated, where then is the main cause of its source? Who among human beings was the first to receive it?

A. This question most likely transitions into the sphere of rational knowledge, because it requires a foundation in previous knowledge; and because knowledge through faith can provide no answer, for it was received directly from the source of everything that exists—from God. This is called revelation.

Q. Is there only one knowledge through faith that people have inscribed in their hearts? Might there not be another expression of this knowledge that people receive from one another?

A. Knowledge through faith was communicated from God immediately to the soul of every human being, as well as mediately, through the transfer of what was expressly revealed to our forebears.

Q. Was the same revelation given by God to all people?

A. Knowledge through faith is revealed by God in the same way in the soul of every individual, but the communication of this revelation to our forebears did not take place homogeneously, because it was the business of reason to communicate this knowledge.

Q. Does sole and true knowledge through faith exist (common to all people)?

A. This knowledge exists in the hearts of men. The knowledge that is common to all human beings is true knowledge through faith.

Q. Is the expression of the Buddhist, Jewish, Christian, and Mohammedan faiths true or not true?

A. The true knowledge through faith is one—it is common to all human beings and has been revealed by God in their hearts, and all expressions of faith are true where they coincide. The external features of faith are but peculiarities that depend on historical and geographical contingencies, and they have the significance of rational knowledge not knowledge through faith.—

Q. Is Christian faith true in its teaching?

A. It is true inasmuch as it reveals the knowledge through faith in human hearts and inasmuch as its teaching does not contradict this knowledge.

Q. How is what was revealed to our forebears communicated?

A. By means of holy scripture, legendary lore, and by way of example.

Q. What is meant by the term "holy scripture"?

A. All the books by means of which our forebears communicated to others that knowledge of faith which was revealed to them in their hearts and which had as its aim the salvation of the soul.—

Q. What is meant by holy lore?

A. Lore (idem).[60]

Q. What is meant by "example"?

A. The actions that demonstrate knowledge through faith for the salvation of the soul.

Q. What is meant in general by the "holy revelation" that is communicated by holy scripture, legendary lore, and by way of example?

A. All that which the true believers who venerate God wrote, said, and did for the salvation of the soul.

Q. Is there a true treasury of the holy revelation?

A. There is: All true believers joined together by holy revelation compose the conciliatory and hereditarily Church that treasures the holy revelation.—

Q. What is the relationship between the Christian Church and the unitary Church of God?

A. The relationship of the particular to the general: The Christian Church is one of the expressions of the Ecumenical Church.

Q. Is the Christian Church corruptible?

A. Not in spirit, but it is corruptible in letter.

Q. Why?

---

60   Sic; in the original.

A. The spirit always corresponds to the heart's knowledge through faith. The letter is the communicative tool.

Q. Is this the same with the others?[61]

A. It is the same.

Q. How is Christianity related to The Teachings of God? Where is it contrary to reason?

A. If the teaching is not contrary to the teaching of the Ecumenical Church and the heart, reason will be humbled before the unfathomable teaching.

Q. And if it is contrary to the knowledge of the heart?

A. Turn it down to remain a member of the Ecumenical Church.—

A Christian Catechism

Q. Of what does the first communication of Christian revelation consist?

A. In the holy scripture of the books of the Old Testament.

Q. Which ones?

A. Genesis.

Q. Why is it holy?

A. [Because it reveals] creation.

---

61 By "others," Tolstoy means non-Christian Churches.

36. Interlocutors[62]
[1877–78]

1. Fet-Strakhov-Schopenhauer-Kant:[63] a healthy philosopher idealist. Strem [illegible]:[64] A wealthy nobleman, a lieutenant resigned from the ranks, 42 years old.

---

62 **Entry 36. "Interlocutors"** [*Sobesedniki*] (1877–78). Published in 1936 in *The Jubilee* 17:369-85, this manuscript is described by V. F. Savodnik later in the same volume (17:732-36). A lot of details provided by Savodnik on the intellectual milieu and dates are inaccurate. For a detailed commentary, see Medzhibovskaya 2008, 184-90; 196.

63 Tolstoy's difficult friend, the poet Afanasy Fet, was a devotee of Schopenhauer and the translator into Russian of *The World as Will and Representation*. Although this translation had not been completed when Tolstoy wrote "Interlocutors," he and Fet spoke—and frequently argued about—both the translation and the ideas of the Frankfurt sage. Fet's translation appeared in 1881: Artur Shopenhauer, *Mir kak volia i predstavlenie*, trans. A. Fet (St. Petersburg: M. M. Stasiulevich, 1881).

64 "*Stremov*" is also a character in *Anna Karenina* (1873–77), the caustic, intelligent, and successful antagonist of Alexey Aleksandrovich Karenin.

2. Virchow,[65] Dubois Raimond,[66] Tyndall,[67] Mill[68] a natural scientist who recognizes the necessity of foundations.—A theory of perfection, progress.—Malikov,[69] 37 years old. Maikov[70]

3. A positivist-Bibikov: progress, but a denial of the necessity of foundations, 35 years old.[71]

4. Archbishop [Russian Archimandrite]: A clever cleric who denies knowledge, 56 years old. Stolnikov.[72]

---

65 The name Rudolf Virchow (1821–1902), the father of cellular pathology, was written by Tolstoy in Cyrillic. Tolstoy was interested in Virchow's scientific persona primarily for his reluctance to admit metaphysics into science.

66 Sic. Tolstoy writes this name in Latin, misspelling Emil du Bois-Reymond (1816–96). Tolstoy shows partiality to du Bois-Reymond's views, who was famous for his studies of animal electricity and for being an astute art critic, renowned for his work on science and literature, on Goethe including. Tolstoy considers him merely a physiological materialist, which is not accurate. Tolstoy attended du Bois-Reymond's lecture in Berlin on July 12, 1860 (Old Style; July 24 New Style) (see *The Jubilee* 48:26). Although he provides no details except to report a general mood of boredom, Tolstoy repeats the incorrect spelling that he had first made in his diary when he mentioned the German scientist's name on a list of his *dramatis personae*. The same indefensible view of du Bois-Reymond is upheld even more emphatically in Tolstoy's *On Life*, which was written a decade later.

67 The name John Tyndall (1820–93) was written by Tolstoy in Cyrillic. Tyndall attracted Tolstoy's attention—and that of his fictional characters—for many years, not only as one of the most prominent physicists of all times, but also for his great scientific versatility, his interest in religion, and in the problems of "demarcation"—that is, the relationship between science and religion, a topic about which Tyndall gave many public lectures, thereby drawing international visibility.

68 The name John Stuart Mill is written by Tolstoy in Cyrillic.

69 Alexander Kapitonovich Malikov (1841–1904) was a Russian industrial worker and socialist, who spent two years living on an agricultural farm in America. Malikov paid Tolstoy a visit in the summer of 1877. Tolstoy mentions him frequently in his diary for many years to come, on numerous occasions closer to the time frame of when he wrote "The Interlocutors" as well as in his letters.

70 This was written in superscript, in a different ink. Maikov is thus a character who combines the traits of Virchow, du Bois-Reymond, Tyndall, and Mill, though Tolstoy attributed to this character an attitude or two of his own, for instance "perfection" and "progress."

71 Alexey Bibikov was an acquaintance of Malikov who had a much stronger positivist and materialistic drive, but in Tolstoy's hands he is becoming more of a typical fictional character.

72 Tolstoy was acquainted with many highly placed hierarchs of the Russian Orthodox Church, but Stolnikov is fictional.

5.   Khomiakov-Urusov:[73] a subtle dialectician, a gentleman who justi-
     fies faith by means of sophisms. Yunovich, 50 years old.[74]
6.   Monk, Father Pimen: meekness, love (is asleep), 70 years old.[75]
7.   I. Ivan Ilyich: 49 years old.[76]

The Course of the Conversation

Strem is busy proving the impossibility of faith, as opposed to pure reason.
Maikov supports this impossibility, from the point of view of experience. For
him, one must conduct observations.

Stolnikov considers this impossibility a done deal.

Yunovich introduces the question of faith as that of the unknowable. See
Khomiakov.

Father Pimen, taken affright, signs himself with a cross and goes to sleep.
Archimandrite condemns science in anger.

Strem denies the possibility of faith.

Ivan Ilyich demands a definition of faith.

The definition by each: Strem defines faith indefinitely, from the point of
view of the history of religions, [and] merges it with philosophy. An objection
by Ivan Ilyich: why are they distinct? Maikov: as one of the sociological forms.

Stolnikov considers faith to be darkness dissolved by the light of knowledge.
Yunovich. Khomiakov. Samarin.

Father Pimen wakes up: let it be done honestly, he says, in a godly manner,
with prayer and the cross.

---

73 This character looks like a composite of two historical personages: the Slavophile Alexey
    Khomiakov and Tolstoy's old society friend and frequent participant in disputes surrounding
    their metaphysical investigations, Prince Sergey (Sergius) Urusov. Urusov was as tradition-
    ally and devoutly religious in the truly Russian Orthodox sense as he was an advocate of
    German idealist tradition in philosophy.
74 While the fifty-year-old "Yunovich" is fictional, his name may be a composite of the then
    recently deceased Pamfil Yurkevich (1826–74), the Russian Christian Platonist, a critic of
    positivism and teacher of Vladimir Solovyov, and a frequent positivist critic of Yurkevich's,
    the younger philosopher Vladimir Lesevich (1837–1905). The name "Yunovich" implies the
    word "iunyi"—"youthful."
75 Elder Pimen of the Optina Pustyn' monastery was personally known to Tolstoy. The kind
    monk here described is more of a generic, harmless, and ineffectual elder who nevertheless
    possesses the main necessary virtues of kindness and love.
76 Tolstoy was indeed 49 in 1877. On this "I"—this seeker who is both Tolstoy's alter ego and
    "Ivan Ilyich," his famous character from the eponymous novella of 1886, see Medzhibovskaya
    (2008, 184-90; 295-332).

Ivan Ilyich finds the definitions wanting: faith is trust in what is said; this is the way it is; and that there are two kinds of knowledge, and the other definition is more narrow.

Strem objects against Kant's definition of knowledge. A critique of Kant, who takes absolute reason, and not the reason as we know it, for his first premise. In real reason, a share of faith is essentially inevitable, and we have to take into account its enormous fruitfulness.

Maikov's objection: There is no distinction, but there must be a necessary hypothesis for the sake of an explanation, and we do not ascribe any significance to such hypotheses.

A response from Yunovich and a proof that faith is the foundation for any kind of knowledge, just as with the basis of experience.

Stolnikov makes no distinction, the impressions being the foundation of everything, for him—a remark that takes them all off track.

Archimandrite: From St. Paul and John Chrysostom.

Ivan Ilyich: I am ready to give up on the division, on giving knowledge a name, but here is what draws attention to itself: faith and knowledge in the historical outcome, which is thus inherited.

Stolnikov rejects this: It stops being inherited, he claims.

Ivan Ilyich affirms by citing the fact of common knowledge. He can see no dissolution possible for philosophy—the kind of dissolution that we effect in chemistry when we amalgamate one substance with another is what we would like to do with knowledge, but knowledge is sharply distinct. While one is inherited through the science of the word, the other is by both means.

Maikov: What do we care if it is inherited if it is contrary to reason? That was our starting point. I cannot have faith in the Creator, and so forth.

Ivan Ilyich cites how faith denies science and how science denies faith and goes back to making affirmations about the method of inheritance.

Yunovich advances to attack: you are not a believer; you are a ratiocinator. Ivan Ilyich explains the difference between the methods of inheritance, and speaks about scientific verification.

Yunovich demands a categorical response: To believe in the Eucharist or not?

Ivan Ilyich on the difference and changes in word meaning.

Archimandrite launches an attack with the help of scriptural [texts].

Father Pimen: He's a kind soul, he will be saved.

Stolnikov declaims his dittos.

Strem. defends I.I., even as he says that he disagrees. But I can see that he agrees, because he is defending the idea that religions develop organically.[77]

Yunovich declines.

Maikov defends the sense of the single ethical foundation.

Ivan Ilyich puts forward other foundations, but subjectively acknowledges the ethical to be chief.

Maikov says that religion is the fruit of reason, that having at first been unaware of how to ration his power,[78] man later came to know it within the sphere of social powers—i.e., religion.

Ivan Ilyich: This is a delusion. Religion resulted in economy, true, but it is not its cause. Religion is not practical in terms of its quality: "I have not come to bring peace but a sword" [Matthew 10:34]. Promises suffering to followers. It does not stem from a practical aim in its essence but from answering the question: What am I? (And what shall I do?)

Stolnikov is furious and expresses loathing.

Maikov is carried away by sociology, Strem by the dialectics of reason.

Archimandrite and Yunovich are trying to prove to each other what they believe in.

Ivan Ilyich grows timid and is in a pitiful state.

—

The next conversation is on the law of ethics. Utilitarianism in the law of ethics. Interlocutors [illegible] Stepa.

Cut off the nose to spite the face.[79]

December 20, 1878[80]

K: What is faith-religion?

I: I don't know: If you ask me about my faith, I will tell you everything, but I can say absolutely nothing about faith-religion in general.

---

77 From this point on, when speakers refer to "I.I." or when the author relates to himself in the third person, they are referring to Ivan Ilyich.

78 Here, Tolstoy uses the word "economy."

79 Tolstoy's phrase "*oserdias' na blokh da shubu v pech'*" "get angry at the fleas and throw your fur overcoat into the furnace" is best translated as "cut off one's nose to spite one's face," though it would more literally translate as "scorch your furs to get rid of the moths." In essence, the saying means stupidly overreacting while trying to fix a minor problem and thereby suffering a greater loss—something like shooting oneself in the foot.

80 The majority of this entry is crossed out: only the last paragraph (K. speaking) remains. In the following part of the December 20 entry, the date is corrected to December 19.

K: But listen: It is superstition, nonetheless. For we cannot believe in the virgin birth, in the divinity of Christ.

I: Why not?

K: Because it is contrary to reason and is thus redundant.

I: I agree completely that it is contrary to reason. But allow me to subdivide further for the sake of clarity: immaculate birth is contrary to the reason of experience; the divinity of Christ is contrary to abstract reason.

K: All right, then let me ask about your personal faith. Do tell us, do you have faith?

I: I do.

K: What do you have in mind by this faith? Why do you distinguish it from your other knowledge? For knowledge it is, if I am not mistaken. Or is this knowledge independent of any existence, perhaps, confirmed to us by history? I confess openly to you that, as someone who has had a certain level of education in our century, there is no way that I can imagine that which is called faith-religion.

I: I cannot but agree that it is contrary to reason, but it has been far from proven that it is of no use.

K: But do you personally believe in what is implied by religion?

I: I do.[81] I have religion and I therefore have faith in everything that it leads me to.

I: So, if, as you say, you cannot imagine what could be called religion in our time, with this you are saying, first, that you know what they call religion, and second, that that which is so called is incompatible with the state of science of our time. In order for me to be able to answer your question with perfect clarity, it is necessary for me to know what you mean by religion. First of all, we must mean one and the same thing by the same term. Once we have clarified that, I will be ready to give you answers. But do tell me why is it that religion is incompatible with our mental development and, above all, what you mean by religion? Pray, speak sincerely of your opinion, and I promise to you that I shall also speak with perfect sincerity. I am

---

81 The name "I" is written twice in a row in the original.

convinced that it is only ever insincerity that interferes with clarity of thought and expression.

K: Perfectly true. Here is why: the concept of divinity does not integrate with the human. The concept of divinity comes from the admission of human weakness and dependence; it is only the destruction of the limits on which human weakness hinges. Man is mortal—God is immortal; man is corrupt—God is incorrupt; man knows not—God is omniscient; man is weak—God is omnipotent; man is delimited by material space—God is omnipresent. And so, in order to compose the concept of God, we have inferred it from juxtapositions with the human, and we then reintegrate this concept with that of man and destroy it in the mind of a thinking individual in so doing, while exhibiting an idol of God to the feeble-minded. The Sabbatians are absolutely right when they deny Christ on the force of the first commandment.

To my surprise, I have noticed that I.I.

—

I was going to hold forth in the form of a conversation developing the thought that visited me today and became confused. The thought is as follows:

—

December 20

Faith is that knowledge on the basis of which any reasonable knowledge rests.[82] Rational knowledge cannot rest on itself; it self-destroys. Infinite divisibility of infinite space, time, atoms, and so on.

Where are the foundations of this knowledge-faith? These foundations exist beyond man, beyond human reason; they exist in our heart of hearts, in faith itself, or in our own self, as we say in common parlance. The answer to the question about the source of faith—which is in faith—is also the main source of distrust toward faith. In essence, this answer is only tempting to those who apply rational methods—namely, causality—to faith, whereas the pillar of reason is the selfsame faith. I believe because I believe altogether irrationally, meaning by this not in accordance with any sort of rational knowing. One should not forget that this answer is only legitimate in relation to questions that are rationally inexplicable. If I am asked why I believe that wine can be turned into blood and I choose to say in response that it is because I have faith, this would be an error, because this particular faith rests not on my belief in the mystery

---

82 I use "reasonable" rather than "rational" to underscore the idea of reasonable doubt of the skeptical, which is reasonable, faith.

of the Eucharist but rather because this belief links itself to another belief that arose out of a question to which reason is not capable of providing an answer for me (and not because it is not insufficiently developed or that it is straining itself thin, but because, in a more straightforward way, it is the wrong addressee for the question). This question is the one eternal question for all humankind: What am I? Why am I alive? What for? I am a part, but what is the whole?

The foundations of rational knowledge are in reason and in all of its functions, all of its distributed devices: experiential, abstract, synthetic, analytical. Just as within the activity of rational knowledge we find different forms, so, too, do we find in the sphere of knowledge of the heart different forms. If the foundations of knowledge-faith are in the heart, as it goes in common parlance, this must be expressed somehow, so that everyone can understand it: The word "heart" completely expresses its main purpose, the delimitation of a known activity of the human soul from the sphere of reason. There is a phenomenon shared by both rational knowledge and knowledge of the heart: neither kind of knowledge is acquired immediately or singly by each individual. For both kinds of knowledge we find that every individual has two separate sources of knowledge, that they have acquired both kinds of knowledge in two ways: through immediate cognition and through assimilation from other people. Let us take the knowledge of aware understanding [*razumenie*] in mathematics, the most exact of the sciences, for example. Being in possession of everything necessary to acquire the knowledge of mathematics, an individual gets to know its indubitable laws thanks to his capacity to assimilate by verbal means that which has become known in the same sphere of knowledge by other people. The exact same thing is true in the case of knowledge-faith, knowledge of the heart. Being in possession of everything necessary to acquire the foundations of faith in his heart, an individual acquires knowledge of everything that has become known before him by other people in this sphere. In both spheres, an individual is in the same position concerning the criteria with which to verify the truth of the knowledge that he receives from preceding generations. To continue with the example of mathematics: Every student recognizes the justice of $2 \times 2 = 4$ when apprehending knowledge, because he recognizes the law of his reason in this formula. In the same way, every student recognizes the formula about future life because he recognizes the law of his heart within it. Just as it is not possible to identify any reason for needing to prove that $2 \times 2 = 4$ or that $1 + 1 = 2$, neither can there be any other proof for the existence of a supreme, omnipotent first cause. This formula cannot have any other proof than its correspondence to the laws of the heart—or the heart, simply put—just as in the former case a simple correspondence to the laws of reason—or reason, simply put—will suffice as the only proof.

The correspondence of the inherited knowledge to the foundational laws of reason and the heart is evidently the main foundation for our assimilation of both types of knowledge from preceding generations. Because the process of bequeathing knowledge through generations is so complex, and because it began at the very dawn of humanity, one should not assume that verification was constantly ongoing and that this bequeathed knowledge was checked, at the point of receipt, against the foundational laws of reason and the heart.

(I am neither professing a theory nor making a hypothesis here; I am merely trying to stick to reality and fact. I am speaking about how man acquires knowledge. The only subdivision I am drawing, between knowledge of the heart and knowledge of reason, is necessary given that there really is a sharp distinction between the two.)

The acquisition of both kinds of knowledge takes place based on trust concerning the results achieved by preceding generations and not so much on the basis of constant verification. Both the child and the grownup—as well as someone being converted to faith—must have trust. They must have trust in positive knowledge where the rational is concerned: for example, they must trust the axiom that the law of integers is expressed completely in raising to the power of 10. Someone who has converted must take it on trust that there is God the Creator and the prophets who have uttered this and that. In any given case, the consciousness of correspondence—or lack thereof—of what is being transmitted to the laws of reason and the heart either supports or violates trust, for both types of knowledge. It is indubitable that two foundations are necessary for the assimilation of both kinds of knowledge—trust and correspondence— and that both of these factors should serve as the foundation of our knowledge in both spheres of cognition. Since we only know anything at all based on these two foundations of knowledge about human beings, the foundation of trust is that incomparable foundation, which serves as the main source for the acquisition and the consolidation of knowledge. (This is what I think about the transfer of knowledge acquired by humankind in all its complexity, not just in our time but always.) Again, this is no theory that I am writing; I am speaking about what is. Let everyone remember what they can about themselves, what they can observe in children and adults.—Let everybody remember their studies: division in mathematics and what results and how, somehow; let them remember how they have acquired historical knowledge, cosmography, and physics, especially. Everybody who has ever studied even through the lower grades of the gymnasia knows about, and has trust in, our conception about the rotation of the earth and the planets. Yet how many people who have completed their university course can explain why this conception is more consonant with the laws of reason than the concept confirmed by our basic instinct that the earth is immobile. The atoms, the ether, the nervous system—with the exception of one case in a thousand, all this knowledge rests on trust.

The same happens in this regard with positive rational knowledge, and with the knowledge of the heart—with faith.[83] The cause for this trust is the same for both spheres of knowledge. We say to ourselves in the sphere of positive knowledge: thousands, even hundreds of thousands, of the cleverest people are preoccupied exclusively with certain subjects in which they toil to achieve results, which they then speak about publicly. They speak and argue about these results, then they confirm them based on those very laws of reason that I know from within myself: that $2 \times 2 = 4$ in mathematics; that the conclusion made in astronomy about "a" in the minus 1 degree $= 1/a$; and that the planets rotate around the sun, after having conducted their observations on the movements of the sun and the celestial bodies correctly. I do not parse the inevitability of these conclusions; I feel obscurely that the conclusion has been made on the basis of rational laws and accept the single conclusion as correct.

I do almost the same thing with questions of faith. I say: more than merely thousands or dozens of thousands, maybe even every human being ever has striven to know cordially that which I know through this foundation in my heart. Over centuries, the best of people with the greatest gift for knowing through their heart, have presented examples of martyrdom, have sought out this knowledge and have transmitted this knowledge to me, in a complex form that might sometimes be inaccessible to my personal knowledge of the heart, but I trust them because I vaguely feel that the direction of their striving is the same as mine.—

The consciousness of correspondence appears to be the main inner foundation for knowing in both cases of knowledge: in the case of external knowing, it is the unity of agreement among all people and, hence, my trust in them. When looking closer at both of these sources of knowledge—that of correspondence and that of trust—we see both merging in essence into one: the correspondence to the laws of reason and the heart, the essence of man, that is. If we accept any knowledge by correlating it to the laws of our mind and heart and foregoing its verification otherwise, it is only because all other people concur on the same knowledge in their cognition. It would suffice for us to conclude that this state of affairs corresponds to the laws of my reason and my heart. Should it correspond to the laws of the mind and heart of all people, then it must

---

83 In Russian, Tolstoy's terms *vèra-dovèrie* [faith-trust] echo one another, and Tolstoy makes good use of this fact.

correspond to mine, even if I haven't had the time to check it. We only quite rarely verify immediately even that which should cohere with the laws of our mind and heart, but rather unite into one general concordance the correspondence of all with my personal own. Through its best representatives, psychiatry recognizes as insanity only the kind of view that is not shared by everyone else. If we alone see that an object is red, while everyone else sees that this object is green, as long as we are healthy, we will not start looking into why the object is red and why we don't see that it is green. Thus, we have no right to claim that any knowledge of ours is our personal knowledge. An imagined savage who grew up in the woods of Germany had no knowledge whatsoever, although he did have the sources of knowledge.

Our knowledge, both rational and cordial, is unthinkable without its antecedents, without our environment, without knowledge that has already been assimilated and that which is in the process of being assimilated; and so we, along with this knowledge of ours, are fruits of this universal knowledge—we are its results, and we may not judge the substance of this knowledge.

We may only judge what this knowledge is composed of, from whence it is partaken, and why we consider it to be true—why we consider it be knowledge, that is. Knowledge is the fruit of our trust; it is partaken from the universal knowledge, which we have considered true only because everyone else, including us, agree about its truth.

For us, nothing else can verify knowledge other than that we all share a conviction in its certitude.—However unpleasant this situation might appear to the lovers of philosophy, it strikes us that there is not any other source of knowledge about which we could speak without taking a flight into the realm of fantasy. This is knowledge, as it is for real. Were we willing to seek another source of knowledge—that of the reason or of the heart, whatever knowledge it may be—we wouldn't delude ourselves but would cut straight to the heart of the matter, in accordance with the essence of what it is to know, to the conviction that it is impossible to search for and find any foundations of knowledge. The foundation of mathematical knowledge is $1 + 1 = 2$. The foundation of empirical sciences is impression. What is the foundation for the equation that $1 + 1 = 2$ or that I can experience a cold, rough surface or that I can see movement? The foundation of these occurrences are the occurrences themselves. What is the foundation of cordial knowledge, the knowledge that I am alive, that I am in search of my destination? None, other than the desires themselves.

Both positive knowledge (that of reason) and cordial knowledge (that of faith) have universal knowledge as their foundation. In the sphere of reason, this knowledge is science; in the sphere of the heart, it is faith. The verification of knowledge may take place only based on its agreement or disagreement with the laws of reason and the heart. This verification is constantly ongoing in reality. We demand that scientific postulates agree with the demands of our reason and that the postulates of faith agree with the laws of the heart. And in the same way as one suffers from seeing a leaf red and looks for possible agreement with the general view, because disagreement destroys one's certitude in one's knowing, so too whenever a scientific postulate contradicts reason, a human being seeks a corrective for his ignorance until he finds unity with the universal knowing, whenever there is a discord between faith and his heart.

Such a disagreement, contradiction, does happen frequently in science and in faith, the source being ignorance, a lack of knowledge about the necessity of conclusive scientific or religious decision, or the falsity of the scientific or religious decision themselves, their discord from reason and the heart and—this happens most frequently—from the transposition of verification of reason by the foundations of the heart, and vice versa.

December 21

Everyone must have encountered the discord within the first kind of science more than once, the discord resulting from ignorance. I can remember a lack of trust, to put it mildly—no, well, a complete conviction in the falsity of—the postulate shared with me about ether and its fluctuations that I encountered, I, who learned physics according to the theory of corpuscular emissions. I was young back then. The one who spoke to me about ether was no authority, in my estimation, and I can remember that his words about the fluctuations of infinitesimally small waves of infinitesimally small corpuscles seemed plain nonsense to me. Similarly, the eucharist seemed to be a still bigger nonsense—something that was not even worth an argument. But out of a desire to consult with competent judges, and having found out that all men of science recognize this postulate, I started learning physics. I read from scholars on this subject and the theory about ether in fluctuation no longer seemed such arbitrary nonsense to me, but something necessitated by the context. The same has happened and continues to happen with individuals who receive fragmentary knowledge. The most striking thing is what happens in cosmography, and with special obviousness, in mathematics. Let someone with good knowledge of arithmetic try to reason out the meaning of assumed means, and it becomes clear that a learner's reason will never be able to allow for a concept so contrary to the laws of reason. To the effect that there should be a minus number resulting from multiplying a like minus quantity with itself, whereas the minus sign could only be the result of an operation when plus is multiplied by a minus. Only as a result of studying the course of the development of thought and its results toward which this postulate leads and predominantly as a consequence of the learners' trust can anyone agree to this postulate at once, without making an inquiry into how everyone else who has studied the subject views this, but with tracing the conclusions from this postulate, there is no way that it could be accepted.

In the sphere of the knowledge of the heart the same sort of doubt creeps in for the same reason of ignorance. They tell a convert to Christianity that Christ is the son of God, that he assumed human flesh and gave a new commandment to people. This postulate cannot be accepted by an individual who neither sees any need for it, nor has any trust in the teacher. The same thing happens as with the assumed numbers and fluctuating ether: an individual can only accept the postulate when it has been demonstrated to him that it originates in a whole series of matters of cordial knowing and entails a whole series of necessary conclusions that concur with the laws of the heart, the conclusions of the Christian teaching, that is, which have, moreover, been reinforced by the trust of millions of people who have studied this cordial knowledge and have arrived at the same postulate.

December 22

The second cause of discord or doubt is the falsity of the postulate of science or religion *per se*, an obvious contradiction with the law of reason and the heart or with other data of science and religion, irredeemable and unjustifiable. For Copernicus, the postulate about the rotation of the sun appeared to contradict both the law of movement of smaller and bigger bodies and his knowledge about planetary movement, and he therefore rejected the postulate. Similarly, it is possible to say with boldness now that a postulate about protoplasm[84] is in place that it is contrary to reason, as is the case with the postulate that our thoughts and desires are organisms. For these postulates make an arbitrary confusion of the realms of the organic and the inorganic—one that, most importantly, is irredeemable and unjustifiable. This is as regards the sphere of science. The postulate in religion that the Pope can exculpate people is likewise legitimately being rejected, because it is contrary to the religion of the heart that senses that consciousness of guilt may not be diminished by any external method and does not coordinate with the religious knowledge of the New Testament, which states that no man has power over the souls of others. The same can be

---

84 Tolstoy has a likely slip here, writing *"protoplason"* instead of *"protoplasm."*

said regarding the whole teaching of exculpation, of redeeming the sins of the human race by the death of Christ.

The third—and main—source of doubt in the truths of both spheres lies in the confusion of one sphere with the other: that is, in the application of the laws of the heart to try to verify rational knowledge, and, vice versa, in the most mundane method that has been, is, and will be the source of any disbelief: the application to faith, or to what the heart knows, of the laws of rational verification. 999 out of one thousand non-believers who falsely reject the postulates of cordial knowledge-faith only reject it because of this very reason. It therefore behooves us to analyze this method of thinking in detail and to consider all the arguments that it cites in its favor.

The method of negating the postulates of science by appeal to the force of faith is known to everybody, is widely used [illegible], and is condemned by the adepts of science, just as the opposite method is. This method is very well known by all. "Well, we have now found out that it is such-and-such billions of miles from here to the sun; so, what's our takeaway? Shall we live better, be kinder or anything?" Those who say so are only saying this: rational knowledge does not satisfy the questions of the heart. And they are not right. Science does not have such an aim at all. "Well, you have studied the nerves and cerebral activity, so what? Will this make people any better?," they say—and they are not right. A true scientist, a physiologist will only say this: "the question about ameliorating humans does not concern me." (The scientist who answers, "yes, this will help people to be better" and then attempts to give reasons as to why, would be a poor scientist trying to straddle his science *entre deux chaises, le cul par terre*;[85] caught between the aims and methods of both science and religion at once, he would accomplish nothing except blabber. And there are many like him.)

The questions of this order that demand answers from science to questions about cordial matters are very common and are for the most part the fruit of ignorance and vanity. To provide a psychological analysis, questions of this sort express the following: "I don't know what you are talking about and I am not willing to admit to my ignorance of something important and essential, and I therefore look for a loophole to excuse my ignorance and indifference to knowledge." This excuse is based on an artificial, sophistic transposition of a question from one sphere to another. "What is my interest? What is the benefit to me and other people from this knowledge?" That is to say that rational

---

85 Sitting between two chairs, one's behind on the ground.

knowledge gifts nothing to my heart. But this goes without saying—this is the starting point.

The opposite thing happens more visibly—I shall not say more frequently, it happens more seldomly if we take all people into account, but yet it happens more visibly—because the rejection of science on the basis of it not offering satisfaction to the demands of the heart is overwhelmingly attempted by the ignorant, by those lacking their organ of self-expression, the press. Thus, the majority of illiterate peasants discuss the uselessness and stupidity of science. The opposite is done by those from the scientific ranks who have weapons of distribution at their disposal—i.e., the words of discourse. Although the number of people who deny the knowledge by faith on the basis of its disagreement with rational demands—and who commit this opposite error—is less numerous, this error has greater visibility, is framed more artfully, and warrants a more careful discussion therefore. This is the argument.—

Such-and-such postulate of knowledge-faith—let us take the Creation, by way of example—disagrees with rational laws. Why would God sit around and sit around some more and then bang, all of a sudden create the world? How could he create it out of nothing? It is not possible to create the firmness of the earth, and so on.

Psychologically, the source is precisely the same as in the case of the denial of science by faith: man is unwilling to confess to his ignorance and to his indifference toward this ignorance, and so he denies all knowledge of the heart, by way of transposing it to the sphere of reason, which is alien to it.

December 23

Let us consider this example: in what does the knowledge of faith consist? In what does rational refutation consist? And how does reason falsely correct the error of faith? (How does it deceive itself?) In the sense of faith, what do the first verses of the Bible mean: There used to be nothing and there was God, and he created the world in 6 days, and so forth? What sort of question does this response answer? The question that called this answer into being (as provided by Moses, Zoroaster, God, the entirety of humankind, or whomever else) is not about when God created the world (reason finds the answer to this question incorrect); not about how, what from, and in what temporal sequence he created it; and whether it was the earth he created first or second. The question lies in the heart of every human being, one and eternal: Who am I? From whence did I and everything surrounding me come into existence? If the question may be ineffable at times and if even nowadays there may be individuals among the savage and Christian peoples alike who never faced this question in all its clarity, one thing is beyond doubt: the question lies, although unconsciously at times, in the heart of every human being. As far as we can tell, centuries had gone by before anyone had any answer to this question. And the answer was variable. One could answer, did indeed answer, and still continues to answer that I am because I am, and everything else exists without a cause. It could be said that I alone am and that everything else is an idea of mine. It could be said that there is a force that created me, and there is another force that created another thing. But in deep antiquity, humankind worked out an answer to this complex question: its gist is that all (moving) forces, perceived and observed by me, have the same source, the force that is called God, that this very source is the source of existence and the origin for everything. But in providing a (verbal) response to the question raised by humankind, the respondent, whoever he may have been, must have conceptualized his response in human terms, in keeping with the knowledge they possessed. The respondent must have answered the question with the feeble faltering word, the predominant instrument of rational knowledge, thus: "I can feel that I am within the power of One Good[86] creature and he created me." He would be answered with: "Not true, you were born of father and mother, grandfather, and so on." In order to communicate with people, he must have spoken their language, and had to say: "God created all people, and he created the first couple." The same considerations forced him to speak about the temporal sequence of the story of creation. The whole sequence and detail of the story of creation is only an inevitable tribute to the weak instrument of expression, the word, and to the weak organ of perceiving, the understanding.

Let us imagine Moses, of all people, engrossed with his inner self, with thoughts about the significance of man, the very same thoughts that serve to answer the question, "what am I?" and who suddenly understood himself integral with the unity of all the elements. Anyone who has experienced such moments, this pressing question and a fleeting clarity of thought, knows this feeling. For a moment, Moses felt God, felt his own position. He saw God (he would have not been able to express the feeling otherwise). But in desiring to transmit this feeling, he had to say it using words, search for and find comprehensible phrasing; and hence he wrote the Book of Genesis. He could not communicate the immediacy of the feeling in this book; he transmuted it into personal aspects, and thus imparted power to the book (all prophets do this). What, then, are those who look in this book and give their rational

---

86 The Good God (*Blagoi*) or of/by/from the Good God (*Blagago*) is the standard way of referring to the omnipotent, kind God. What is unusual here is Tolstoy's reference to God as also a "Creature," and, thus, the creating creature, spelled with a small "he."

critique to the details of the narration doing? They are looking for answers as to how God created the world. But Moses uttered his "how" unwittingly, against his will even, paying tribute to the tool of the weak: the word. He meant to say one thing only: that there is one God, the source of everything throughout time and space, and man is his creation. (And now, in trying to correct Moses, I am paying an even more inferior tribute to the weakness of words, feeling all the while that each word that I use is inadequate to the concept.) One thing is clear and certain: the fulcrum point, the meaning, the purpose of Moses's words is not and cannot be the exposition of the theory of the origin of the world but only the answer to the question, "What am I? From whence do I come? And what for?" We could only be in denial of Moses's answer in the Bible (Zoroaster in Zend Avesta) had the question remained unanswered, been wrong, or disagreed with another known answer to the questions of the heart. But we cannot deny this because the form of the details to the questions of the heart disagrees with the questions that reason has to ask, questions that are completely different from those of the heart and have nothing to do with them. This is exactly what science is busy doing when it celebrates its finding within faith any disagreements with its own postulates. You claim that there is no firm ground— fine! Well then, God created precisely what Moses meant when he used the term "firm ground." It doesn't matter what it was that he meant by firm ground without a knowledge of astronomy; what matters is that he said that God had created that also, that all that exists has the same source. If this was God's revelation, why wasn't it aware of astronomy? Assuming that this was God's revelation in the narrowest sense: it did not behoove God to speak about the system of the Hercules Constellation or about Cancer[87] to the Jews, who could see the earth and were asking where it came from. (Our own concept about celestial bodies will appear very ridiculous and crude some 10,000 years from now, I am afraid; if so, we could not use our language to reveal).[88]

This objection explains only why God would not speak scientifically. Yet this does show exactly why the sphere of science is not the same as the sphere of faith. The answer was given to the question of the heart, not reason, and the answer is complete and clear where the question is concerned. <"Faith is not inherited through the word but immediately through the legend, the act, and the example. On this rests its spread which would be inexplicable otherwise,

87 Tolstoy spelled "o rake" in small letters; it could equally have meant "*Racha*": a sacrificial ewe, a female sheep, or a term of contempt. He uses the word "*ràka*" in the nominative in his other passing comments on Judaism.
88 Tolstoy forgot to add a closing parenthesis here, which is now added in the text.

and from it begins the rite.">[89] If the answer is incomplete or unclear as it happens, then clarify it, make it complete, but don't forget the question. Geological investigations will not advance me a hair's width toward clarifying the question about whether I am alone or live in conjunction with the whole world and am codependent on the same force. What am I? It is only this question for which the answer is sought. Science makes the same mistake in this case as does faith when it denies science from the foundation of its demands. Having gained mastery of discourse and dialectics, science plays its sleight-of-hand tricks better than faith. Frequently, false science pretends that it corrects the errors of faith by covering up the illegality of its transfer of the question from the sphere of the heart to the sphere of reason, and it deceives itself based on this false change of tracks. It says: "The creation of the world in one fine day makes no sense. The creation of animal couples in one day makes even less sense. We can see that everything exists and develops; based on this, we have no right to infer that there once was a time when there was nothing. We come to the conclusion when tracing the process of development, however, that there used to be lower forms out of which higher forms developed, including man. A reasonable theory of the development of the forces of nature comes forward replacing for us the creation fable." A strange manipulation takes place: holding on tight to the questions of faith, man finds himself, many manipulations later, with a heap of sundry rational questions; questions of faith and its answers are left behind—not to say rejected—but put completely aside. The scientific scaffolding[90] slipped underfoot to uphold faith is so complex and bulky that many fail to notice the fraud and naively accept that one is an organism wherein unknown forces develop according to unknown laws in response to the question of who one is. Anyone who would trouble himself to reduce this scaffolding to the first question of faith would see that there is no answer from science in essence; that there can be none ever in the sphere of science, of rational knowledge. My starting point was this: What am I? What is my life—that is, my separation from others? What are the forces that I experience when I act and suffer? And from whence do I come?

Science says: "you are an organism, you are individuated, you are a force acted upon by forces of an unknown nature, and you come from your mother's womb, and your mother from the womb of her mother." In its desire to solve questions science inadvertently washed its hands of them, which is inevitable given the nature of its rational occupations. Instead of an answer, it repeated

---

89 Tolstoy adds the phrase in brackets as a marginal comment circled in ink.

90 Here, Tolstoy uses the French term *échafaudage*.

the words of the question to me. And it answered the main question with non-sense, which was also inevitable due to the nature of its occupations. To the question, "From whence do I come?," it answered: "you are a chinking link on an infinite chain of being"; that's what it sees in the creature of man ahead of everything, that's what makes him afraid, and why he starts asking his questions in the first place.

PART 5

Writings of the 1880s

37. The Kingdom of God[1]
[1879–86]

The kingdom of God[2] is something that we will see arrive; it exists within people (Luke 16:20-21).

To enter the kingdom of God, the son of man should be risen.[3] The son of man is the spirit in every individual that is not composed of the flesh. Whoever

---

1   **Part 5: Writings of the 1880s. Entry 37. The Kingdom of God**" [*Tsarstvo Bozhie*] (1879–86). The manuscript copy of "The Kingdom of God" did not survive. The publication of this fragment alongside fragments 38 and 39 that follow in volume 90 of *The Jubilee* in 1958 was well justified (90:125-26). However, it must be borne in mind that the "expedited" volume 90—the so-called "appendix volume"—was rushed to print to meet the government's deadline and directives for marking *The Jubilee's* thirtieth anniversary in 1958. The scholarly principles and instructions that guided the editorial process of *The Jubilee*, which were increasingly compromised after 1946 by constant intrusions by the apparatchiks, were here gravely violated, with the quality of annotations and the commentary clearly suffering as a result. V. S. Mishin's unusual decision to change the attribution date for the fragment published in Tolstoy's lifetime from 1886 to 1879 was arbitrary. To redress the violation, we offer a date range (1879–86) for the composition of fragments 37-39, based on the guiding principles of *The Jubilee* edition. The content and ideas in the fragments cannot be limited to the year 1879 alone (that there is a line in the notebook from 1879 resembling these ideas was Mishin's sole rationale for this change [see *The Jubilee* 1958; 90:400-1]). It is just as plausible that these are the same ideas and terms that Tolstoy developed through the middle of the 1880s. The 1886 date is based on Chertkov's edition of fragments 37-39, published by Free Press in 1904, about which Chertkov consulted with Tolstoy. Remarkably succinct, Tolstoy's summaries in fragments 37-39 from the gospels are, critically, part of the work he developed in famous longer works like *A Confession* (1879–82), *The Critique of Dogmatic Theology* (1879–80; 1884); *What I Believe* (1882–84), and his commentaries on, and harmonization of, the gospels (1880–81; 1883; 1884). Despite their brevity, these articles are complete statements in themselves. The articles were most likely started toward the end of 1879 or in the early 1880s, aligning well with critical studies Tolstoy was then conducting of Church teaching and the dogmatics as well as shorter recaps of these that he wrote throughout 1887.
2   Here and elsewhere in this piece, Tolstoy does not capitalize the word "God" in the original.
3   Here, Tolstoy uses the verb *vozvysit'* meaning "to raise" or "elevate."

raises this spirit in themselves shall receive life outside of time and shall enter the kingdom of God.

The kingdom of God has always been; all who rely on the son or, put otherwise, live in awareness[4] shall enter; those who do not rely on the son, who commit evil deeds or, put otherwise, do not live according to their awareness, are separated from the kingdom of God (John 3).

The kingdom of God is not to be understood as if each individual shall in some place or at some point in time enter it, but as if some individuals all over this world always become sons of the kingdom yet others do not.

God the spirit is the father of the spirit that is in a human individual and is only God and the father of those who recognize themselves as his sons.

And only those who hold on to what God gave to them exist for God.

As the father, he throws seed and gathers what grows to keep the grain (Matthew 13).

He gave all people a chance to become his sons and does not interfere with the affairs of the world (Mark 4).

The human world is, for God, the same while humans are alive as a kneading trough is for a peasant woman. There is nothing you can do to sourdough; it must become sour on its own. God does not eradicate evil in the world, because God does not destroy anything and nothing is evil to him; for him, there is only that which yields fruit. The human world with all the evil that people see in it is the same for God as the field seeded by its owner: The owner seeds the field and waits for the harvest; he knows nothing of that for which he did not plant a seed. The owner knows his own and gathers from his seed when the harvest is ripe; everything for which he did not plant a seed gets destroyed.

The kingdom of God is like a net: He who gathers all fish can select the fish that he needs (Matthew 13:47).

This is what the kingdom of God is for God. But for each individual man, his kingdom of God is within him.

The kingdom of God consists in the reliance on the son and on holding forth in one's awareness.[5] The one who does not accept awareness is like a road upon which lie fallen seeds: Whoever accepts awareness only then to stomp it away becomes like rocky soil; when seeds fall into it, they will grow in this soil, but the soil will not trap the plants by their roots. Whoever accepts awareness but does not observe it in their life is like soil overgrown with thorns, the stalk of the plant that grows is hollow, and they do not enter the kingdom of God.

---

4   The term here is "awareness" [*razumenie*], which Tolstoy used from the end of the 1870s onwards to describe human understanding of our spiritual purpose.

5   On *razumenie*, see the previous note.

Whoever accepts awareness despite all misfortunes and cares is like good soil that grows a hundred grains out of one seed; those shall enter the kingdom of God (Matthew 11).

The kingdom of God prophesied by John consists in this: Here, men live in the spirit and not in the flesh; despite their seeming privations, men are blessed who see other than with their eyes and hear other than by their ears; the unhappy become blessed because blessed is he who lives in the spirit. There used to be prophets to carry out the will of God, but John was no prophet. He announced the kingdom of God on earth and showed us how to enter it.

John was more than a prophet: he made the law and its prophesies obsolete; he announced that the kingdom of God is always on earth; and he himself entered it.

All the prophets and the laws—all of this had been necessary before John. The kingdom of God was announced starting with John; it became manifest, blessed happiness for men; it is in anybody's will to enter it. Wise men and scribes search for signs of the kingdom of God based on the prophecies and the law. But they don't see what's in front of them, their wisdom and bookishness shame-faced. The whole mystery of the kingdom of God is not in the teaching of the law and the prophets but in recognizing your father, and this mystery became concealed from wise men and was revealed to those who acknowledge that they are the children.

"Nobody knows the son from the father. Only the father knows the son. And this son reveals what the father is."

"I am the son of the father-spirit. I shall lead you to enter the kingdom of God, all ye who are tormented and oppressed with your labors; come and learn from my teaching. Do as I do, and you shall see how light it is for me to live. For I am obedient and humbled of soul. Be the way I am and you shall find peace in your lives, you shall feel how simple and easy it is to live just as I do."

And thus, having explained what the kingdom of God is as such, what the kingdom of God is for each man, and how to enter it, Jesus offers yet another teaching, a clearer and simpler one, for entering the kingdom of God. He says, "Do as I do, be what I am," and he explains in the Sermon on the Mount the way he lives, how one must live, what he does, and what should be done.

38. What a Christian Should and Should Not Do[6] [1879–86]

1800 years ago, a new law was unveiled to people by Jesus Christ. Jesus Christ demonstrated to people through his teaching, and through his own life and death, what should and should not be done by a disciple of his, a Christian.

The teaching of Christ is, as it was back in the day, contrary to the teaching of the world. According to the teaching of the world, rulers govern their peoples. To govern them, they force some men to kill, execute, and punish others, and force men to take an oath that they will always fulfill the will of the incumbent governor. According to the teaching of Christ, no individual can kill; moreover, nobody can coerce another nor resist another using force: nobody can do harm to his neighbors or even to his enemies. The teaching of the world and the teaching of Christ have always been contrary to each other. Christ was aware of this and told his disciples so, foretelling how he would suffer for the truth himself (Matthew 20:18), that they would also be tortured and put to death (Matthew 24:9), and that the world would hate them as it hates him, for they shall serve the father, not the world (John 15:19-20).

All of this came true, just as Christ foretold. The world was fanned by hatred toward him and sought to ruin him.

All of them—the Pharisees and the Sadducees, the Scribes and the Herodians—piled reproaches on him for being an enemy of Caesar, for forbidding his followers to pay taxes to him, for inciting and corrupting the people. They called Christ a villain, who had appointed himself king and was therefore an enemy to Caesar (John 19:12).[7]

Before his sentence to death by execution, they sent "cunning people who, pretending to be pious, aimed to set him up and seize on his word and then deliver him to the authorities and the governor's office. They asked him: Rabbi!, we know how truthfully you speak and teach, and that you do not cower but teach the godly way. Are we allowed to pay taxes to Caesar or not? But he could see through their cunning and told them: 'Why do you tempt me? Show me a denarius: whose image is minted there and what is the inscription? They

---

6   **Entry 38. "What a Christian Should and Should Not Do"** [*Chto mozhno i chego nel'zia delat' khristianinu*] (1879–86). Although undated, the manuscript of "What a Christian Should and Should Not Do" (Tolstoy's own title) did survive. Like entry 37, "The Kingdom of God" published above, this text appeared in Tolstoy's lifetime in 1904 with a date (1886). We follow the same publication logic with this fragment as with fragment 37. This text was published in volume 90 of *The Jubilee* in 1958 (90:123-24).

7   Tolstoy has "Tsar" in the original Russian, for, in Russian, "*Tsar' Iudeiskii*" means "the King of the Jews." Here, Tolstoy intentionally paraphrased the gospels in his own words.

answered: Caesar's. He told them: Render unto Caesar the things that are Caesar's, and to God the things that are God's'" (Luke 20: 20-25).

They marveled at his answer and fell silent.

They had expected him to say that it was the law to pay taxes to Caesar, which would destroy his teaching about the sons being free in so doing (that man should live like the birds do, taking no care for tomorrow, and so on). Either that, or they had expected him to say that it is forbidden to pay taxes to Caesar, which would expose him as Caesar's enemy. But Christ said: give to Caesar the things that are Caesar's and to God what is God's.

He said more than had been expected of him. He divided the human domain into two parts: the human and the godly, and he said that what is human can be returned to a human, but what is godly must not be returned to a human but only to God. With these words, he told them that if man believes in God's law, he will only then fulfill Caesar's law when it does not contradict God. Although they did not know the truth, the Pharisees respected the law of the Lord, which they would not trespass even if the law of Caesar commanded them to. They would never disavow circumcision, the Sabbath, fasting, and much else. If Caesar demanded that they work on Saturday, they would say: "we shall give every day to Caesar except Saturday." The same with circumcision and the rest. Christ showed to them with his answer that the law of the Lord is superior to Caesar's law and that man can render unto Caesar only that which is not contrary to the law of the Lord.

So, what is Caesar's and what is God's, for Christ and his disciples?

Terror overwhelms you at the response that you shall hear from the Christians of our time.

According to the judgment of the Christians of our time, what is God's never interferes with what is Caesar's, and what is Caesar's always agrees with what is God's. All life is given to serving Caesar and only that which doesn't interfere with Caesar's ways is given to God. This is not how Christ reasoned this meaning out. [8]All life belonged to God, for Christ, and only what was not God's could be rendered unto Caesar. To Caesar what is Caesar's, to God what is God's. What is Caesar's? A coin, things of the flesh, that which is not yours. Give up all that is of the flesh to anyone who takes it, but your life, which is God-given, is not yours; it is all Godly. You should not give this away to anyone but to God—because human life, according to his [Christ's] teaching, exists to serve God (Matthew 4:10).

And no one can serve two masters (Matt. 6:24).—

---

8   The verb here is the past tense of *razumel*, which is more common to poetic diction, but not very common in regular parlance. It is related to Tolstoy's term *"razumenie,"* which is explained above.

39. To Whom Do We Belong?[9]
[1879–86]

Whose subjects are we: God's or the devil's? Who do we believe in: God or the devil? Who do we serve: God or the devil? Or is there neither God nor the devil, neither good nor evil? Is it not given to us to know what is good and what is evil? We would love to say the latter, but this is not possible for us, the miserables. If we did not know what is good and what is evil we could not live. Every day, every hour we must choose: to go or not to go; to take or to give; to kill or to forgive. Take a look at your day and think about how you lived through it: You shall see that everything you did you did because you knew what was good and what was evil.

It is said in the Bible that in paradise, before the fall, Adam did not know what was good and what was evil; in that state, he could say that he did not know what was good and what was evil. But we can't imagine this for ourselves. We only see cattle behaving in such a way: living without knowing what is good and what is evil. Where there are human beings there is the law. When I look at an individual, I can see that he knows what is good and what is evil and he conducts his life in accordance with this. When I look at people all at once, the law is even more distinct: it is written, and every individual either accepts it or doesn't accept it when he is aware of a better law.

Where, then, is the law according to which we live? Don't say that it is a law to placate one's body: to eat, drink, copulate, and take care of progeny. This is no law but simply the needs of the flesh, needs that exist in cattle—precisely that for which the law is needed. Cattle don't have laws; their lusts are all the same—they all want the same thing. Lest people fight over the same piece of food, for the same body to sleep with, lest they fight one another to death, and neither of them eats or sleeps fully, they must share; they need the pillar of the law between them. For them to share, lust must have limits imposed on it: the law is born in the hearts of men with a view to limiting lust. When there is lust there is law; the law is nothing other than a humbling—the conquest of lust for the other. There are many such laws in the heart of every man. Cattle don't have the law and nor do they need it. Whether for good or bad, man cannot be without the law: the law is inscribed within him. And there has never been man

---

9   **Entry 39. "To Whom Do We Belong?"** [*Ch'i my?*] (1879–86). The rationale for this chron-
ological placement and the date attribution for this fragment is the same as with entry 37,
"The Kingdom of God" and 38, "What a Christian Should and Should Not Do." Since these
appeared in Tolstoy's lifetime with the date of completion shown as "1886," this date has
been honored. This text was published in volume 90 of *The Jubilee* in 1958 (90:127-31).

without the law. Whether or not he existed, when Adam was alone—or when man was alone—he could live without the law: his lusts were his alone and interfered with nobody else's. But as soon as two, and then three, people come together, their lusts collide: "I want to eat this apple." "Me, too." One grabs a stone and kills the other. And then a third shows up who tries to intervene. The soul of the man will register whether what he has done was good or bad. One wolf will tear another wolf to pieces; a third will do nothing, will unthinkingly feast on the flesh of the killed with the killer. But a man will speak up, will think: Is this good or evil? Having found the law in his heart, don't say there is no law. The law is inscribed in your heart. If you live a day among people and become engaged in any activity, you will find the law. There is no human affair for which you do not have the law of yours in your soul, and no business of yours for which you do not know the law.

If you say that there is no law, you are saying that too many laws have come about and hence that all are without sense. There are such cases—indeed, there are many—when one legal order conflicts with another. And, besides, there are statutes that establish provisions for satisfying lusts instead of quenching them. And these are called laws. People live amid a sea of laws, and to stay afloat without following any, they can blend statutes with laws and live according to none, live by lust.

If you say so, this must be true. It is true that there are a multitude of laws and statutes, that no one real law is in view, and that one can live without the law. This is true and this is precisely what I want to speak about; it is for this reason that I am asking: Whose subjects are we—God's or the devil's?

Do we live by law or by lust? Don't forget: the law exists—not one law but an enormity of laws, and we follow thousands; man has never lived and can't live without laws. Indeed, there are so many laws and we become so confused by them that we opt to live by lust. So many have lived by choosing a law that is handy to follow and substituting handy laws for the "keep your hands off" laws. Laws cannot but exist. Even if there were only two humans alive for three days, they would have laws. Moreover, millions upon millions have lived over the course of 5000 years, according to the Bible—for millions of years, according to science—and surely they have found laws? To suggest otherwise is guff that is not worth discussing.

I am sitting in my house writing, my children are studying and playing, and my wife is working around the house while I write. All of this transpires as it does because there are laws for all of this, accepted by everyone. No stranger can move into my house because it is mine: As per the 10th commandment, nobody should desire another's property. The children study work I have assigned, as per the 5th commandment. My wife is safe from the advances of other men, as per the 7th. I work on what I can, as per the 4th. I have listed Moses's tablets, but I could have named thousands of state and customary laws that affirm the same things, at least in part. Should I want to, I could immediately find laws and customs that render the above laws null and void. I might say to myself: Why do you have a house? Christ showed us the example of living with no bed on which to rest his head at night. Why do you have a house when there exist poor people without shelter? Why do you have a house if it is said that we should care about no earthly possessions? I might ask myself: Why do you care about children? For, not a hair on their head will perish.[10] Why do you teach them if blessed are the poor in spirit? Even more simply: Why do you teach them pagan wisdom if you are a Christian? I might say: Why do you teach them out of vanity, if it is better to work the land? Why do you have a wife when happy are those who do not marry?[11] Why do you have a wife when it is said: "If one comes to me and does not hate his . . . wife, he cannot be my disciple".[12] Why are you working, writing this very text, if this goes against humility and caring nothing for worldly affairs?

I could abandon my wife, my children, my work, and could support this by appealing to divine law or to state laws and customs. I could abandon my wife and children and join the monastery. Or I could abandon my wife and children, get divorced, take another wife, and live a debauched lifestyle—finding confirmation for all of this in divine and human laws. And so, do as you please and what suits you—laws can be fit retroactively.

This is our situation, and it is no good. It is not that there are no laws but that there are too many, and we've grown too clever. And this is why I ask myself: Do we belong to God or the devil?

But then you shall ask me again: "What is it to belong to God or the devil?" You will say: "It is time to let go of this hoary verbiage: much has been said about these tall tales of God and the devil; much evil has been done and blood spilt in the name of these tales. But we now have grown too clever and have stopped believing in these tales about God and the devil. So, if you wish to speak about such things, kindly speak so that you are understood and get rid of the big and senseless words from your speech. What is God and what is the devil? Nobody has ever seen either and nobody can even imagine what it would be to

---

10 Luke 21:18.

11 In the original, Tolstoy writes *"blago luchshe ne zhenit'sia?"* See (Matthew 19:10: "It is not expedient to marry."

12 Luke 14:20, 26.

see either. God and the devil are figments of people's imagination, and we have given up on them as useless. If you wish to speak, speak about humans."

It is about humans that I wish to speak, and this is why I speak about God and the devil: they are inseparable and indivisible from humans. I speak as I do because I want to call God and the devil by their names; it's impossible for me to say what I would like to without doing so.

You say: "one cannot comprehend how God could have sat around somewhere for eternity only at some stage to have thought, 'I know, I'll create the world,' and then to have got down to business creating it in seven days, uttering that it was good."[13] True, this is incomprehensible for you and I when we are not inquiring but are just flatly told as much. But do tell, can we make sense of the idea that everything has existed for eternity and had no beginning? No, we cannot. Moreover, you say that "everything has a beginning." You say that moving back from beginning to beginning, you've traveled far back, further even than 7,000 years ago, much further based on guesswork and conjecture, and there you can see not only the formation of the earth and of the vital element on it, but also the formation of the sun, and further back still. But however far back you have travelled, you shall admit that the beginning of all beginnings is even further, inaccessible. Yet you still search for the beginning of all beginnings; your gaze is fixed there, from it—so you say—originates everything. Well, this very thing, which is not a part but is the beginning[14] of all beginnings, is what I call "God." As such, when I say "God," you cannot fail to understand me and cannot condemn me. Neither of us know him but both of us have the same faith; nobody can demand from us the same comprehension of God as can be found in the Book of Genesis. We would need to let go of what we understand with—in other words, our mind—in order to understand him as such. We can no more do this than we can demand of Moses that he comprehend the heavens, the sun, the moon, and the stars more than he does the earth. But Moses's answer to the question, From whence do we come?, is the same that you have provided: from the beginning of all beginnings, from God.

"But," you shall say, "this beginning of all beginnings is far from what most people mean by the word 'God.' By 'God,' they mean a person who cares about human people. They say that he wrote the law with his finger, walked in the bush, sent his son, etc. All this is missing in the rational concept of the origin."

And I agree with this: There is no such God at the beginning of all beginnings. A personal, living, pitying God, one who lives and gets angry with human

---

13 Sic, Tolstoy here speaks of seven rather than six days of creation.
14 "Not a part but is the beginning" corresponds to "*ne chast', a nachalo*" in the original Russian.

beings, is incomprehensible to you: the human mind cannot grasp what he is and what his life is as such. Tell me what life is and I shall tell you what a living god is. You say that "life is man's consciousness—an abiding, if false consciousness—of his freedom, the satisfaction of his needs, and the choices he makes." But from whence does this life come?

You say: "This life developed out of the lower organisms." But if consciousness was born in the lower organisms, from whence did these organisms come? You say: "they emerged from the infinite beginning." I call the same thing "God": I say that the consciousness of my life, the consciousness of freedom, is God.

But this is not the whole of God. Not only is He the creator, but He lives too.[15]

But aside from my existence, my being alive, my pursuit of satisfying my needs, I am conscious of my freedom of choice, and I have reason that guides me in this choice. From whence does reason come? This reason, that which searches for the beginning, is in conflict with man himself, conquers man and his lust, places laws in his face—laws that are nothing other than struggles to conquer lust. Tell me from whence comes this reason of man which establishes the laws that oppose lust?

You say: "These laws originate in man." But where does human reason come from? From the evolution of the animate? And the animate from the inanimate? But the inanimate was already pregnant with the embryos of reason. Were there embryos of reason in the severed particles of the moving sun? And in the sun and the stars from which the sun tore itself? If there is reason and it was the product of evolution, its origin is hidden in infinity. This very beginning of all beginnings also is God. You and I have the same concepts for the beginning of that which exists—to wit, that the beginning of life and of reason merge into one. Only you point out the train of your thought and I call it all God. But I call it so because I somehow need to give a name to what you point out and what becomes divided into three tracks of thought for you.

You ask: "Why the devil? Man is flesh, has life and reason, and evolves. That is all." But here I must stop you. It is okay to say that a rope unfurls, that an embryo develops in an egg, but to apply such words to human beings and humanity is unscrupulous.[16] If you are human, you live. Therefore, stop talking

---

15 According to the Russian text published in *The Jubilee*, Tolstoy writes in Russian: "*On tol'ko tvorets i zhivoi.*" This might be a handwritten slip on the writer's part where an obvious "not" [*ne*] is missing before "only." This might also be either an error by V. F. Savodnik, the editor responsible for editing this text originally for volume 17 of *The Jubilee*, or an error committed by typesetters during the production of the later volume 90.

16 Tolstoy makes excellent use of the polyvalent meaning of the substantive derivatives "*verevka*" (rope) and "*razvitie*" (development) from the verbs "*vit'*" (to weave something)

about development, look at yourself and indicate what is it that you are doing while in possession of life and reason? If you can do that, you will answer that you are looking for a reasonable choice for all of your bodily needs; our life consists in this. When there is a choice (there is no life for man without this consciousness) man is on the lookout for what best—and most harmoniously—agrees with reason and its laws (the laws of God). It is this very thing, that which disagrees with the laws of reason, that I call the devilish . . .

40. The Sermon on the Mount[17]
[1884]

Sermon to the people by Our Lord Jesus Christ:
Having stepped out, Jesus saw a multitude of people and had pity on them because they were like sheep without a shepherd, and so he started to teach them at length (Matthew 6:34).[18]

Our Lord Jesus Christ spent his earthly life spreading his teaching among the people, through the sum of his deeds and the whole of his life. He taught them at the synagogues—in Nazareth, Capernaum, and Jerusalem—at the temple, and at the seashore, in the boat, and on the mountain, in towns, and in villages. He taught them and the Jews marveled (I. VII, 15).[19] The Jews

---

and "*vit'sia*" (a reflexive and intransient derivative meaning "to stretch out," "to unfurl"). There is a great Russian proverb (or ditty) frequently used in fairy tales that grasps perfectly the magic depths of the word: "*dolgo verevochke vit'sia*" (the rope takes a long time to unfurl), meaning "do not rush the story, be patient with its digressions and detours." Tolstoy uses these semantic potentials as if to say: "do not rush the unfolding of the story; this is far more complicated than just a linear phenomenon."

17 **Entry 40. "The Sermon on the Mount"** [*Nagornaia propoved'*] (1884). This fragment, completed during the last days of April 1884, was among a group of short didactic inscriptions published in the form of cheap paper pocketbooks that were produced by the then-newly created publishing house Posrednik (The Intermediary) initiated by Vladimir Chertkov, for broad dissemination among the masses of Russian readership. The fragment was likely meant to serve as an illustration, one of a series of visual commentaries to "The Sermon on the Mount" scenes by I. P. Keller, an academic artist and professor of fine arts in St. Petersburg. Banned by the censors, who demanded unacceptable excisions from Tolstoy's text, the fragment was at long last published in 1936 in volume 25 of *The Jubilee* (25:530-31) and was edited by the veteran folklorist and academician Vsevolod Izrailevich Sreznevsky (see 25:881-82).

18 Tolstoy's reference to Matthew is inaccurate and must be a reference for himself. The verses about the gathered multitudes in Matthew occur at the end of chapter 4, and then in chapters 5 and 6, and the Sermon on the Mount runs through chapters 5, 6, and 7 of the New Testament. Here, I have retained Tolstoy's original references.

19 Tolstoy means John 7:15.

marveled because He taught them as the king in power and not as the Scribes (Matthew 6:22), and they marveled and said: From whence come his wisdom and power (Matthew 13:54)?[20] In the morning, he came to the temple, and the whole multitude of people came to him. He sat down and started to teach them (I. VII. 2).[21]

What did Jesus teach? Could the gist of the teaching that he gave in response to the wicked questions of the Scribes and the Pharisees suffice for us?[22] Could what he said in response to the doubts of his disciples, the parables he gave to the people and then explained to his disciples—face to face—be sufficient? Might it be that not all of this teaching at which the populace marveled and through which he preached the Gospel of the Kingdom to all common people has survived to reach us? Could only those who lived when he lived and could hear Him, who knew His entire teaching, be happy? Can we, weak sinners as we are, only make guesses about him[23] and comprehend Him only through the interpretations of other people? Could it be that after His coming down to earth to save us, God did not leave us a chance to hear His divine voice? This could not have been the case and is not. God came down to earth and revealed the truth to all of us, and we can hear His divine voice as long as we have ears to hear. Many times over, Christ spoke his teaching through parables as something already comprehended by His disciples; many times over, He explained what was unclear about His teaching; many times over, He spoke about us, whether on the occasion of healing a blind man, the resurrection of Lazarus, or when giving an incomplete message to the disciples, people who already knew him. [This is] not what The Son of Man said.[24] He said (Matthew 11:28, 29, 30):[25] Come to Me, all you who labor and are heavy laden, and I will give you rest. Take my yoke upon you and learn from Me, for I am gentle [krotok],[26] and lowly in heart, and you will find rest in your souls."[27] He said: "For my yoke is easy

---

20 This reference is correct, but Tolstoy substitutes "power" for "mighty works."
21 This reference is erroneous: the relevant place in the New Testament is John 8:2 or Luke 21:38 and not John 7:2.
22 Here, there is no capitalization in Tolstoy's original.
23 I have maintained Tolstoy's spelling to make it clear that his capitalizations were not intuitive or consistent.
24 This is Tolstoy's fragment of a sentence. He can only mean the following when we take his context into account: "This is not what Jesus (aka The Son of Man) said."
25 This reference is correct.
26 Tolstoy uses "krotok" to mean "gentle," though the word is translated in Russian NT standard as "humble."
27 Tolstoy did not provide closing quotation marks in the original.

and My burden is light."[28] How can we say our load is "heavy"?[29] Who is right: He or we? He will judge us; he judges and chastises us. We say "heavy," but do we really know his burden and the yoke he told us to assume? We did not lift a finger to touch this yoke and we yet say that it is heavy. What yoke did He want us to put on? His commandments—wherein are they?

41. On Charity[30]
[1885]

The publisher of *Detskaia Pomoshch'* [*Aid to Children*][31] solicited my participation in an issue of this journal, in light of a newspaper article that I wrote in 1882 during the census, regarding charity work for the poor. When I received this invitation, I was putting the finishing touches on an article for the journal *Russkaia Mysl'* [*Russian Thought*], a sequel to my article on the census. And I was thus already writing on the topic to which the present issue is devoted.

In the latest article, I described in detail my experiences of my attempted charity work during the census and the conclusions at which I arrived. The article could not be published. Here, I shall once again try to briefly adumbrate my thoughts about charity work as such.

What follows are the conclusions I have arrived at concerning charity. I have become convinced that one cannot be charitable without living the good

---

28 Tolstoy writes: "*ibo igo moe blago i bremia budet legko*," which is the Russian standard version of Matthew 11:30.

29 Here, I have added quotation marks, which were absent in the original.

30 **Entry 41. "On Charity"** [*O blagotvoritel'nosti*] (1885). This translation is based on the version of this piece that was published in 1937 in volume 25 of *The Jubilee* (536-37). Tolstoy wrote this résumé about charity somewhere between the end of 1884 and May 24, 1885, at the request of the priest G.P. Smirnov-Platonov, publisher of the periodical *Aid to Children*. Tolstoy's article summarizing his experiences during his participation in the census work in Moscow in 1882 was initially published in the January 20, 1882, issue of the newspaper Sovremennye Izvestiia [Contemporary News]. This longer article of 1882 by Tolstoy is one of his better-known works on urban poverty and relief work. The article he mentions for the journal *Russian Thought* is a selection from his *What Then Shall We Do?* ["*Must Do*" in Maude's translation], his famous tract of 1885, which was banned from publication. This text appeared, with significant cuts, in the last volume of the new edition of his collected works (1886), which also included *The Death of Ivan Ilyich*. The present short article did not make it into Smirnov-Platonov's journal. Instead, in issue 8 of the journal, which was released on May 24, 1885, Tolstoy published a translation of "The Teaching of the Twelve Apostles," along with a preface and commentary. See the summary of this publication in *The Jubilee* by N. K. Gudzii (25:886).

31 See the previous note.

life, and certainly not if one is conducting a bad life or is using the conditions of one's bad life to justify an excursion into the domain of charity for the sake of adorning this bad life. I have become convinced that charity is justified and does justice to the needs of others only when it ensues as an inevitable consequence of the good life, and that the demands of this good life are very far from the conditions in which I currently live. I have become convinced that an opportunity to do charity is the crown privilege and the highest distinction of the good life; a long winding staircase leads all the way up to this goal, but I haven't really done as much as take the first step. You can render welfare unto others only when neither they nor you are conscious of doing so—as when your right hand is not conscious of what your left is doing. As it is said in the teaching of the twelve apostles: charity must issue from your hands without your knowing whom you have benefited. You can create charitable welfare only when your whole life is in the service of the happiness of good works. Charity cannot be a goal: being charitable must be the inevitable consequence and fruit of the good life. What kind of fruit can there be on a dry tree that lacks living roots, living bark, boughs, buds, leaves, and florets?

You can suspend fruits, such as oranges and apples, on a Christmas tree garland, but this will not turn the tree into a living orchard that gives birth to oranges and apples. Before one even starts to think about fruit, one needs to help the tree to take root in the soil, to graft it, and then to grow it. For the tree of good works to be planted, grafted, and grown, much else needs further thinking through, much groundwork completed before the good fruits to be given by us to others may be marveled at. One can parcel out the fruits of the work of others and suspend them on the garlands of a dry tree, but there is nothing in this even remotely like goodness. For this, much else should and must be done first.

42. Preface to *Tsvetnik* [*The Flower Garland*][32] [1886]

Brood of vipers! How can you, being evil, speak good things?
For out of the abundance of the heart the mouth speaks. A good

---

32 **Entry 42. "Preface to The Flower Garland"** [*Predislovie k sborniku* Tsvetnik] (1886). This text is based on the version published in 1936 in volume 26 of *The Jubilee* (26:307-9). A description of this manuscript can be found in the commentary provided by P. V. Bulychev (see 26:746-47). The title of this collection might, more literally, be translated

man, out of the good treasure of his good heart, brings forth good things, and an evil man out of his evil treasure brings forth evil things.[33]

But I say to you that for every idle word men may speak, they will account for it on the day of judgment.[34]

For by your words you will be justified, and by your words you will be condemned.[35] [Matthew 12:34-37]

This book collects stories that describe true incidents as well as historical tales, legends, oral lore, myths, fables, and the kind of tales that have been drawn up and written for the good of the people.

We have gathered those that we consider concordant with the teaching of Christ and which we therefore consider to be good and truthful.

When reading a story, a fairy tale, a legend, or a fable, many people—children, especially—tend to ask first of all whether what is being described is true. Frequently, and whenever they see that what is being described could not possibly have happened, they say: this is windbag fiction; it's all untrue.

People who so judge are not judging correctly.

Only those shall know the truth who come to know how things should be according to the will of God—not how things used to be, are, or how they might be.

Only those shall write the truth who show what people do well is what is in accordance with God's will and what they do badly is what is contrary to God's will—not he who describes how things had to happen or what such-and-such a man did.

Truth is the way. Christ said: "I am the way, and the truth, and the life."[36]

---

as *The Constellation of Flowers*. This publication venture owes its beginning to Alexandra Kalmykova, an activist in the sphere of popular education, of whose efforts Tolstoy was very supportive. *The Flower Garland* contained various legends, histories, and anecdotes of a didactic character. With Tolstoy's preface and the serious emendations that he made to its composition, the collection was published in Kiev (Kyiv) in 1886. In further editions before 1917, Tolstoy's preface was banned from publication. On the "flower garland" question, see also entry 5 and entry 41 on the garlands of charity.

33 Here, Tolstoy joins Matthew 12:34-35 into one paragraph.

34 At this stage in the text, Tolstoy sets off Matthew 12:36 in a separate paragraph.

35 Here, Tolstoy sets off Matthew 12:37 in a separate paragraph. Though Tolstoy is quoting from The New Testament, he doesn't use any quotation marks, creating the illusion of a totalizing authority that even transcends the words spoken by Jesus, an effect that Gary Saul Morson has dubbed "absolute language" in his influential writings on Tolstoy.

36 Here, Tolstoy doesn't add the reference, namely John 14:6, though he does provide quotation marks.

And the truth is known not by someone who looks at his feet but who knows where to walk by looking at the sun.

Literary works are good and necessary not when they describe how things used to be but when they show how things should be; not when they describe what people used to do, but when they evaluate the good and the bad; when they show the one narrow way that accords with the will of God, leading people toward life.

One must not only describe what happens in the world to show the way. The world lies in evil and temptation. Should you describe these lies, there will be no truth in your words. For there to be truth in what you describe, you must describe what should be and not what is, not the truth of that which is but the truth of the Kingdom of God, which is close to us but is not here yet. This is why there are mountains of books that speak about what certainly used to be the case and about what likely was, but all these books are lies if those writing them do not better know what is good and what is evil, if they neither know nor show the only way that leads to the Kingdom of God. But then, there are fairy tales, parables, fables, and legends describing the marvelous, things that have never been and could not have been—, and these legends, fairy tales, and fables are true because they show in what the will of God has always been, is, and will be; they show the truth of the Kingdom of God.

We can imagine a book—there are lots of them around—containing a story, a novel or novella, in which it is described how a person lives for his passions, tolerates torture, tortures others, endures danger and misery, resorts to cunning, combats others, rises in his fortunes, and is joined toward the end with his love interest, becomes a notable and happy rich man. A book like this and everything it describes may well have nothing improbable in it, but it would still be lies and untruth: however beautiful his wife and however distinguished and rich he might become, a man living for himself and his passions cannot be happy.

Meanwhile, we can imagine a legend like this: Christ and the apostles roamed the world and stopped in to visit a rich man, who did not let Him in. And then they stopped in on a poor widow, who let them in. And He then ordered for a barrel of gold to roll toward the rich man, and he sent a wolf to the widow to eat her last remaining heifer. And the widow felt happy, and the rich man felt wretched. It felt good for the widow because nobody could take away from her kind deed and her happiness. And it felt wretched for the rich man because an evil deed lay heavy on his conscience, and the bitter aftertaste from the evil deed was not quenched by the barrel of gold.

This story is all around improbable, because none of what it describes occurred and could not have occurred. Yet it is entirely true, because it shows what always should be, in what goodness consists, in what evil consists, and what man should strive to do to fulfill the will of God.

No matter what marvels are described, no matter what beasts speak like men, what flying carpets carry people through the air—legends, parables, and fairy tales will be right if they contain the truth of the Kingdom of God. And when there is none of this truth, let anyone whatsoever certify it as truth, it will all be lies: it lacks the truth of the Kingdom of God. Christ himself spoke in parables and His parables remain truth eternal. He only used to add: "and so observe as you listen."

43. The Concept of Life[37]
[1887]

Let us assume the impossible, [. . .][38] let us assume that everything that the science of life today wishes to know, all is clear as day! It is clear how organic matter is born through adaptation from inorganic matter; how forces are transformed into feelings, will, and thoughts; and all this is known not only to the students at gymnasia but also to peasant children.

---

37 **Entry 43. "The Concept of Life"** [*Poniatie zhizni*] (1887). This is a translation of the version of Tolstoy's talk that was originally published in 1887 as "L.V., 'The Concept of Life.' A Talk by L.N. Tolstoy. New Time (Novoe Vremia), No. 3973 March 23 (April 3), 1887 (pp. 2-3)." I thank the *Tolstoy Studies Journal* for allowing me to reprint my recent translation of Tolstoy's talk from Inessa Medzhibovskaya, *Tolstoy's* On Life: *From the Archival History of Russian Philosophy* (Toronto and de Land, FL: Tolstoy Studies Journal. Volume 30, 2019), 354-63. The talk is a summary of earlier drafts of Tolstoy's book *On Life*, which Tolstoy completed in the autumn of 1887.

Tolstoy delivered the talk soon after his election to membership at The Moscow Psychological Society at its session on February 26, 1887, at Moscow University. Tolstoy volunteered at the session on March 5, 1887, to make his presentation on March 14, 1887, at the conclusion of a prolonged discussion of Nikolai Grot's talk on the freedom of the will, which went on for several sessions in a row. This report on Tolstoy's paper, taken in longhand by the Society Secretary Professor Legonin and based on the version from which Tolstoy read, was published in three columns in the cultural life and events section of the authoritative St. Petersburg newspaper Novoe Vremia. (The initials "L.V." are those of the Secretary of the Session, V. Legonin, only inverted.) All further details about this talk and other extant versions of it, and, more generally, of Tolstoy's participation in the work of the Moscow Psychological Society may be found in Medzhibovskaya 2019, my long archival study cited above. For Tolstoy's book *On Life*, see "Further Reading" in this volume.

This is the third talk by Tolstoy in this volume. See also entries 18, "A Talk Delivered at the Society of the Lovers of Russian Literature" (1859) and 23, "A Speech in Defense of Soldier Vasilii Shibunin" (1866). "The Concept of Life" is the last known public talk delivered by Tolstoy in front of formal audiences. We do not include in the volume the more intimate and informal talk that Tolstoy gave at one of the meetings for the members of a newly formed publishing house Posrednik in February 1884 that he convened at his Moscow home in Khamovniki. In his comments devoted to the topic of popular literature, Tolstoy criticized the propagandistic character of the brochures for the people published by the Church and sectarians alike, as well as the lowbrow "lacquer box" ["lubochnaia"] type of literature. The text of the talk, which appeared under the title "A Speech about Popular Editions" ["Rech' o narodnykh izdaniiakh"] may be found in volume 25 of *The Jubilee*, which appeared in 1937 and reprinted the text from the 1933 edition of Tolstoy's unpublished texts (25:174-79), with a commentary by P. S. Popov (25:523-29). Tolstoy's own variant of the satirical "lacquer box" can be found in entry 74, "Two Different Versions of the History of a Beehive with a Lacquer-Painted Lid" (1888/1900).

38 I have removed "said the Count" from the first sentence, the phrase from the stenographic protocol of Tolstoy's talk by V. Legonin. See note 40 below.

It is known to me that such and such thoughts and feelings happen because of such and such movements. So what? Can I or can I not control these movements in such a way as to excite in myself these and other thoughts? The question about the kinds of thoughts and feelings that I need to excite in myself and others remains not only unresolved, but even untouched.

But this question is the sole question of the central concept of life. Science has chosen for its subject matter certain phenomena attendant to life and having accepted a part for a whole has called these phenomena the totality of life.

The question that is inseparable from the concept of life is not the question from whence life has begun but the question about how one should live, and only if one starts with this question is it possible to come to any sort of decision about what life is.

The answer to the question about how one should live appears so well known to man that it seems to him that it is not worth talking about. . . . To live as would be better. This seems at first very simple and understood by all, but it is far from being either simple or understood . . . [39]

The concept of life appears as most simple and clear to man at first. First of all it seems to man that life is within him, in his body. I live in the body, and therefore life is in my body. But as soon as man begins looking for this life in a specific part of his body, complications emerge.

There is no life in nails or hair; neither is there life in a leg or in an arm, which can be amputated; and there is no life in the blood, in the heart, or in the brain. Life is everywhere and nowhere. And it turns out that it cannot be located in the place of its domicile.

Then, man looks for life within time, which at first seems very simple also . . . But then again, as soon as one begins looking for life within time, one sees that things are not simple here either. I have lived 58 years, according to my birth certificate. But I know that I slept 20 years out of these 58. So did I live or did I not during this time? And then in my mother's womb, or when with my wet nurse, did I live or did I not? And then out of the remaining 38 years, the greater half of which I spent sleepwalking, and I don't know whether I was living or not. I lived somewhat, and somewhat I did not, and so within time also [life] is everywhere and nowhere. And then a question arrives involuntarily: from whence does this life, which I can find nowhere, come [?] [40]

---

39 Ellipsis in the original.
40 For readability's sake in English, I have added the question mark that was missing in the original.

Here, I am indeed going to find out . . . But here as well, it turns out that what appeared to be so easy is not only difficult but impossible. It turns out that I have been looking for something other than my life. It turns out that if one is bent on searching for life, one should search neither in space nor in time and not as [if it were a matter determined by] a consequence or a cause, but as something that one knows in oneself absolutely, independently of space, time, and causality. And so should I study myself ? So, how do I know life in myself ?

This is how: I know, first of all, that I live and that I live wishing good things for myself, and I have been wishing this for myself ever since I can remember up until now, and I wish this morning through evening. All that which lives outside me is important to me only insofar as it enables that which does good to me. The world is important to me only because it brings me joy.

But with this knowledge of my life yet another kind of knowledge is connected. Inseparably connected with this life that I feel within me is the knowledge that besides me there lives around me a whole world of other living creatures each of which has the same consciousness of its own life, each of which lives for its own aims that are alien to me.

These creatures don't know and don't want to know about my claims for exclusive life; for the sake of attaining their own aims, these creatures are all ready to annihilate me any minute. And moreover, by watching the annihilation of other creatures similar to me, I also know that a very rapidly approaching and inevitable annihilation faces me, this precious me in whom alone life appears [to be contained] . . . [41]

It is as if there are two "I"s in man that do not seem to be able to get on with each other in life and that seem to fight with each other and exclude one another.

One "I" says: "Only 'I' live for real, all else only seems to live and therefore the whole meaning of the world is my well-being."

The other "I" says: "The whole world is not for you, but for its own aims and wants to know nothing about whether you are well or ill."

And life becomes terrifying.

One "I" says: "I want my needs and desires to be satisfied. The desires and needs of animals are satisfied at the detriment of other animals, and therefore all animals fight against one another. You are an animal and must fight eternally. But however successfully you should fight, some fighting creature will sooner or later crush you."

It is even worse—and it becomes ever more terrifying.

---

41 Ellipsis in the original.

The most terrible thing that encompasses all the preceding is that the situation is like this:

One "I" says: "I want to live, to live eternally." The other "I" says: "You will certainly die very soon—maybe now—, and all those whom you love will die, and you and they are annihilating your life with your every movement and are on your way toward suffering, death, the very things that you hate and that you fear the most." This is the worst of all . . .[42]

It is impossible to change this situation. It is possible not to move, not to sleep, not to breathe even, but it's impossible not to think. One thinks, and every thought—every thought of mine—poisons every step of my life as an individual person.

As soon as man begins living consciously, [his] reasonable consciousness states the same thing over and over again to him: you can no longer live the life as you feel it and as you see it in your past, the life that animals and many people live, the life from which you became what you are now and what you used considering as life. If you attempt to walk away from the struggle with the whole world of creatures that live just as you do for their personal aims, you will not succeed, and these creatures will inevitably destroy you.

An individual cannot change this situation, and one thing remains, the one thing done by man when he begins to live and transfers his aim beyond his self and strives for other creatures . . . But however far man posits his aims beyond his self, as his reason becomes more illuminated, not a single aim satisfies him.

If reason had illuminated his activity for him, then even after having unified Germany and ruled over all of Europe, Bismarck would have felt the same unresolved contradiction between the futility and unreasonableness of everything he had accomplished and the eternity and reasonableness of everything that exists, just as the cook who had prepared Bismarck a dinner that would be eaten up within an hour [would have felt]. Either one, as soon as they think about it, will see clearly that, first, the wholeness of Prince Bismarck's dinner, just like the wholeness of the mighty Germany, are held together—the former by police, the latter by the army, for as long as both of these forces are vigilant, since there are hungry people that want to eat the dinner and there are other nationalities that want to be as mighty as Germany. Second, Prince Bismarck's dinner and the might of Germany not only fail to cohere with the meaning of life in the world but contradict it. And third, both the one who cooks dinner and the might of Germany [43] will soon perish, and so will their dinner and Germany,

---

42 Ellipsis in the original.

43 A clause of the sort "and the one who is responsible for the might of Germany" might be missing from the transcript. I have simply provided a direct translation of the original.

and the world will remain living, reminiscing neither about the dinner nor Germany, and even less so about those who cooked these things up.

As his reasonable consciousness grows stronger, man arrives at the thought that no happiness connected with his individuality is a heroic deed, but a necessity . . . An individuality is only the first condition from which life begins, and life has an ultimate limit . . . [44]

"But where does life begin and where does it end?"—they will ask me. Where does the night end and day begin? Where on the shore does the sphere of the sea end and the sphere of the land begin?

There is day and night, there is land and sea, there is life and not-life.

Our life, from when we are conscious of it, is a movement between two boundaries.

One boundary is the complete lack of concern for other lives in this limitless world and relates to activity that is directed only at the satisfaction of the needs of one's individual person. The other boundary is a complete renunciation of one's individual person, the greatest attention to other lives in this limitless world and concordance with them, the transfer of the desire for happiness from one's individual person to the limitless world, and other creatures. The closer one adheres to the first boundary, the less there is of life and happiness; the closer one adheres to the second boundary, the more there is of life and happiness. And therefore, every man is always moving from one boundary to the other, i.e., he lives. This very movement is life itself.

If I speak about life, the concept of life is inseparably connected within me with the concept of reasonable life. I do not know any other life but a reasonable one, and nobody can know it otherwise.

We call animal "a life" and the life of an organism "a life" . . . But this is not life, it is only a certain condition of life that is revealed to us.

But what is this reason—the demands of which preclude personal life and transfer the activity of man beyond himself, onto the condition that is recognized by us as the joyous condition of love?

What is reason? Whatever we define, we define only through reason. And therefore, with what would we define reason? . . . [45]

---

44 Ellipsis in the original.
45 Ellipsis in the original.

If all that we have been defining we have defined through reason, we cannot define reason in the same way. But all of us not only know what reason is, reason alone is something that we all know without doubt and in the same way . . .[46]

Reason is a law, in the same way in which there is a law of life of every organism and plant, with the only difference being that we see the law of reason fulfilling itself in the life of a plant. We cannot see the law of reason to which we are subject as a tree is to its law, but we nevertheless fulfill it.

We have decided that life is what is not our life. Herein lies the root of delusion. Instead of studying the life that we know within ourselves as completely exclusive—since we do not know any other—we look for that which lacks the main quality of our life—reasonable consciousness . . . We are doing what a man would do if he were to go about studying an object by looking at its shadow or reflection . . .[47]

If we find that the material parts are undergoing change in obedience to the activity of the organism, we found that out not because of watching and studying the organism, but because we are in part an animal organism—a part of us that is familiar to us as the material of our life, i.e., what we have been called to do work upon, by subjecting it to the law of reason . . . As soon as man has doubts about his life, as soon as he transfers his life onto what life is not, he becomes unhappy and sees death. But the man who is aware of his life as it has been put into his consciousness knows neither unhappiness nor death, because the happiness of his life is vested solely with making his own animal side obey the law of reason, and this is not only within his power but is inevitably fulfilled within him . . . We have knowledge of the death of the material parts of the animal creature. We have knowledge of the death of animals and of man himself as an animal. But we do not know of the death of reasonable consciousness and we cannot know this because it is life itself. And life cannot be death . . . [48] An animal lives blessedly, does not see death, and dies without seeing it. For what purpose has man been given the gift of seeing death? And why is it so terrible for him that it tears his soul apart, forces him to kill himself out of fear of death? Why is that? This is because the man who sees death is a sick man who has violated the law of his life, who is not living the life of reason. He is the same as the animal that has violated the law of its life.

---

46 Ellipsis in the original.
47 Ellipsis in the original.
48 Ellipsis in the original.

Man's life is a striving for happiness, and what he is striving for is given to him. The light kindled in the soul of man is happiness and life, and this light cannot be darkness because there is truly for man only this integral light that burns in his soul.[49]

49 The protocol remark below precedes Tolstoy's comments at the session: "Among various sessions of learned societies that so abound in Moscow at the end of the academic year, the sessions of The Psychological Society especially stood out this year. After a period of abatement—its activity having been terminated for a while—, the Society lives again thanks, in particular, to the work of Prof. N. Ia. Grot and our venerable writer, Lev Nikolaevich Tolstoy. Professor Grot presented to the Society his essay "On the Freedom of the Will," which took up two entire sessions and the beginning of a third. This presentation—in the discussion of which L. N. Tolstoy took part—gave rise to Tolstoy's wish to share his own thoughts with The Psychological Society. And thus, a week later, a new session was scheduled and devoted to the Count's paper on 'The Concept of Life.' To avoid the concourse of a multitudinous public, it was announced that this session would be a closed one. This session was attended only by members of The Psychological Society, almost all the professors from all departments of the University, and several persons by special invitation. At 8 pm, when everyone with the exception of the Count was assembled, Deputy Chairman of the Society and Dean of the Faculty of Law, V. Legonin, announced the session open and the Society proceeded to discuss the talk by N. Ia. Grot. This debate continued for about two hours until Count Tolstoy's arrival (Tolstoy had made known by an advance notice that he would not be able to arrive on time at the beginning of the session). The Count entered the discussion hall after everyone present had already taken their seats following the intermission. He quickly walked over to his reserved seat, apparently unwilling to draw any attention to himself. Upon taking his seat, Tolstoy addressed the audience with the following words: "I must beg your forgiveness, gentlemen, that I could not appear on time, and therefore, in order not to keep you here for long, I will begin my presentation starting with its second part." "Better from the beginning, Count," voices of protest were heard. "No, really, it would be better this way," the Count objected, "permit me to abide by my decision." He then proceeded with his reading. Here are the most interesting parts of the Count's paper in their original form." On Tolstoy's opinion about Grot, see also entry 61, "Reminiscences about N. Ia. Grot" (1910) in this volume.

PART 6

Writings of the 1890s

44. On Science and Art[1]
[1889–91]

Imagine someone who loves music, who has dedicated his entire life to its service, and who therefore has at least some understanding of it. One day, he hears a man producing an ugly cacophony instead of nice sounds and tells him that what he is producing is no good. Convinced that he is producing music, we can easily imagine this man responding with disapproval to the music lover, putting his judgment down to his being the enemy of music. All the arguments that the lover of music puts forward about why it is not nice to produce ugly sounds, and about what real music is, would be futile, since they would simply be ascribed to his being the enemy of music.

Something similar has happened to me in relation to science and art. As a lover of both, and having dedicated my whole life to them, I endeavored to

---

1   **Part 6: Writings of the 1890s. Entry 44. "On Science and Art"** ["*O Nauke i Iskusstve*"]. This text is one of several notes and articles on this question that Tolstoy wrote in response to multiple requests resulting out of the discussions at the Moscow Psychological Society toward the end of the 1880s. One of these requests was from Vladimir Goltsev, editor of the journal *Russkaia Mysl'* [*Russian Thought*] who was planning to give a lecture at the Moscow Psychological Society where he and Tolstoy were active members. It would take Tolstoy several years of thinking back and forth and making what appeared to him to be false starts before he wrote something more substantial—and not for Goltsev's journal but for *Voprosy Filosofii i Psikhologii* [*Questions of Philosophy and Psychology*], the main publishing organ of The Moscow Psychological Society. His bipartite response, which was published in 1897 and 1898 in the journal's two installment issues, would become none other than his famous tract *What Is Art?* The fragments from 1889–91—and the current entry is a good example—articulate the role that Tolstoy unveiled for science and art in the religious sense. Among the other six related beginnings of *What is Art?* of the late 1880s and the very early 1890s, this article appeared in volume 30 of *The Jubilee* (240-42). For other essays on art (and art and science), see 30:213-39; 434-85. In the same volume, V. S. Mishin wrote a sizable commentary describing in one long breath what he treated as preparatory writings for *What is Art?* (30:509-54).

point out that not everything that takes place in our time under their guise of science and art are good and estimable things. In response, it has been resolved by the majority of individuals to whom my comments have been directed that I am the enemy of the sciences and the arts and that my arguments are best left ignored. And since these individuals control the press and so direct public opinion, the opinion that I am the enemy of the sciences and the arts holds sway and has become nearly universal: all of my efforts to explain my view only call forth indignant resistance in the face of my alleged desire to return people to their prehistoric ignorance.

The majority of books that appear today draw this conclusion. Moreover, except for the select few, most individuals hardly read—or cannot catch up on—original authors or follow how they express their ideas; the majority only read criticism, reports, or surveys that paraphrase original authors. And, given their own lack of time for reading, their own degree of comprehension, and their own attention span, the paraphrasers skip over much and fast forward through the material, replacing the original thought with their own. However hopeless this situation, I shall nonetheless make an effort to express my thoughts on science and art—which is always a topic of enormous importance, especially in our time when they, ousting all else, are becoming the sole guide of our life—for the sake of those who love them.

The sciences and the arts belong to the most important of human activities; a human being would not be the same without them. Everything from the naming of objects, calculation, the ability to understand and express shadings of meanings—not just in words, but also through intonations—through the most complex conceptual forms of knowledge is the result of what is transmitted through the domain of science and art, in the broadest sense. In the broadest sense, everything that makes human beings distinct from animals, makes us capable of infinite perfection, is the consequence of the transmission of knowledge from the domain of the sciences and the arts.

In the broadest sense, then, the domain of sciences and arts embraces the entirety of human life within its fold. All that man possesses is the consequence of this knowledge transmission. So, the question concerning the sciences and the arts is not about whether they are useful or harmful *per se* but about what we currently single out and appreciate as most important and essential from within this enormous domain—what we might call science and art in the narrow sense (only an insane person could doubt that the sciences and the arts are generally useful). It is the narrow sense of science and art that both the ancient philosophers and Rousseau in modern times, as well as others, discuss. It is not science and art in the broad sense that are condemned but only that which has been singled out as preferred by certain people at certain times, and thus put in the limelight, that is judged to be unfit. It cannot be denied that the knowledge of all the subtleties of scholastics is not science, and that the mastery of cover jacket design or coverlet embroidery is not art: No exceptional or prime significance in the domain of the arts and the sciences should be ascribed to such things.

We are liable to think that what we now consider and call the sciences and the arts, in the exclusive sense, is, always has been, and must be a singular activity, distinct from all others, according to its importance, and that this could not be otherwise. But one must provide foundations for such a claim.

One should not be content simply with being sure. In all times, people have been completely certain that what they consider science and art are, indubitably, science and art. But it has almost always turned out that this certitude was in error. What was considered science and art in antiquity and in the Middle Ages no longer has for us the same meaning.

The science of our time is especially proud of its exactitude and its critical method: not taking anything on faith, it substantiates its postulates, subjecting them to a multilateral critique. It is this very peculiarity of the science of our time that I would like to apply to the most essential question of science and art, namely to the question concerning the foundations: Why is it that out of the whole enormous domain of human knowledge some knowledge is singled out exclusively and considered to be *the* science and art of our time, in the narrow sense?

We are so accustomed to considering only such art and science that even this question appears strange to us.

45. Concerning the Freedom of the Will[2] (from the unpublished work) [1894]

I.

No matter what he does, in all of his conscious deeds, man acts one way and not another only for one of two reasons: because he takes it that he must so act since

---

2   **Entry 45. "Concerning the Freedom of the Will (From the Unpublished Work)"** ["*K voprosu o svobode voli (Iz neizdannogo sochineniia)*"] (1894). Inexplicably, this work of Tolstoy's slipped the attention of *The Jubilee* editors as an independent article. With its enigmatic subtitle, it was published in the January issue of the journal *Voprosy Filosofii i Psikhologii*

the deed is just or because he previously recognized that this is how he should act and the inertia of habit causes him to act so again.

Whether man eats or abstains from food, works or rests, flees from danger or exposes himself to it, he acts as he does only because—as a conscious man—he thinks this to be obligatory and reasonable; he thinks it just to act thusly and not otherwise, or at one stage long ago he did think so already. The acceptance or rejection of it being just to act in one way and not in another is independent of external causes subject to man's observation but depends on some other causes found within man himself, those not subject to his observation. And so, the whole set of external circumstances that might sometimes seem conducive for accepting certain deeds as just are rejected by one individual, while another

---

[*Questions of Philosophy and Psychology*] (see notes to entry 44 above) ("*K voprosu o svobode voli*," L'va Tolstogo. *Voprosy Filosofii i Psikhologii*. Year Five, 1894, Volume 21 [1]: 1-7). The article consists of two short parts, as indicated. Elsewhere in the papers of Tolstoy's closest disciples—for example, among the papers of Pavel Biriukov—the article is referred to as "excised from correspondence." The article must be one of the responses written by Tolstoy on the question of free will from a set of letters to Nikolai Grot, Chairman of The Moscow Psychological Society and editor of the journal in 1894 that are considered irretrievably lost (see Medzhibovskaya *Tolstoy's* On Life [2019, 41-53; 277-80]). The freedom of the will was one of the topics that Grot exercised throughout his life. It was precisely a series of discussions of his presentation on this topic that delayed the delivery of Tolstoy's talk, "The Concept of Life," in March, 1887 (see entry 43 and the notes to it). Grot edited a collection of talks on the freedom of the will in the "Transactions" volume of the Moscow Psychological Society in 1889, which included articles by Grot, Lev Lopatin, Nikolai Bugaev, Sergey Korsakov, Ardalion Tokarsky, and Petr Astafiev (see *O svobode voli. Trudy Moskovskogo Psikhologicheskogo Obshchestva* [Moscow: Tipografiia A. Gatsuka, 1889]). On this book, see Medzhibovskaya *Tolstoy's* On Life (2019, 107-12). The publication of Tolstoy's article in Grot's journal in the year 1894 was a very brave step. Its subtitle "from the unpublished work" should have read "from the work categorically banned by state and religious censorship." Lengthy sections of the article are to be found in Tolstoy's *The Kingdom of God Is within You* (1890–93), arguably one of Tolstoy's most famous tracts. Although the work became known very quickly and very widely thanks to illegally circulating copies and its speedy publications abroad in Russian and in translation, it was dangerous to advertise it in the legal press within Russia. The publication of selections from this tract as selections from a "private letter" reveals the very skilled practice of Grot, Lev Lopatin, and other editors of the journal. The employment of language so subversive in such a deliberately clandestine manner was a political act that could have resulted in the complete closure of the journal. Quite inexplicably—and wondrously too—the censors missed their chance to punish a transgression. Interestingly, while publishing *The Kingdom of God Is within You* in his complete collections of Tolstoy's work in 1913, Biriukov did not set the matter straight that Tolstoy's article was not a letter and was instead an undercover section of the tract. *The Jubilee* is also silent on this score: See volume 28 of *The Jubilee*, published in 1957 and edited by N. V. Gorbachev, especially section 5 of the concluding chapter 12 (28:278-86).

individual, on the contrary, accepts these as just and acts accordingly, even when the circumstances are most disadvantageous.

And so, while feeling himself unfree in his acts, man always feels independent of external circumstances—free, that is, as regards what causes his acts, what causes him to accept them as just or reject them as such. And he feels free not simply from the external events that take place without him but also from his own acts.

And thus an individual who has committed an act contrary to what he accepts as just still remains free to accept or reject the act: he may consider his act to be good, that is, not contrary to what is just, and justify himself in having committed his act; or, he may, on accepting justice, consider his act evil, contrary to justice, and condemn himself for his act.

In this way, a gambler or a drunkard who has not withstood temptation and has caved to his passion remains free to accept gambling and drinking as just, to consider them evil, or to deem them a harmless amusement.

Quite similarly, a man who bolts out of a house on fire because he is unable to endure the heat and who thus abandons his comrade inside is still free to accept it as just that an individual must endeavor to save other lives even if it imperils his own; he is free to judge his own behavior evil and condemn himself for it. Alternatively, he is free to reject the justice of this course of action and consider his own act completely natural and necessary, and thus to justify himself in his act.

In the first case, man paves a whole series of good deeds that are consonant with what is just for himself, which follow inevitably when he accepts justice despite his lapse; and in the second case, he paves a whole series of evil deeds that are contrary to justice.

It is not as if man were always free to accept or reject any justice for true justice. There is a distinction between truths that are accepted by man as is and those that are inherited by him during his upbringing, as a matter of tradition, or that are taken by him on faith. Following these latter truths has become second nature for him: man cannot fail but accept these truths and is therefore unfree in their face. There are other truths still: these loom far away and have not yet fully revealed themselves; man cannot willfully accept them. He is equally unfree as regards accepting both of these kinds of truth: he cannot fail but accept the former and is still unable to accept the latter. But there is a third kind of truth: truths that have not yet become an unconscious motive for man's acting but have nonetheless been revealed to him with such clarity that he cannot evade them and should relate to them thusly or otherwise, accept or reject them. It is in his relationship toward these truths, these truths alone, that human freedom is revealed.

Every individual finds himself throughout the course of his life in the position of a wanderer moving in the dark following the light of a lantern advancing ahead of him: he cannot see what he has passed and what has fallen into darkness behind him, and he cannot see what he has not reached either and what is not yet illuminated by the lantern; moreover, it is not within his power to change his relationship toward one or the other. But whenever he stands still, he can see what is illuminated by the lantern, and it is in his power to choose this or that side of the road along which he is walking. The same is the case for each individual advancing in his spiritual life: there are always truths that he has already experienced, absorbed, and that make up part of his consciousness; there are other truths that have not yet been revealed to his mind's eye and of which he is only prescient; and there is a third kind of truth—truths that have to such an extent revealed themselves to him that he must inevitably relate to them, by accepting or rejecting them. And in the accepting or rejecting of these latter truths that become revealed, we are conscious of our freedom.

The whole difficulty and the seeming insolubleness of the question concerning human freedom arises because, in trying to solve the question, people imagine that man is immobile in relation to truth.

Man is certainly unfree should we imagine him immobile, only assuming that the life of humankind is not a constant movement from darkness toward light, from the lowest to the highest degree of truth, from the truth with an admixture of superstition toward the truth that is more and more free from superstition.

Man would be unfree if he knew no truth, but he would be similarly unfree, and indeed would not even have a concept of freedom, were the truth that were to rule his life opened to him in all its purity, admixed with no superstition.

But man is not immobile in relation to truth: as each individual advances in life, they, and humankind as a whole, constantly make themselves freer and freer of superstition, and they obey the truth. And therefore all people find themselves in this triple relationship with truth: some truths are already appropriated by them so as to have become the unconscious causes of their acts; others are only beginning to be revealed to them; and the third kind, although they haven't yet become appropriated, are exposed to people to such a degree of clarity that it is inevitable that they should develop a relationship toward them thus or otherwise, should acknowledge or not acknowledge them. And so, human freedom consists in either acknowledging or not acknowledging these truths.

II.

Human life advances in accordance with a single, definite, and immutable law. And it is therefore not free in general: Everyone will inevitably walk the same path of the law. There can be no life beyond this path. But the law of human life appears to people as a truth that is gradually revealed, and it can be accepted by them or not; therefore, people can walk the path of the law of life in two ways: they can either obey it of their own will, consciously and freely submitting to the law of life, or they can obey it unwittingly and unconsciously. Human freedom rests within this choice.

It is not that man can act arbitrarily regardless of the course of life and the causes that exist and exert their influence on him. But he can accept the law of life as it reveals itself to him in the form of truth in his consciousness and profess it, becoming a free and joyous fulfiller of the cause of not just his life but of the life of the whole world. Or he can refuse to accept the truth, becoming a slave of the law of life and be torturously dragged and coerced where he is not willing to go.

This freedom, within such narrow bounds, seems to people so trifling that it is not worth noticing. Some (the determinists) consider this share of freedom so infinitesimal that they reject it entirely; while others—those in support of absolute freedom—hold this seemingly trifling share of freedom in contempt by comparison with their notion of freedom.

The freedom bounded by the limits of truth, which has become an instinct, second nature, and the truth not yet exposed to the consciousness of man, the freedom that only consists of admitting a known degree of the truth that is in the process of being revealed, seems to people an unfreedom. This is all the more so because whether he wills it or not, to acknowledge the truth revealed to him man will be inevitably brought to carrying it out in his life.

The horse harnessed to a cart with other horses is unfree in that it cannot help but walk in front of the cart. And if it does not draw it, the cart will hit its hind legs, and the horse will end up walking where the cart is headed, drawing it willy-nilly. But despite this bounded freedom, the horse is free to draw the cart or be drawn along by it.

The same is true of man.

Whether this freedom is great or not compared to the fantastic freedom we would rather have, it is the sole freedom that exists and is freedom indeed. It is not enough to say that this is true freedom: it is also true life. According to the teaching of Christ, the man does not have true life who sees the meaning of life in that sphere in which it is not free, in the sphere of consequences—[his] acts, that is. Only that person has true life, according to the Christian teaching, who has transferred his life into the sphere in which it is free, into the sphere of the causes where truth is cognized and acknowledged as revealed, where this truth is professed and inevitably fulfilled (followed as inevitably as the cart follows the horse).

By staking his life in the affairs of the flesh, man commits to affairs that are always dependent on spatial and temporal causes that are external to him. This man does not even know what he is committing himself to: it only seems to him that he is the doer, but in reality all the deeds he thinks has performed are performed through him by the Supreme force;[3] he is not the master of life[4] but its slave. Yet in staking his life in the acknowledging and professing of the truth that opens up to him, he enters into a union with the source of universal life. He thus fulfills the deeds that are no longer his personal and private ones—which depend on the conditions of space and time—but the deeds which have no other cause than his own consciousness, which in themselves constitute the cause of all the rest,[5] and which have an infinite significance unbounded by anything.

The Kingdom of God is conquered by effort and only those who make the effort accede to it. Every human can and must make this effort to conquer the Kingdom: this effort consists not in external feats but only in accepting and professing the truth.

Straining one's effort to improve the conditions of life through external actions and holding the essence of true life in contempt, human beings are like those folk on a steamship that has built up plenty of steam, who wish to arrive at their destination. Instead of just running off the accumulated power of the steam, they throttle down the engine to allow the rowers to row—rowers whose oars cannot reach the water due to the tempest that is raging.

People only need to understand this: They should stop taking care of their external and general affairs in which they are unfree, and they should apply all their energy to external affairs in which they are free—to accepting and professing the truth that confronts them and to liberating themselves and others from the lies and hypocrisy that obstruct the truth. In this way, the individual

---

3   These are "performed through him by the Supreme force" ["*tvoriatsia cherez nego Vyssheiu siloi*"].

4   The Russian original phrasing is "*ne tvorets zhizni*," which usually translates as "not the creator of life," but can in this context also be rendered as "not the master of life."

5   In the original, Tolstoy wrote "*I sami sostavliaiushchie prichinu vsego ostal'nogo*," which translates as "in themselves constitute the cause of all the rest."

can achieve the highest attainable happiness, and moreover people will thereby arrive at the first stage of the Kingdom of God for which they are ready already according to [the state of] their consciousness.

46. A Letter to Alexander Macdonald about Resurrection[6] [1895]

To Alexander Macdonald. Y[asnaya] P[olyana]. July 26, 1895.[7]
Dear Sir,

You write that you wish me encouragement in my work. There is no more joyful encouragement for me, than the receiving of such letters as yours.

As for your questions, I will very gladly try to answer them as well as I can.

---

6   **Entry 46. A Letter to Alexander Macdonald about Resurrection [1895].** This is the title of the letter that I have assigned for this anthology. This is the first English translation of one of four entries in this anthology that were prepared under Tolstoy's supervision; the version that was sent to the addressee was personally corrected and authorized by Tolstoy. Like the other three entries, this letter was translated by members of Tolstoy's family and close circle whom he not only trusted but whose translation he could check, easily dispute, and change where necessary. Alexander Macdonald was a casual correspondent and is not to be confused with Greville MacDonald (1856–1944), a well-known English otolaryngologist, scholar of religion, and writer, author of *The Religious Sense in Its Scientific Aspect* (1903/1904)—a book that Tolstoy read on December 19, 1903.
The letter from Alexander Macdonald is one among hundreds that Tolstoy wrote in response to strangers, domestic and foreign, who were seeking his opinion or advice. This letter is chosen for its care, length, and detail, despite the near-anonymity of the inquirer. The response offers an exhaustive account of Tolstoy's view on the matter of the "hereafter" or "afterlife," and thus represents his eager return to earlier findings of his which survive in a few fragments from the 1870s, which are also included in this anthology. See entries 28, 29, 30, and 36. In what follows, I have only translated several paragraphs written by Tolstoy that did not make it into *The Jubilee* volume 68 where Macdonald's letter was first published. Nothing else is known of this correspondent except that he wrote to Tolstoy in English on June 12 Old Style/June 24 New style, 1895, asking Tolstoy to clarify a few questions that arose out of his reading of the following major works by the writer in English translation: *The Kingdom of God Is within You*; *What I Believe*; and short stories, such as "Where Love is, God Is."
The letter was translated into English by Tolstoy's daughter Maria Lvovna Tolstaya, and it appeared in volume 68 of *The Jubilee* in 1954 (68:123-27), edited by A. S. Petrovsky (see 68:130-31). The Russian original, which was printed next to a translation by Maria Lvovna (68:127-30), is not the final copy. The final copy sent to Macdonald must have included the corrections in Russian and English that Tolstoy made to his daughter's translation. All the variances and additions made by Tolstoy are included in my comments in the notes that follow and that supplement the annotations by A. S. Petrovsky in *The Jubilee*.

7   The address and date are written in a mix of English ("To Alexander Macdonald") and Cyrillic ("Y[asnaya] P[olyana]"). The date is written in Russian and in English: July 26, 1895.

1) I have got nothing against the usual assembling of people confessing the Christian doctrine on Sundays in halls that they call churches. But I think, that these assemblies ought not to be devoted, as they usually are, to public and uniform public prayers,[8] firstly, because the repetition on Sunday in the same words is perfectly useless, as it very soon becomes a mechanical procedure; secondly and chiefly, because in the Gospels this error is plainly pointed out and it is there definitely said (Math. VI), that one should not pray in public places, but in solitude, which is corroborated both by the reason and the experience of every man, who has ever sincerely prayed to God, as the assembly of people only distracts, makes one's thoughts wander and diverts them. I think that Sunday rest and dedication of this day to spiritual exercise may take place in the most various forms. One may suggest, that men of the same spirit, meeting together on Sunday, should bring to their meeting such religious books or articles which they find in ancient and modern literature and read and discuss them together; one may suggest, that meeting together on Sunday men of the same spirit should arrange dinners for the poor and themselves serve those dinners; one may suggest, that meeting together men of the same spirit should confess their sins to each other and discuss them. In short one can think of a hundred different forms of worship,[9] which should all have for their aim a mutual spiritual help and should not be mechanical, but sensible.

2) Do I believe in the resurrection and that there is a hereafter? I believe in true, i. e. indestructible life which Christ has disclosed to us and for the[10] which death does not exist. But this life should in no-wise be understood as a resurrection to *future* life, as a *hereafter*. One cannot

---

8   In a slightly different Russian opening, Tolstoy mentions the repetitious Sunday worship, writing the word "worship" in English. In the English translation by Maria Lvovna, he crossed out the line with a blue pencil, adding the following notation: "But I think that these assemblies should not be devoted as they usually are to common prayers that are always the same. First, because the repetition every Sunday of the same words is completely useless, very soon becoming a mechanical thing done by rote. Second, and most importantly, this delusion is pointed out directly in the Gospel where it is said distinctly (Matthew 6) that one should not pray in public places, or in meetings, but should pray in solitude. Anyone who has ever prayed to God sincerely, would know, after giving it some thought and through personal experience, that a human assembly only distracts and entertains one's reasoning" (68:130-31; my translation).

9   In the first (Russian) version, Tolstoy used the word "worship" in English, adding a Russian Genitive masculine declension through an apostrophe: *"worship'a."*

10 Sic in the original: "and for the which."

be too cautious in the use of terms for the definition of the true, indestructible, eternal life. If we were to say, that it will be a personal life, that we shall pass into other bodies or beings, as the Buddhists understand it in their metam-psychosis,[11] we should be making *a gratuitous assertion.*[12] If, on the other hand, we were to assert, that death destroys all that which composes our "ego," it would be a yet more gratuitous assertion altogether contrary to reason, for in our "ego," as in all which exists, there is a certain element, which is true and abiding. And if I accept as my "ego" this abiding element, it is evident, that that, which I consider as my "ego," will not be destroyed. The essence of Christ's teaching consists precisely in the acceptance of this abiding and indestructible element as our "ego." The chief fallacy of our judgement about the state in which we will be after death proceeds from our not being able to renounce the conception of a separate personality and the ensuing therefrom conceptions of space and time. It is the proper to every individuality, that it cannot conceive itself otherwise,[13] than in space and time. Whereas death destroys the personality and therefore destroys also the conditional conceptions of space and time, proper only to personality. And therefore when we ask: *where shall* we be after death?[14] we wrongly put the question, for we are asking: in what space and time shall we be when there will be for us no space and time? The word *"where"* expresses a demand for fixing space; the word *"shall"* a demand for fixing time. And therefore Christ's definition of life, expressed in the words: "I am the resurrection[15] and life," and "before Abraham was I am," not only is wiser and more elevated, but also much more accurately defines the true and therefore eternal life of man, than the teaching of the churches about the soul of man rising after death and going to purgatory, to heaven or to hell. According [to] Christ's teaching, true life is and therefore cannot be infringed by death. Death destroys for us only space and time and therefore those bars, which in this life limited our personality. What will this state without space and time be we cannot imagine, but according to John, Christ says: "in my Father's house are many mansions." And these

---

11 Sic. This word should be "metempsychosis."
12 The phrase was also written by Tolstoy in English in his original Russian version.
13 The punctuation of the original is preserved.
14 In this paragraph, Tolstoy highlights the words "gde," and "*bùdu*" in his original.
15 Sic. There is no capitalization.

"mansions," i.e. states other, than our own, without space and time, we cannot in this life represent to ourselves; but nevertheless [we] may be quite sure that they exist. From another point of view life cannot cease with the destruction of personality for the reason, that if in the universe there is an eternal element, which I know without myself as order and mutuality, within myself—as reason and love, this eternal element, if I take it as my "ego," cannot be destroyed by death.

3) You write: "You seem to condemn business or commerce and, in that case, if a man is so engaged, would you have him give up his business and live upon the land," which, you say, would be very pleasant, but often difficult and even impossible, especially for those who have a family. *How to steer clear of the present network which surrounds us?*[16] That is the question. To steer clear of all the temptations of the world is impossible, because every one of us has got former ties and has learnt the truth after having had time to become entangled in the seductions of the world; and these temptations hinder each of us from doing that good which we regard as our duty; but the circumstance, that we cannot altogether liberate ourselves from the temptations of the world and cannot completely fulfil the good which we regard as our duty, does not prove, that man cannot fulfil the law of Christ and do God's work. The law of Christ lies in one object—in fulfilling the will of the Father who sent us into the world. His will is, that men and beings should not be in mutual enmity, but should be united in love, "that they may be one even as we are one" . . . The only obstacle to this unity are the temptations of the world, and therefore for the attainment of this aim there is only one means: the destruction of those temptations, which separate men and all beings and leading them to enmity in the place of joy, which is proper to them, and love which is good for

---

16 In the original version of his response in Russian, Tolstoy wrote this phrase in English as stated. He also added the following in English to the margins next to Maria Lvovna's translation: "That is the question. Steer[ing] clear off [*sic*] all the seductions of the world is impossible, because every one of us," he writes, before continuing in Russian, "has pre-existing connections and has come to know the truth only after already having had time to become entangled in the temptations of the world, and these temptations prevent each of us from doing the good that we think we should do. But that we are unable to quite fulfill the good that we think we should be doing does not prove that we are unable to fulfill the law of Christ and do godly deeds. The law of Christ consists in fulfilling the will of the father" (68:131; my translation).

them.[17] What then can we do for the destruction of those tempta-tions? First of all—acknowledge, that deceit is deceit—elucidate it so that all the falsity of deceit should become evident to ourselves and to everyone. And it is necessary to do so not only independently of the fact of one's participating in it, but on the contrary with all the more energy, the more one participates in it. If I am caught in the net of deceit of state service, landownership, military service, or, as you say, commerce—the first and chief thing, which I should do is not to conceal from myself the unlawfulness[18] and sinfulness of my position; but on the contrary use all the power of my intellect in order to see it. And if such a man will bring the consciousness of the unlawfulness and sinfulness of his position to full lucidity, he will no more be able to continue the activity, which his conscience condemns. And if he be not able to continue it, he will either find means of leaving it ("where there is a will, there is a way"),[19] or, if he does not find the means, he will suffer and search for it and feel himself guilty. And this is the most advantageous state of mind for a Christian.[20]

In miracles I do not believe, because I believe in reason. One cannot believe in both, you must believe the one or the other. And I prefer to believe in reason: firstly, because reason is undoubtedly given to us by God, whereas[21] we receive miracles by hearsay, from people, who very often are not deserving of our credit, and secondly, because reason is common to all men, whilst every group of men have their own special miracles; and thirdly, because reason is convincing, whereas miracles are not. Upon this subject I have written in the detail in the introduction and notes to my translation of the Gospel, which is now published by Walter Scott.[22]—

---

17 In the original Russian, Tolstoy made a reference in English to his description of the non-Christian attitude in the same paragraph to John Ruskin: "Unto this last. J. Ruskin." He means Ruskin's *Unto This Last* (1862), his four lectures on religious economy and the "eleventh hour laborers" that provides a robust answer to Macdonald's hesitance about commerce.

18 "Unlawfullness" is how Tolstoy spells the word in the original.

19 Tolstoy wrote the phrase in English in his original Russian version.

20 A small letter is used in the original.

21 "Whereas" is in the original.

22 Walter Scott's surname alone (first name missing) is written by Tolstoy in English.

Are you acquainted with the activity of John [23]Kenworthy? He is one of the most near to me in his views and has written excellent articles about questions, which probably will interest you. (I enclose his address and a list of some of his books).

I greatly wish that my answers may satisfy you: and yet more do I wish, that you should yourself find the answers to these questions in the one and only source, from which we draw all our answers to the questions of life, namely from our heart.

Wishing you true welfare. I am, with love, yours truly.[24]

47. How Should the Gospel Be Read and Of What Does Its Essence Consist?[25] [1896]

In what is taught as the teaching of Christ, there is so much that is strange, improbable, incomprehensible, contradictory even, such that it is hard to know how to interpret it.

Moreover, this teaching does not enjoy a universal interpretation: Some say that its crux is in retribution; others that it is in grace; the third that it is all about obeying the Church. Furthermore, different Churches interpret Christ's teaching differently: for the Catholic Church, the Spirit issues from the Father and the Son, the Pope is incorruptible, and salvation is possible in the realm of acts; for the Lutheran Church, the former is not the case and salvation is

---

23 Tolstoy mistakenly abbreviated Kenworthy's first name to "G." in his Russian version of the letter. On Kenworthy, see my "Editor's Introduction" to this volume along with entries 46 and 48 of this anthology.

24 Tolstoy's original letter had "With love. Jours truly" (sic), written in English at the conclusion.

25 **Entry 47. "How Should The Gospel Be Read and Of What Does Its Essence Consist?"** [*Kak chitat' evangelie i v chem ego sushchnost'?*] (1896). Tolstoy uses the singular "Gospel" in his title. Although the Russian "*evangelie*" borrows from the Greek, the word that Tolstoy uses here instead of "*Novyi Zavet*" for "The New Testament" is usually singular, he does consider the New Testament only as a work of harmony, always making a point of exterminating any disharmonies among the evangelists, as he does precisely in this master class of close reading where the word "harmonization" is indeed present. The text of Tolstoy's instruction originally appeared in Chertkov's London publication in 1897. Here, I have translated the corrected *Jubilee* version, which was published in 1956 in volume 39 (39:113-16) and was edited by V. S. Mishin (39:241). Mishin used the latest extant version of the two original manuscripts of this note, incorporating all of Tolstoy's final corrections.

possible only through faith; and for the Orthodox Church, it is that the Spirit issues from the Father alone, and salvation requires acts and faith.

The Anglican, Episcopal, Presbyterian, and Methodist Churches—not to mention the hundreds of various other Churches—each interprets Christian teaching in its own way.

Having begun to doubt the truth of the teaching of the Church in which they are brought up, young people and common folk frequently turn to me to ask about my teaching—how do I interpret Christian teaching? Such questions always aggrieve and even offend me.

Christ is God[26]—according to the teaching of the Church—who descended to earth to reveal divine truth to guide people in life. Assuming that he desired to transmit guidance that is important to people, to guide every human—however simple and silly—, he must have been able to transmit the message in such a way that he is understood. All of a sudden, God comes down to earth with the sole purpose of saving people, and yet he somehow fails to communicate in such a way that people reach the same understanding rather than misinterpreting his words, arriving at inconsistent interpretations.

This simply can't be so if Christ were a God.

This would also suggest not just that Christ weren't a God, but that he wasn't a great teacher, either. A great teacher is great only because he is able to express the truth in such a way that it is as certain as the sun, and it is neither possible to eclipse nor darken it.

Either way, it should therefore be the truth in the gospels that communicates Christ's teaching to us. And verily so, truth is to be found in the gospels by anyone who reads them with a sincere desire to know the truth without bias, especially without thinking in the back of their mind that there is some special wisdom hidden therein that is inaccessible to the human mind.

This is the way in which I read the gospels, finding in them the truth that is accessible to infants, as it says in the gospels. And when people ask me what my teaching consists of and how I interpret Christian teaching, I answer: I have no teaching whatsoever; I interpret Christian teaching the way it is expressed in the gospels. I have written books about Christian teaching, though only in order to prove that the exegeses of the New Testament commentators are not right.

To comprehend the truth of Christian teaching, one must not interpret the gospels but understand them the way they are written. As to the question about how to interpret the teaching of Christ, I therefore answer: If you wish to understand the teaching of Christ, read the gospels; read them without bias,

---

26 Here and elsewhere in this piece, the word "God" is not capitalized in Tolstoy's original.

with the sole desire of comprehending what is said in them. But precisely because The Gospel is a holy book, it must be read thoughtfully, sensibly, with discrimination, and not haphazardly or superficially through ascribing the same significance to its every word.

To comprehend any book, it is necessary to be discerning, separating out everything that is readily comprehensible from that which is incomprehensible and tangled. One must then draw for oneself from that extrapolated clarity a notion about the meaning and spirit of the book as a whole; and on the basis of that which is fundamentally comprehensible, one should then clarify for oneself the places that are not quite comprehensible, as well as that which is tangled. This is how we read books of all sorts. It is all the more necessary to read The Gospel in this way, given that the book has passed through multiple and complex harmonizations, translations, and transcriptions, and the fact that it was drawn up 18 centuries ago by people as poorly educated as they were superstitious.**[27]

Thus, in order to understand the gospels, one must first of all single out that which one finds quite simple and clear from that which is tangled and unclear. One must then read that which one clearly understands a few times in a row, trying to absorb the meaning of that simple and clear teaching. Only then should one try to clarify for oneself, on the basis of the meaning of Christ's teaching as a whole, the meaning of those spots that previously seemed complex and uncertain. This is how I approached the gospels, and the meaning of Christ's teaching was revealed to me with such clarity, in the light of which no uncertainty could remain. I therefore advise those wishing to comprehend the true meaning of Christ's teaching to do the same.

Let everyone take a blue pencil, and during their reading of The Gospel, underline everything that appears quite simple, clear, and comprehensible to them. Then, to complement their blue pencil marks, they should use a red pencil to single out, using double underline, the words of Christ himself as distinct from the words of the evangelists. They should reread the remarks underlined in red a few times. Only after they have reached a good understanding of these spots, let them reread the rest of those passages in Christ's teachings that were left unmarked, due to the fact that the reader did not previously understand them, and let them now underline in red what has become comprehensible. They should leave unmarked those passages containing Christ's words that continue to remain completely incomprehensible, along with the unclear wording of the gospel writers. The passages in red highlight will yield the essence of

---

27 See Tolstoy's Footnote at the end of this entry 47 in the main text of the anthology.

Christ's teaching to the reader, will yield to the reader what everyone needs, and what Christ has therefore said so that everyone could understand it. The passages that are underlined in blue will yield what the gospel writers had to say of what was comprehensible to themselves.

It may very well be that while highlighting that which is quite clear as opposed to that which is not quite clear, different people will underline different things—that that which is clear for one person will seem obscure for another. But people shall see eye to eye about the most important things, which will be clear to everyone, one and the same. The things that are quite clear to everyone comprise the core of Christ's teaching.

There are highlights in my copy of The Gospel that correspond to my understanding.

Lev Tolstoy.
Yasnaya Polyana.
June 22, 1896

[**28]As is well known to anyone who has studied the genesis of these books, The Gospel is not a flawless expression of divine truth. Rather, it is the blemished, human-made product of countless hands and wits that may therefore never be accepted to be the production of the holy ghost, as the churchmen assert. If this were so, God would reveal it directly, through his own channel, the way he revealed the commandments on Mount Sinai; or he would present this book ready for people's use by means of some miracle, as for example, the Mormons claim about their holy scripture. With regards to us today, we know how these books were recorded and collected, how they were corrected and translated; and so we can therefore never accept it as uncorrupted revelation. Instead, we are obligated—as long as we respect the truth—to correct the flaws that we encounter in these books.

---

28 Tolstoy added this footnote at the conclusion of the paragraph: "To comprehend any book . . ." See the double asterisk mark "**" at the conclusion of the sentence "as they were superstitious."

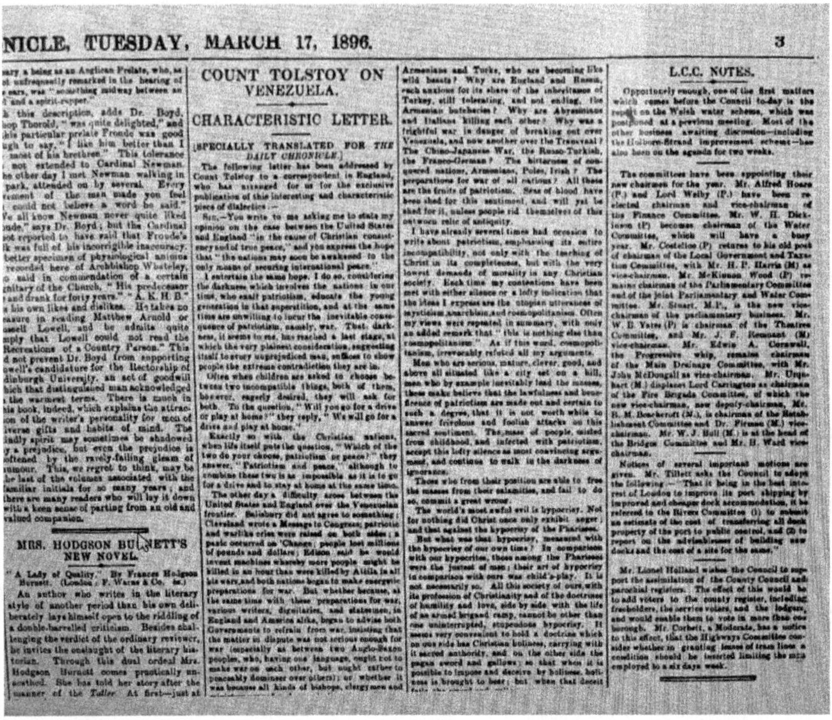

NICLE, TUESDAY, MARCH 17, 1896. 3

COUNT TOLSTOY ON VENEZUELA.

CHARACTERISTIC LETTER.

[SPECIALLY TRANSLATED FOR *THE DAILY CHRONICLE*.]

The following letter has been addressed by Count Tolstoy to a correspondent in England, who has arranged for us for the exclusive publication of this interesting and characteristic piece of dialectics :—

SIR,—You write to me asking me to state my opinion on the case between the United States and England "in the cause of Christian consistency and of true peace," and you express the hope that "the nations may soon be awakened to the only means of securing international peace."

I entertain the same hope. I do so, considering the darkness which involves the nations in our time, who exalt patriotism, educate the young generation in that superstition, and at the same time are unwilling to incur the inevitable consequence of patriotism, namely, war. That darkness, it seems to me, has reached a last stage, at which the very plainest consideration, suggesting itself to every unprejudiced man, suffices to show people the extreme contradiction they are in.

Often when children are asked to choose between two incompatible things, both of them, however, eagerly desired, they will ask for both. To the question, "Will you go for a drive or play at home?" they reply, "We will go for a drive and play at home."

Exactly so with the Christian nations, when life itself puts the question, "Which of the two do your choose, patriotism or peace?" they answer, "Patriotism and peace," although to combine these two is as impossible as it is to go for a drive and to stay at home at the same time.

The other day a difficulty arose between the United States and England over the Venezuelan frontier. Salisbury did not agree to something; Cleveland wrote a Message to Congress; patriotic and warlike cries were raised on both sides; a panic occurred on 'Change; people lost millions of pounds and dollars; Edison said he would invent machines whereby more people might be killed in an hour than were killed by Attila in all his wars, and both nations began to make energetic preparations for war. But whether because, at the same time with these preparations for war, various writers, dignitaries, and statesmen, in England and America alike, began to advise both Governments to refrain from war, insisting that the matter in dispute was not serious enough for war (especially as between two Anglo-Saxon peoples, who, having one language, ought not to make war on each other, but ought rather to peaceably domineer over others); or whether it was because all kinds of bishops, clergymen and

Armenians and Turks, who are becoming like wild beasts? Why are England and Russia, each anxious for its share of the inheritance of Turkey, still tolerating, and not ending, the Armenian butcheries? Why are Abyssinians and Italians killing each other? Why was a frightful war in danger of breaking out over Venezuela, and now another over the Transvaal? The Chino-Japanese War, the Russo-Turkish, the Franco-German? The bitterness of conquered nations, Armenians, Poles, Irish? The preparations for war of all nations? All these are the fruits of patriotism. Seas of blood have been shed for this sentiment, and will yet be shed for it, unless people rid themselves of this outworn relic of antiquity.

I have already several times had occasion to write about patriotism, emphasising its entire incompatibility, not only with the teaching of Christ in its completeness, but with the very lowest demands of morality in any Christian society. Each time my contentions have been met with either silence or a lofty indication that the ideas I express are the utopian utterances of mysticism, anarchism, and cosmopolitanism. Often my views were repeated in summary, with only an added remark that "this is nothing else than cosmopolitanism." As if this word, cosmopolitanism, irrevocably refuted all my arguments.

Men who are serious, mature, clever, good, and above all situated like a city set on a hill, men who by example inevitably lead the masses, these make believe that the lawfulness and beneficence of patriotism are made out and certain to such a degree, that it is not worth while to answer frivolous and foolish attacks on this sacred sentiment. The mass of people, misled from childhood, and infected with patriotism, accept this lofty silence as most convincing argument, and continue to walk in the darkness of ignorance.

Those who from their position are able to free the masses from their calamities, and fail to do so, commit a great wrong.

The world's most awful evil is hypocrisy. Not for nothing did Christ once only exhibit anger; and that against the hypocrisy of the Pharisees.

But what was that hypocrisy, measured with the hypocrisy of our own time? In comparison with our hypocrites, those among the Pharisees were the justest of men; their art of hypocrisy in comparison with ours was child's-play. It is not necessarily so. All this society of ours, with its profession of Christianity and of the doctrines of humility and love, side by side with the life of an armed brigand camp, cannot be other than one uninterrupted, stupendous hypocrisy. It seems very convenient to hold a doctrine which on one side has Christian holiness, carrying with it sacred authority, and on the other side the pagan sword and gallows; so that when it is possible to impose and deceive by holiness, holiness is brought to bear; but when that deceit

L.C.C. NOTES.

Opportunely enough, one of the first matters which comes before the Council to-day is the report on the Welsh water scheme, which was postponed at a previous meeting. Most of the other business awaiting discussion—including the Holborn-Strand improvement scheme—has also been on the agenda for two weeks.

The committees have been appointing their new chairmen for the year. Mr. Alfred Hoare (P.) and Lord Welby (P.) have been re-elected chairman and vice-chairman of the Finance Committee. Mr. W. H. Dickinson (P) becomes chairman of the Water Committee, which will have a busy year. Mr. Costelloe (P) returns to his old post of chairman of the Local Government and Taxation Committee, with Mr. H. P. Harris (M) as vice-chairman. Mr. McKinnon Wood (P) remains chairman of the Parliamentary Committee and of the joint Parliamentary and Water Committee. Mr. Stuart, M.P., is the new vice-chairman of the parliamentary business. Mr. W. B. Yates (P) is chairman of the Theatres Committee, and Mr. J. F. Remnant (M) vice-chairman. Mr. Edwin A. Cornwall, the Progressive whip, remains chairman of the Main Drainage Committee, with Mr. John McDougall as vice-chairman. Mr. Urquhart (M.) displaces Lord Carrington as chairman of the Fire Brigade Committee, of which the new vice-chairman, new deputy-chairman, Mr. R. M. Beachcroft (M.), is chairman of the Establishment Committee and Dr. Firman (M.) vice-chairman. Mr. W. J. Bull (M.) is at the head of the Bridges Committee and Mr. H. Ward vice-chairman.

Notices of several important motions are given. Mr. Tillett asks the Council to adopt the following :—"That it being in the best interest of London to improve its port shipping by improved and cheaper dock accommodation, it be referred to the Rivers Committee (1) to submit an estimate of the cost of transferring all dock property of the port to public control, and (2) to report on the advisableness of building new docks and the cost of a site for the same."

Mr. Lionel Holland wishes the Council to support the assimilation of the County Council and parochial registers. The effect of this would be to add voters to the county register, including freeholders, the service voters, and the lodgers, and would enable them to vote in more than one borough. Mr. Corbett, a Moderate, has a notice to this effect, that the Highways Committee consider whether in granting leases of tram lines a condition should be inserted limiting the men employed to a six days week.

...kindly spirit may sometimes be shadowed by a prejudice, but even the prejudice is softened by the rarely-failing gleam of humour. This, we regret to think, may be the last of the volumes associated with the familiar initials for so many years; and there are many readers who will lay it down with a keen sense of parting from an old and valued companion.

MRS. HODGSON BURNETT'S NEW NOVEL.

"A Lady of Quality." By Frances Hodgson Burnett. (London: F. Warne & Co. 6s.)

An author who writes in the literary style of another period than his own deliberately lays himself open to the riddling of a double-barrelled criticism. Besides challenging the verdict of the ordinary reviewer, he invites the onslaught of the literary historian. Through this dual ordeal Mrs. Hodgson Burnett comes practically unscathed. She has told her story after the manner of the *Tatler*. At first—just at

FIGURE 3. Caption for 48. "Patriotism, or Peace?" Currently known as "Patriotism, or Peace?" this text was first published in English as "Count Tolstoy on Venezuela. /Characteristic Letter/ (Specially translated for The Daily Chronicle)." The letter was published with an unsigned editorial preface: "The following letter has been addressed by Count Tolstoy to a correspondent in England, who has arranged for us for the exclusive publication of this interesting and characteristic piece of dialectics" (The Daily Chronicle and Clerkenwell News [London], Tuesday, March 17, 1896, 3). Tolstoy's letter is featured prominently in the upper right of page 3, in a two-column newspaper layout, next to reviewed biographies of British dignitaries and following the headlines and major news briefs on births, deaths, industry statistics, gallery and museum exhibitions, and stock exchange quotes in the opening two pages. Credits: The Daily Chronicle. March 17, 1896. 12 pages, one penny. Permission to reproduce page 3 granted February 2, 2022: Courtesy by The British Library Board for shelf item MFM.MLD10.

48. Patriotism, or Peace?[29]
[1896]

Sir,- You write to me asking me to state my opinion on the case between the United States and England "in the cause of Christian consistency and of true peace," and you express the hope that "the nations may soon be awakened to the only means of securing international peace."

I entertain the same hope. I do so, considering the darkness which involves the nations in our time, who exalt patriotism, educate the young generation in that superstition, and at the same time are unwilling to incur the inevitable

---

29 **Entry 48. "Patriotism, or Peace?"** [from the Russian *Patriotizm ili mir*] (1896). This is the second entry in the anthology which reprints, with minor emendations, an authorized English translation published during Tolstoy's lifetime, reproducing the text that originally appeared in the London Daily Chronicle on March 17, 1896. The story of the letter is interesting. On Christmas Eve 1895, the British journalist and editor of The Daily Chronicle John Manson asked Tolstoy to comment on the dispute between the United States and England over the spheres of influence in Venezuela and the country's gold mines and rich deposits of oil in the Guiana Highlands and Andes territories. President Grover Cleveland sent a note to London and delivered several speeches interpreting the application of the Monroe Doctrine to the quickly unfolding crisis. Manson's request arrived on the heels of Cleveland's well-known "Message Regarding Venezuelan-British Dispute," addressed to Congress on December 17, 1895. Tolstoy obliged Manson's request and quickly wrote his response in Russian as "*Patriotism ili mir*" ("Patriotism, or Peace"), signing it on January 5, 1896, in Moscow. In the meantime, John Kenworthy was on his first visit to Russia (on Kenworthy, see my "Editor's Introduction" to this volume and entries 46 and 47 in part 6 of this anthology) and happened to be passing through Petersburg just when Chertkov was headed there with Tolstoy's response in hand. The plan was to translate the article into English with Kenworthy's expert help. This is exactly how it transpired, and Tolstoy approved of the translation. Upon Kenworthy's return to London, something of a dispute broke out over Tolstoy's letter with the peace plan for Venezuela between Manson and Kenworthy. Tolstoy found a wise solution for that conflict, too, just as he had with Venezuela. Tolstoy's letter granting rights to Kenworthy for everything from Tolstoy's hand that he would be willing to translate in perpetuity placated Kenworthy into ceding the right of the first publication of "Patriotism, or Peace" to Manson. On March 17, 1896, the date of the publication in the Daily Chronicle, Manson wrote to Tolstoy thanking him for the honor and expressing regret that his dispute with Kenworthy caused discomfort to Tolstoy. Here, I have reprinted the Chertkov-Kenworthy translation version published by the Daily Chronicle. The curious backstory of this article is excellently summarized at greater length than would have been possible here in 1958 by V. S. Mishin in volume 90 of *The Jubilee* (90:360-63), which also included some of the substantial drafts of the Russian text of the article (90:163-68)—these are discussed in my introduction to this volume. However, only the Russian text by Tolstoy that formed the basis for the translation into English is published in *The Jubilee* (90:45-53). The year was 1958 and the Cold War was heating up. To my knowledge, this is the first reproduction of the accurate version from The Daily Chronicle in English since the date of its original publication in 1896.

consequence of patriotism, namely, war. That darkness, it seems to me, has reached a last stage, at which the very plainest consideration, suggesting itself to every unprejudiced man, suffices to show people the extreme contradiction they are in.

Often when children are asked to choose between two incompatible things, both of them, however, eagerly desired, they will ask for both. To the question, "Will you go for a drive or play at home?" they reply, "We will go for a drive *and* play at home."

Exactly so with the Christian nations, when life itself puts the question, "Which of the two do you choose, patriotism or peace?" they answer, "Patriotism *and* peace," although to combine these two is as impossible as it is to go for a drive and to stay at home at the same time.[30]

The other day a difficulty arose between the United States and England over the Venezuelan frontier. Salisbury did not agree to something; Cleveland wrote a Message to Congress; patriotic and warlike cries were raised on both sides; a panic occurred on 'Change;[31] people lost millions of pounds and dollars; Edison[32] said he would invent machines whereby more people might be killed in an hour than were killed by Atilla in all his wars, and both nations began to make energetic preparations for war. But whether because, at the same time with these preparations for war, various writers, dignitaries, and statesmen, in England and America alike, began to advise both Governments to refrain from war, insisting that the matter in dispute was not serious enough for war (especially as between two Anglo-Saxon peoples, who, having one language, ought not to make war on each other, but ought rather to peaceably domineer over others); or whether it was because all kinds of bishops, clergymen and ministers prayed and preached on the subject in the churches; or because both sides considered themselves unprepared—at all event it has fallen out that this time there will be no war, and people have calmed down.

But one would be deficient in perspicacity not to see that the causes which led to this difficulty between England and America remain the same; and that

---

30 These are very much the overtones of Grover Cleveland's address to the United States Congress. See my "Editor's Introduction" to this volume.

31 Stock Exchange is meant.

32 Tolstoy is referencing the famous inventor Thomas Edison (1847–1931). Edison would surely have been aware of this criticism in such a high-profile international forum. If he missed it in the Daily Chronicle, then he is likely to have caught it in central American newspapers, which tended to reprint Tolstoy's new articles from the British press. This makes Edison's gift to Tolstoy in 1908 of a phonograph and his invitation to the writer to make recordings of his philosophical thoughts all the more remarkable. On Tolstoy, Edison, and the benefits of philosophy for life, see my "Editor's Introduction" to this volume.

though this difficulty be settled without war, yet inevitably, to-morrow or next day, other difficulties will arise between England and America, or England and Germany, or England and Russia, or England and Turkey. Some one of these numberless possible situations, as they daily arise, must inevitably precipitate war.

For if two armed men live side by side, who have from childhood been taught that power, wealth, and glory are the highest distinctions, and that therefore to gain these by arms at the expense of their neighbors[33] is most praiseworthy; and if, further, these people acknowledge no moral, religious or political limitation—then is it not evident that such people will consistently wage war; that their normal inter-relations will be war; and that if, having flown at each other's throats, they have separated for a time, it is only, as the French proverb has it, "pour mieux sauter,"[34] that is, they draw back to take a better leap, to rush upon each other with the greater ferocity?

Terrible as is the egoism of individuals, the egotists of private life are yet not armed, they do not think well to prepare or to use arms against their rivals; their selfishness is controlled by the powers of the State and of public opinion. A private individual who should, with weapons in his hands, deprive his neighbor of a cow or an acre of field, would be at once seized by the police and imprisoned. More than this, he would be condemned by public opinion; he would be called a thief and a robber. With States it is quite otherwise. All of them are armed; power over them there is none—more than is exerted in those ludicrous attempts to catch the bird by sprinkling salt on its tail in these efforts to establish international congresses, which evidently never will be acknowledged by the powerful States (armed, forsooth, to be independent of advice). And what is more important still is that the public opinion which condemns every act of violence by the private individual, praises, extols as the virtue of patriotism every appropriation of other people's property made with the view of advancing the power of one's own country.

Open the newspapers at any time you choose, and you will see always some black spot, a possible cause of war. At one time it is Korea, at another time the Pamirs, Africa, Abyssinia, Armenia, Turkey, Venezuela, or the Transvaal. The work pf brigandage does not cease for a moment; now here, now there, some

---

33 Here and throughout, I have changed British spellings—e.g., "neighbour," "skilful" to contemporary American English. The capitalization pattern that Tolstoy approved for this translation in The Daily Chronicle has been left intact.

34 Here, Tolstoy is referencing the French idiom, "[il faut] reculer pour mieux sauter," meaning "one must take a step back in order to better jump."

small war is always waging: like skirmishing in the front lines. A great, real war may begin at any moment: must begin.

If the American desires the greatness and prosperity of the States before all other nations, if the Englishman desires the same for his nation and likewise the Russian, Turk, Dutchman, Abyssinian, Venezuelan, Boor, Armenian, Pole, Czech; if all of them are convinced that these desires ought not to be concealed and suppressed, but rather to be gloried in and encouraged in oneself and others; and seeing that the greatness and prosperity of one country or nation cannot be obtained except at the expense of another, or it may be of many others—if all this is fact, then how can war fail to be?

Obviously, to prevent war, it is not necessary to preach sermons and pray God for peace, not to adjure the English-speaking nations to keep the peace with each other in order that they may domineer over other nations, nor to make double and triple alliances of nations against each other, nor to inter-marry Princes and Princesses of different nations; but it is necessary to destroy the cause of war. That cause is the desire for the exclusive welfare of one's own people; it is called patriotism. Therefore to destroy war patriotism must be destroyed. But to destroy patriotism the conviction that it is an evil must first be established, and this is difficult to do. Tell people that war is evil and they will laugh at you, for who does not know this? Tell them that patriotism is evil, and the majority will agree, but with some reserve. "Yes, there is an evil patriotism which is undesirable, but there is another and good patriotism, that which we hold." But what this good patriotism is no one explains. If its character is unaggressiveness,[35] as many say, nevertheless all patriotism, even if "unaggressive," must remain "retentive." That is, people must wish to keep their former conquests. Now that nation does not exist which was established without conquest; and conquests can only be held by the means which effected them—namely, violence, murder. But if patriotism cease to be even retentive, then it can only be the "rehabilitative" patriotism of conquered, oppressed nations—of the Armenians, Poles, Czechs, Irish, and so on. And this kind of patriotism is perhaps the very worst, because most embittered and most calling for violence.

Patriotism cannot be good. Why not as well say that selfishness is good? This proposition, indeed, might be more easily maintained, because selfishness is a natural instinct, born in man, whilst patriotism is an artificial feeling engrafted on him.

It will be said: "Patriotism has united men into States, and is the bond of States." But men have by now formed themselves into States, the process

---

35 Sic: in the original.

is accomplished; why then should we still maintain the exclusive devotion to one's own State, when this produces terrible evils for all States and peoples? The same patriotism which produced States is now destroying them. If there were but one patriotism, say that of the English only, it would be possible to deem it unifying and beneficent; but when, as now, there is American patriotism, English, German, French, Russian, all opposed to each other, patriotism no longer unites, but disunites. To say that patriotism was beneficent, unifying, when it flourished in Greece and Rome, and that therefore it is still equally so, despite our 1800 years of Christianity, is as much as to say that because ploughing the field was good and useful before sowing, it is as much so now, when the crop is rising.

It might be well, indeed, to maintain patriotism as a memento of the benefit it once brought to man, just as we preserve ancient monuments, temples, tombs, and so on. But those last continue to stand without doing any harm; while patriotism ceases not to cause immeasurable calamities.

Why these sufferings, these massacres, among Armenians and Turks, who are becoming like wild beasts? Why are England and Russia, each anxious for its share of the inheritance of Turkey, still tolerating, and not ending, the Armenian butcheries? Why are Abyssinians and Italians killing each other? Why was a frightful war in danger of breaking out over Venezuela, and now another over the Transvaal? The Chino-Japanese War, the Russo-Turkish, the Franco-German? The bitterness of conquered nations, Armenians, Poles, Irish? The preparations for war of all nations? All these are the fruits of patriotism. Seas of blood have been shed for this sentiment, and will yet be shed for it, unless people rid themselves of this outworn relic of antiquity.

I have already several times had occasion to write about patriotism, emphasizing its entire incompatibility, not only with the teaching of Christ in its completeness, but with the very lowest demands of morality in any Christian society. Each time my contentions have been met with either silence or a lofty indication that the ideas I express are the utopian utterances of mysticism, anarchism, and cosmopolitanism. Often my views were repeated in summary, with only an added remark that "this is nothing else than cosmopolitanism." As if this word, cosmopolitanism, irrevocably refuted all my arguments.

Men who are serious, mature, clever, good, and above all situated like a city set on a hill, men who by example inevitably lead the masses, these make believe that the lawfulness and beneficence of patriotism are made out? and certain to such a degree, that it is not worth while[36] to answer frivolous and foolish

---

36 Sic: "Worth while" is the spelling found in the original English translation.

attacks on this sacred sentiment. The mass of people, misled from childhood, and infected with patriotism, accept this lofty silence as most convincing argument, and continue to walk in the darkness of ignorance.

Those who from their position are able to free the masses from their calamities, and fail to do so, commit a great wrong.

The world's most awful evil is hypocrisy. Not for nothing did Christ once only exhibit his anger; and that against the hypocrisy of the Pharisees.

But what was that hypocrisy, measured with the hypocrisy of our own time? In comparison with our hypocrites, those among the Pharisees were the justest of men; their art of hypocrisy in comparison with ours was child's play. It is not necessarily so. All the society of ours, with its profession of Christianity and of the doctrines of humility and love, side by side with the life of an armed brigand camp, cannot be other than one uninterrupted, stupendous hypocrisy. It seems very convenient to hold a doctrine which on one side has Christian holiness, carrying with it sacred authority, and on the other side the pagan sword and gallows; so that when it is possible to impose and deceive by holiness, holiness is brought to bear; but when that deceit fails, the sword and gallows are set in motion. Such a doctrine seems very convenient; but a time comes when this tissue of lies breaks asunder and it becomes impossible to keep up both sides; one or the other must be held to. This event is at hand with respect to the doctrine of patriotism.

Whether mankind wish it or not, the question stands early in front of them—*How can this patriotism, from which proceed human sufferings incalculable, both physical and moral, be needful and a virtue?* This question must perforce be answered.

Hither it must be shown that patriotism is so great a blessing as to recompense all the sufferings it inflicts on mankind, or it must be acknowledged that patriotism is evil; not to be grafted into people, drilled into them, but, instead, to be struggled against for deliverance with all our powers.

C'est à prendre ou à laisser,[37] as the French say. If patriotism is good, then Christianity, which gives peace, is an empty dream, and the sooner we root out the Christian doctrine the better. But if Christianity really has peace in gift, and we really desire peace, then patriotism appears as a survival of barbarism, which must not be excited and cultivated as now, but exterminated in every way, by preaching, persuasion, contempt, ridicule. If Christianity is truth, and we wish to live in peace, then. not only must we not desire power for our nation, but we must rejoice at the weakening of that power, and further its

---

37 Here, Tolstoy uses the French "*c'est à prendre ou à laisser,*" meaning "take it or leave it."

weakening. A Russian should be glad for the separation, freeing, of Poland, the Baltic Provinces, Finland, Armenia; and an Englishman should rejoice likewise for Ireland, India, and other possessions, and should help their liberation, because the greater the State the profounder and more cruel is its patriotism, and the greater the amount of suffering upon which its power is built. Therefore, if we really would live up to our professions, we must not desire the growth of the State we live under, but we must seek its diminution, its weakening, and help towards this with all our power. And in this faith we must educate the rising generation, educate them so that, just as now a young man is ashamed to betray coarse selfishness (as, for instance, by eating everything, and leaving nothing for others, by pushing aside the weak to make his own way, or by forcibly taking what another needs), so, then, he shall be equally ashamed to desire the growth of his own country's power. And just as it is now considered stupid, ridiculous to praise oneself, it shall then be considered equally foolish to praise one's own nation in the style of divers of the best national histories, pictures, monuments, textbooks, essays, verses, sermons, and silly "national hymns." Let us understand that so long as we praise patriotism and cultivate it in the young, so long we shall have militarism, destroying the physical and moral life of nations, producing wars, calamitous, awful wars, such as we are making ready for, and into the circle of which we are now drawing, while debasing them in our patriotic interests, now and to-be-dreaded combatants from the Far East.

The Emperor William, one of the most comic personages of our time— orator, poet, musician, dramatist and painter, above all, a patriot—lately made a sketch showing all the nations of Europe, armed with swords, standing on the sea-shore, and gazing, directed by the Archangel Michael, at figures of Buddha and Confucius, seated in the distance.[38] In William's intention, this signifies that the nations of Europe must unite to oppose the danger moving upon them from the direction shown. He is perfectly right, from his own—these eighteen centuries obsolete—pagan, gross, patriotic point of view.

The nations of Europe, having forgotten Christ for the sake of patriotism, have ever more and more aroused and stimulated patriotism and war in these peaceful peoples of the East; and now they have as much provoked them that

---

38 "Emperor William" is the anglicized name of Kaiser Wilhelm II, "King of Prussia" and the last German Emperor (1888–1918). During his rule, Kaiser Wilhelm's drawings exhorting the Western nations to defend their holiest possessions from what he infamously labeled "The Yellow Peril" inundated Anglo-American and European periodicals. Tolstoy alludes to the infamous cartoon of 1895 that provoked numerous counter-cartoons in publications such as *Harper's Weekly*, *Le Petit Journal*, and *Punch*, *Puck* depicting Wilhelm as Archangel Michael, Confucius, as well as in more ignoble, satirical representations.

really, if only Japan and China forget the teachings of Buddha and Confucius as completely as we forget the teaching of Christ, they will ere long master the art of killing, which is quickly learned, Japan to witness. And being brave, skillful, strong, and numerous, they cannot be prevented from doing with the countries of Europe (unless Europe can oppose something more effective than armaments and the devices of Edison)[39] what the countries of Europe are doing with Africa. "The disciple is not above his master, but every one that is perfect shall be his master."

To this question of a small king, as to how many, and in what way, he should add to his troops, in order to vanquish a tribe in the south which had not submitted to him, Confucius replied, "Disband all the army, use what thou now spendest on troops to educate thy people and to improve agriculture; and the tribe in the south will drive out its king, and without war, will submit to thy authority."

Thus Confucius taught: he whom we are advised to fear. While we, having forgotten Christ's teaching, having renounced Him, wish to subdue nations by force: thereby only preparing for ourselves new enemies still more powerful than our neighbors are.

A friend of mine, having seen William's picture, said: "The picture is excellent. Only it does not at all signify what is written beneath. It really means that the Archangel Michael is pointing out to all the Governments of Europe, represented as brigands hung round with weapons, that which will destroy, annihilate them: namely, the meekness of Buddha and the reasonableness of Confucius." He might have added, "And the humility of Lao-Tzu."[40] Indeed, thanks to our hypocrisy, we have so far forgotten Christ, and corroded out of our lives all that is Christian, that the teaching of Buddha and Confucius stand incomparably higher than that bestial patriotism which guides our pseudo-Christian nations.

The salvation of Europe and the Christian world comes not of their being girt with swords, like brigands, as William has represented them: not of their rushing to kill their brethren across the sea: but, to the contrary, it will come of their renouncing that survival of barbarism, patriotism, and in this renunciation, disarming: to show the Oriental nations an example no more of savage patriotism and ferocity, but of that brotherly life taught to us by Christ.

LEO TOLSTOY.

---

39 The inventions of Thomas Edison are implied. "The disciple is not above his master, but every one that is perfect shall be his master" is an extract from the Gospel of Luke 6:40 that Tolstoy quotes to upturn the absurdities of "the little king" Kaiser Wilhelm.

40 In this volume, I have changed the spelling of "Lao-Tse" (as found in The Daily Chronicle publication) to "Lao-Tzu."

49. Preface to *Modern Science* by Edward Carpenter[41]
[1897–98]

I think this article of Carpenter's on Modern Science should be particularly useful in Russian society, in which, more than in any other in Europe, a superstition is prevalent and deeply rooted which considers that humanity for its welfare does not need the diffusion of true religious and moral knowledge, but only the study of experimental science, and that such science will satisfy all the spiritual demands of mankind.

---

41 **Entry 49. "Preface to *Modern Science* by Edward Carpenter"** [*Predislovie k stat'e Eduarda Karpentera "Sovremennaia nauka"*] (1897–98). This is the third entry in the anthology which reprints, with minor emendations, an authorized English translation published during Tolstoy's lifetime, reproducing the text that Tolstoy authorized for publication as "Modern Science" in Aylmer Maude's *Essays and Letters by Count Leo Tolstoy*, translated by Aylmer Maude (London: Grant Richards/Henry Frowde, 1903), which was reprinted by New York's Funk and Wagnalls in 1904. I use the latter edition, in accordance with Tolstoy's general preference for copyright-free dissemination of his views: *Essays and Letters by Count Leo Tolstoy*, translated by Aylmer Maude (New York's Funk and Wagnalls, 1904), 219-29. Tolstoy acknowledged the translation, expressing his thanks and approval to Maude on December 11, 1903, from Yasnaya Polyana: "Thanks to you, Maude, my dear friend, for sending the book of *Essays* to me. It is very well edited" (74:256). A copy of the book (*Essays and Letters* by Leo Tolstoy, trans. Aylmer Maude [London: Henry Frowde, 1903]) may be found in Tolstoy's personal library at Yasnaya Polyana (*Biblioteka Tolstogo* 3 [2], 446). After receiving from Maude a copy from Funk and Wagnalls of Aylmer Maude, *A Peculiar People: The Doukhobors* (New York: Funk and Wagnalls, 1904), on January 31, 1905, Tolstoy wrote to Maude to share his admiration for Carpenter, perhaps prompted by the name of the publisher to make this connection: "I am swept by admiration" (75:214) for "Edw. Carpenter's *Civilization, Its Cause and Cure* [. . .] I knew only 'Modern Science' from what's there between the covers," calling Carpenter "a worthy heir to Carlyle and Ruskin" and asking Maude to send him more information about the author (ibid.).
Maude added this note to his translation: "Written as preface to a Russian translation, by Count Sergius Tolstoy, of Edward Carpenter's essay, *Modern Science: A Criticism: Its Cause and Cure*, published by Swan Sonnenschein and Co." (Maude, *Essays and Letters*, 219). "Sergius Tolstoy" was Tolstoy's elder child Sergey Lvovich (1863–1947), who was a graduate of the Mathematical and Physics Faculty of the University of Moscow in 1886, where he worked under the guidance of the legendary chemist Dmitry Mendeleev.
Edward Carpenter (1844–1929) was a prolific, polymathic—and Bohemian—socialist thinker raised in the late Victorian era who also wrote poetry and drama. His interest in *eros* was arguably as strong as his interest in industrial freedom, the two topics on which his works frequently focused. It is not a given that Tolstoy chose to comment on this recent volume by Carpenter. They are very different in most important respects. However, Carpenter's warnings against the spuriousness in the condition of the scientific animal who is playing his "games of the intellect around phenomena" and does not notice his losing the intrinsic connection to the eternal certainly appealed to Tolstoy. Here, I am quoting from a comparable edition that was available to Tolstoy in 1896: Edward Carpenter, *Modern Science: A Criticism* (London: John Heywood, 1885), 74.

It is evident how harmful an influence (quite like that of religious superstition) so gross a superstition must have on men's moral life. And, therefore, the publication of the thoughts of writers who treat experimental science and its method critically is specially desirable in our society.

Neither Tolstoy nor Maude nor Sergey Lvovich had any intention of "prefacing the Preface"—so to speak—with a rather unfitting epigraph from Sextus Empiricus's adage from his outlines of Pyrrhonism, *panti logos (logos) isos antikeitai,* "To every argument an equal argument is opposed," which Maude translated as "To every argument an equal argument is matched" (*Essays and Letters* [1904, 219]). The original Latin phrasing was transposed and back translated into Greek to underscore the relation of Sextus Empiricus to Diogenes by generations of more pretentious sophists. In the nineteenth century, the practice received a revival through an influential dissertation by Immanuel Bekker, *Sextus Empiricus* (Berlin: Reimer, 1842), with the author's preface in Latin and the main text in ancient Greek. Carpenter's flamboyant side is evident by his peppering his "Modern Science" with short Greek quotes, but this quote from Sextus Empiricus disappeared from later editions of the essay.

None other than John Kenworthy supplied Tolstoy with Carpenter's *Civilization: Its Cause and Cure and Other Essays* in 1896, which included "Modern Science" at Carpenter's own request. Tolstoy called it "fabulous" in his diary on October 23, 1896 (53:115). How did the epigraph end up being in the essay? From 1894 onward, Tolstoy was often pestered with requests for new contributions by a rather ostentatious St. Petersburg journal, *The Northern Messenger* (*Severnyi Vestnik*), which was then run by two assimilated Russian Jews, Liubov Gurevich and Akim Volynsky (Flekser). Tolstoy sympathized with the editors and asked Sergey Lvovich to translate "Modern Science" into Russian for the journal to publish it. That was not good enough for the editors, who wanted Tolstoy to provide a preface as the cherry on top. Over Sophia Andreevna's vehement protests and after long delays, Tolstoy did write the preface, which was published, with errors, on March 1, 1898 (199-206). As if this were not bad enough, Sergey Lvovich refused to be listed on the translation and the journal editors credited Tolstoy as the party responsible both for the translation and the preface.

In corrected form, Tolstoy's "Preface" was published by *The Jubilee* in volume 31, which came out in 1954 and was edited by N. V. Gorbachev, L. P. Grossman, and V. S. Mishin (31:87-95). N.V. Gorbachev provided the description of the manuscripts (31:282-85). *The Jubilee* editors removed the Sextus Empiricus epigraph from the text.

There is a later edition of *Civilization: Its Cause and Cure* in Tolstoy's personal library at Yasnaya Polyana that came out through the London-/New York-based Swan Sonnenschein and Charles Scribner's in 1903. There are four other books by Carpenter in Tolstoy's personal library: *Angel's Wings: A Series of Essays on Art and Its Relation to Life* (London and New York: Macmillan/William Brendon, 1899); *Prisons, Police, and Punishment: An Inquiry into the Causes and Treatment of Crime and Criminals* (London: Arthur C. Fifield, 1905); *Towards Democracy.* 3rd ed (London: T. Fisher Unwin, 1892), which includes a handwritten dedication to Tolstoy in Carpenter's writing; and the Russian translation by Tolstoy's follower Ivan Nazhivin of *Civilization: Its Cause and Cure* [no date]. See *Biblioteka Tolstogo* 1, no. 1, 343, 3, 202-4. Tolstoy included selections from Carpenter's works in his editions of several of his wisdom readers, including *The Path of Life.* For details on these selections, see *The Jubilee* (41:548; 42:194; 43:185, 284; 45:195, 398).

Carpenter shows that neither Astronomy, nor Physics, nor Chemistry, nor Biology, nor Sociology, supplies us with true knowledge of actual facts; that all the laws discovered by those sciences are merely generalizations, having but an approximate value as laws, and that only as long as we do not know, or leave out of account, certain other factors ; and that even these laws seem laws to us only because we discover them in a region so far away from us in time and space that we cannot detect their non-correspondence with actual fact.

Moreover, Carpenter points out that the method of science, which consists in explaining things near and important to us by things more remote and indifferent, is a false method which can never bring us to the desired result.

He says that every science tries to explain the facts it is investigating by means of conceptions of a lower order: "Each science has been (as far as possible) reduced to its lowest terms. Ethics has been made a question of utility and inherited experience. Political Economy has been exhausted of all conceptions of justice between man and man, of charity, affection, and the instinct of solidarity; and has been founded on its lowest discoverable factor, namely self-interest. Biology has been denuded of the force of personality in plants, animals, and men; the 'self' here has been set aside, and the attempt made to reduce the science to a question of chemical and cellular affinities, protoplasm, and the laws of osmosis. Chemical affinities, again, and all the wonderful phenomena of Physics are emptied down into a flight of atoms; and the flight of atoms (and of astronomic orbs as well) is reduced to the laws of dynamics."

It is supposed that the reduction of questions of a higher order to questions of a lower order will explain the former. But an explanation is never obtained in this way, and what happens is merely that, descending in one's investigations ever lower and lower, from the most important questions to less important ones, science reaches at last a sphere quite foreign to man, with which he is barely in touch, and confines its attention to that sphere, leaving all unsolved the questions most important to him.

What takes place is as if a man, wishing to understand the use of an object lying before him—instead of coming close to it, examining it from all sides and handling it—were to retire further and further from it, until he was at such a distance from the object that all its peculiarities of color[42] and inequalities of surface had disappeared, and only its outline was still visible against the horizon; and as if, from there, he were to begin writing a minute description of the object,

---

42 Here and throughout, I have changed the spellings of "colour," "neighbour," "skilful," "labour" to bring them into conformity with contemporary American English and in compliance with the style of this volume.

imagining that now, at last, he clearly understood it, and that this understanding, formed at such a distance, would assist a complete comprehension of it.

And it is this self-deception that is partly exposed by Carpenter's criticism, which shows, first, that the knowledge afforded us by the natural sciences amounts merely to convenient generalizations, which certainly do not express actual facts; and, secondly, that the method of science by which facts of a higher order are reduced to facts of a lower order, will never furnish us with an explanation of the former.

But without predetermining the question whether experimental science will, or will not, by its methods, ever bring us to the solution of the most serious problems of human life, the activity of experimental science itself, in its relation to the eternal and most reasonable demands of man, is so anomalous as to amaze one.

People must live. But in order to live they must know how to live. And all men always obtained this knowledge—well or ill—and in conformity with it have lived, and progressed; and this knowledge of how men should live has from the days of Moses, Solon, and Confucius been always considered a science—the very essence of science. And only in our time has it come to be considered that the science telling us how to live, is not a science at all, but that only experimental science—commencing with Mathematics and ending in Sociology—is real science.

And a strange misunderstanding results.

A plain, reasonable working man supposes, in the old way which is also the common-sense way, that if there are people who spend their lives in study, whom he feeds and keeps while they think for him—then no doubt these men are engaged in studying things men need to know; and he expects of science that it will solve for him the questions on which his welfare, and that of all men, depends. He expects science to tell him how he ought to live: how to treat his family, his neighbors and the men of other tribes, how to restrain his passions, what to believe in and what not to believe in, and much else. And what does our science say to him on these matters?

It triumphantly tells him: how many million miles it is from the earth to the sun; at what rate light travels through space; how many million vibrations of ether per second are caused by light, and how many vibrations of air by sound; it tells of the chemical components of the Milky Way, of a new element—helium—of micro-organisms and their excrements, of the points on the hand at which electricity collects, of X rays, and similar things.

"But I don't want any of those things," says a plain and reasonable man—"I want to know how to live."

"What does it matter what you want?" replies science. "What you are asking about relates to Sociology. Before replying to sociological questions, we have yet to solve questions of Zoology, Botany, Physiology, and, in general, of Biology; but to solve those questions we have first to solve questions of Physics, and then of Chemistry, and have also to agree as to the shape of the infinitesimal atoms, and how it is that imponderable and incompressible ether transmits energy."

And people— chiefly those who sit on the backs of others, and to whom it is therefore convenient to wait—are content with such replies, and sit blinking, awaiting the fulfilment of these promises; but a plain and reasonable working man—such as those on whose backs these others sit while occupying themselves with science—the whole great mass of men, the whole of humanity, cannot be satisfied by such answers, but naturally ask in perplexity: "But when will this be done? We cannot wait. You say yourselves[43] that you will discover these things after some generations. But we are alive now—alive to-day and dead to-morrow—and we want to know how to live our life while we have it. So teach us!"

"What a stupid and uneducated man!" replies Science. "He does not understand that science exists not for use, but for science. Science studies whatever presents itself for study, and cannot select the subjects to be studied. Science studies everything. That is the characteristic of science."

And scientists are really convinced that to be occupied with trifles, while neglecting what is more essential and important, is a characteristic not of themselves, but of science. The plain, reasonable man, however, begins to suspect that this characteristic pertains not to science, but to men who are inclined to occupy themselves with trifles and to attach great importance to those trifles.

"Science studies *everything*,"[44] say the scientists. But, really, everything is too much. Everything is an infinite quantity of objects; it is impossible at one and the same time to study all. As a lantern cannot light up *everything*, but only lights up the place on which it is turned or the direction in which the man carrying it is walking, so also science cannot study *everything*, but inevitably only studies that to which its attention is directed. And as a *lantern* lights up most strongly the place nearest to it, and less and less strongly objects that are more and more remote from it, and does not at all light up those things its light does not reach, so also human science, of whatever kind, has always studied and still

---

43 (Sic): In the original, the particle "to" is missing from the phrase: "You say to yourselves." The phrase means, in somewhat dated British English, "You are yourselves saying" or "You are the ones who are saying," etc.

44 The term *vsé* ("everything") is highlighted by Tolstoy in the original of the preface.

studies most carefully what seems most important to the investigators, less carefully what seems to them less important, and quite neglects the whole remaining infinite quantity of objects.

And what for men has defined and still defines the subjects they are to consider most important, less important, and unimportant, is the general understanding of the meaning and purpose of life (that is to say, the religion) possessed by those who occupy themselves with science. But men of science to-day—not acknowledging any religion, and having therefore no standard by which to choose the subjects most important for study, or to discriminate them from less important subjects and, ultimately, from that infinite quantity of objects which the limitations of the human mind, and the infinity of the number of those objects, will always cause to remain uninvestigated—have formed for themselves a theory of "science for science's sake" according to which science is to study not what mankind needs, but everything.

And, indeed, experimental science studies everything, not in the sense of the totality of objects, but in the sense of disorder—chaos in the arrangement of the objects studied.

That is to say, science does not devote most attention to what people most need, less to what they need less, and none at all to what is quite useless, but it studies anything that happens to come to hand. Though Comte's and other classifications of the sciences exist,[45] these classifications do not govern the selection of subjects for study, but that selection is dependent on the human weaknesses common to men of science as well as to the rest of mankind. So that, in reality, scientists study not everything, as they imagine and declare, but they study what is more profitable and easier to study. And it is more profitable to study things that conduce to the well-being of the upper classes, with whom the men of science are connected; and it is easier to study things that lack life. Accordingly, many men of science study books, monuments, and inanimate bodies.

Such study is considered the most real "science." So that in our day what is considered to be the most real "science," the only one (as the Bible was considered the only book worthy of the name), is, not the contemplation and investigation of how to make the life of man more kindly and more happy, but the compilation and copying from many books into one of all that our predecessors wrote on a certain subject, the pouring of liquids out of one glass bottle

---

45 Tolstoy must be referring to Auguste Comte's complicated tabulation of human knowledge in the four volumes of his *System of Positive Polity* (*Système de politique positive*, 1851–54), which posits primary distinctions between religion, metaphysics, science, and the evolutionary scale on which human knowledge elevates itself in the modern age.

into another, the skillful slicing of microscopic preparations, the cultivation of bacteria, the cutting up of frogs and dogs, the investigation of X rays, the theory of numbers, the chemical composition of the stars, etc.

Meanwhile all those sciences which aim at making human life kindlier and happier—religious, moral, and social science—are considered by the dominant science to be unscientific, and are abandoned to the theologians, philosophers, jurists, historians, and political economists; who, under the guise of scientific investigation, are chiefly occupied in demonstrating that the existing order of society (the advantages of which they enjoy) is the very one which ought to exist, and that, therefore, it must not only not be changed, but must be maintained by all means.

Not to mention Theology and Jurisprudence, Political Economy, the most advanced of the sciences of this group, is remarkable in this respect. The most prevalent Political Economy (that of Karl Marx), accepting the existing order of life as though it were what it ought to be, not only does not call on men to alter that order—that is to say, does not point out to them how they ought to live that their condition may improve—but, on the contrary, it demands an increase in the cruelty of the existing order of things, that its more-than-questionable predictions may be fulfilled, concerning what will happen if people continue to live as badly as they are now living.

And, as always occurs, the lower a human activity descends—the more widely it diverges from what it should be—the more its self-confidence increases. That is just what has happened with the science of to-day.

True science is never appreciated by its contemporaries, but on the contrary is usually persecuted. Nor can this be otherwise. True science shows men their mistakes, and points to new, unaccustomed ways of life. And both these services are unpleasant to the ruling section of society. But present-day science not only does not run counter to the tastes and demands of the ruling section of society, but it quite complies with them: it satisfies idle curiosity, excites people's wonder, and promises them increase of pleasure. And so, whereas all that is truly great is calm, modest and unnoticed, the science of to-day knows no limits to its self-laudation.

"All former methods were erroneous, and all that used to be considered science was an imposture, a blunder, and of no account. Only our method is true, and the only true science is ours. The success of our science is such that thousands of years have not done what we have accomplished in the last century. In the future, travelling the same path, our science will solve all questions, and make all mankind happy. Our science is the most important activity in the world, and we, men of science, are the most important and necessary people in the world."

So think and say the scientists of to-day, and the cultured crowd echo it, but really at no previous time and among no people has science—the whole of science with all its knowledge—stood on so low a level as at present. One part of it, which should study the things that make human life kind and happy, is occupied in justifying the existing evil order of society; another part is engaged in solving questions of idle curiosity.

"What? —Idle curiosity?" I hear voices ask in indignation at such blasphemy. "What about steam, and electricity, and telephones, and all our technical improvements? Not to speak of their scientific importance, see what practical results they have produced! Man has conquered Nature and subjugated its forces . . ." with more to the same effect.

"But all the practical results of the victories over Nature have till now—for a considerable time past — gone to factories that injure the workmen's health; have produced weapons to kill men with, and increased luxury and corruption" — replies a plain, reasonable man — "and, therefore, the victory of man over Nature has not only failed to increase the welfare of human beings, but has, on the contrary, made their condition worse."

If the arrangement of society is bad (as ours is), and a small number of people have power over the majority and oppress it, every victory over Nature will inevitably only serve to increase that power and that oppression. That is what is actually happening.

With a science which aims not at studying how people ought to live, but at studying whatever exists — and which is therefore occupied chiefly in investigating inanimate things while allowing the order of human society to remain as it is — no improvements, no victories over Nature, can better the state of humanity.

"But medical science? You are forgetting the beneficent progress made by medicine. And bacteriological inoculations? And recent surgical operations?" exclaim the defenders of science, — adducing as a last resource the success of medical science to prove the utility of all science. "By inoculations we can prevent illness, or can cure it; we can perform painless operations: cut open a man's inside and clean it out, and can straighten hunched-backs," is what is usually said by the defenders of present-day science, who seem to think that the curing of one child from diphtheria, among those Russian children of whom 50 percent, (and even 80 percent, in the Foundling Hospitals) die as a regular thing apart from diphtheria — must convince anyone of the beneficence of science in general.

Our life is so arranged that from bad food, excessive and harmful work, bad dwellings and clothes, or from want, not children only, but a majority of people, die before they have lived half the years that should be theirs. The order of things is such that children's illnesses, consumption, syphilis and alcoholism seize an ever-increasing number of victims, while a great part of men's labor is taken from them to prepare for wars, and every ten or twenty years millions of men are slaughtered in wars; and all this because science, instead of supplying correct religious, moral and social ideas, which would cause these ills to disappear of themselves, is occupied on the one hand in justifying the existing order, and on the other hand—with toys. And, in proof of the fruitfulness of science, we are told that it cures one in a thousand of the sick, who are sick only because science has neglected its proper business.

Yes, if science would devote but a small part of those efforts, and of that attention and labor which it now spends on trifles, to supplying men with correct religious, moral, social, or even hygienic ideas, there would not be a one-hundredth part of the diphtheria, the diseases of the womb, or the deformities, the occasional cure of which now makes science so proud, though they are effected in clinical hospitals, the cost of whose luxurious appointments is too great for them to be at the service of all who need them.

It is as though men who had ploughed badly, and sown badly with poor seeds, were to go over the ground tending some broken ears of corn and trampling on others that grew alongside, and should then exhibit their skill in healing the injured ears, as a proof of their knowledge of agriculture.

Our science, in order to become science and to be really useful and not harmful to humanity, must first of all renounce its experimental method, which causes it to consider as its duty the study merely of what exists, and must return to the only reasonable and fruitful conception of science, which is, that the object of science is to show how people ought to live. Therein lies the aim and importance of science; and the study of things as they exist can only be a subject for science in so far as that study co-operates towards the knowledge of how men should live.

It is just to the admission of its bankruptcy by experimental science, and to the need of adopting another method, that Carpenter draws attention in this article.

L. Tolstoy.

PART 7

Writings of the 1900s

50. On Religious Tolerance[1]
[1901]

I.

There are missionaries in Russia whose duty is to convert all heathens to the Russian Orthodox Church.

At the end of 1901, a congress of such missionaries convened in the town of Orel. Mr. Stakhovich,[2] Chairman of the Governorate Nobility, delivered a speech at the conclusion of the meeting in which he motioned for a vote to

---

1   **Part 7: Writings of the 1900s. Entry 50. "On Religious Tolerance"** [*O Veroterpimosti*] (1901). Translated from the version published in 1952 in volume 34 of *The Jubilee* (34:291-98), edited and with comments by N. N. Gusev (34:586-87). Signed "December 28, 1901," the article was written in the same year as Tolstoy's own falling away from [*otpadenie*] the Church by the determination of the Holy Synod of Russia on February 20-22, 1901. Although not a formal and ritualized excommunication, it has been interpreted as such since it was issued. Notably, Tolstoy wrote this essay after, but not about, his excommunication. His famous response to the Holy Synod in which he stood by his convictions was written in March of 1901. "On Religious Tolerance" was published abroad in 1902, and not until 1906 did it appear in Russia.

2   A graduate of the prestigious Law Academy [*Uchilishche Pravovedeniia*], Mikhail Alexandrovich Stakhovich (1861–1923) was introduced to Tolstoy in 1880 and quickly became a member of his inner circle. Stakhovich accompanied Tolstoy on his trips, advised him on sensitive copyright issues, and prepared translations into Russian for Posrednik Publishing House. From 1895, Stakhovich served as Chairman of the Nobility of the Orel Governorate. Known as a pious Orthodox believer, he delivered a speech at the opening of the Congress of the Missionaries of Orel calling on the Congress to initiate a petition to the Church hierarchs in support of religious tolerance. The enormous resonance of this speech resulted in attacks on Stakhovich by the right-wing and conservative press. Stakhovich served as Deputy of The Duma, as Vice Governor of Finland, and in various diplomatic roles for the Provisional Government after the fall of the Romanovs. After the Bolshevik takeover, he emigrated to France where he died.

recognize the absolute freedom of conscience, by which he meant not only the freedom to choose one's faith but also a reconversion to confessions and the freedom to confess in one's own words, and even the right to lapse from the Russian Orthodox Church, all of which contradicts Russian Orthodoxy.[3] Mr. Stakhovich claimed that only such liberty [*svoboda*] could contribute to the triumph and spread of Russian Orthodoxy of which he considers himself a believer and confessor [*veruiushchim ispovednikom*].

The members of the congress disagreed with Mr. Stakhovich's motion and did not even proceed toward discussing it. Eventually, however, a lively debate and exchange of opinions broke out about whether the Christian Church should or should not be tolerant of other religions. The first group—the majority of them Orthodox, both clerics and laity—spoke against religious tolerance in journals and newspapers, claiming, for a number of reasons, that it was impossible to end the prosecution of defectors from the Church. The other group—the minority—were in agreement with Stakhovich's opinion and attempted to prove the desirability and even the necessity of the Church recognizing freedom of conscience.

Those who disagreed with Stakhovich's motion claimed that, as the provider of eternal bliss [*blàgo*], the Church cannot afford *not* to resort to all the devices in its power when it comes to saving its members, who have such little sense, from eternal perdition. They claimed, moreover, that erecting a fence is one of the only safeguards against trespassers, the only way to stop members from straying outside the pale of the true Church and getting lost. "The Church has received from God the power to bind and rule," was their main argument, "and it knows what it is doing when it uses violence against its enemies. Lay people's discussions about the justice or injustice of employing violence only demonstrate the delusion of those who dare to condemn the actions of the incorruptible Church." So spoke the opponents of religious tolerance.

Meanwhile, the supporters of religious tolerance assert that it is unjust to use violence to forbid those confessions of faith that disagree with Russian Orthodoxy, and that the division made by the proponents of religious intolerance between faith and the open profession of faith has no basis, because each belief finds its inevitable expression in external actions.

---

3   Tolstoy uses pungently strong words, which literally translate as "corrupt into conversion to confessions contradicting Russian Orthodoxy" "*sovrashcheniia v nesoglasnye s pravoslaviem veroispovedaniia.*" While "*sovrashchenie*" is corruption, "*vrashchenie*" translates as "conversion," "co-rotation," and "turning together." And thus, "*sovrashchenie*" here means "falling together," or even "caving into, perdition together."

Additionally, they claim that, for the true Church with Christ at its head, crowned with his promise that nobody will prevail over his Church, there can be no danger from the lies professed by a handful of heretics and apostates. Moreover, persecutions achieve none of their goals, since martyrdom further undermines the moral authority of the Church and amplifies the might of the persecuted.[4]

II.

The supporters of religious tolerance say that in no case should the Church use violence either against the dissenters among its members or among those who practice other faiths. *The Church should not use violence!* A question necessarily arises here: How could it be possible in the first place for the Church to use violence?

According to its own definition, the Christian Church is *the God-ordained society of the people, which has as its aim the communication of the true faith to people, which saves them in this age and in the future.*[5]

How can this society, which has blissful grace [*blagodat'*] and the spread of the word of the gospel as its weapon, intend and then indeed commit violence against those who do not accept its beliefs?

Advising the Church against persecuting its apostates or those who proselytize to others would be like advising the Learned Academy not to persecute, execute, and exile, etc., those people who do not share its views. The Learned Academy cannot desire such violence; and even if it did, it would still be unable to enact it, for it has no devices for this. The same is true of the Church. By its very definition, the Christian Church cannot use violence against dissenters, and even if it wanted to, it would not be able to do so without being in possession of the necessary means.

How, then, do we understand the still-ongoing persecutions that the Christian Church has been committing since the time of Constantine, from which supporters of religious toleration advise that the Church desist?

---

4   Here, Tolstoy assumes that his readers have a general familiarity with the contents of Acts, Romans, Corinthians, Galatians, Ephesians, and Colossians, and the apostolic epistles.

5   There is some ambiguity here in the pharse "*v vek i v budushchem*": "*i v budushchem*" may relate to "*vek*" as an adjective or it might be the accusative of the substantivized adjectival "*budushchee.*"

III.

After citing the nice, clear words of Guizot in his speech about the necessity for freedom of conscience for the Christian religion, Mr. Stakhovich goes on to cite the less nice and less coherent words of Aksakov, who substitutes the concept of *the Church* for the concept of the *Christian religion*, and tries, after having made this slippery substitution [*podstavka*], to prove the possibility and necessity of religious toleration for the Christian Church.[6] But the Christian religion and the Christian Church are not one and the same thing, and we have no right whatsoever to suppose that what befits the religion also befits the Church.

Christian religion is man's supreme consciousness of his relationship to God, a state of consciousness to which humanity has ascended from a lower level of religious consciousness. Knowing that they have reached a certain degree of lucidity and loft in their religious consciousness only thanks to the ceaseless movement of humanity from darkness toward light, both the true Christian religion and all those who profess it cannot help but be tolerant. When such people encounter novel beliefs that disagree with theirs, given that they can only lay claim to a small portion of the truth—the truth that unfolds in its clarity and loft through the universal effort of all humanity—not only can they not condemn and toss aside these novel beliefs but should greet them with joy, studying them, checking them against their own beliefs, throwing aside whatever disagrees with reason, and embracing whatever clarifies and elevates the truth professed through them, thus becoming even more assured of what is the same in all faiths.

---

6   Tolstoy must be referring to the multiple statements—in oral deliveries and in press—by the Slavophile Ivan Aksakov (1823–86) on the problem of religious tolerance and Russian Orthodox statehood. The volume of articles by Aksakov that Tolstoy owned includes several that fit the description of Aksakov's views that he criticizes. See "*Pochemu v pravoslavnoi Rossii ne dopuskaetsia svoboda sovesti*" [Why Freedom of Conscience Is Not Allowed in Orthodox Russia]; "*Svoboda sovesti—samaia stikhiia i uslovie zhizni pravoslavnoi tserkvi*" [Freedom of Conscience: The Very Element and the Vital Condition of the Russian Orthodox Church]; and "*O svobode sovesti i veroterpimosti s tochki zreniia gosudarstvennoi*" [On Freedom of Conscience and Religious Tolerance from the Point of View of Statehood] in I. S. Aksakov, *Sochineniia*. 7 vols. (Moscow: Tipografiia M. G. Volchaninova, 1886), vol. 4:63-66, vol. 4:82-87, and vol. 4:88-94, respectively. On Ivan Aksakov, also see my editorial commentary to entries 66-67. The mention of "Guizot" here likely refers to the noted historian and statesman François Guizot (1787-1874). Tolstoy must be thinking of the ideas in Guizot's representative works such as *L'Église et la société chrétienne en 1861* (1861), *Méditations sur l'essence de la religion chrétienne* (1864), *Méditations sur l'état actuel de la religion chrétienne* (1866), and especially *Méditations sur la religion chrétienne dans ses rapports avec l'état actuel des sociétés et des esprits* (1868).

This is the quality of Christian religion in general, and in this way does the entire Christian confession behave.

Things are not the same with the Church. Having appointed itself the sole keeper of the complete divine truth revealed to people by God Himself, eternal and unchanging for all times, the Church cannot help but view any religious teaching that is different from its dogmatic proclamations as false and harmful—ill-intentioned, even, should it issue from those knowledgeable of the postulates of the Church—a teaching that condemns people to eternal perdition. Thus, based on its very definition, the Church cannot be tolerant: It cannot but resort to using devices against those who confess and proselytize dissenting religious teachings.

Therefore, Christian religion and the Christian Church are completely different concepts. Granted, every Church asserts that it is the sole exponent of Christianity, but the Christian religion, or, in other words, those who confess the liberated Christian religion, can in no way recognize the Church as a stand-in for Christianity. Those confessing Christianity would not, in any case, be able to pull off this equivocation, for there are so many churches, and each considers itself to be the sole bearer of the whole divine truth.

The clerics constantly conflate these two different concepts: All of their talk about the desirability of toleration for the Church suffers from obscurity, pomposity, understatement, and, as a result, complete unconvincingness.

Such are the discussions on this score here in Russia by the likes of Khomiakov, Samarin, the Aksakovs, and so on, and the speech by Mr. Stakhovich is no different.[7] All of this is not just vapid and injurious rubbish but it fans the smoke of incense into the eyes of those who are just beginning to free themselves from illusion.

---

7   Tolstoy names key figures in the Slavophile movement of Ivan Aksakov's generation: Ivan Aksakov's elder brother Konstantin Aksakov (1817–60), Alexey Khomiakov (1804–60), and Yuri Samarin (1819–76), all of whom wrote extensively on the correctness of the existing hierarchies among the Russian Orthodox Church, the Russian monarchy, and the people of Russia as well as within Russian statehood. Are they conciliatory? Only under the ecumenical dome of the Church? Are Russian Orthodoxy and Christianity one and the same? On Konstantin Aksakov and Khomiakov, see also my editorial commentary to entry 18. Tolstoy mentions these and the other Slavophiles in his writings of the 1860s and the 1870s in this anthology.

IV.

In light of the foregoing, only the following answer exists to the question as to how the Church that defines itself as a human communion of those who profess the truth, which has no and can have no weapons of coercion, can yet apply violence against dissenters: The institution that calls itself the Christian Church is not a Christian institution but a secular institution that disagrees with Christianity and is, if anything, hostile to it.

I did not believe this to be true when the thought first crossed my mind, because the veneration of the Holy Church has been strongly inspired in all of us since childhood. At first, I thought it paradoxical and thus assumed that I had made a mistake in defining the Church. But once I looked at the question from many sides, I became ever more convinced of the precision of the definition: the Church is a non-Christian institution, which is, moreover, hostile to Christianity. Without recognizing this, it is impossible to explicate to oneself all the contradictions that the past and present activity of the Church contains.

What, indeed, is the Church? The Church adepts say that it is the community established by Christ, which is exclusively entrusted with safeguarding and professing the indubitable divine truth certified by the descent on the members of the Church of the holy ghost, and that this certificate by the holy ghost is passed on from generation to generation by means of the ordination established by Christ. But simply glancing at the evidence presented in the proof of this will convince you that all these assertions are completely arbitrary. The two texts from the scripture that the Church considers holy and on which rest the proof alleging the establishment of the Church by Christ himself have none of the meaning that is ascribed to them; in any case, they cannot justify the establishment of the Church, since the very concept of the Church did not exist at all when the Gospels were written or during the times of Christ. The third text on which they base the exclusive right of the Church to teach the divine truth are the concluding verses from the Gospels of Mark and Matthew,[8] which have been confirmed as forgeries by all researchers of holy scripture. Even less provable is the idea that tongues of fire appeared over the heads of the disciples, which they alone could see, and ensured that everything that they had to say, as well as everything said by those upon whom they placed their hands, was spoken by God, the holy ghost, that is, and was thus certainly and eternally true.

Even if all of the above could be proven—which is completely impossible—vitally, there is no possibility whatsoever of proving that the Church

---

8   Tolstoy has it in this order.

is gifted with incorruptibility, which is what it asserts about itself. The main insolvable conundrum is that the Church is not singular: each Church asserts about itself that it alone is the truth and that the rest are false. And thus, properly speaking, the assertion of any Church that it alone is the truth has as much weight as someone's assertion that "by God, I am right, and all who disagree with me are wrong."

"By God, we are the only ones who form the true Church": this is in what the full proof of the incorruption of the Church consists. This foundation—a very rickety and false one—has an additional drawback: the Church's claims of incorruptibility are completely unverifiable, which opens the door for a limitless number of the strangest fantasies to pass as truths. When irrational and fantastic assertions pass as true, individuals protesting these assertions are sure to appear. And there is but one means to coerce people into believing in irrational and fantastic assertions: violence.

The entirety of the Nicene Creed involved the weaving together of irrational and fantastic assertions, which could only have arisen among individuals who considered themselves incorrigible, and which could have only been spread by means of violence.[9]

God the Father eternally begat the Son of God, and from him all things were made. He was sent down from heaven for the salvation of men to earth where he was born incarnate through virginal birth, was crucified, resurrected, and then ascended back to heaven, where he remains seated at the right hand of the father. At the end of the world, this son shall come again to judge the living and the dead. All of this is the indubitable truth revealed by God Himself.

Many of us living in the twentieth century cannot accept any such dogmas, which contradict both common sense and human knowledge. But even during the times of the Nicene Creed there were those who were not devoid of common sense and could not accept such strange dogmas, who also voiced disagreements.

Considering itself alone to be the keeper of the whole truth, the Church could not allow this and utilized the fastest means to quash dissent and its spread: violence. In combination with power, the Church has always resorted to violence—often covert violence, but yet no less definite or real: It has levied

---

9   The Nicene Creed (325 A.D.) defined the Trinity and defended Jesus's deity. It is considered the main Creed of Christianity and precedes the Athanasian Creed (ca. 400 A.D.) and the Chalcedonian Creed (451 A.D.). In the latter, the Church Fathers completed their definition of the "two natures of Christ" through which Christ is to be recognized: as fully God and fully Man.

taxes on all by force, caring not whether people agreed or disagreed with the state religion but demanding that they profess it.

Having levied its taxes, the Church used the funds to devise and implement the most powerful hypnotizing technology upon children and adults, to institute a faith monopoly. If and when those means fell short, it applied the violence of state power directly. Thus, there can be no question about religious toleration when it comes to the Church that is supported by the state. And this cannot be otherwise for as long as churches continue to be churches.

Some might respond that the churches of the likes of the Quakers, the Wesleyans, the Shakers, the Mormons—and, especially, today's Catholic Church—raise donations from their members without violence and maintain their churches without resorting to violence. But this is not correct: The donations raised by the rich and within the Catholic congregation for many centuries, thanks, in particular, to the hypnotism of money, are not free sacrifices of the members of the Church but are the result of a violence most crude.[10] Money is only ever raised by means of coercion; it is always the instrument of coercion. In order for the Church to be able to consider itself tolerant, it must be absolutely free of any monetary influence: "You got this for free—give it away for free."

V.

In its essence, the Church does not possess instruments of violence; if and when it resorts to violence, it leans on the state with which it is conjoined. This raises the question: Why do the state and the ruling classes join forces with the Church and support it? It might seem that the beliefs professed by churches should be a matter of indifference for governments and the ruling classes. It might seem to be a matter of indifference for governments and the ruling classes what their people believe in, whether they are of the reformed churches, the Catholics, the Orthodox, or the Mohammedans. But this is not so.

At all times, religious faiths correspond to the social order and the social order is set up in accordance with religious beliefs. The religious beliefs of a nation directly correspond to its social order. Governments and the ruling classes know this, and they therefore support whatever religious teaching is

---

10 Tolstoy uses the word "*zhertva*" (meaning both "victim" and "donation") to imply victimhood and to take advantage of the second meaning of the word in Russian: the doing of *blàgo* (*blagodeianie*), as well as the doing of *zherva* become the donation-doing, i.e., charity, sacrificing for the sake of what is good.

most convenient for their situation. Governments and the ruling classes know that the true Christian religion rejects power that is based on violence, rejects division into classes, the accumulation of wealth, executions, and wars—everything to which they owe their profitable status—and they therefore consider it necessary to support whatever faith justifies their status. Christianity perverted by the churches fulfills this task. The added benefit is that, by having perverted it, the churches conceal the access point to true Christianity.

Governments and the ruling classes could not exist without this perverted Christianity that they call faith, which is sponsored by the Church. The Church and all of its deceit could not survive without the direct or indirect support through violence of governments and the ruling classes. In some countries, this violence is manifested in persecutions, in others with the preferential patronage of the rich classes and holders of wealth. The possession of wealth is always the result of violence. And this is why the Church, the government, and the ruling classes give mutual support to one another. The opponents of religious toleration are hence perfectly right to defend the right of the Church to commit violence and persecution, for its existence rests upon it. The supporters of toleration would only then be right if they addressed themselves to the state and not to the Church and if they demanded what is incorrectly called *the separation of church from state*, but what is in fact only the termination of exclusive support by the state, whether by direct or indirect violence and its subsidizing of but one religion.

To demand of the Church that it renounce violence of any form would be like demanding that a besieged enemy surrounded on all sides put his weapons down and relinquish himself to his attackers.

The only Christianity that can be tolerant is one that is true and free from all ties with secular institutions, that fears nothing and nobody, and that has as its aim only the gaining of greater and greater knowledge of divine truth and the greater and greater implementation of it in life.

December 28, 1901

51. On the Consciousness of the Spiritual [1903][11]

1. Life is consciousness of the immutable spiritual elements that are manifested within the bounds that delimit it from everything else.

---

11 **Entry 51. "On the Consciousness of the Spiritual"** [*O soznanii dukhovnogo nachala*] (1903). Published in 1958 in volume 90 of *The Jubilee* (90:141-42), with commentary by

2. The bounds of this element that is delimited from everything else appear to a human being as his own moving body and the bodies of other creatures.

3. The individuation, the indissolubility, and the impenetrability of one creature from and to another may become manifest only as a corporeal body (matter), moving independently of the movements of other creatures.

4. And therefore: like corporeality and space, movement and time are only the conditions for the possible manifestation of the separateness of our spiritual essence from everything else—from the unbounded, incorporeal, non-spatial, immobile, non-temporal, spiritual essence, that is.

5. And therefore: our life appears to us as the life of a spatial body moving through time.

6. It appears to us that—forming a part of the corporeal world infinite in time—our body is born, grows, develops, then weakens, shrivels, and dies when it loses its former corporeality and transitions into another state, when it stops moving, when it dies, that is.

7. In reality, only the consciousness of the spiritual creature that is separated from everything else and is bounded by its body and movement comprises our true life.

8. This spiritual creature is always equal to itself and is not subject to changes; it seems to us that it grows and expands in time, that it moves, that is. Whereas only the bounds are moving within which it is positioned; this is akin to how it seems to us that the crescent moon is moving when the clouds fly past it.

9. At first, life appears to man as material and spatial, moving and temporal. Man accepts at first that those bounds separating him from everything else are his life; this appears as matter in movement

---

V. S. Mishin (90:406-8). Tolstoy formulated a total of seventeen points in his diary of 1903, and Tolstoy's daughter Maria Lvovna (Obolenskaya) then reformatted these drafts into a publishable fragment provisionally titled "On Consciousness" [*O soznanii*]. Tolstoy added an eighteenth point and sent the expanded list to Chertkov in England for publication in 1903 in the September-October issue of *Free Word* (issue 7, pp, 16–17). Working with a version published in 1906 by Posrednik (issue 633, pp, 9–11), Tolstoy revised the list yet again in 1906-8 to scale the number of points down to fifteen. Although the title of Chertkov's publication was retained, *The Jubilee* used the latter revision, which is now considered the final and definitive version of the fragment and on which my translation is based.

to him, supposing that his life is material and spatial,[12] and that it self-propels through time.[13] He sees the cessation of his life in the sensation of the movement of this matter.

10. Whereas true life is the manifestation of consciousness beyond the bounds of space and time. And it always is. The intermissions when consciousness ceases to appear to us are such only when we view them as the moving bounds of consciousness within ourselves and other creatures. Whenever we take a view from within the self, we know that consciousness is one and does not change; it neither begins nor ends.

11. And so, people ascribe two different meanings to the word "life." The one meaning is the concept of movable matter separated from everything else, acknowledged as the self by a human being; the second is the immobile spiritual creature always congruent to itself that a human being recognizes to be the self.

12. These concepts seem different, but, in reality, they are not two but one: the concept of being conscious of oneself as a spiritual creature bounded within limits. The recognition of life as only the spatial and temporal existence of a separate creature is but thought left incomplete. The consciousness of the self as a creature separated from everything else is possible only for a spiritual creature. Therefore: life is always the life of a spiritual creature. The spiritual creature can be neither spatial nor temporal.

13. And therefore: taking the material and temporal existence of man to be the whole of his life is a mistake of thinking, involving the recognition of a part for a whole, the effect for a cause. It is the same error in thinking as accepting that it is the force of the waterfall that rotates the wheel of a mill rather than the force of the river.

14. Religious teachers have always drawn a difference between accepting the immutable spiritual element as life as opposed to its manifestation within the bounds in which it is manifested. It is upon this elucidation of the difference of two concepts of life that the teaching about true life is based in the Gospels: of the life in the spirit and the false life—the life of the flesh, temporal life.

---

12 This is written as "material and spatial" in the feminine gender [*material'no-prostranstvenna*] in the original.

13 The original reads as "self-propels through time" [*samodvizhno-vremenna*]. More literally, this translates as "self-propels through its [own] temporality."

15. This elucidation is very important, because the good life, that which gives the greatest happiness [*blàgo*] to people, follows from the consciousness that true life is contained only in the spiritual creature. What follows from this consciousness is what comprises the basis of the good life: love follows, that which recognizes the unity of one's life with all the creatures of the world.

52. Introduction to *A Short Biography of Garrison*[14] [1903–04]

I thank you very much for sending me your biography of Garrison.[15]

Reading it, I lived again through the spring of my awakening to true life. While reading Garrison's speeches and articles I vividly recalled to mind the spiritual joy which I experienced twenty years ago, when I found out that the law of non-resistance—to which I had been inevitably brought by the recognition of the Christian teaching in its full meaning, and which revealed to me the

---

14 **Entry 52. Introduction to *A Short Biography of Garrison*** [*Predislovie k biografii Garrisona*] (1904) is the last translation into English of the four inclusions of this type in the present anthology that Tolstoy personally participated in and authorized. Vladimir Chertkov and Florence Holah translated Tolstoy's letter written at the end of 1903. They then incorporated what Tolstoy had sent as a follow-up with additions and corrections on or before January 11, 1904. That month, Tolstoy signed the final copy, and later the same year, the letter was published in English as follows: "By Leo Tolstoy. Letter To V. Tchertkoff." *A Short Biography of William Lloyd Garrison* by V. Tchertkoff and F. Holah. With an Introductory Appreciation of His Life and Work by Leo Tolstoy (London: The Free Age Press, 1904), vi-xii. The Russian text of Tolstoy's letter appeared in volume 36 of *The Jubilee*; published in 1936, this volume offered a commemoration to Chertkov who had died that year and featured his obituary. Nikolai Gudzii, the editor of the volume, assigned the following title to the entry: "*Predislovie k angliiskoi biografii Garrisona, sostavlennoi V. G. Chertkovym i F. Khola*" ["An Introduction to the English Biography of Garrison Compiled" by V. G. Chertkov and F. Holah] (36:95-99). Gudzii also wrote a very detailed commentary to this letter that was published in the same volume of *The Jubilee* (36:599-603).

15 William Lloyd Garrison (1805–79). Since becoming acquainted in 1886 with the biography of Garrison written by his son Wendell Phillips Garrison, Tolstoy experienced the exhilaration and joy that he describes in this entry of discovering a kindred Christian non-resistor. Communicating regularly with Wendell Phillips and his three other siblings, Tolstoy became a convinced and tireless proponent of Garrison's ideas in Russia. He also listed Garrison's *Declaration* among the most important literature on nonresistance in *The Kingdom of God is within You*. Many of the collections of wise sayings that Tolstoy edited starting in 1887 feature extensive selections from Garrison's works. Tolstoy's correspondence with Garrison's children is equally valuable.

great joyous ideal to be realized[16] in Christian life—was even as far back as the forties not only recognized and proclaimed by Garrison (about Ballou I learnt later),[17] but also placed by him at the foundation of his practical activity in the emancipation of the slaves.

My joy was at that time mingled with bewilderment as to how it was that this great Gospel truth, fifty years ago explained by Garrison, could have been so hushed up that I had now to express it as something new.

My bewilderment was especially increased by the circumstance that not only people antagonistic to the progress of mankind, but also the most advanced and progressive men, were either completely indifferent to this law, or actually opposed to the promulgation of that which lies at the foundation of all true progress.

But as time went on it became clearer and clearer to me that the general indifference and opposition which were then expressed, and still continue to be expressed—pre-eminently amongst political workers—towards this law of non-resistance are merely symptoms of the great significance of this law.

"The motto upon our banner," wrote Garrison in the midst of his activity, "has been from the commencement of our moral warfare 'Our Country is the World; Our Countrymen are all Mankind.'[18] We trust that it will be our only epitaph. Another motto we have chosen is, 'Universal Emancipation.' Up to this time we have limited its application to those who in this country are held by Southern taskmasters as marketable commodities, goods and chattels, and implements of husbandry. Henceforth we shall use it in its widest latitude—

---

16 British spellings of words such as "realised," "endeavoured," "organisation," etc., have been amended to American English.

17 Adin Ballou (1803–90) was an American Unitarian pastor and abolitionist, author of *Standard of Practical Christianity* (1839) and *Christian Non-Resistance* (1846), and a proponent of non-resistance whom Tolstoy admired and frequently cited. Although Ballou had read Tolstoy's religious writings prior to 1886, Tolstoy did not learn of Ballou's major texts until a year before the American writer's death. They nonetheless had a whole year to exchange a letter each: Tolstoy's to Ballou of February 21–24, 1890 began with "Dear friend and brother" (the correspondence with both praises and objections to each other may be found in *The Jubilee* [65:34-36]). For Tolstoy's other correspondence discussing Ballou's ideas, see the following in particular: June 22/July 5, 1889, letter to Lewis Gilbert Wilson in 64:270-72; letters to Prince Dmitry Khilkov from June 23, 1889, in 64:276-79 and from February 21, 1890, in 65:28-29). In Tolstoy's ranking of most important works on nonresistance in *The Kingdom of God is within You*, Ballou's "Catechism of Nonresistance" is listed after Garrison's *Declaration*.

18 Tolstoy quotes one of Garrison's most famous phrases from his "Declaration of Sentiments" (September 28, 1838) published in *The Liberator* magazine founded by Garrison in 1831. These words served as the magazine's motto until it ceased publication in 1865.

the emancipation of our whole race from the dominion of man, from the thral-dom of self, from the government of brute force, from the bondage of sin, and the bringing it under the dominion of God, the control of an inward spirit, the government of the law of love ... "[19]

Garrison, as a man enlightened by the Christian teaching, having begun with the practical aim of strife against slavery, very soon understood that the cause of slavery was not the casual temporary seizure by the Southerners of a few millions of negroes, but the ancient, and universal recognition, contrary to the Christian teaching, of the right of coercion on the part of certain people in regard to certain others. A pretext for recognizing this right has always been that men regarded it as possible to eradicate or diminish evil by brute force, i.e., also by evil. Having once realized this fallacy, Garrison put forward against slavery neither the suffering of slaves, nor the cruelty of slaveholders, nor the social equality of men, but the eternal Christian law of refraining from opposing evil by violence, i.e., of "non-resistance."[20] Garrison understood that which the most advanced among the fighters against slavery did not understand: that the only irrefutable argument against slavery is the denial of the right of any man over the liberty of another under any conditions whatsoever.

The Abolitionists endeavored to prove that slavery was unlawful, disad-vantageous, cruel: that it depraved men, and so on; but the defenders of slavery in their turn proved the untimeliness and danger of emancipation, and the evil results liable to follow it. Neither [the][21] one nor the other could convince his opponent. Whereas Garrison, understanding that the slavery of the negroes was only a particular instance of universal coercion, put forward a general prin-ciple with which it was impossible not to agree—the principle that under no pretext has any man the right to dominate, i.e., to use coercion over his fellows. Garrison did not so much insist on the right of negroes to be free as he denied the right of any man whatsoever, or of any body of men, forcibly to coerce another man in any way. For the purpose of combating slavery he advanced the principle of struggle against all the evil of the world.

This principle advanced by Garrison was irrefutable, but it affected and even overthrew all the foundations of established social order, and therefore those who valued their position in that existing order were frightened at its announcement, and still more at its application to life; they endeavored to ignore it, to elude it; they hoped to attain their object without the declaration of

---

19 Tolstoy quotes Garrison's words spoken on December 15, 1837, and published in *The Liberator*.

20 I have used a hyphen to recognize Tolstoy's spelling of the term.

21 The phrase is written as "neither one nor the other" in the original.

the principle of non-resistance to evil by violence, and that application of it to life which would destroy, as they thought, all orderly organization of human life. The result of this evasion of the recognition of the unlawfulness of coercion was that fratricidal war which, having externally solved the slavery question, introduced into the life of the American people the new—perhaps still greater—evil of that corruption which accompanies every war.

Meanwhile the substance of the question remained unsolved, and the same problem, only in a new form, now stands before the people of the United States. Formerly the question was how to free the negroes from the violence of the slaveholders; now the question is how to free the negroes from the violence of all the whites, and the whites from the violence of all the blacks.

The solution of this problem in a new form is to be accomplished certainly not by the lynching of the negroes, nor by any skillful and liberal measures of American politicians, but only by the application to life of that same principle which was proclaimed by Garrison half a century ago.

The other day in one of the most progressive periodicals I read the opinion of an educated and intelligent writer, expressed with complete assurance in its correctness, that the recognition by me of the principle of non-resistance to evil by violence is a lamentable and somewhat comic delusion which, taking into consideration my old age and certain merits, can only be passed over in indulgent silence.

Exactly the same attitude towards this question did I encounter in my conversation with the remarkably intelligent and progressive American Bryan. He also, with the evident intention of gently and courteously showing me my delusion, asked me how I explained my strange principle of non-resistance to evil by violence, and as usual he brought forward the argument, which seems to everyone irrefutable, of the brigand who kills or violates a child. I told him that I recognize non-resistance to evil by violence because, having lived seventy-five years, I have never, except in discussions, encountered that fantastic brigand, who, before my eyes desired to kill or violate a child, but that perpetually I did and do see not one but millions of brigands using violence towards children and women and men and old people and all the laborers in the name of the recognized right of violence over one's fellows. When I said this my kind interlocutor, with his naturally quick perception, not giving me time to finish, laughed, and recognized that my argument was satisfactory.

No one has seen the fantastic brigand, but the world, groaning under violence, lies before everyone's eyes. Yet no one sees, nor desires to see, that the strife which can liberate man from violence is not a strife with the fantastic brigand, but with those actual brigands who practice violence over men.

Non-resistance to evil by violence really means only that the mutual inter-action of rational beings upon each other should consist not in violence (which can be only admitted in relation to lower organisms deprived of reason) but in rational persuasion; and that, consequently, towards this substitution of ratio-nal persuasion for coercion all those should strive who desire to further the welfare of mankind.

It would seem quite clear that in the course of the last century, fourteen million people were killed, and that now the labor and lives of millions of men are spent on wars necessary to no one, and that all the land is in the hands of those who do not work on it, and that all the produce of human labor is swal-lowed up by those who do not work, and that all the deceits which reign in the world exist only because violence is allowed for the purpose of suppressing that which appears evil to some people, and that therefore one should endeavor to replace violence by persuasion. That this may become possible it is necessary first of all to renounce the right of coercion.

Strange to say, the most progressive people of our circle regard it as dan-gerous to repudiate the right of violence and to endeavor to replace it by persua-sion. These people, having decided that it is impossible to persuade a brigand not to kill a child, think it also impossible to persuade the working men not to take the land and the produce of their labor from those who do not work, and therefore these people find it necessary to coerce the laborers.

So that however sad it is to say so, the only explanation of the non-understanding of the significance of the principle of non-resistance to evil by violence consists in this, that the conditions of human life are so distorted that those who examine the principle of non-resistance imagine that its adaptation to life and the substitution of persuasion for coercion would destroy all possibil-ity of that social organization and of those conveniences of life which they enjoy.

But the change need not be feared; the principle of non-resistance is not a principle of coercion but of concord and love, and therefore it cannot be made coercively binding upon men. The principle of non-resistance to evil by vio-lence, which consists in the substitution of persuasion for brute force, can be only accepted voluntarily, and in whatever measure it is freely accepted by men and applied to life i.e., according to the measure in which people renounce vio-lence and establish their relations upon rational persuasion—only in that mea-sure is true progress in the life of men accomplished.

Therefore, whether men desire it or not, it is only in the name of this prin-ciple that they can free themselves from the enslavement and oppression of each other. Whether men desire it or not, this principle lies at the basis of all true improvement in the life of men which has taken place and is still to take place.

Garrison was the first to proclaim this principle as a rule for the organization of the life of men. In this is his great merit. If at the time he did not attain the pacific liberation of the slaves in America, he indicated the way of liberating men in general from the power of brute force.

Therefore Garrison will for ever[22] remain one of the greatest reformers and promoters of true human progress.

I think that the publication of this short biography will be useful to many.

Yasnaya Polyana, January, 1904.

53. On the Social Movement in Russia[23]
[January 13, 1905]

Two months ago, I received a cablegram from a North American newspaper, along with a prepaid receipt for a response of one hundred words sharing my

---

22 Sic in the original and published translation.

23 **Entry 53. "On the Social Movement in Russia"** [*Ob obshchestvennom dvizhenii v Rossii*] (1905). Published in 1936 in volume 36 of *The Jubilee* (36:156-65), with expert commentary by N. K. Gudzii (36:629-36). Tolstoy finally expressed his slow-brewing anger against the agitation in the zemstvos to limit autocracy and call for a constitutional assembly, which he viewed as half-measures that did not address the very foundation of the power structure. He sent a cable to Philadelphia's The North American newspaper on November 18, 1905: "Scope Zemstvo agitation restriction of despotism and establishment of representative government. Probable results cannot be foreseen. Will the agitation's leader attain their aim or only continue stirring public in both cases sure results of whole matter will be delay of true social amelioration. True social amelioration can be attained only by religious moral perfectionment of all individuals. Political agitation putting before individuals pernicious illusion of social improvement by change of forms habitually stops the real progress as can be observed in constitutional countries France, England, America" (36:635). The draft of his article was signed off with the finish date "January 13, 1905," but Tolstoy continued correcting until February 18, 1905. Conservative papers in Russia took advantage of equivocations in the reactions to Tolstoy's cable from abroad—either accusing Tolstoy of foaming revolution or intimating that he was doing the reverse, pouring cold water on the expressions of indignation at the government's brutal overreaction. Because of technical delays, Chertkov did not publish the article until April 18, 1905, even though Tolstoy had given Chertkov carte blanche to proceed as early as January 22, 1905: "Do what you will with it" (89:9-10). The horrific event described by Tolstoy is known as The Bloody Sunday in the history of social movements: on January 9, 1905, troops fired at close range at a peaceful rally of workers and their sympathizers near Winter Palace in St. Petersburg, triggering a quick unfolding of the revolutionary situation in Russia.

thoughts about the significance, purpose, and the probable consequences of the Zemstvo agitation.[24] Because I have a very definite opinion on this matter, one that departs from the opinion of the majority, I considered it necessary to express as much.

Here is what I wrote in response:

What is at stake in the Zemstvo agitation is the reach of despotism and the establishment of representative government. Will the agitation leaders attain their aim or will they only continue to stir up the public? In both cases, what is certain to happen is a delay of true social amelioration, because this can only be truly attained by the religious-moral perfection of all individuals. Political agitation presents people with a pernicious illusion of social improvement, by means of changing merely external appearances; it habitually stops real progress, as can be observed in constitutional countries like France, England, and America.

The content of the cablegram was published in The Moscow News,[25] albeit not exactly as I had expressed it. Following this, I have begun to receive letters full of reproaches for the ideas that I expressed, along with novel inquiries from American, English, and French newspapers about my further thoughts about current affairs in Russia. Initially, I was leaning toward leaving both sorts of response unanswered. But after the massacre in Petersburg—and the complex feelings of indignation, fear, anger, and hatred caused by the outrage in society—I consider it my duty to dwell with greater detail and definitiveness on what I spoke about succinctly in the space of one hundred words in the American newspaper.[26] Perhaps what I have to say may help at least to rid some individuals of the tormenting and accusatory emotions of shame, irritation, and hatred, of the desire to struggle and take revenge, of the consciousness of one's helplessness that the majority of Russian people are now experiencing—that it may channel their energy in the direction of spiritual activity within. For this alone is truly beneficial[27] to individuals and society alike; it alone is all the more necessary the more complex and grave current affairs are.

---

24 *Zemstvo* is the state institution of Muscovite Russia (1564–1699) created under Ivan IV. *Zemstvo* is a collective name for organs of local governance in pre-revolutionary Russia (1864–1917). The *zemstvo* movement was given a second life under Alexander II. The liberal *zemstvo* was the main force in the call for reforms using legal means to pressure the Russian autocracy.

25 The arch-conservative Moscow paper Moskovskie Vedomosti published a slanderous article "L. N. Tolstoy on Constitution" (*L. N. Tolstoy o konstitutsii*) on November 30, 1904 (36:635).

26 "But after the massacre in Petersburg": see the first note for this entry 53.

27 Written as "truly beneficial" (*daet istinnoe blàgo*) in the original.

Here is what I think about current affairs:

I consider any government—not just the Russian government—to be a complex institution that has received sanction to commit, through violence and with impunity, the most terrible crimes of murder, robbery, stupefaction by drink and corruption, and exploitation of the populace by the rich and those in power, a sanction supported by the anecdotal lore of legend and by custom. And I therefore suppose that all human efforts to improve social life must be directed at liberation from governments—from their evil and, vitally, their redundancy, which is becoming more and more evident in our time. This aim is achievable by one means only: through the religious and moral self-perfection of individuals. The more exalted people are in religious and moral respects, the better the social forms that will emerge, and the less there will be of governmental violence and the outrage it triggers. And vice versa: the less developed are people of a given society in the religious and moral sense, the mightier the state and the greater the evil it commits.

And so, the evil that people experience from the outrageous crimes of the government is also proportionate to the religious and moral state of society— no matter what form or shape it takes.

When they witness the evil-doing committed nowadays by the Russian government—as uncommonly cruel, flagrant, stupid, and deceitful as it is— some people tend to think that this is because of misalignments in the structure of the Russian government, as they understand them, and that it should thus be reconfigured in line with other existing governments. (The same institutions that commit crimes that go unpunished against their own nations.) They think that any means at hand will do, imagining that changing the form will ameliorate the content.

I consider such activity of changing the external form of government purposeless, unreasonable, incorrect (meaning that people ascribe unavailing rights to themselves), and harmful.

I consider it purposeless because the violent struggle carried out by external means, rather than by spiritual might alone—by a pitiful handful of people, who are up against a mighty government that will defend its life with millions of armed people and billions of rubles that it has at its disposal—is both ridiculous, considering its chances at success, and pathetic, considering the death of those arrant miserables who will perish in this unequal struggle.

I consider such activity unreasonable because, even if today's militants were to achieve an improbable triumph over the government, this still cannot improve the condition of the people.

The violent government that we have today has only become as much because the society that it rules over consists of morally weak individuals. Some of these people lack any scruples and are governed by ambitions, self-interest, and pride, prepared to use any means whatsoever to grab or maintain power. Others, meanwhile, help the former by obeying out of fear, because of the same self-interest and vanity, or due to their stupefaction. No matter how you reshuffle these individuals, or in which configuration, the very same violent government will be formed out of such people.

I consider this activity incorrect because those who are now warring against the government—the liberal Zemstvo, doctors, lawyers, writers, students, revolutionaries, and the few thousand workers who have gone too far, poisoned by brainwashing propaganda—have no right to call themselves or claim to be representatives of the common people. These individuals make demands for freedom of the press, freedom of conscience, freedom of assembly, the separation of church and state, eight-hour workdays, and the right of representation, etc., to the government on behalf of the people. But go ask the people, the greater mass of a hundred million-strong peasantry, what they think about such demands. The real people—the peasantry, that is—will be hard-pressed to answer, because these demands for the freedom of the press and freedom of assembly, the separation of church and state, and even the eight-hour workday, are of no interest to the greater mass of them.

Real people don't need any of these things, but instead crave something else—something which they have been awaiting and desiring for a long time, about which they never stop thinking, and never stop speaking, but about which there is nary a word in any of the liberal addresses and speeches, and which is mentioned only tangentially in revolutionary and socialistic programs. It awaits and desires but one thing: the liberation of the land from private property, common ownership of the land. When a man is availed of land, his children will not leave for the factory, and if they do, they will negotiate their hours and wages by themselves.

They say: "Give them liberty, and the people shall state their demands." This is not true. England, France, and America enjoy complete freedom of the press but there is no discussion taking place in the parliaments or in the press about the liberation of the land, and the question about the universal right of the people to own the land retreats further and further into the background.

The liberal and revolutionary leaders who draft programs with demands on behalf of the people have no right whatsoever to claim to represent them: they represent themselves; "the people" is simply the pretext they use on their unscrupulous banners.

And thus, their activity is purposeless, unreasonable, and incorrect. It is also harmful: for it distracts people from the only activity through which and thanks to which the aims of the individuals who struggle against the government can be achieved—the moral perfection of individual persons.

They will say: "one thing does not preclude the other." This is untrue. You cannot multitask here: You cannot rise in the moral sense while participating in political affairs that seduce people into intrigue, scheming, infighting, and into the kind of embitterment that can even lead to assassinations. Political activity, far from contributing to the liberation of the people from the violence of governments, only renders them incapacitated for the sole activity that could lead to their liberation.

For as long as people remain incapable of resisting the temptations of fear, stupefaction, self-interest, ambition, and vanity that enslave some and corrupt others they shall remain socially configured as, on the one hand, deceivers and perpetrators of violence, and on the other hand, as the deceived and the victims of violence. For this not to happen, every individual must make efforts at self-control. In the depths of their souls, people are aware of this, yet they typically attempt to bypass or find a shortcut for what only effort can achieve.

Clarifying one's relationship toward the world and holding on to it, establishing one's relationship toward other people on the basis of the eternal law that commands that we do unto the other what we desire for ourselves, suppressing the evil lusts that make us slaves to others, not being anyone's master or slave, not pretending, not lying for the sake of fear or for profit, not recoiling from the demands of the supreme law of one's conscience—all of this requires effort. It goes without saying that it requires no effort to imagine the establishment of certain social forms that will mystically lead all humans, including me, toward the greatest possible justice—and nor does it require any effort to simply repeat what members of one party tell you, training yourself not to think but instead to just fuss, argue, prevaricate, verbally abuse and fight others.

People so long for a shortcut that they persuade themselves that this is how it is: A new theory will appear that will show that one need make no effort to achieve the fruits of labor. This theory is perfectly akin to the idea that you can improve yourself simply by saying prayers, that the sins of your imperfection have already been washed away and expiated by the blood of Christ, or that, through faith, you receive the holy gift of grace that can stand-in for your personal effort. The astonishing theory about the improvement of public life by means of changing its external form is based on the same psychological illusion. It is to blame for the horrific outrages that are in question here, and, more than anything else, it slows down the true progress of humankind.

People are aware that something is amiss and that their lives require improvement. There is just one thing that is within our power to improve: one's self. To improve the self, one should recognize that one is no good, and that this is undesirable. But attention turns away from what is always in one's power—one's self—toward that which is beyond one's power to control: external conditions. Changes in external conditions can do as little to improve the human condition[28] as the shaking of wine and pouring it into another container can do to change its quality. What follows this shifting in attention are corrupt activities: first, idleness; second, harmful pride (correcting other people); and third, evil (killing those who stand in the way of general happiness).

"We shall rebuild social forms, and then society will prosper." Wouldn't it be nice if the happiness of humankind could be achieved so easily! Unfortunately, or rather, fortunately (given that individuals whose lives are arranged by others are the unhappiest individuals around), this is not so: the condition of human life changes not with the change of external forms but only thanks to the internal work of each individual on their own self. Any effort to influence the external forms of other people will not improve the condition of those people but will only make them corrupt, diminishing the life of those who submit to this ruinous delusion—as has happened with political leaders, kings, ministers, presidents, MPs, all sorts of revolutionaries, and the liberals.

Supercilious and superficially judgmental individuals are especially shaken by the internecine carnage and the events attendant to social outrage. They think that the despotism of the Russian government is the main cause for these events and that if the autocratic monarchy of the Russian sovereignty were replaced by a constitutional or republican government, such events would never happen again.

But once you consider its significance, the main disaster that causes the suffering of the Russian people is not the events in St. Petersburg, but the senseless, disgraceful, and cruel war waged by a dozen immoral individuals. This war has already killed or maimed hundreds of thousands of Russian people, and it threatens to kill and maim many more. This war not only continues to desolate the people of our time but also imposes a huge debt burden on future generations in the form of taxes on their labor; it kills human souls and corrupts the people. What took place in Petersburg on January 9 is nothing compared to what is taking place out there. Out there, a hundred times more people are killed and maimed every day than the number of those killed on January 9 in Petersburg. The fate of these people who have perished, however, does not make society as

---

28 Written as "the human condition" [*polozhenie liudei*] in the original.

indignant as the Petersburg massacres. Indeed, society seems at best indifferent and at worst sympathetic to this war, in which thousands and thousands more people are hastily being sent off for senseless and aimless extermination.

This is a terrible disaster. If we are going to talk about the disasters suffered by the Russian people, the main disaster is this war—the events in St. Petersburg are only a collateral, attendant circumstance of this great disaster. If we are going to talk about a panacea for such disasters, think about what would provide a cure. The switch from a despotic to a constitutional or republican form of governance will cure Russia of neither disaster. Like the Russian government, all constitutional governments are engaged in a permanent arms race; as soon as it crosses the mind of a few individuals in power, they send their peoples into fratricidal combat. The Abyssinian war, the Boer War, the Spanish wars with Cuba and the Philippines, wars in China and Tibet, wars with the peoples of Africa—all of these wars are fought by constitutional and republican governments. Whenever they find it propitious, these governments use violence to suppress insurrections and the self-determined will of the people. Indeed, these governments consider the latter to be illegal—that is, a violation of what these governments consider, at any given moment, to be legal.[29]

Whenever there is an organization of violent power that can be seized by several individuals in one way or another, regardless of the constitution of the state, events similar to the ones we are currently experiencing in Russia are bound to happen—both the wars and the crackdowns.

The significance of the Petersburg events consists in something other than what the many supercilious individuals have assumed and alleged. Rather than demonstrating the special wickedness of Russia's despotic government, and making clear that it should therefore be replaced by a constitutional government,

---

29 Tolstoy mentions some of the most notorious colonial wars and conflicts of the turn of the century, including the Russian war against Japan in Manchuria in which his own son Andrey Lvovich participated. The Russo-Japanese War (1904–05) was a military, political, economic, and moral fiasco for Russia. It concluded with considerable territorial concessions to Japan, yielding one of the main causes of the rapid growth of the revolutionary situation in Russia. In the aftermath of a two-week-long campaign at the end of World War II in 1945, the Soviet Union recovered some of the land and sea territories it had lost to Japan. Other wars and conflicts mentioned by Tolstoy include "The Abyssinian War," the First Italo-Ethiopian War (from 1895 to 1896), as a result of which Italy lost control of the African territory; The Boxer Revolt in China and its crackdown in 1901; the Spanish wars against Cuba following the 1895 Cuban revolution against Spain that prompted the United States war against Spain over Cuba (or rather, over its investments in the Cuban economy) and resulted in Spain losing control of Cuba and the Philippines in 1898; and The Boer War (1899–1902) led by the British Empire against the Republic of Transvaal and the Orange Free State, ending the independence of these two republics and subjugating them to British rule.

the significance of the events is greater by far: the actions of the exceptionally stupid and brutal Russian government allow us to see much clearer than would the actions of a more dignified government the wickedness and futility of every government—not this or that form but every form of government—that is, the wickedness and futility of every assembly of individuals that has the capacity to force a majority of people to obey its will.

In England, America, France, and Germany, the wickedness of the government is so well masked that the subjects of these nations point at Russia and naively imagine that what is happening here is only happening in Russia, that they enjoy complete liberty, and that their situation requires no improvement. In short, they find themselves in the most hopeless situation of enslavement: the enslavement of slaves who are not aware that they are slaves and who even take pride in their enslaved condition.

The condition of us, the Russians, is harder in this regard (in the sense that we are suffering the more brutal brunt of violence), but it is also better because it is easier to understand what's going on.

The condition, situation, and mindset of the Russian, European, and especially of the American people, is exactly what is described in the gospel of Luke about the Pharisee and the tax collector—the condition, situation, and the mindset of the two individuals who once walked into a temple, Luke 8:10, 11, 13 (The Pharisee and the tax collector).

The fact of the matter is that any violent government is essentially a liability and an enormous evil. Our task as Russian people, which is also the task of all people who are oppressed by their governments—is not to substitute one form of government for another but to get rid of government, to destroy it.

Thus, this is my opinion about current events in Russia: Just like any other government, the Russian government is horrifically inhuman, a mighty marauder whose wicked actions have been always on show. The wicked activity of all existing governments—the American, French, Japanese, and English— are part of this same show. And this is why every reasonable person should do everything in their power to get rid of governments, and the Russian people should get rid of the Russian government.

To get rid of governments, one should not participate in them, support them, or resist them with external devices, which are pitiful when compared to the devices at governments' disposal, which they will use to destroy people.

In order not to participate in governments and to avoid supporting them, one should rid oneself of the frailties that allow governments to capture and control people, turning them into their slaves and accessories.

Only that individual who has established his relationship to the All, to God, who lives by the single supreme law that is born in this relationship—a religious and moral individual, that is—can be free of the frailties that make people fallible, make them slaves to the governments and their accessories.

Therefore, the more acutely people see and feel the evil of governments—as we, the people of Russia, feel the acute pain of the wickedness, stupidity, cruelty, and deceit of the Russian government, which has murdered hundreds of thousands of human beings, and which devastates and corrupts millions of people, inciting the Russian people to fratricide—the more intensive should be our attempts to establish within ourselves a clear and firm religious consciousness and to never waver from fulfilling the divine law prompted by this consciousness. This law does not demand that we rectify the extant government or establish a social order that would guarantee universal happiness, as we see such a state through our narrow lenses. Instead, it demands moral self-perfection, and nothing more than this self-liberation from all the frailties and vices that enslave us to governments and incriminate us as accomplices to their crimes.

I had barely finished this note, unsure of whether or not I should publish it, when I received a remarkable, unsigned letter.

Here it is:
"For how many days now have I been beside myself?"
"Whenever anyone starts talking about the workers, I start to detest him and I feel physical revulsion."
"[In Petersburg], there were heaps of corpses—those of women and children, too—and their bloodied bodies were carried by horse-driven hearses. But is this the horror? The horror is in the ordinary faces of the soldiers, their non-thinking and kindly, obtuse faces, as they hop to keep warm in the frosty weather, awaiting orders to start shooting people. The horror is in the public and its ordinary inquisitive faces. Even the kindliest of people go there to see for themselves or to learn more about the grizzly details and gossip about the bloodied and trampled corpses, etc. . . . As if there could even be anything more terrible than these soldiers, ready for business as usual, than these kindly people who long for one thing only—to be over-stimulated by the gruesome titillation."
"I am at a loss as to how to define what is most terrible, but perhaps it is the soldiers' incomprehension and the fact that their faces are emotionless despite the fact that, an hour from now, they will be shooting and killing people, spattering blood on the cobblestones. Perhaps even more terrible is the feeling that there is no bond between people."

"Some of these people are from the same village—though some of them are clad in grey uniforms and others are in black overcoats. What is difficult to wrap one's head around is how those dressed in grey could make jokes in the frost, casting seemingly peaceful glances at passers-by dressed in black, even though each of them knows that they have ten gun cartridges and that, within an hour or two, all of these cartridges will have been spent. And the people in black look back at those in grey as if everything is just as it should be. You read in books about this thing that alienates people; you can speak about it and yet not feel how terrible it is. But when everything else is disappearing around you—as is happening these days—only one thing remains: grey uniforms, black overcoats, and dressy furs; all are busy with one thing, albeit in different ways; nobody feels astonished, nobody knows why one person shoots first, why a second falls down, and why a third stares on. At other times, life is just as terrible and incomprehensible—when, for example, it is business as usual to open fire when ordered to do so, without feeling any animosity or hatred at all. But these days, everything has come to a temporary standstill and only this terror remains. There is a feeling of an abyss that separates you from other people and there is no crossing it, even though you are so close. This feeling is intolerable."

"I have started to write this letter about five times and quit every time, but I am finally managing to finish it. Perhaps simply because keeping silent day in and day out is unbearable. Everybody is talking about giving aid to the workers and sympathizing. But it is not the workers' condition that is terrible; it is not to them that aid is due but to those who shot people and trampled them down, and to those who took a leisurely stroll the day after to gaze at the shattered glass, the lanterns, the bullet pockmarks, oblivious to the frozen blood on the pavement, shuffling along, walking all over it."

Yes, the vital issue is that something that alienates people, the fact that there is a bond missing between people. It is all about removing that which disunites people and fostering that which unites them.

What alienates people is any external coercive form of government; what unites them is but one thing: their relationship toward God and their orientation of striving toward Him, because God is one for everyone and the relationship of all people toward God is also one and the same.

Whether or not human beings are willing to recognize this, we are all faced with one and the same ideal of the highest perfection and its pursuit is what destroys alienation and brings us closer to each other.

54. **Discourses with Children on Moral Questions**[30] [1907]

The following describes how I attempted to teach ethics to children: I started by assembling moral truths uttered by various thinkers and rendering them into comprehensible language for children aged around 10. Next, I divided these truths into sections. Then, every day I would read one thought at a time from each section sequentially, and I would ask the children to recite what I had read in their own words, to clarify anything that was unclear, and to answer any questions that arose from the reading.

Roughly twenty such sections were formed in my assembly. I say roughly twenty because I am not quite finished with the sections, now adding to and now subtracting from them.

The following are the main sections:

> 1) God; 2) Life in the will of God; 3) Man as the son of God; 4) Reason; 5) Love; 6) Making perfect; 7) Effort; 8) Thoughts; 9) Words; 10) Actions-acts; 11) Inner temptations; 12) External temptations; 13) Humility; 14) Self-resignation; 15) Non-resistance; 16) Life in the present; 17) Death; 18) Happiness in life; and 19) Faith.

I have over 700 of these moral truths in my collection; and so, if divided by day, I will read 2 of them per day.

Here is an excerpt of one thought from each section, by way of examples.

From the first section:
Once upon a time, the fish of the water heard humans say: "Fish may only live in the water." And so the fish got to asking one another: what is water? And not a

---

30 **Entry 54. "Discourses with Children on Moral Questions"** [*Besedy s det'mi po nravstvennym voprosam*] (1907). Translated from the version published in 1956 in volume 37 of *The Jubilee* (37:31-38), edited with commentary by V. S. Spiridonov (37:413). Tolstoy wrote a number of shorter versions of his religious writings for younger audiences, including his abridgment of the harmonization of the gospels such as "Christ's Teaching for Children" ["*Uchenie Khrista, izlozhennoe dlia detei*"] (1907–8). Separately, his conversations and readings of the gospels with peasant children at Yasnaya Polyana motivated Tolstoy to write a more general summary on moral questions. The managing editor of Posrednik Ivan Gorbunov-Posadov (1864–1940) invited Tolstoy to provide a contribution for his newly founded journal *Svobodnoe Vospitanie* [*Upbringing Liberated*]. Its first issue was published on November 8, 1907, with this summary by Tolstoy, which was reprinted in *The Jubilee*. On Gorbunov-Posadov, who edited many later works by Tolstoy, see also commentary for entries 62 and 63.

single fish could say what water was. An old and wise fish then said: "The wisest fish of all lives in the sea. It knows everything. Let's ask it: what is water?" And so the fish swam to the old fish who was the wisest of all and asked it: "How might we know what water is?" Thus said the wisest fish of all: "You don't know what water is because you live in the water. You can only know what water is when you jump out of the water and can thus feel that you can't live without it. Only then will you understand that we live by water and that there is no life without water."

The same is true with humans when they think that they don't know God. We live in God and by God; when we jump away from this, it's as bad for us as it is for a fish out of water.

From the second section:
In a world beset by highwaymen robbers, travelers avoid hitting the road alone: rather, each traveler waits to see if anyone else is traveling with a bodyguard company that he can join; that way, he won't fear the robbers.

Similarly, this is how a person with reason acts in their life. He says to himself: "There are many troubles in life. Where can I find protection from everything? For what fellow traveler can I wait so that I may travel safely? In whose stead should I travel—A rich person? An important person? A courtier? Even a tsar, perhaps? But will they shield me and keep me safe? For they, too, might get robbed and killed, and they suffer just like other people. It is also possible that my fellow traveler will attack and rob me. So, how can I find a loyal fellow traveler who will not attack me, who will always protect me? Whom should I follow?" There is one such loyal friend: It is God. He is to be followed so that one doesn't get into trouble. But what does it mean to follow God? It means desiring what he wills and not desiring what he wills not. How to achieve this? By understanding his laws and following them.

From the third section:
Christ said that every man is the son of God. This means that the divine spirit lives in every human being—that every human being is the son of their parents in the body but is the son of God in the spirit. The more that men understand the divine spirit within themselves, the more they acknowledge their sonhood to God, and the more they approach God and true happiness.

From the fourth section:
The more filled with goodness is the life that man leads, the more reason lives within him. The more reasonably that man lives, the more filled with goodness is his life.

The light of reason is necessary for a good life. For reason to be enlightened, a good life is necessary: One helps the other. And should reason be of no help to the good life, this means that this reason is therefore inauthentic. And should life be of no help to reason, then this life must be no good.

From the fifth section:
Make an effort to love those who have done you wrong. And if you succeed, you will feel very good and joyous in your soul. As light shines brighter after darkness, so does the soul feel especially good when you feel love instead of anger and annoyance for someone who did not love you and who wronged you.

From the sixth section:
We all know that we don't always live the way we should or could have lived. And one ought to always remember that one's life may and must be better.

One ought to remember this not in order to reproach one's life or the life of other people, without reforming it, but in order to try to become just a little bit better every day and every hour, so as to reform oneself.

This is the main and most joyous deed in life.

From the seventh section:
It may feel unpleasant when you are praised for something you haven't done, just as it may feel unpleasant to be scorned undeservedly. But it is possible to find a use for undeserved praise and scorn. If you haven't done a good deed and yet are praised for it, make an effort to accomplish that deed. And if you are scorned for a deed you haven't committed, try not to commit that deed in the future.

From the eighth section:
Just as we rein in a horse with a bridle in its mouth and we steer a ship with a steering wheel, we use our tongue to command our whole body. You can degrade or sanctify yourself with your tongue. You should therefore never say what's on the tip of your tongue, but rather should watch your words.

A word is a great thing indeed. As a small fire can burn whole villages down to the ground, a single word may cause a great misfortune.

From the ninth section:
In order not to commit evil deeds, one should hold back from not just the deeds themselves but from evil talk, too. Yet in order to avoid committing evil deeds and evil talk, one must learn to hold back evil thoughts. When you

reason alone with yourself and unkind thoughts visit you—you reproach someone or are angry—remember that it isn't nice to think like this; stop it, and try to start thinking about something else. Only then will you be able to rein in evil deeds by learning to rein in evil thoughts. The root of evil deeds is evil thoughts.

From the tenth section:
Once they asked a Chinese sage if there was a word that could grant happiness for life.
The sage responded: "There is a word, 'shu,' and the meaning of this word is this: what we do not wish to be done unto us, we should not do unto others."

When Christ was asked about the main commandment of the law, he said: "As you wish people to do to you, so should you do to them. This is in the law and in the prophets."

The Chinese sage said not to do unto others what you do not wish for yourself: do not step away from love. And Christ said: Do not do unto another what you do not wish for yourself, but do unto another what you wish for yourself: commit acts of love.

From the eleventh section:
There is a proverb that reads thus: "Good deeds won't build you a palace made of marble. Labor gives you only a hunched back and won't enrich you one bit." There is truth in every proverb. Huge wealth is not earned through labor but through sin. Huge wealth is worse than a yoke and is no joy for a good person. You can't squeeze into the kingdom of heaven weighed down by the yoke of huge wealth.

From the twelfth section:
One must not be infected by what others do; one must live by one's own wits. There is no trouble when we laugh for no reason if another person is laughing or if we yawn upon seeing someone else yawn. Yet it is bad when we give in to an evil feeling of a person who is angry with us or is hurting us. He's angry; we're angry. The most important thing is not to give in to an evil feeling, but to answer anger with kindness. If you are evil to evil people, you will become like them, soon becoming evil also to people who are good.

From the thirteenth section:
It is said in the gospels (Luke 16:15) that what is great among men is an abomination in the eyes of God. This must always be remembered so that we don't fall

into error and hold in high esteem what is small and slight. This must be remembered, for men always extol and decorate that which they know will be overlooked and regarded poorly without the embellishment. This is how all kinds of temples, parades with music and flags, and rich garments are bedecked. One should not be tempted by this glitter. One should know and remember that all that is true and good needs no ornament; all that is good is simple and modest.

From the fourteenth section:
Men live by the common labors of all. Cast iron, scythes, plowshares, textiles, paper, matches, candles, kerosene—among thousands of other goods—are all products of human labor. If we use these products, we must pay for them through our own labor, and not simply take from others the products of their labor.

There is a proverb that goes like this: "If one person lives by doing no work, there is another person somewhere who is dying of hunger because of it."

How is one to keep an account of whether one takes more than one gives? One simply cannot keep track of all this. So, in order not to be a thief or a murderer, it is better for this reason to give more than one takes—to work as much as possible and to take as little as possible from other people.

From the fifteenth section:
"You have heard that it was said, 'An eye for an eye and a tooth for a tooth. But I tell you not to resist an evil person. Whoever slaps you on your right cheek, turn the other to him also'" (Matthew 5:38-39). This teaching forbids us from doing anything that magnifies evil in the world instead of putting a stop to it. When one man attacks another and hurts him, he sparks a feeling of hatred, the root of all evil, in that person. What is to be done to extinguish this evil feeling? Is it really by doing precisely what caused the evil feeling, by repeating an evil deed, that is? To do so would mean to magnify evil instead of destroying it.

Non-resistance to evil with evil is therefore the sole means to win victory over evil: for, it alone can kill both the evil feeling in the one who committed evil and in the one who suffered from it.

From the sixteenth section:
Never postpone a good deed if you can do it now. Death does not distinguish between what man has or hasn't done from what he should have done. Death is not lying in wait for anyone or anything. Death has neither foe nor friend. A human's deeds are what he had the time to accomplish; they become his

destiny, good or bad. And so, the most important thing for a human being is what they are doing right now.

From the seventeenth section:
Man sees that everything in the world—plants and animals alike—germinates, grows, becomes stronger, bears fruit, but then grows weaker, begins to rot, grows old, and dies.

Man sees the same thing when he looks at his body and at other people when they die: he knows that his body will grow old and decay, just as everything else that is born and lives in this world.

But aside from what he sees in other creatures and human beings, every man also knows that within him there is something incorruptible that doesn't grow old, but rather that becomes better and stronger the longer it lives: every man knows his soul within himself.

What happens to our soul when we die, nobody can know. But one thing we do know for sure is that only the flesh gets corrupted, stews in its foulness, and rots; the soul isn't embodied and so what happens to the body cannot happen to it. Death feels scary only to someone who lives only in their body.

For someone who lives by his soul, there is no death.

From the eighteenth section:
Know and keep in mind that if man is unhappy, it's his fault: For God created human beings for happiness and not for them to be unhappy. People are unhappy when they desire what they can't always have. They are happy when they desire that what they can always have. So, what is it that people can't always have? And what can they always have when they desire it?

People can't always have what's not in their power, that which others can take away from them. People can't have everything at all times. People can only always have what others can't take away from them.

The former are all the goods of this world: wealth, honors, health. The latter is your own soul, your own desire to always fulfill God's will. And God endowed us with the power of what is most necessary for our happiness because nothing, no goods of this world, give true happiness to us, but always only deceive us. Only fulfilling God's will brings true happiness. God is no foe to us; he treats us as a kind father: he doesn't give us only that which can't bring true happiness to us.

From the nineteenth section:
The teaching about how men should live is one and the same in all religious doctrines. Rites are different, but faith is the same.

A person with reason sees what is universal in all these doctrines; a stupid person sees only what's different in them.

Lev Tolstoy.

55. Introduction to the Collection, *Selected Thoughts of La Bruyère*, with an Addendum of Selected Aphorisms and Maxims by La Rochefoucauld, Vauvenargues, and Montesquieu[31] [1907]

I have compiled the present book on the advice of my recently deceased friend Gavriil Andreevich Rusanov, who passed away when this book was still being assembled at the press.[32] I was sent a copy for proofing. Having perused all of Rusanov's translations and the original texts themselves, I am permitting myself to make a few additions: I have added some thoughts by La Rochefoucauld, La Bruyère, and Vauvenargues, which were omitted by Rusanov, as well as adding to this volume selections from the thoughts by the famous Montesquieu, with which I had not been familiar before and which struck me not only with their profundity but also with their simplicity and spontaneity.

---

31 **Entry 55. "Introduction to the Collection, *Selected Thoughts of La Bruyère*"** (1907). The text of "Introduction to the Collection, *Selected Thoughts of La Bruyère, with an Addendum of Selected Aphorisms and Maxims by La Rochefoucauld, Vauvenargues, and Montesquieu*" [Predislovie k sborniku *Izbrannye mysli Labriu'era, s pribavlenim izbrannykh aforizmov i maksim Laroshfuko, Vovenarga in Montesk'e*] was published in 1956 in volume 40 of *The Jubilee*, following the text of the 1907 publication in Posrednik for which Tolstoy wrote this introduction (40:217-18). N. N. Gusev's commentary in this volume of *The Jubilee* (40:490-96) is for the entire collection of aphorisms and has less to say about the text of Tolstoy's introduction per se. Introduction was one of many such editions prepared by Tolstoy and his circle for dissemination among the "intelligent readership" [*dlia intelligentnykh chitatelei*], a category used by Posrednik for its more sophisticated illustrated publications.

32 Gavriil Andreevich Rusanov (1846–1907) met Tolstoy in 1883. He held degrees in science and education and was among the most prominent purveyors of popular enlightenment in pre-revolutionary Russia. Rusanov wrote more than seventy known letters to Tolstoy and was a great sympathizer of his ideas. In 1903, Tolstoy consulted with Rusanov during his work on the collection *Wise [Men's] Thoughts for Every Day [Mysli mudrykh liudei na kazhdyi den']*. When a spinal illness forced Rusanov to resign from his full professorship, he concentrated his energies on providing translations and selections of literature for editions of popular books.

In relation to the elucidation of the laws that govern human life, the activity of human reason has always manifested itself in two different ways. Some thinkers have attempted to bring into a certain system of connections all the phenomena and laws of human life. Such are the compilers of philosophical theories from Aristotle through Spinoza and Hegel.

Others have contributed to knowing the laws of human life with detached observations of this life, and with apposite expressions pointing out the eternal laws that govern it. Such were the sages of antiquity who compiled collections of gnomic observations, the mystic Christian writers, and, especially, the French writers of the sixteenth, seventeenth, and eighteenth centuries, who have elevated this genre to the most sublime degree of perfection.

Setting aside the astonishing Montaigne, whose writings partly belong to this latter genre, the thoughts and maxims of La Rochefoucauld, La Bruyère, Pascal, Montesquieu, and Vauvenargues all belong to this latter group.

If we were to compare the sum of knowledge of the laws of human life to a sphere that is continually enlarged by newer acquisitions, then thinkers of the first, systematic class should be likened to men who try to plaster the sphere with a stodgy and more or less gooey substance in order to evenly expand its whole surface. Thinkers of the second category, meanwhile, are like men who do not care about the even expansion of the entire sphere and who increase its surface unevenly, making their additions at different points along the radii where it was proper for their thought to function, outstripping the thinkers of the first kind for the most part and supplying future systematizers with material that they can later work upon.

The advantage of the thinkers of the first category is the coherence, completeness, and symmetry of their teaching. But the downside is the artificiality and forced connections they draw between parts, their frequent deviations from truth for the sake of observing the slender stature of the entire teaching, and their frequent opacity and hence vagueness of exposition. To secure the coherence of their systems, they often need to deviate from the truth.

The advantages of the second type of philosophy are spontaneity, sincerity, novelty, audacity, a dashing flight of thought—as if it is not tied down by anything—and power of expression. And the downsides are fragmentariness and a sporadic outward contradiction—for the most part, an apparent contradiction rather than an internal one.

The main advantage of this second type is that whereas the writings of the first type—the philosophical systems—frequently repel with their pedantry (well, if they don't repel, they enfeeble the mind of the reader, subduing it and depriving it of its ingenuity), the writings of the second always attract with the sincerity and elegance of their pithy expressions, and, most importantly, far from subduing the independent activity of the mind, they pique it, forcing the reader either to draw further inferences of their own from the reading, or, if they are in complete disagreement with the author on a given occasion, to argue with him, arriving at new and unexpected conclusions.[33]

Such are most of the isolated thoughts of the ancients and the moderns, as well as the French writers collected in the book here offered.

L. Tolstoy.
March 9, 1907

56. Religion and Science[34]
[August 1908]

A thought has kept crossing my mind from various angles, seeming like a paradox at first: that the science of our time is not just not useful but is downright harmful, contributing, quite like false religion does, to the debauched state in which humanity is currently living. The longer I live and the older I become, the more seriously I consider the questions of life, and the less paradoxical this thought seems to me: I can now bravely say that I cannot but consider this paradox to be a truth, an important and certain truth. Indeed, there is within the sum of human knowledge one piece that is not merely important but is vital; in its absence, no knowledge can be useful and can only be harmful. The situation is like when a person pours anything at hand into a flour sack to substitute for flour: not only is the other stuff inedible but it diminishes the quantity of the

---

33 This paragraph is preserved syntactically as is. It reveals the breadth of Tolstoy's power and weakness: he knows the "right" way to write and yet writes differently when he chooses to write his didactic works verbosely.

34 **Entry 56. "Religion and Science"** [*Religiia i nauka*] (1908). Tolstoy dictated this text to his secretary N. N. Gusev in the middle of August 1908; several days later on August 17, Gusev made a corresponding note in his diary. See N. N. Gusev on the history of its writing (40:515; N. N. Gusev, *Two Years with Tolstoy* [Moscow: Khudozhestvennaya literatura, 1912], 186). The dictated text was first published by Gusev in the 1956 volumes of *The Jubilee* (37:360-62) with V. S. Spiridonov's commentary (37:467, 40:427-29) which is identical in both volumes. Duplication of the commentary must have resulted after Spiridonov's passing and the rush to complete and "over-coordinate" the edition from 1956 to 1958.

"real flour" and thus ruins its overall quality. The one piece of knowledge that is inevitable and vital for all living people has always been one and the same: the knowledge of one's purpose in the condition in which one finds oneself in this world, and in the activity or the abstention from activity that results from one understanding this purpose. This knowledge has always appeared central to man, has always enjoyed the greatest respect, and has for the most part been called "religion" or sometimes "wisdom." It is true that in our current situation of close communication between nations, the old disagreements and contradictions between religious teachings have become more apparent to us, and they naturally undermine—more and more so—our trust in the teachings professed by these nations and others. The enlightenment that has increased our understanding of our relationship across space (i.e., the differences between faiths), on the one hand, has necessarily increased our understanding of the relationship of these faiths through time, on the other hand. Paying attention to the temporal historical origin of these teachings, which now appear contradictory to us, helps us to see that the contradictions are not in the foundations of the religious teachings but in the temporal distortions of these foundations, which become all the more gross as time passes.

The progressive people of our time who are accustomed to being guided by their reason cannot help but feel doubtful about the truth of these teachings whenever they encounter their horrid perversions that run contrary to common sense—for example, by our Church, which perverts even the most primitive morality. On becoming doubtful, they took these teachings to be false and threw them away, supposing that any other kind of knowledge would be better than perverted knowledge of the most vital things. This error was most natural and perhaps even unavoidable. And yet, by acting in this way, those who lead our young generations are like the man with the sack of flour: Even if the flour offered to the man was the best on offer, he can clearly see that it is all rotten, inedible, and bad for one's health. And so he substitutes for this wood shavings and grass. Fresh as these might be, these substitutes are inadequate as nourishment, unsuitable for human beings. Upon seeing that all existing religious teachings contradict one another and don't live up to their promise, they are pushed aside, just as in the proverb: get angry at the fleas, throw your furs into the oven fire.[35] Instead of investigating the essence of these teachings and absorbing their foundational truths, which are the same in all religions, instead of endeavoring to unite these foundations with everything that humanity has achieved in this regard up until today, instead of making these foundations

---

35 See footnote 79 to entry 36 in part 4 of this book.

the pillar of knowledge and the guide for human life, these progressive people either tossed them away or studied them merely as a curious historical phenomenon that is otherwise irrelevant for the current moment. Instead of endeavoring to understand that the contradictions between teachings do not arise out of the falsity of the teachings *per se* but thanks to the falsity of their perversions, progressive people have decided that the teachings answering to the questions concerned with life's purpose and guidance are false *per se*, and therefore redundant, irrelevant, or even harmful. This is without a doubt the direction of European science, which has now, taken as a whole, overtaken the world as a whole. I speak of the science that started at the end of the eighteenth century. This direction consists in—strange to say—the principle that any knowledge, the more the better, is useful to man and can substitute for the sole knowledge that appears vital for every step a human being has to make in life. That is: pour whatever into your sack; the more tightly your sack is filled, the more food you can take home.

And thus, the task for progressive thinkers (thinkers and not scientists, these being two incompatible concepts) is not so much to demonstrate the futility of what is called the sciences but to demonstrate the vital inevitability of what has always been considered knowledge. Progressive thinkers must demonstrate that this knowledge has always been known to humankind and was revealed through religious teachings, as well as the teachings of the sages—the Egyptians, the Greeks, and the Romans, as well as later ones—down through the most recent times—Kant, Schopenhauer, Vivekanda,[36] Amiel,[37] etc. To demonstrate that this knowledge has always existed for the select few among humankind, and more so, that it is essentially the same: This is the main task of the thinking people of this humankind of ours. Without fulfilling this task, neither science nor intellectual nor political effort can advance humankind. The fulfillment of this task will grant the same understanding of life to all people. (I am wrong to say that this will *grant* a common understanding of life; rather, it will *reveal* to people that this common understanding has always existed among them.) And this will effortlessly lead to the awareness of the condition that is characteristic of, and satisfactory for, humanity.

L. Tolstoy

---

36 Swami Vivekananda (1863–1902) was a chief disciple of the nineteenth-century Indian mystic Ramakrishna.

37 Henri-Frédéric Amiel (1821–81) authored *Journal Intime* and was one of Tolstoy's favorite contemporary spiritual writers. Tolstoy frequently quoted Amiel and propagated his thoughts, ideas, and writings. Increasing Amiel's renown, Tolstoy's daughter Maria Lvovna translated his work into Russian while Tolstoy provided an introduction to the volume.

57. Reminiscences about the Court-Martial of a Soldier[38] [1908]

Dear friend Pavel Ivanovich,

I am very glad to grant your wish and to relate to you what I have thought and felt repeatedly about the incident in which I served as defense counsel for a soldier, about which you write in your book. This incident has had a much greater influence on my life than other seemingly more important events—whether that is the loss or restoration of assets, my success or failure in literature, or even the loss of loved-ones.

I will relate the way the incident transpired; and afterwards I shall attempt to express the thoughts and feelings that the incident caused in me back then, and what its reminiscence causes in me now.

I can't recall exactly what it was in particular that I was preoccupied with at that time, for you know this better than I; I only know that, at the time, I lived a quiet, self-contented, and quite egoistic life. We were visited in the summer of 1866, rather unexpectedly, by Grisha Kolokoltsov, an acquaintance of my wife, who used to visit the Behrs family while he was still a military cadet. Turns out, he served in the infantry regiment billeted in our neighborhood. He was a merry, good-hearted boy, preoccupied in particular at the time with his riding horse, a Cossack horse that he enjoyed showing off, and on which he visited us often.

It was thanks to him that we became acquainted with his regimental commander, Colonel Youth, and with the demoted A. M. Stasiulevich who served in the same regiment, brother of the famous editor (he may have been conscripted to the rank-and-file infantry for political reasons—I don't remember).[39] Stasiulevich was a youth no more. Recently, he had been promoted to a

---

38 **Entry 57. "Reminiscences about the Court-Martial of a Soldier"** [*Vospominaniia o sude nad soldatom*] (April 1908) was edited by V. S. Spiridonov and published in 1956 in volume 37 of *The Jubilee* (37: 67-75). This text expresses the gist of Tolstoy's teachings on nonviolent resistance to evil. In response to the request of his follower and biographer Pavel Ivanovich (Posha) Biriukov, Tolstoy relates the painful memory of his botched defense of the soldier Vasilii Shibunin in 1866 (also see entry 23 and the related annotations 26-33 in part 3 of this volume). Biriukov had intended to publish this text (of the current entry 57) in 1908 in the second volume of his Tolstoy biography. [On Biriukov's work, see Spiridonov's commentary in *The Jubilee* (37: 421-22)]. "The Behrs family" mentioned in the reminiscences refers to Tolstoy's in-laws; his wife's maiden name was Sophia Andreevna Behrs.

39 Tolstoy means Stasiulevich's famous brother Mikhail Matveevich Stasiulevich (1826–1911), a man of letters and editor of *Vestnik Evropy* [*The Messenger of Europe*]. On the "famous brother," see also my editorial commentary to entry 36.

sub-lieutenant and assigned to the regiment of Colonel Youth, an old friend of his, who was now his chief superior. Both Youth and Stasiulevich would also occasionally pay us a visit. Youth was a well-fed, pink-complexioned, and good-natured man, still a bachelor. He was one of those people, frequently to be encountered in life, in whom nothing human can be discerned because of their constant striving to fulfil the conventions of their position as their top aim in life. For Colonel Youth, the convention of being a regimental commander was that position. One cannot tell about such people, in human terms, whether they are kind or reasonable, because it is unknown what they would be if they were just human, and stopped being colonels, professors, ministers, judges, or journalists. That's how it was with Colonel Youth also: He was a conscientious regimental commander, a decent guest. But as to what kind of man he was, one couldn't tell. In fact, I don't think he knew, either, and nor did he care to find out. As regards Stasiulevich, he was a vivacious person, albeit crippled to the point of deformity on all sides, most of all by misfortunes and humiliations that he had endured emotionally as an ambitious man full of self-conceited pride. That is how it appeared to me, but I didn't know him well enough to be able to gain a deeper understanding into his psychic state. I only know that it was a pleasure to socialize with him, although it called forth a mixed feeling of pity and respect. I fell out of touch with Stasiulevich but I soon found out—when their regiment had been reassigned to another station—that he had taken his own life, without any apparent personal reason, or so they said, and he did so in the strangest of manners. One early morning, he put on a thick, heavy-padded military coat underneath his outerwear, walked into the river and drowned himself once he reached the river's deepest point, for he didn't know how to swim.

I don't remember which of the two it was, Kolokoltsov or Stasiulevich, but one of them told us about an event most terrible and extraordinary for people in the military: a soldier striking his commanding officer, a captain and an academy graduate, in the face. Stasiulevich in particular spoke with such ardent sympathy for the soldier and his lot, which, according to Stasiulevich, was death by execution; he kept telling me about it and suggested that I serve as the soldier's defense attorney at his court martial.

I have to say that the condemnation to death of some people by others and the condemnation of yet other people to carry out capital punishment has not only always filled me with indignation but has always appeared as something impossible to me—a fiction, one of those deeds whose reality you completely refuse to believe in, even though you know that they have been and continue to be committed by people. Long has capital punishment been, for me, one of those deeds that even the news of its actual occurrence does not destroy the consciousness in me of the impossibility of its being committed.

I have long understood that man is capable of killing when it comes to the defense of someone close to him or his own self, whether under the influence of irritation, anger, vengefulness, or after losing consciousness of his own humanity. I can also understand how man is capable of endangering his life and participating in collateral murder during war, under the influence of a patriotic herd hypnosis. But that people could calmly and in full control of themselves premeditate as necessary the killing of a human being like themselves and could force other human beings to carry out this deed that is contrary to human nature—this I could never understand. Nor did I understand it back in 1866 while living my life as a limited egoist, which is why I jumped at the opportunity[40] hoping for success, however strange that may sound now.

I remember arriving in the village of Ozerki where the man about to be tried was being kept (I cannot recall whether this was a special place of detention or the very place where the incident had occurred). Having entered a brick hut with low ceilings, I was met by a short man with high cheekbones who was closer to being overweight than to being thin, a thing rare among soldiers, a man with the simplest, most unchanging facial expression. I was in the company of Kolokoltsov, it seems—I can't remember. The man rose to stand at attention like a soldier would when we entered. I explained that I wished to be his defense lawyer and asked him to give me his rundown of the affair. He had little to say of his own and answered my questions unwillingly, in a soldierly manner: "Yes, sir." His answers conveyed the sense of someone who felt very bored and whose commander was very demanding toward him: "He was very hard on me," the man said.

It was just like you had described it, except that the claim that the soldier had had a little something to drink for courage right before the occasion is hardly true.

Here is how I came to understand the cause of this soldier's action back then: His commanding officer, the outwardly calm man, drove this soldier copyist utterly irate by demanding, in his soft and even voice and over the course of several months, the repetition of tasks that the copyist considered to have been correctly and fully completed. The core of the matter, as I understood it then, was that their service relations apart, the two developed very tense human relations: the relations of mutual hatred. The commanding officer experienced antipathy toward the defendant, as is often the case, aggravated still further by an intuition that the man's hatred toward him was on account of the officer's being an ethnic Pole who hated his inferiors. Taking advantage, the commander

---

40 Tolstoy means that he "jumped at the opportunity" to defend the soldier.

pulled rank, finding pleasure in showing displeasure with anything that the copyist would do, making him prepare several new drafts of work that the copyist considered to have been drafted fairly and irreproachably. For his part, the copyist hated the commanding officer—not only for being a Pole and for the officer's insults in not acknowledging the copyist's handwriting expertise, but most of all for his calm demeanor and his unassailable position. This hatred had no outlet; its flames were fanned more and more with every reproach. And when it reached its zenith, it erupted in a manner that surprised even the copyist. In your version, you report that the outburst was incited by the commander's threat to have the copyist flogged with a rod. This is not true. The company commander merely returned some copy to the copyist, telling him to correct it and make another.

The trial soon took place. Youth was its Chairman, and Kolokoltsov and Stasiulevich were the two members. The defendant was brought in. I read my speech after some formalities that I don't remember, and though it's not a strange occurrence for me, I simply feel ashamed reading it now. The judges listened with boredom, poorly veiled by civility, to all the vulgar trivialities that I recited, citing articles such-and-such from volume such-and-such, before withdrawing to a conference after having heard me out. I later found out that it was only Stasiulevich, who insisted during the conference on the application of the stupid article that I cited, namely that the defendant was to be acquitted on the ground of his demonstrated insanity. Kind and good boy that he was, I thought Kolokoltsov was sure to rule in my favor, but he kept obedient to Youth whose voice decided the matter. The condemnation to a sentence of death by firing squad was read out loud. Just as you have it described, right after the trial I wrote to Alexandra Andreevna Tolstaya, a Lady in Waiting as close to me as she was to the court, asking her to petition the Sire for Shibunin's pardon (Alexander II was Emperor at the time). I wrote to Tolstaya but forgot to write the name of the regiment in which the affair had taken place.[41] Tolstaya turned to the War Minister Miliutin,[42] but he said that the Emperor could not be petitioned without the name of the defendant's regiment. She wrote to me about this and I hurried to write a response. Yet those at the top of the regiment sped things up, and as soon as no more petition obstacles were in their way, the execution was carried out.

---

41 Alexandra Andreevna Tolstaya (1817–1904) was Tolstoy's second aunt and one of his closest friends. Their correspondence lasted forty-seven years and is witness to their passionate disagreements on religious matters.

42 Tolstoy is referencing Russian War Minister Dmitry Alekseevich Miliutin (1816–1912).

The rest of the details, as well as what you have written in your book about the Christian treatment of the defendant on the part of common folk, are completely true.

Yes, it was terrible and infuriating for me to reread this pitiful, abominable defense speech of mine that you published. I had nothing better to offer than some stupid verbiage called "laws" that somebody had written when speaking about the most obvious violation of all divine and human laws that these people were about to commit toward their brother.

Yes, it is shameful to read this pitiful and stupid defense of mine. As soon as I became aware of what the uniformed people who took their seats at the three sides of the table were intending to do—people who imagined that because they were so seated and had their uniforms on, and that because they knew certain words written on the headlined leaves within various books, people who, because of all this, thought they may violate the eternal universal law that is not inscribed in books, but yet is indelible in each human heart—the only thing that might and should have been said to such people would have been to beseech them to remember who they were and what they were about to do. I should not have tried to prove with the help of contrivances based on the false and stupid words we call laws that it would also be quite all right not to murder this man. Everyone knows that the life of every human being is sacred, that there is no vested right in one individual to take the life of another—this is beyond proof given that such proof is not needed. But one thing may, should, and must be done: human judges must be liberated from the insane hypnosis that could have led them to having such a wild, inhuman intention. To prove this is the same as proving to a human being that he must not do what is contrary to and uncharacteristic of his nature: for example, walk about naked in winter, nourish himself from the contents of a cesspool, or amble around on all fours. That this is uncharacteristic and contrary to human nature has been long demonstrated to people in the story of a woman about to be stoned.

Have people come into existence since then—Colonel Youth and Grisha Kolokoltsov on his hobby horse—who are so righteous that they are not afraid to cast the first stone?

Back then, I could not understand this. Neither did I understand this when I petitioned for Shibunin's pardon with the tsar through Tolstaya. I cannot but be astonished at the delusion that I was then under—that what was being done to Shibunin was quite normal and that the participation in this affair, albeit indirect, of a man who was called tsar was just as normal. I begged this man to pardon another man from death, as if such a pardoning was within anybody's power. Had I been free from that universal insanity, I would have seen that there was only one thing that I could have done where Alexander II and Shibunin were concerned: not to ask Alexander to pardon Shibunin, but rather to pardon his own self, by rejecting that terrible, shameful condition in which he found himself as an involuntary participant in all the "legal" crimes that are committed, even though he could have put an end to them.

I did not understand any of this back then. I only had a dim feeling that what had happened should not have happened, and must not happen again, that this affair was not a chance occurrence but is connected deeply with all the other delusions and misfortunes of humankind, that it is the very bedrock underlying all the delusions and misfortunes of humankind.

I dimly felt back then that capital punishment, a consciously calculated and premeditated murder, is directly opposed to the Christian law that we allegedly profess, something that clearly violates the possibility of a life governed by reason or any kind of ethics. Because it is clear that if an individual or a collective can decide that it is necessary to murder another individual or many other people, there is no reason why another individual or group of people won't find it just as necessary to murder still other people. What kind of life with reason and ethics might there be among people who can make it their decision whether or not to kill someone? I could already dimly feel that the justification of murder by the Church and by science proves the falsity of the Church and science rather than affirming them. I had the first vague feeling of this when I was in Paris, witnessing an execution from afar; but I could feel it much more clearly when I took part in this affair.[43] Yet, I was still afraid to trust in myself and to divorce myself from the judgments of the world. Only much later did I come to see the necessity of having trust in myself and of rejecting the two terrible lies that keep people of our age in power and produce all the misfortunes from which humankind suffers: the lie of the Church and the scientific lie.

It was only much later when I started investigating more carefully the premises with which the Church and science try to uphold and justify the existence of the state; that I could see those manifest and crude lies with the help of which both the Church and science conceal the evildoing committed by the state. I saw the elucubrations within the catechisms and scholarly books circulated by the millions which explain the necessity and legality of the murder of some people at the will of others.

---

43 "Witnessing an execution from afar": Tolstoy witnessed a public execution in Paris in the spring of 1857 during his first trip abroad. He wrote about this experience many times. The first and better-known reflection is in his letter to Vasilii Botkin on March 24–25 (Old Style)/April 5–6 (New Style), 1857 (60:167-69).

Here, in the very first lines of the catechism with regards the sixth commandment—thou shalt not kill—people get taught to kill.

"Q: What is forbidden in the sixth commandment?

A: Murder, or the taking of the life of thy neighbor in any manner.

Q: Is any taking of life a law-trespassing murder?

A: Murder is not lawless when life is taken by duty; for example: 1) when a criminal is punished according to the court of justice; or 2) when an enemy is killed during a war for the tsar and the fatherland."

And further:
"Q: Which cases may fall under a law-trespassing murder?

A: When a murderer is being harbored or allowed to go free."

With regards so-called "scholarly" writings, there are two relevant sorts: those produced under the name of jurisprudence with its own criminal right, and the theoretical scholarly writings proper that are even more limited and bold in proving the same thesis. There is no need to talk about criminal law: It is a series of the most obvious sophisms in its entirety and has as its goal the justification of violence toward, and the murder itself, of one human being by another. The same is implied in the scientific literature beginning with Darwin, who puts the struggle for existence as the law at the basis of the progress of life. Some *enfants terrible* of this teaching, such as the noted Jena Professor Ernst Haeckel[44] in his famous work, *The Natural History of World Order*, a gospel for atheists, makes the argument explicitly like this:[45]

> Natural selection has been exerting a rather beneficial influence
> on the cultural life of humankind. How great in the complex

---

44 Ernst Haeckel (1834–1919) was a world-famous zoologist who taught at Jena. His system of monism as Gott-Nature [God-Nature] treats nature as an evolutionary and self-guiding process and does not admit of the guiding hand of God. According to Tolstoy, *Natürliche Schöpfungsgeschichte* [The Natural History of World Order] (1868) is Haeckel's atheistic Bible; this critique can be applied to Haeckel's other works including *Die Lebenswunder* [Life's Miracles (1904); Russian translation *Chudesa zhizni* (1908)]. Tolstoy's passage is thus a medley of critique in which he tears apart a series of points from several works by Haeckel which are justifying the efficacy of capital punishment from the point of view of evolution.

45 Tolstoy here provides a rather free, incomplete, and even dodgy paraphrase of Haeckel's points about military and medical selection. I thank Joel Thomas Paxton de Lara for his comments on Tolstoy's overly liberal rendition. See also the previous note.

course of civilization is the influence of good school education and upbringing, for example. Alongside natural selection,
capital punishment, too, is exerting the same beneficial influence. Nowadays, however, many voice their ardent defense for
the "liberal measure" of abolishing capital punishment, citing
nonsensical arguments in the name of a false humanism. Yet
in reality, for the vast majority of incorrigible criminals and
scoundrels, capital punishment is not only just retribution but
is also a saving grace for the better part of humankind, in the
same way that for the successful cultivation of an orchard, the
uprooting of harmful weed is required. In the same way that
the meticulous annihilation of weed overgrowth yields more
light, air, and space for the plants of the field, the unflagging
annihilation of incorrigible criminals shall not only alleviate
"the struggle for existence" for the better part of humankind
but shall also carry out the natural selection beneficial for it,
because these degenerate human castaways shall be deprived
of the possibility of hereditary transmission of bad qualities
within humankind.

People read this, learn it, and call it science; it crosses nobody's mind to ask
the question: if it is useful to murder bad people, who is to decide who qualifies as harmful? Take me: I can think of nobody worse and more harmful than
Mr. Haeckel. Shall I and other people with my convictions sentence
Mr. Haeckel to death by hanging? On the contrary: the crasser Mr. Haeckel's
delusions, the more I wish him to come to his senses and would on no condition
wish to deprive him of this opportunity.

It is these very lies of the Church and science that have brought us to the
state in which we are now. It is not simply something that happens in any given
month: whole years go by in which not a day goes past without executions and
murders. Some people rejoice that government-sanctioned murders outweigh
the revolutionary ones; meanwhile, others rejoice when more generals, landowners, merchants, and policemen are murdered. For the former, murders
garner bonuses—10 and even 25 rubles a piece; and revolutionaries honor
the murderers and expropriators among them, glorifying them as great saintly
heroes. Freelance henchmen get paid 50 rubles per execution. I know of a case
when a man came to see the Chairman of a trial in which 5 people had been
condemned to death, asking him to outsource the execution to him since his

rates were cheaper: he charged 15 rubles per person. I don't know if the leadership agreed to the offer.

Yes, be afraid not of those who kill the body, but of those who kill the body and the soul. . .

All this I have come to understand only much later, though I could already dimly feel it at the time when I so stupidly and shamefully conducted the defense of this unfortunate soldier. This is why I said that this incident has had a very powerful and important influence on my life.

Yes, this incident had an enormous and most beneficial influence on me. The incident allowed me to feel the following for the first time: First, that every act of violence presupposes murder or its threat, that every act of violence is inevitably tied to murder. Second, that state order is unthinkable without killings, and hence is incompatible with Christianity. Third, that what is called science with us is nothing but the same justification of the existing evil, by the same falsity as employed by the Church.

This is all clear to me now, but back then I had only a vague consciousness of the untruth in the midst of which my life was unfolding.

58. A Variant of the Article "On Upbringing"[46] [1909]

Everything boils down to one question: What kinds of knowledge are we justified in passing on to learners as useful? To answer this question, let us imagine the whole sphere of knowledge, even at its most general level.

---

46 **Entry 58. "A Variant of the Article 'On Upbringing'"** [*Varianty k stat'e "O Vospitanii"*] (1909). Published in 1936 in volume 38 of *The Jubilee* (38:283-84), which contained Tolstoy's 1909–10 writings and was edited by A. I. Nikiforov, B. M. Eikhenbaum, and V. S. Shokhor-Trotskaya. Chertkov died the same year, and the volume features his obituary as the frontispiece. Eikhenbaum's annotations, specifically where they relate to the questions of education and upbringing (38:504-6), indicate he may have been forced to leave this fragment without commentary. This brief reflection was inspired by "On Upbringing," a longer article that Tolstoy wrote in April and signed on May 3, 1909, via a detailed response to his last secretary Valentin Bulgakov. Yet, after finishing his response, Tolstoy decided to keep the draft apart from the article. Nikolai Gusev, the penultimate secretary of Lev Nikolaevich, had mediated communication between Bulgakov and Tolstoy, but he was soon exiled by a police order for disseminating Tolstoy's work. Throughout Tolstoy's life, the image of the sphere of knowledge remained one of his favorite figural representations of intrinsic harmony of learning and thinking.

I imagine this whole sphere—of the knowledge of an individual or of all humankind—consisting of an infinite number of infinite lines, the infinite sphere consisting of infinite radii that diverge from the one central point of consciousness of an individual or of humankind. Knowledge can be more or less perfect based on the quantity of these radial lines and the tangents that diverge from the center. It is clear that since the quantity of the radii and their lengths are infinite, there can be no perfect knowledge, nor even a knowledge that comes close to perfection; there can only be more or less harmonic knowledge, with its own internal agreement. The knowledge that attains the most internal agreement is one where the radii issuing from the center, whether more or less frequent, are equidistant from one another and, being of a more or less equal length, embrace all the sides of the sphere in such a way as to form a sphere that is more or less regular in shape. Such a distribution of knowledge with equidistant radii forming a sphere, would represent the most edifying upbringing. An uneven distribution of knowledge—with radii that are shifted more to one half, quarter, or eighth of the sphere, with some radii shorter and some longer— would signify false upbringing and mis-edification.

Here, I am only concerned to imagine the distribution of knowledge in its crude form, and I do not in the least insist on the legitimacy of this scheme, admitting that it is quite probable that other representations exist. It is not the distribution *per se* that is important to me for depicting the best kind of upbringing, but rather that there should be a distribution that embraces all spheres of knowledge in their mutual dependence.

I imagine this as follows:[47]

---

47 Please see on the next page, clockwise from the top: Natural Sciences; Life; Religion; The literary arts; Philosophy; Social; Life; Mathematics. See my "Editor's Introduction" for a detailed explanation of Tolstoy's drawing of the sphere and its working principles. See the previously reproduced image of this figure with English captions and explanations in "Editor's Introduction," p. 11.

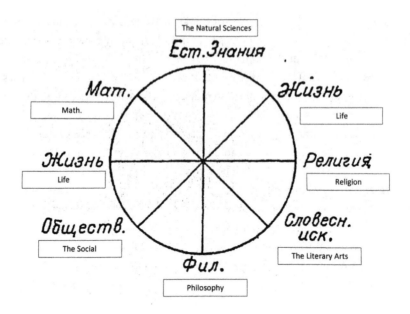

The first diameter consists of two radii: one marking the religious comprehension of life and the other, on the opposite side, marking the activity of life, its main guidance. Perpendicular to this diameter is the knowledge of the natural sciences, with philosophical knowledge on the opposite side. The third crossing diameter signifies social life at one end, and history, geography, ethnography, and the life of nations at the other end. The fourth diameter marks the literary arts at one end, and mathematics at the other. This is how [I envision the best distribution of the spheres of knowledge in their mutual dependence].

59. A Letter to a Student Concerning Law[48] [1909]

I have received your letter and answer it with pleasure.

48 **Entry 59. "A Letter to A Student Concerning Law"** [*Pis'mo studentu o prave*] (1909) is Tolstoy's response to a letter he received on April 17, 1909, from Isaac Krutik, a law student at the University of St. Petersburg. Upon reading the first volume of the newest book on the theory of right by the influential and prolific legal scholar Leon Petrazycki (1909), Krutik asked Tolstoy to clarify several questions regarding the relation of right to moral emotions and personal duty. He specifically asked Tolstoy to publish his response in the press. Tolstoy's response, which includes extensive quotations from Krutik's letter, was written accordingly and yet was legally unpublishable in Russia owing to its content. Thus, the letter

Allow me to quote your excerpts from the book by Mr. Petrazycki:[49]

The substantive meaning of ethical emotions of the moral and legal type in human life consists in that they:

1. Act as behavioral motives (the motivational effect of ethical emotions);
2. Produce certain modifications in the psyche of individuals (the pedagogical, edifying effect of ethical emotions) ...

"The purely moral and non-presumptive psyche is a very lofty and ideal psyche, but it requires yet another, presumptive, legal psyche for the normal and healthy development of character. There is no healthy ethics without this supplement, or, more correctly, without such an imperative-attributive foundation, there exists soil for the growth of various deformities—frequently, repellent ones.[50] It is a custom in society to treat law as something inferior compared to morality, something less valuable, less deserving of respect. And then there

---

was first published abroad in 1910 by the Swiss *Journal Franco-Russe* (no. 26:1-4; no. 27:3-7) in Geneva. The second publication was in a brochure translated into German: L. N. Tolstoi, *Ueber das Recht* (Heidelberg: L. M. Waibel, 1910). *The Jubilee* published the text based on the latest typed redaction (no. 8), corrected and signed by Tolstoy. My translation is based on *The Jubilee* version published in 1936 in volume 38 (38:54-61). On the history of writing and publication, including Krutik's original letter and a description of the manuscripts, see Eikhenbaum's commentary (38:500-03).

49 Lev (Leon) Iosifovich Petrazycki (1867–1931) was an influential and prolific legal scholar and the most outstanding representative of the psychological school of law in Russia. Petrazycki was Professor at St. Petersburg University (1898–1918), serving as Chair of the Encyclopedia and Philosophy of Law. He was also Deputy of the First State Duma. After the 1917 revolution, he left Russia for Warsaw, where he continued to teach and publish. Petrazycki introduced a distinction among ethical-moral commanding [*velenie*], the personal order of the will, and external orders. He also wrote extensively on moral emotions classified as imperative-attributive. Presenting a positive legal account, Petrazycki treated moral retribution [*vozdaianie*] as distinct from punishment. By the time of Tolstoy responded to Krutik's letter, the following works by Petrazycki had already been published: Leon Petrazycki, *Bonafides v grazhdanskom prave* [The Bona Fides in Civil Law] (St. Petersburg: N. I. Martinov, 1897); *O motivakh chelovecheskikh postupkov* [On the Motives of Human Behavior] (St. (Petersburg: E. L. Prokhovshchikov, 1904); *Universitet i nauka* [The University and Science] (St. Petersburg, 1907); *Vvedeniie v izucheniie prava i nravstvennosti* [The Introduction to the Study of Law and Morality]. 3rd ed. (St. Petersburg: J. N. Erlich, 1908); *Teoriia prava i gosudarstva v sviazi s teoriei nravstvennosti* [The Theory of Law and State in Connection with a Theory of Morality], 2 vols. (St. Petersburg: Ekateringofskoe Pechatnoe Delo, 1909-10).

50 The professor's writing style is one such "deformity," and Tolstoy does not spare him in these citations. The citations are in Tolstoy's paraphrase.

are teachings (as, for example, that of L. Tolstoy, various anarchic teachings) that treat law with outright negativity."

As follows from the aforementioned, it is ignorance about the nature and importance of this or that branch of human ethics that lies at the foundation of these views.

With their imperative-attributive, ethical, and otherwise emotive tone, these excerpts struck me as supremely amusing, especially when I imagined both the imposing gravity with which such ideas are taught by dignified and frequently older individuals, on the one hand, and the obliging obeisance with which all of this is absorbed and learnt by rote by thousands of young people who aren't stupid, and indeed are considered educated, on the other hand. Aside from their amusingness, there is a serious side to this matter, a very serious one indeed, about which I would like to speak my mind. The serious side is this: This so-called "legal science" is nothing but the greatest rubbish, invented and circulated not with what the French call *gaieté de cœur*[51] but with a distinct and not as nice a purpose: to justify the evildoing committed constantly by people from non-working backgrounds. Moreover, nothing else allows for such a vivid proof of the true baseness of the enlightenment of the people of our time, nothing but this astonishing phenomenon: that a collection of such tangled, confused discourses, expressed with such contrived, meaningless, and ridiculous words passes for "science" in our world and is taught with seriousness at universities and the academies.

Law? Natural law, state law, civil law, criminal law, Church law, military law, international law, *das Recht, le droit*, right. In English, the word "right"—*das Recht, le droit*—is rendered with the word "law." The English have, with perfect grounds, united into one the two concepts that have been artificially sundered, because what is called "right" is only that which has been legislated by the law.

What does this strange word mean? Should we think it over "unscientifically," and, letting go of the attributive-imperative emotions, define what is truly implied by the word "right" according to the common sense possessed by all people? If so, the response to the question about what right is would be simple and clear: In reality, what is called "law" is the right that individuals in power give to themselves to coerce other people into doing what is profitable for those in power. For the subjects of power, law is the right they receive to do that what they have not been prohibited from doing. State law is the right to take the fruits of the producers' labor, to dispatch them to butcheries called wars. For those

---

51   The usual Russian translation of the idiom is: "*s legkim serdtsem*." Tolstoy provides the negative of the same: "not light-heartedly" ["*ne s legkim serdtsem*"].

on the receiving end, who have the fruits of their labor expropriated and are dispatched to war, law is their right to use only those products of their labor that haven't been expropriated from them as of yet, and not to go to war until dispatched. Civil law is the right of some individuals to own land, thousands, dozens of thousands of acres, the right to own the tools of labor, and the right of those who own neither land nor labor tools to sell their labor and their lives to those who own the land and the capital, dying from destitution and hunger. Criminal law is the right of some individuals to exile, incarcerate, and hang all those people whom they consider necessary to exile, incarcerate, and hang; for those sent into exile, put behind bars, and hanged, there exists the right not to be exiled, incarcerated, and hanged, so long as this seems unnecessary to those who have the right and the means. The same is true of international law: This is the right of Poland, India, Bosnia and Herzegovina to live independently of alien powers, but only until individuals in command of armies with considerable manpower change their mind about this. All of this is clear to any individual who thinks not in accordance with the attributive-imperative emotions but according to the common sense possessed by all people. It is clear for such a person that what is concealed by the word "law" is nothing other than a crude justification of the various kinds of violence that are committed by some individuals on others.

"But these rights are defined by laws," the "scholars" respond. Laws? Yes, but these laws are invented by the very same human beings—the emperors, kings, advisors to the emperors and kings, or the members of parliament who live off of violence and can hide their coercive rights behind the laws they make. These are the very people who execute the laws, provided they are profitable to them; and whenever these cease to be profitable, they invent other laws, those that they need.

The whole affair is very simple: There exist the coercing and the coerced,[52] and those who coerce like to justify their violence. They call "laws" those resolutions of theirs with which they currently plan to coerce other people; they call "right" the permission that they give to themselves to commit this violence and the rescripts issued to the coerced to only do those things from which they are not forbidden.

Thousands upon thousands of young people study all these stupidities assiduously. It would be only half as bad were this merely stupid nonsense, but this filth provides the foundation on which crude and ruinous deceit is erected. And scores of millions of simple trusting people, without making a peep,

---

52 Written as "*nasiluiushchie i nasiluemye*" in the original Russian.

embrace this unnatural and oppressive life, accept the deceit professed to them as "scientific" by the "scientists."

When a Persian Shah, Ivan the Terrible, Genghis Khan, or Nero put people to the sword and kill them by the thousands, this is terrible. But it is not as terrible as what Messrs. Petrazycki and Co. are doing: Although they are not murdering people, they are murdering that which is holiest of holy within them.

In processions on the way to the people, they promote the wretched superstition—which is really a kind of fraud—about the miracle-making icon of the mother of God, the Tsarina of heaven. Yet at least there is a whiff of poetry about this superstition and deceit, and besides, it calls forth kind feelings in people. But there is nothing in the superstition and fraud that is the "law": nothing except the filthiest of swindling, the intent to not simply conceal the moral and religious truth of which all human beings are conscious but to pervert it, to disguise as truth the cruelest of deeds that are contrary to morality: plunder, violence, and murder.

The arrogance, stupidity, and the neglect of common sense on the part of the scientific Messrs are striking, as are their unperturbed and self-confident assertions that the very fraudulence that corrupts people the most in fact morally edifies them. This could have been said—even if this would have been somewhat sinful—when the origin of law was believed to be divine. But now that what is called "right" finds expression in laws—that are either invented by individuals or by the parties of parliamentary disputants—to accept as absolutely just and to speak about the edifying significance of "law" would seem totally impossible. The main point is that one should not speak about the edifying quality of "right," because the decisions of "justice" are enacted violently, by means of exile, imprisonment, and executions—the most immoral of acts, that is. Speaking about the ethical and edifying meaning of the "law" is like speaking about the ethical and edifying significance of the rule of slave-owners over slaves (something that has indeed been said). But now we can fully see the edifying significance of the rule of "law" in Russia: We can witness the unceasing corruption of the populace by means of the never-ending crimes committed by the Russian government—putatively justified by their "right." The corrupting influence of actions based on "right" is especially clear in Russia, but the same is everywhere visible and always will be—it being ubiquitous—wherever the legality of any kind of violence is accepted, including murder based on "right."

Yes, how "edifying" is the significance of "right"!

Hardly in any other case has the arrogance of human lies and stupidity reached the same limits.

How terrible it is to speak of the ethical and edifying significance of "right"! The main cause of the immorality of the population of our Christian world is the terrible fraud called "right," and yet they claim it has edifying significance.

Putting aside love, nobody will ever enter a dispute about the first and most basic moral demands: Do not do unto another what you do not want to be done unto yourself; commiserate with the poor and the hungry; forgive insults; don't rob people; don't appropriate what others have as much right to; and, in general, don't commit what every aware and uncorrupted human being recognizes as evil. But what is triumphantly chosen as a model of justice and the fulfillment of moral demands by the people who consider themselves teachers and leaders of the people? The protection of the wealth of large landowners, factory owners, capital owners, who have made their fortunes by stealing the land that, by natural right, is common property, or the theft of the workers' labor once they have become fully dependent on the capitalists after their land has been stolen. The protection of property is so zealous that whenever one of the robbed, the downtrodden, the deceived, those who are drunk into stupefaction by substances that are proffered to them from all sides—whenever he tries to appropriate even 0.0000001% of the goods expropriated from him and his comrades by constant plunder, he is "by law" put on trial, locked up, or sent away.[53]

Consider the man who owns some 2,700 acres of land: This individual has violated every possible justice and blatantly seized as his own what is the treasury of the many, those especially who live on that very land; he is someone who has openly robbed and continues to rob people. And then consider the brutalized, illiterate person, brainwashed by the fraudulent "faith" that is passed on to him generation after generation, whom the government corrupts out of his wits with drink, and who only wants for very basic necessities. This man takes an axe, walks out into the woods one night, and cuts down a tree to build something or to sell so that he can afford those necessities. This man is captured. They, the connoisseurs of "right," say that he violated the "right" of the owner of the 2,700 acres of forest; they try this man, put him in prison, and his family is condemned to hunger, having lost its last breadwinner. This very thing happens all over the place, hundreds and thousands of times, in the cities and in the plants and factories.

It would seem that no morality could exist without justice, kindness, compassion, and the forgiveness of insult. But now, all of this is violated in the name

---

53 When Tolstoy writes about "exile," he means Russian exile, which ranged from the more civil extradition and deracination to the more punitive deportation and assignment to faraway places where a person could be sentenced to serve their term.

of "right." And these thousands of cases of "right," processed on a daily basis, are supposed to constitute an edifying morality for the people.

How edifying is the ethical influence of "right"!

There is nothing—even theology is not an exception—that could have succeeded so inevitably in corrupting human beings.

One can only marvel that the true understanding of justice still holds sway among the working people, despite this constant and intensive bilateral corruption—an understanding that is perfectly lost on those from the idle social stratum.

The train of thought of the commoners proceeds like this:

If the scholarly lords, who know all divine and human laws, and who want for nothing, who are rich, if these men judge that a pauper, driven by need—or out of stupidity, drunkenness, or ignorance—who cuts down a tree in the forest or steals two rubles worth of merchandise from a plant, should be put in prison, unforgiven, and his family should be tortured by famine, what can I do, uneducated as I am? I would be stripped of all my belongings if someone were to steal my horse. In that case, it would not be enough to merely try this horse thief or sentence him to prison: he should be killed!

But despite the corruption that pours forth under the name of "right" and theology—with "right" predominating—the common people retain their true moral human qualities, nonetheless, qualities that are entirely absent from the individuals who erect "rights" and live by them.

Kant used to say that the confabulations at institutions of higher learning consist, for the most part, in an agreement to steer clear of difficult questions by imparting evasive meanings to words. Half of the problem here is that those who talk, emptily, of "right" mean to evade the hard questions. But such talk also has a deliberately immoral aim: justifying the existing evil.

This is how it goes, in the moral sense. But from the point of view of reason, a faith in some miracle-making mother, the Tsarina of heaven, or in Joan of Arc, who was sainted just days ago, is still not as insensate as the faith in the attributive and imperative emotions, etc. I would have thought that the obvious imprecision and sophistry of these concepts, and the artificiality of their neologisms, would have repelled the fresh and young minds of our time, weaning them from the study of such subjects. But your letter shows to me that it is the same now as it was 60 years ago. I was a lawyer myself and I remember, in my second year, becoming interested in the theory of right. It was not merely to pass my examination that I started studying it: I thought that through such theory I would be able to make sense of what seems strange and murky to me in the order of human life. But I recall that the further I penetrated the meaning of the theory of law, the more I became convinced that something was out of whack in that science—either that, or that I lacked the wherewithal to comprehend it. Put simply: I became convinced that either the author of the encyclopedia of law that I studied, Nevolin,[54] must be very stupid or that it was me who lacked the capacity to comprehend the wisdom of that science. I was 18 years old then, and I could not avoid admitting that it was me who was stupid; I thus decided that jurisprudence was above my mental capacity, and so I dropped those studies. After having kept busy for a few decades, pursuing completely different interests, the science of "right" somehow slipped out of my memory, and I vaguely imagined that the majority of people in our time had become too mature for this fraud. Your letter shows me, to my regret, that this "science" still exists, continuing its ill-making influence. And I am therefore glad to speak up on this occasion and say everything that is on my mind about this science now—thoughts that I suppose I am not alone in thinking but also share with other people.

I will not go as far as suggesting that the professors of various "rights" abandon this foul occupation: they have spent their life studying and teaching this fraud and made careers at universities and academies, thinking naively that when they teach the motivational actions of ethical emotions, and so on, they are doing something important and useful. I shall not advise them to abandon this, just as I would not go as far as suggesting that the priests and archpriests should abandon their foul occupation, given that they, too, like the former gentlemen, have spent their lives disseminating and giving support to what they consider necessary and useful. But to you—and young men like you—and to all your comrades, I cannot help but advise that you abandon this vapid, stupefying, harmful, and corrupting occupation, before your mind becomes completely confused and your moral feeling becomes obtuse.

You write that, in his lectures, Mr. Petrazycki mentions what he calls my teaching. I have no such thing and have never had such a thing as a teaching. I know nothing more than what everyone already knows. This is what I know, along with all people, with the enormous majority of humankind across the whole world: that all human beings are free and rational beings, that one and the same supreme law, which is very simple, clear, and accessible to all has been

---

54 Tolstoy recalls the lectures of Konstantin Alekseevich Nevolin (1806–55), his professor at the University of Kazan, legal and governmental historian, and Hegelian Right scholar. Nevolin authored a two-volume encyclopedia of jurisprudence (1839–40), and by the time of Tolstoy's admission to the faculty of law, he had written a text on the Russian governmental administration spanning from Ivan III to Peter the Great (1844). Nevolin's three-volume history of Russian civil laws was published in 1851, after Tolstoy's departure from Kazan. Curiously, the root in the surname of the professor suggests "lack of freedom" [nevòlia].

implanted in every soul, and that this law has nothing in common with the manmade prescriptions called rights and laws. This Supreme Law, the simplest and most accessible law to any man, consists in loving thy neighbor as he loves himself, and therefore not doing unto him what you do not desire him to do to you. This law is so dear to the human heart, so sensible, and its fulfillment so faultlessly establishes the happiness of every individual person across human-kind, and it has been so similarly proclaimed by all the sages of the world—from the Vedantists in India, the Buddha, Christ, Confucius, up to Rousseau, Kant, and the most recent thinkers—that had it not been for the cunning and mean-spirited harm inflicted by the theologians and the scholars of right to con-ceal this law from men, it would have long been internalized by the majority of human beings, and the morality of the people of our time would not have sunken as low as it has now.

These are the thoughts that your letter called forth in me and which I am glad to have the opportunity to say to you.

I would like to publish this letter. If you permit me, I will publish it along with your letter.

April 27, 1909. Yasnaya Polyana

60. On *Signposts* [*O Vekhakh*][55]
[1909]

We expect that the teacher will make a sensible man out of his listener first of all, then a reasonable one, and, finally, one that

---

55 **Entry 60. "On *Signposts*"** [*O Vekhakh*] (1909) was written in May 1909 but first published in 1936 in volume 38 of *The Jubilee* (38:285-290). See commentary by B. M. Eikhenbaum (38:571-75). *Signposts* was subtitled "A Collection of Essays on Russian Intelligentsia" and featured a preface and article on creative self-consciousness by the editor Mikhail Gershenzon (1869–1925), with submissions by Nikolai Berdyaev (1874–1948), Sergey Bulgakov (1871–1944), Bogdan Kistiakovsky (1868–1920), Petr Struve (1870–1944), Semyon Frank (1877–1950), and Alexander Izgoev (1872–1935). *Signposts* was one of the main prerevolutionary forums of the Russian liberal intelligentsia. The volume was convened and edited by Mikhail Osipovich Gershenzon, a literary and intellectual historian, originally from Kishinev (Chişinău), who paid Tolstoy a discomforting visit on January 5, 1909. Except for Kistiakovsky's essay, which was left unmarked, Tolstoy went over every line of all the con-tributions with pencil in hand. His judgments in this privately made review that he did not consent to be published are strong, yet hardly rushed. Tolstoy's copy of *Signposts* is preserved in his personal library: *Vekhi. Sbornik statei o russkoi intelligentsii* (Moscow: Tipografiia V. M.

is educated. This kind of method has the following advantage: that even if the student never reaches the final stage, as usually happens in reality, he will nevertheless benefit from his studies and will become more experienced and intelligent, even if not for school. But for life. And if we reverse the method, the student grasps something, which is part of the species of reason, before he has developed his intellect and he emerges from his studies, his borrowed learning stuck to him, as it were, instead of its fusing with him. And so his spiritual capacity stayed as barren as before, and, at the same time, strongly contaminated by his imagined learning. Herein lies the reason why, not infrequently, we encounter learned people (rather, people who have been taught something) who display very little intelligence; and here is why academe launches into life more lamebrains than any other social class. Kant.[56]

Something happens to those who turn to modern science with direct, simple, and vital questions—something that doesn't happen to those who turn to it simply to satisfy an idle curiosity or because they want to play a certain role as a scientist, writing, arguing, and teaching. What happens is this: Science provides a thousand sundry answers, even crafty and tricky ones, yet it provides no answer to the one question that every reasonable human being has—namely, the question: what am I? and how should I live?[57]

The other day, I read in the newspapers about a writers' forum in which the views of the so-called old and new intelligentsia are discussed. Apparently, the new intelligentsia recognize the necessity of our committing to internal moral work to improve the life of men, whereas the old guard claim that such improvements depend rather on changes in external forms.

Because I have been firmly convinced for a long time that one of the chief obstacles to progress toward reasonable life and happiness is precisely the widespread superstition that has taken root according to which it is external changes in the forms of social life that improve the life of men, I became overjoyed upon

---

Sablina, 1909), 209 pages. An understanding of Tolstoy's marginalia can be gleaned from their description in *Biblioteka Tolstogo* (1 [1], 150-53).

56 Tolstoy must be paraphrasing Kant's words regarding catechistic and didactic knowledge from *The Metaphysics of Morals*.

57 This anonymous epigraph belongs to Tolstoy himself.

reading the newspaper announcement. I hastened to procure the literary collection *Signposts* in which, the article said, the views of the young intelligentsia
are expressed. In the introduction, this thought, with which I am very much in
sympathy, about the superstition concerning external change and the necessity
of internal work by each of us is expressed. And so I read on.

But the further I read, the more disillusioned I became. Much is said here
about the caste of the intelligentsia, a caste that seemingly considers itself separate from the rest of humanity. Accounts are squared and arguments are fired
back-and-forth between members of this caste, and there is lots of fashionable
name-dropping of Russian and European authors, signal authorities like Mach,
Avenarius, Lunacharsky,[58] etc. There are also very keen explications of disagreements and misunderstandings, ongoing refutations of refutations from those
who have been refuted, and an abyss of learnedness of the trendiest sort is presented, which manifests, in particular, in the invention of tricky new coinages—
words without precise or definite meanings. Authors talk about the "piety in the
face of the martyred intelligentsia"; about how, through some know-how, they
"outwardly project an heroic maximalism"; about how "the psychology of the
heroism of the intelligentsia makes an impression on this or that group"; about
how "religious radicalism appeals to the internal existence of man" (page 139);[59]
and how the areligious maximalism "sweeps aside the problem of upbringing."
There is talk about "the ideology of the intelligentsia;" about "political impres-
sionism;" about "staged provocation" (pp. 140, 141);[60] about the artificially
isolating process of abstraction" (p. 148);[61] about the intellectually adequate
representation of the world (p. 150);[62] about the "metaphysical absolutization
of the value of destruction;" and so forth. There is also an extraordinary self-
assuredness professed by both individual authors and the caste of the intelligentsia itself. On page 59, for example, an author writes:

> Whether for good or bad, the fate of Russia is in the hands of
> the intelligentsia, no matter how persecuted and harassed,

---

58 Tolstoy names the proponents of the doctrine known as empirical criticism formulated
   by Richard Avenarius (1843–96), developed by Ernst Mach (1838–1916), and followed by Russian Marxist Anatoly Lunacharsky (1875–1933), the future Commissar of
   Enlightenment in Soviet Russia.
59 Tolstoy refers to Petr Struve's "Intelligenstia and Revolution" [*Intelligentsiia i revoliutsiia*]
   (*Vekhi* 1909, 127-45).
60 Tolstoy refers to "The Ethics of Nihilism" [*Etika nigilizma*] (*Vekhi* 1909, 146-81), a well-
   known essay by Semyon Frank.
61 Ibid.
62 Ibid.

however weak and even powerless it might seem at the moment. This handful of people are responsible for the monopoly of European acculturation and enlightenment in Russia; they are the main conduit for reaching the thicket of the million-strong populace. Faced with the threat of political and national death, Russia cannot do without this enlightenment. And so, lofty and meaningful indeed is the historic vocation of the intelligentsia: it has an enormous, historic responsibility for the future of our country, in both the short and long term.[63]

There is, as such, lots in this volume that could have been omitted. And yet it contains no trace of precisely what it promised and what I had a right to expect: an account of how the improvement of life comes about through internal, rather than external, change—a truth that every individual recognizes and that all the sages of the world expressed hundreds of times even before the birth of Christ. The volume—written by individuals who call themselves the intelligentsia, in whose hands the fate of Russia supposedly rests—contains no account of how to look, or find guidance for, this internal work. The volume's introduction makes it seem as if this internal work is supposed to substitute for the very external forms of change that the compilers of the collection deny. (I say "as if" because the collection includes an article about law that not only supports the foundations of external social order but that also denies that anything should or could replace such external forms.) Yet not a single article in the collection provides such an account.

Despite being expressed in the same confused and unclear jargon in which all the articles are written, only the contributions from Berdyaev and Bulgakov come close to grappling with this issue. Berdyaev's article claims that

> our spiritual need right now is to recognize the intrinsic value of the truth, to make meek before the truth, and to prepare oneself for sacrifice in its name. This would open up the possibility of a fresh stream in our cultural creativity. For what is philosophy if it is not an organ of self-consciousness of the human spirit—not an individual organ but a supra-individual one, a conciliatory [*sobornyi*] one. The supra-individuation and conciliatoriness of philosophical consciousness is realized only on the soil of the

---

63 The quote occurs not on page 59, but on page 25 of the collection. This is from Sergey Bulgakov's "*Geroizm i podvizhnichestvo*" [Heroism and Religious Striving] (*Vekhi* 1909, 23-69).

universal and national tradition. The strengthening of this tradition must contribute to Russia's cultural renaissance.[64]

A similar account is provided in Bulgakov's article[65]—albeit in a very strange and unexpected form. Bulgakov speaks (on pp. 66, 67)[66] about "the mass exodus of the intelligentsia from the Church and the cultural isolation of that latter as a result, which also accounts for the further deterioration of the historical situation." "It goes without saying," the article continues, "that for anyone who has faith in the mystical life of the Church, its particular empirical shroud does not have a decisive significance in any given historical moment." Whatever its manifestation, it cannot and should not arouse doubts about the ultimate triumph of the Church and its "coming into the light manifest to all." And so, "to answer our vital needs, both historical and national" the intelligentsia must become clerical—they must combine true Christianity with an enlightened and clear comprehension of cultural and historical tasks, something that contemporary leaders of the Church so frequently lack.

While reading all of this, I am reminded of my late old friend Siutaev,[67] a peasant from the Tver' region. In his twilight years, he came to his own understanding of Christianity—one that was lucid and firm, and that contradicted that of the Church. He posed the same question for himself as do the authors of the *Signposts* collection. And he responded to it, in his Tver' dialect, with a few simple words: "All's in thee," he said, "thine love." Everything to say has thus been said.

By a strange coincidence, on the same day as I was reminiscing about Siutaev, spurred by reading the collection, I received a letter from Tashkent, a letter of substance the likes of which I often receive from peasants. Tashkent's letter discusses the very same questions as are discussed in the collection, responding as lucidly and definitively as Siutaev had, only in greater detail.

Here is the letter (a copy is attached):

The basis of human life is love; a human being should love everyone without exception. Love can unite anyone, even a

---

64 Tolstoy quotes from "The Philosophical Truth and the intelligentsia's Sense of Right" [*Filosofskaia istina i intellihgentskaia pravda*] (*Vekhi* 1909, 1-22) by Nikolai Berdyaev.

65 See note 62.

66 Sergey Bulgakov, *Vekhi*, 66-67.

67 Tolstoy's acquaintance Vasilii Kirillovich Siutaev (1819–1902), a sectarian Christian radical and peasant, served prison time and held very strong views: Tolstoy humbly submitted himself to Siutaev's frequent criticism of his aristocratic softness.

beast, and this love is God. Nothing can save a human being but love. As such, there is no need to pray to the empty space or to the wall; one should simply beseech oneself not to be a fiend but to be a human being. And one should try on one's own to lead a good life, not to appeal to judges and pacifiers: Let each man be his own judge and pacifier. If you are peaceful, meek, and full of love, you will unite with everyone. Try doing this, and you shall find another world and another light [*svet*] and will achieve great happiness—a happiness by comparison with which your former life will seem like wild bestiality. Don't consult others; reason with yourself as to what's good and what's bad. Don't do unto others what you don't wish for yourself. We all sit at the same table as guests, are sated by the same food, live the same way in the world, on the same earth; we must all use the same light and labor and eat together, because nothing belongs to anybody [*vse nich'e*] and we are all temporary guests in this world. There is no need to put a limit on anything except pride, which should be replaced by love. Love will bring any malice to naught. Nowadays, we only complain about and condemn one another, but maybe we are worse than those whom we condemn. Nowadays, we all hate each other—the higher-ups and the lowly are all ready to kill one another. The lowly think they might become rich by such murder, and the rich only want to pacify the working folk. These are delusions: One can only become rich through justice, and the folk can only be pacified by loving admonition, by support, and not by murder. People are so deluded that they think of other people—whether the Germans, the French, or the Chinese—as enemies against whom we should go to war. But people ought to rise to their life in the spirit, forget about their flesh, and come to understand that the spirit is the same in everyone. If people were to come to understand this, all would love one another, there would be no evil between them, and Jesus's words would be fulfilled—the Kingdom of God would exist within each person and within all human beings.

This is what an uncultured peasant thinks and writes—one who knows nothing about Mach, Avenarius, or Lunacharsky, nothing even about Russian orthography. Yet the supposed carrier of the destiny of the Russian nation is confident in its calling (p. 59)[68]—confident that it is guiding and determining the fate of the hundred-million strong mass of people, staging its provocations, and isolating its processes of abstraction. The intelligentsia have the goal of bringing into the thicket of the illiterate hundreds of millions of people, their philosophy, which is a supra-individual and conciliatory organ actualized only on the soil of universal and national traditions, as well as a mystical kind of Church in which the intelligentsia, too, must take part.

What the intelligentsia can do, of course, is corrupt the people: this is precisely what they have done and continue to do. But fortunately, they don't accomplish this corruption as successfully as they might, thanks to the spiritual force of the Russian people, in light of which no "enlightenment" is possible. Nothing reveals the impotence of these otherwise good, intelligent, and self-assured individuals than the most reasonable and essential truth of our time: that true life takes place in the souls of men and not in the external order. Caught in the tangle of their own obscure concepts, using words that are even more obscure, the intelligentsia can say nothing about what this inner life of the soul should consist of. When they do speak about this, they utter only the most pitiable and empty nonsense. And yet these individuals are eager to enlighten the people, considering their vocation unfulfilled until they have imparted to them the empty, puffed-up, and unwieldy verbiage that they call science and enlightenment. Please come to understand who you are and who the people are upon whom you take pity, those you are unwilling to deprive of your enlightenment. Come to understand this and it will become clear to you that instead of enlightening the people, you yourselves stand to learn a thing or two from them. Specifically, you stand to learn a major life lesson concerning something at which you are completely unskilled but without which no reasonable mental activity can be conducted—something that the better representatives of the people practice and have been practicing throughout history: how to truthfully pose the fundamental, essential questions about life, and how to answer them simply, directly, and sincerely.

However unpleasant it may feel for someone who has travelled so far along a false path, he must not just arrest such a journey but, first of all, backtrack, before turning onto the right road—unless, that is, he wants to drive himself to death. The same is true of our learning and refinement and the limitless contradictory theories about how to mold the human race.[69] I am becoming ever more convinced in this opinion when observing, on a daily basis, the ever-growing

---

68 See Bulgakov in *Vekhi* 1909, ibid.

69 The original states: "to mold the human race" [*ustroit' rod chelovecheskii*]. It is a likely reference to Kant's winged phrase the "crooked timber of humanity."

confusion and perversion of the feelings and ideas of the individuals from the so-called educated world—here with us, and across Europe and America. Along with this, I am witnessing the ever-greater awakening of the people, with every passing day, especially the Russian people, who are becoming more and more aware of their divine spiritual nature and, as a result, are forging a new relationship with life, one that is completely different from their former consciousness. We, the so-called educated classes—not only in Russia, but throughout the Christian world—must come to admit that we have gotten ourselves into confusion, that we have lost our way, that we have been walking the wrong path and must try and get onto the right one. In order for this to be possible, we must, first of all, recognize as redundant, empty, and harmful the entire complicated codex of useless knowledge that we have proudly called "science." Let us try to use our own heads, think for ourselves, rather than accepting whatever ideas happen to have popped into the heads of idlers, learning their ravings by rote or disputing them. Let us think about what human beings really need to live a reasonable and good life. Once we do this, we will no longer concur with the likes of Darwin, Haeckel, Marx, and Avenarius in how we pose questions and answer them but rather will agree with all the greatest religious thinkers throughout history and across all nations.

May 9, 1909

61. Reminiscences about N. Ia. Grot [1910][70]

Konstantin Iakovlevich,

I have received your letter and the part of the volume dedicated to the memory of your brother. You were quite correct to assume that the

---

70 **Entry 61. "Reminiscences about N. Ia. Grot"** [*Vospominaniia o N. Ia. Grote*] (1910). The reminiscences about Nikolai Grot (1852–99), a younger philosopher friend of Tolstoy's from 1885 until his untimely death, reflect an unusually tender tribute. Tolstoy genuinely cherished Grot, although primarily for his human qualities rather than his philosophical insights. Since 1886, Grot served as the Chair in Philosophy at the University of Moscow and as Chairman of the Moscow Psychological Society. For many years, he was also editor of the journal *Voprosy Filosofii i Psikhologii* [*Questions of Philosophy and Psychology*] (see commentary notes to entry 45). On Grot and Tolstoy, see commentary to entries 44 and 45 in his anthology and Further Reading. Tolstoy wrote this commemoration in September 1910 at the request of Grot's younger brother Konstantin Iakovlevich Grot (1853–1936) for a volume in Grot's memory. Although the first published version bears the date "September 18, 1910," Tolstoy's final corrections to the text were made on September 27, 1910; see "*Vospominaniia gr. L. N. Tolstogo*" in *Nikolai Iakovlevich Grot v ocherkhakh, vospominaniiakh i pis'makh*. ed. K. Ia. Grot (St. Petersburg: Tipografiia Ministerstva Putei Soobshcheniia, 1911), 207-10. Based on the text from the initial 1911 publication, *The Jubilee* text was published in 1936 in volume 38 (38:421-25), edited and with commentary by B. M. Eikhenbaum (38:589-91).

collection you forwarded would call forth in me memories about sweet Nikolai Iakovlevich. This is exactly what happened. I read what I received this morning and, while on my customary morning walk, never once stopped thinking about Nikolai Iakovlevich. I shall attempt to write down my thoughts.

I can't remember through whom I made N. Ia.'s acquaintance and under what circumstances, but I very well remember that we became fond of one another from our very first meeting.[71]

Aside from his learnedness and, to be forthright, despite his learnedness, Nikolai Iakovlevich was dear to me because the same questions that captivate me captivated him, too, and he dealt with them for himself and for his soul, and not for his cathedra, as do the majority of scholars.

It was difficult for him to liberate himself from the superstition of science in which he had been reared and matured, in the service of which he garnered outstanding worldly success. But I could see that his live, sincere, and ethical nature was, against his will, making unceasing efforts to accomplish this liberation. Having learned through inner experience about the narrowness and—simply put—the stupidity of the materialist worldview, its incompatibility with any ethical teaching, Nikolai Iakovlevich was inevitably led to accepting that the spiritual foundation is the basis of everything and that man bears a relationship toward it. He was led to ethical questions, that is, and he became more and more preoccupied with these questions in his later years.

Essentially, it turned out that by a tortuous and long route of academic philosophical thought, N. Ia. was led to a simple premise recognized by everybody—even by the illiterate Russian peasant: that one must live for the soul, and that one must know what should and shouldn't be done to live for the soul.

N. Ia.'s stance was perfectly correct, but he failed time and again to liberate himself from the scientific ballast he had internalized as something necessary and valuable, that demanded utilization, and that blocked his thinking, getting in the way of its free expression. Sharing with the "scholars" the superstition that philosophy is the science that establishes the foundation of all other truths—all of them, really—N. Ia. never ceased trying to establish these truths, constructing one theory after another, without arriving at any definite result.

---

71 The reader should not feel dismayed by Tolstoy's use of "N. Ia." for "Nikolai Iakovlevich" after the first paragraph. The abbreviated spelling is not a sign of disrespect or laziness on Tolstoy's part. On the contrary, this is a more familiar and intimate rendering of a person's full name and patronymic, very appropriate in less formal communications between adult individuals. In similar situations and for the same effect, the peasants of Tolstoy's time would use only a person's patronymic without their first name to express their feeling of cordiality toward the person being referred.

His great erudition and his still greater suppleness and the inventiveness of his mind did much to encourage him in this regard. The main cause for the futility of this work, which ended in no result, was the false conviction—as I see it— that has gained traction among academic philosophers and that N. Ia. shared: to wit, that religion is nothing other than faith—in the sense of trust—in what is asserted by these people or others, and that faith or religion can have no significance for philosophy. And so, philosophy should be completely independent of religion, if not hostile toward it. Together with other philosopher scholars, N. Ia. failed to see that, aside from the meaning of dogmatic postulates and the instantiation of blind trust toward some sort of scripture imputed to how it is understood today, religion-faith has another, much more important meaning: that of recognizing and clearly expressing the indefinable origins of everything (the soul and God) of which everybody is aware. Therefore, all the questions that passionately preoccupy philosopher scholars—along with countless theories constructed already (still counting), including mutually contradictory and frequently very stupid theories—have for many centuries been resolved by religion and resolved in such a way that there is neither need nor possibility to re-solve them.

Like all of his fellow philosophers, N. Ia. failed to see this: he failed to see that in the sense of accepting and expressing the indefinable primary elements—the soul and God that everybody is aware of—and not in the sense of the perversions to which these elements have been everywhere subjected, there is an unavoidable condition for any reasonable, clear, and fruitful teaching of life, a teaching, indeed, from which alone clear and firm ethical foundations can be drawn. Therefore, he failed to see that not only can religion not be hostile to philosophy in its true meaning but that philosophy cannot be a science unless it takes for given the foundations established by religion.

However strange this may seem to individuals who have become accustomed to considering religion as something imprecise, "unscientific," fantastic, infirm, yet who consider science to be something firm, precise, and indisputable, it pans out quite differently with philosophy.

According to the religious conception, there is above all and most indubitably an indefinable something known to us: this something is our soul and God. Exactly because we know this above all and most indubitably of all, it is not possible for us to define this: having faith that it is and that it is the foundation of everything, we construct everything else that follows in our teaching on the foundation of this faith. Out of everything that can become known by man, the religious conception singles out what is not subject to definition, and it says about this: "I don't know." With regards to that which it is not given to man to know, this device comprises the first, most necessary condition of true knowledge. Such are the teachings of Zoroaster, the Brahmins, Buddha, Lao-Tzu, Confucius, and Christ. Failing to see or closing its eyes to the distinction between the cognition of external phenomena and the cognition of the soul and God, philosophy reflects on chemical compounds and the human consciousness of one's "I," and on astronomical observations and calculations and the assumption of the primary cause of everything—treating all of this as equally subject to rational and verbal definitions. Philosophy confuses the definable with the indefinable, cognizable with the consciously recognizable [*poznavaemoe s soznavaemym*], and never stops heaping its fantastical theories on top of its constructs, wherein one decries the other, in trying to define the indefinable. Such are the teachings on life by the Aristotles, Platos, Leibnizes, Lockes, Hegels, Spencers, and many, many others whose names are legion. In essence, in and of themselves, all these teachings are vapid deliberations about that which cannot be deliberated; they should be called "philosophistry" and not philosophy, not the love of wisdom [*liubomudrie*] but "luvofwisecraft" [*liubomudrstvovanie*]; they are merely a bad repetition of what was so much better expressed concerning moral laws in religious teachings.

However strange this may indeed seem to those who have never given it a thought, the conception of life of a pagan who recognizes the personification of the indefinable beginning of all in any kind of an idol is immeasurably superior to the conception of life of a philosopher who is in denial of the indefinable foundations of knowledge. The religious pagan recognizes something indefinable, has faith that it is and is the foundation of everything, and he builds his conception of life—whether well or poorly—on this basis, obeys this indefinable, and is guided by it in his actions. The philosopher, meanwhile, tries to define everything else, everything that is indefinable for this reason, and he lacks any firm grounding either to construct his conception of life on its foundation or to be guided by it in his actions.

This cannot be otherwise, because any knowledge is the establishment of a relationship between cause and effect; the chain of causes is infinite and it is therefore obvious that the investigation of a known series of causes along the infinite chain cannot be the foundation of a worldview.

How to be? Where to get this foundation? An inference, or the activity of the mind, cannot provide such a foundation. Might there be some other kind of cognition in man beside the rational? The answer is evident: everybody knows this cognition within themselves—so altogether distinct is it from the rational and independent of the infinite chain of causes and effects. This cognition is the consciousness of one's spiritual "I."

A human being calls this immediate discovery of his "consciousness," the cognition that is independent of the chain of causes and effects. When he discovers this consciousness in religious teachings, he calls it "faith," to make a distinction between this consciousness—common to all people—and rational cognition. Such are all faiths from the most ancient to the newest. Their essence consists in the fact that despite the frequently incongruous forms that they have perversely assumed, they nonetheless provide to the perceiver foundations for cognition that are independent of the chain of causes and effects; indeed, only they provide an opportunity for a reasonable worldview. And thus, the academic philosopher who is in denial of religious foundations is inevitably condemned to making rounds on an infinite chain of causes, trying to locate on it an imaginary and impossible cause of all causes. The religious person is already aware of this cause of all causes, believes in it, and has, as a consequence, a firm understanding of life and as firm a guidance for his actions. The academic philosopher does not have and cannot have either one or the other.

The other day, a learned philosopher tried to explain to me that all psychic qualities have now been tied down to mechanical causes: "only consciousness hasn't been explicated quite fully," so said the learned professor, with such astonishing naïveté. "We already know everything about the entire machine; we just don't fully know what it is that brings it into movement or how." How marvelous! It is only consciousness that hasn't been tied down to mechanical processes (this "only" is so very good). It hasn't been tied down yet, but the professor is evidently certain that information will arrive one of these days that a Professor Schmidt of Berlin or a Professor Oxenberg of Frankfurt has discovered the mechanical cause of consciousness or God in the soul of man.[72] Is it not obvious that the cute old woman who believes in the Mother of God of Kazan, Our Heavenly Tsarina, is not only morally but also mentally superior to the learned professor, beyond measure?

Forgive me, Konstantin Iakovlevich, for venting these old man's rants. I can only say in self-defense that this subject, namely the false conception about the significance of religion, which is so widespread among our so-called educated society, has always preoccupied me, still preoccupies me, and preoccupied me when I was friends with Nikolai Iakovlevich. I remember pointing out to him this false conception of the significance of religion that he shared with all men of science, in my opinion. I don't remember the exact form in which I expressed these thoughts to him, likely not in the same form as I am doing so

---

72 Professors "Schmidt" and "Oxenberg" are Tolstoy's inventions.

now, but I remember having expressed them to him, and that he was more or less in agreement with me.

I think that Nikolai Iakovlevich and I, despite moving along different radii, were both advancing toward the same center that unites us all, that we were both aware of this, and that our friendly relations were never interrupted because of this. And I am glad to reminisce with sincere love on this occasion about this man who was not only intellectually gifted but had the dearest of all gifts: kindness and sincerity of heart.

September 18, 1910 Kochety

62. On Insanity[73]
[1910]

> *Ce sont des imbéciles. Un imbécile est avant-tout un homme q'on ne comprend pas.*
> [These are the insane. An insane individual is, above all else, a man who is not understood.]

I.

For many months, and especially so recently, I have been receiving no fewer than 2 or 3 letters every day—I have received 3 today—in which, for some reason, young men and young ladies write to me expressing their decision to end their lives.[74] They write to me with this in the hope that I shall rescue them

---

73 **Entry 62. "On Insanity"** [*O bezumii*] (1910) remained unfinished by the time of Tolstoy's death. It was first published in 1936 in volume 38 of *The Jubilee* (38:395-411). The commentary by B. M. Eikhenbaum (38:584-87) is uncharacteristically sketchy—as if itself unfinished—perhaps because madness and the state of asylums, both popular topics among the top Marxist leadership in the early 1930s, were quickly becoming dangerous subjects in Stalin's Soviet Union. An old topic of Tolstoy's writings was the connection among lack of purpose or opportunity in life, the debilitating effects of pessimism and depression, and the pursuit of dissident choices [consider, for example, entry 43, "The Concept of Life" (1887) and entry 50, "On Religious Tolerance" (1901)]. The most immediate trigger for reconsidering "insanity" was a stay on Vladimir Chertkov's estate Otradnoe in the Moscow suburbs from June 10 to June 23, 1910, located near the state of the art asylum wards and hospitals for mental patients run by the rich local *zemstvo*. Tolstoy paid multiple visits to these medical institutions from June 14 to June 21 during his stay.

74 One of these letters received on March 10, 1910, was by Raisa Samuilovna Labkovskaya, a young Jewish woman and doctor's assistant from the deeply provincial city of Sterlitamak.

with some advice. These letters are of three different kinds. The first kind is the most common: A village teacher desires to abandon her current occupation and enroll in a course of study (she says that she is insufficiently educated to enlighten common folk). Her idea of her desire is that it is so powerful and noble that she will take her life should she fail to realize this plan. Or there is the rapturous youth who is ready to call it quits unless he is helped to develop what he sees as his mighty potential. Or there is the inventor who desires to make humankind happy; the poet who has experienced his own genius; the maiden desirous of either dying or enrolling in studies; the woman in love with another woman's husband; the man in love with the married woman. The gender, age, and status of these letter writers change, but they have one feature in common: a blind, crude egoism that prevents these people from seeing anything besides themselves. "There is injustice everywhere, cruelty, lies, deceit, baseness, debauchery, everyone is evil—except me. The conclusion that follows is natural: my soul is too sublime for this corrupt world or the corrupt world is too filthy for my sublime soul, and I can remain in it no longer."

Such is the first kind of letter. The second kind of letter is from people who desire to serve the common folk yet find no method for engaging their energies—mighty energies, supposedly.—This kind of letter writer is so noble, so lofty, that it is impossible for them to live simply for themselves; they wish to dedicate their life to serving others, yet they fail because other people are in their way—or something else is in the way that prevents this individual from losing himself in self-sacrificial service.[75]

Imagine: For a long time, no human being existed. And then one day, he appears suddenly and sees the whole of this divine world around him: the sun, the sky, the trees, the flowers, the animals, and human beings just like him who love and whom he can love, and he is conscious of himself and his capacities of reason and of love that he can bring to the supreme degree of perfection. All this has been gifted to him from somewhere, given for free, despite the fact that he could have done nothing to deserve such gifts. The gifts must be for some purpose, but it does not cross his mind to ask such questions.

Labkovskaya was informing Tolstoy of her decision to end her life unless she was able to enroll in the additional professional training necessary to become a doctor. Perhaps realizing that his rebuttal taking into account the quotas for Jews and for women to study medicine in Russia would be too devastating, Tolstoy never sent the letter he wrote on March 23, 1910. His response to Labkovskaya survives as a copy published in *The Jubilee* (81:179-82) and was one of the building blocks of this unfinished essay.

75 Tolstoy barely explained the third kind of letter he received, but implies this category and some other varieties in the next two paragraphs.

Such a being never before existed. Never. And he is suddenly conscious of being alive, and he sees the whole world with all its joys: the sun, nature, plants, animals, and human beings like himself. These things attract him, promising the joy of mutual love, true happiness; nothing more blessed can be imagined. But he says:

"All of this is no good, and I don't need any of it. I want something else, something way more important. I want to have as much money as Ivan Ivanovich; or, I want Maria Petrovna to love me and not Semyon Ivanych; or, I want Semyon Ivanych to love nobody else but me; or I want to be able (he or she says) to learn various sciences and to become certified with a piece of paper that will allow me (he or she says) to harness the common people into supporting this sacrifice of mine; or, as happens most customarily among the so-called young intelligentsia, I wish that I could set up the republic the logistics for which Tikhonov, Mishin, and myself have rationalized so well in our party faction.

But no, this won't be. And therefore: this world is good for nothing and must be destroyed. And because it's not in my power to destroy the world, I shall destroy myself. And for this, there is liquid ammonia, there are train cars running on rails, there are buildings with windows on third floors and above, there are revolvers. I am done living. You stay here; I'm gone. So long!"

This is not a joke but a terrible, scary truth.

Man seeks happiness[76] (if he is alive, he seeks happiness—life is exclusively a striving for happiness). Man seeks happiness, happiness is possible for man only in life, and here there is man, surrounded by happiness that he can attain simply by opening his arms instead of pushing away that happiness that is given to him for free. But this man not only does not accept this happiness but instead elects to exit from the very conditions in which he could have received this happiness. It is like someone who is parched with thirst and knows that he can only get water from the river to quench his thirst, and yet he flees further and further away from the only place where he could obtain what he seeks.

II.

Sometimes people ask: Does a human being *have the right* to kill himself? The word "right" is out of place here. Rights belong only to the living. As soon as a

---

76 Written as "*blàgo*" throughout this paragraph.

human being has killed himself, he is beyond rationalizing what is right.[77] And the question is therefore only about whether a human being *can* kill himself. We see truly that he can; we see that people never tire of abusing this possibility, doing little bits of gradual self-killing through depravity, with vodka, tobacco, and opium, sometimes dueling so that his life becomes more like a war with the increased probability of being killed attached, and sometimes ending his life in one fell swoop, as in suicide. This capacity to kill oneself has been given to human beings to act as a safety valve. Armed with this capacity, a human being has no right—here is an apposite occasion for the expression of "having a right"—to say that it is unbearable to live. Unbearable to live? Well, kill yourself; you can do so, after all, and then there will be nobody left to say that this life is unbearable. The question, it turns out, is not about the right to commit suicide as much as it is about whether it is reasonable and ethical to do so (the reasonable and the ethical always coincide). The answer is unequivocal: it is both unreasonable and immoral.

It is unreasonable, first of all, because life is beyond time and space and cannot be destroyed with the death of the body. By putting an end to their manifestation of life in this world, someone who commits suicide cannot know whether this life will manifest in a more pleasing way in the next world. Second, it is unreasonable because, by ending his life in this world, man deprives himself of the possibility of experiencing and acquiring everything for his "I" that can be experienced and acquired in this world. Furthermore, it is unreasonable because—and this is key—by ending his life in this world given that it appears *unpleasant* to him, man shows how fallacious his idea about the purpose of his life is: he supposes that the purpose of life is pleasure and not service to the life of everything that exists throughout the entire world. Having taken advantage of life only to the extent that it seemed pleasant, man refuses to take advantage of life to serve the world as soon as it begins to appear unpleasant to him. And it begins to appear unpleasant to him only because he did not stake his life upon that of what it really consists, and instead places his happy stock not simply where it draws on nothing but where it cannot be. Almost always, people commit suicide for one of two reasons: either because life does not deliver the happiness that the individual desires or because it seems to him that his life is without purpose, that he cannot serve the world in the form that he has chosen. But both reasons presuppose a false concept about the purpose of life.

---

77   The Russian word *pravo* used by Tolstoy can be a noun, an adjective, and an adverb. It can mean "right" as a legal allowance and "what is right;" "just" (as in "correct") and "justice."

Consider the paralyzed monk who had control only of his left arm and who spent over 30 years lying on the floor of his cell at Optina Pustyn'. Doctors said that his suffering must have been great. Not only did he never complain about his situation but he happily spent his time looking at the icons, crossing himself constantly, and expressing his gratitude to God; with a smile on his face, he showed obvious joy at the spark of life that kept itself warm within him. Tens of thousands of visitors came to him, and it is hard to imagine all the good that this man, impaired for active work, has spread in the world.

While there is life in man, he can have true happiness and he can give it to other people. He can obtain this true happiness: By making perfect through love, he cannot help but experience the supreme happiness that is common to all human beings who stake the aim of their life on it, cannot help but contribute to the happiness of other people at the same time, by infecting them with that quality that only true happiness can grant to people.

III.

It is inevitable that either man recognizes himself as unavoidably dependent on an immaterial yet indubitably existing unknowable element and sees the meaning of his life in fulfilling the law of this element, or, on the contrary, takes himself alone to be the primary element of everything and knows no other law than his desires. Because there can exist an unlimited number of such miscellaneous desires—desires that are unattainable, given that their fulfillment depends on conditions of the external world, which are not within man's control—it is clear that life has no meaning and no value for an individual who so understands life, given that it is then a life in which his desires do not get fulfilled and so must be destroyed.

Yes, it is astonishing the stupefaction in which the people of our Christian world find themselves; this stupefaction becoming ever greater with every passing day and year. This cannot be otherwise given that this stupefaction is produced from two opposing sources, which nevertheless lead human beings to the same terrible consequences: from what is called the Church, on the one hand, and, on the other hand, from what is called science.

The stupefaction produced by the Churches—the Catholic, Greco-Russian, as well as all those different Protestant nomenclatures—is known and clear to all. Under the name of the true Christian faith, something else, incompatible even with the worldview of the least enlightened people of our time, is inspired assiduously and stubbornly: the idea of the creation of the world in

6 days, the Trinity, redemption, resurrection, mysteries, and much else that both the so-called educated classes and working people alike have stopped believing in after having become powerless to isolate religious truth from its admixture with lies. And so people remain without any kind of religion, in a state most uncharacteristic for human beings, without any explanation of the meaning and purpose of life and the internal ordering of that which is.

This is the doing of the Church. The teaching called science bridges the shortcomings in the project left unfinished by the Church. This teaching consists in the idea that the law of human life can be inferred from the laws that we observe in the natural world. Because we observe creatures in the external natural world struggling for existence, and there occur modifications and progress among the species that evolve, science invites us to see that the same should be the case with the law of the human species—that is, that what humans do, in essence, is and should be the same as what animal creatures do.

As a result, not only does there not exist among the entire Christian world a single reasonable religious conception of life that is proper to the reasonable creature called man but instead a conception of life reigns that quite excludes any possibility for the existence of an understanding that should be proper to man as a reasonable creature. Only this can explain the existence and the would-be renaissance in our time of a sundry of quasi-Christian beliefs,[78] including the Catholic, Lutheran, and Baptist, as well various theosophical, spiritualist, and other quasi-religious teachings. Only individuals with a keen self-consciousness can sense the inanity and inner contradiction of the reigning conception of life: evolution, progress, the acceptance of whatever the majority of people do as good and obligatory. Without anything else at their disposal, they snatch at the weirdest superstitions within reach that somehow respond to the higher demands of their soul. With obstinacy and imperviousness, the majority of people persist in their delusion, something that they have in common with the insane, becoming less and less penetrable by reasonable arguments, and more and more self-confident and self-conceited.

IV.

Aside from the aforementioned letters that arrive in the mail every day with threats of suicide addressed to me, I receive no fewer than a dozen letters every

---

78 Sic, written as *vèrovanii* ["beliefs" in the genitive plural], not *ver* ["faiths" in the genitive plural].

day from young—or not so young—men and women asking the same unbelievably tedious questions: What is the meaning of life? Why live? These questions sometimes strike me with their naïveté and absurdity: After they have read the latest bestsellers and not found in them any explanations as to the meaning of life—and indeed, on the contrary, having for the most part discovered the negation of the meaning of life in these books, most of them works of fiction—, the letter writer is confident that there is no meaning whatsoever and that denying the existence of any meaning to life is endearing and is the clearest indication that they are highly cultured, in the contemporary sense. The other day, I received in the mail a book titled *On the Meaning of Life*.[79] In this book, the author searches for the meaning of life in the writings of Sologub, Andreev, and Shestov. To show that they are not oblivious about the various sources for the topic of the meaning of life, the author also uses Chekhov's writings, and quotes other writers who are equally competent with regards to the question— as if neither the Brahmins, nor Buddha, nor Solomon, nor Marcus Aurelius, nor Socrates, nor Plato, nor Christ, nor Rousseau, nor Kant, nor Schopenhauer, etc., ever existed. The author writes as if prior to Sologub, L. Andreev, Shestov,[80] and Leo Tolstoy, humans lived without nary a concept of the meaning of life, which is only now on the verge of being disclosed to people by the likes of Shestov, Andreev, Sologub, and Tolstoy.[81] The same idea is expressed in the letters that I receive in the mail. I can sense that there are forgone conclusions hiding behind the question about the meaning of life in these letters: namely, that there is no such meaning and cannot be. One writer, for example—in a real letter—asks whom to believe: the Christ of the gospels or Sanin from Artsybashev's novel?[82] The author's sympathy is clearly with Sanin. In such letters—which, for the most part, are written by people posturing as writers—the author expresses their "gotcha" answer to the question about the meaning of life. The answer is always, essentially, that there is no meaning to life; that there is simply is and can be no such thing for truly educated individuals. Instead, there is evolution, which takes place in accordance with the laws discovered by science, and which renders null and void the old and obsolete notions of the soul, God, and other such superstitions, as well as the ideas about the vocation of man and his moral duties. And all of this is uttered with infinite self-confidence and smugness.

---

79 There is no record of a book by this title in Tolstoy's personal library.

80 Tolstoy means his younger contemporaries writing on the meaning of life (or lack thereof), including novelists and fiction writers Fedor Sologub (1863–1927) and Leonid Andreev (1871–1919) as well as philosopher Lev Shestov (Leib Isaakovich Shvartsman, 1866–1938).

81 Tolstoy uses plurals here: the Shestovs, the Andreevs, the Sologubs, and the Tolstoys.

82 Tolstoy means Mikhail Artsybashev's novel *Sanin* (1907).

"All of this is outmoded and has overstayed its welcome. What we need now is a new definition of the meaning of life, a new account that concurs with Darwinism, Nietzscheanism, and with the most up-to-date conceptions of life. We should think up a novel explication of the meaning of life that would only recognize at its foundation material laws, ones explored across the infinity of space and time." This is uttered by the sort of man who would bet that it is incumbent upon them to think up a new type of geometry wherein the sum of the angles of a triangle is equal to three rather than two square angles. Indeed, despite all costs, these are the kind of people who would even attempt to devise such a brand of novel geometry. The best among the young, poor sorts, vacillate between the smug smarts in the blabber of the likes of Darwin, Haeckel,[83] Marx, and, variously, Maeterlinck, Knut Hamsun, Weininger,[84] Nietzsche, and so on—thinkers whom they esteem as great sages, on the one hand, but whose teachings, they vaguely recognize, are meaningless for their quest to understand the meaning of life, on the other hand. These young people are nevertheless still searching—in vain, it goes without saying—for the explication of the meaning of life, and, increasingly and inevitably, they come to despair. And the most fervid and unhinged among them end up committing suicide. According to Krose's book *Der Selbstmord im 19. Jahrhundert*,[85] in Europe alone, not including statistics from Russia and the other uncultured countries of Europe, there were 1,300,000 suicides in the nineteenth century—a number that continues to increase.[86] Manifestly, this could not have been otherwise.

What is hard for people living in our world to understand is the cause of their disastrous situation. It is hard for people to become conscious that their situation is disastrous as the main result of the major disaster of our time called "progress." "Progress" is expressed in feverish anxiety, rush, the intensity of work whose object is completely useless or is obviously harmful, permanent self-intoxication with ever-newer and all-consuming amusements,[87] and—the key thing—smug self-confidence. Dirigibles, submarines, dreadnoughts, 50-story buildings, parliaments, theaters, wireless telegraphs, congresses of peace, million-strong armies, fleets, professors of various schools, billions of books,

83 On Haeckel, see notes to entry 57.

84 Otto Weininger (1880–1903), author of *Geschlecht und Charakter* [Sex and Character] (1903). By bringing up of Weininger's example, Tolstoy is underscoring his condemnation of spectacular suicide.

85 Tolstoy means Hermann Anton Krose (1867–1949), a German Catholic mathematician, priest, and member of The Society of Jesus.

86 Whether appropriately or not, Tolstoy is being ironic and even sarcastic yet again about the true meanings of "culture" and "cultured."

87 The Russian word "*zatèi*" means both "gadgets" and "pastimes."

newspapers, discussions, speeches, research investigations: In all of these we see feverish fuss, haste, anxiety, and an intense mode of work whose object is always not that which is necessary—or more likely, that which is harmful. All the while, and incessantly so, people conducting such affairs are in a bent-over-backward state of self-delight: they do not see their own insanity, and nor do they wish to nor are they capable of seeing it; they are proud of it, and they expect all sorts of happy outcomes from it. In anticipation of these great happy outcomes, these people intoxicate themselves with ever-newer brands of amusement whose aim is always the same: to stupefy them into oblivion as they sink deeper and deeper in the quagmire of political, economic, scientific, aesthetic contradictions—without exit or solution.

We have so ordered—or rather, disordered—our life[88] that we stand in need of a countless number of the most strange and unnecessary things, and we have run out of space for the one thing we really need, the one thing that cannot help but be needed by a human: Religion! "Oh, that thing, no, we don't need that in our enlightened age—not now that we know about the descent of man and the origin of the earth, that we can transmit nonsense and filthy rubbish from one end of the world and back to the other, and not now that we shall soon fly around the sky like birds of the air."

V.

Yes, the thousands of suicides that take place every day are terrible and very pitiful. But more pitiful still is the lot of those who are in this psychic state and are thus preparing for the same thing—either for a swift suicide or for a meaningless and unhappy life, which is inevitably in store for individuals in such a perverse psychic state. And the enormous majority of the populace of the pseudo-Christian world of our time find themselves in just this situation.

In his fine book, *Suicide as a Social Phenomenon of Modern Civilization*, a well-known Czech writer, Masaryk, arrives at the perfectly just conclusion that the main cause for suicide among Christian nations is the absence of religion.[89] The conclusion at which he arrived in this book, which he wrote 30 years ago,

---

88 Tolstoy plays on the rhyming in Russian of "ordered-disordered" [*ustroili-razstroili*].

89 Thomas Garrique Masaryk (1850–1937), well-regarded intellectual historian, future President of Czechoslovakia (1918–35), and author of *Der Selbstmord als soziale Massenerscheinung der Modernen Civilization* (Wien, 1881). Masaryk paid several visits to Tolstoy over the years. During his last visit to Tolstoy in March 1910, the two men discussed questions of spiritual education and culture.

is unfortunately indefinite and far from complete. If the cause for the increased number of suicides is the absence of religion, then salvation must lie in the assimilation of religion. But what religion? He speaks about a Christianity "cleansed of the clerics' churchly daub" (*gesäubert von Pfaffengeschmiere*)—or, cleansed intuitively, on the spur of their gut feeling—such a religion. Although he presumes that salvation lies in one of the Christian sects, he does not decide which one it is; more precisely, he does not tell us which religious content will satisfy the requirements of our time. This book contains the very same lack of definitiveness of opinion, the same temerity, and, essentially, the same lack of faith in anything that characterizes the major disaster of our time. How can you expect a religion to evince itself? I am not alone—what about the billions of other more people who are alive? Shall we all continue to perish without any comprehension of the meaning of our life, living this nasty, animal, criminal life of ours, taking consolation only in the idea that a new religion will one day come together for our progeny and that their requirements will be satisfied within its fold? The error of such reasoned schemes is the same scientific perversion of thinking that looks at plainly vital phenomena as if they were something external, subject to research and investigation. For any living individual—but not for the learned—religion is never the subject of investigation but is the vital, inevitable condition of life: Religion is for the soul of man what air and food are for the body. Just as we cannot defer to future generations when it comes to breathing and eating, we should not defer to them when it comes to the issue of a new religion, all the while living with empty souls. While there are animals, there is air for them to breathe and food for their sustenance; while there are humans, there is, and always has been, a religious conception of life that allows for human—rather than cattle-like—existence. This conception has always been there in response to the degree of man's intellectual and moral development, so it is here now as well, in response to the degree of the development of the people of our time. This religion exists, and we all know it for as long as we are unwilling to conceal its demands from ourselves. These demands appear impossibly excessive to us because they are directly opposed to the entire order of our life, exposing all of our customary transgressions and sins. This religion has always been and still is: it is in the Vedas, in Confucianism, in Taoism, in the teaching of the sages of ancient Greece and Rome, in Christianity, in Mohammedanism, in Bahaism, in the teachings of Rousseau, Pascal, Kant, Schopenhauer, Emerson, Ruskin, Lamennais,[90] and many, many others. Mainly,

---

90 The American Transcendentalist Ralph Waldo Emerson (1803–82), the British champion of the Arts and Craft Movement John Ruskin (1819–1900), and the French Catholic Socialist Félicité Robert de Lamennais (1782–1854) were among Tolstoy's favorite

however, it exists in the heart and reason of every individual of our time. This religion can be very easily defined: Its postulates are the same as those of every religious-moral teaching that has ever existed, before it became perverted, and they are all clear, short, and they are as comprehensible to the illiterate workman and the child as they are to the learned old man. These teachings all concern but one thing, which is uttered in unison by the greatest teachers of the world and not by Christ alone: being conscious of one's divine element within and recognizing it within all human beings, loving them all, and not doing unto any human being what you would not want done unto yourself. The one universal religion common to all people consists in this and always has. True, there is a metaphysical side to this, to provide substantiations for these demands of love, but these metaphysical postulates have never been rendered into verbal expression in such a way that they are naturally and similarly understood by everybody. They resist this rendering and continue to do so today. The more carefully people attempt to express these postulates, the fewer obstacles they encounter in their pursuit of a universal conception of religious truth common to all humankind. And so, the chief cause of the disastrousness of our life—the absence of religion—does not stem from the fact that a new religion proper for our "enlightened" time has not yet been "invented," but only from the fact that our life is so immoral and unreasoned that we are unable to accept the one eternal religion common to all people with which we cannot be unfamiliar.

The main cause for the disastrousness of the life of the humankind of our time is in our living through an inevitable transition from one age to the next, something that individuals and whole nations alike experience when transitioning from one worldview and order of life to another, newer, more reasonable one, one that is better suited for the more perfect stage of development experienced by the humankind of our time.

VI.

There once was a time when my view of the insanity of our life was so discordant with the inflexible self-confidence of the enormously overpowering majority of those living their lives insanely, and it appeared such an exception to me that it felt strange and scary for me to speak up. As of late, I have started

---

contemporary thinkers, whose ideas and works he frequently cited and included in his collections of wisdom.

feeling completely the opposite: it is becoming strange and scary for me not to speak up about my view. It has thus become evident to me that the majority of humankind, and of the Christendom of our time, especially, live life directly and glaringly contrary to reason, feeling, and to human benefits and comforts. The majority live in a state of madness, insanity—perhaps temporary, but total nonetheless.

A few months ago, I did something I had not done for quite a long time: I picked up a newspaper and read through it. Everything in it was so strange to me that I could hardly believe that anything described in it did indeed take place. I read about the following (extracted from my erstwhile jottings):

The first matter in question is the annexation of Bosnia and Herzegovina. In the headline article, it is written, in a most serious tone, that a few individuals calling themselves the Austrian government are willing to annex a couple of million people to what they call the Austrian Empire, even though other small group of individuals who call themselves, respectively, the Serbian, the Turkish, and the Bulgarian governments, do not want this. To resolve the dispute, the few individuals who desire that the annexation take place, and the other few individuals who do not desire that the annexation take place, collectively agree to forcing hundreds of thousands of people of several different ethnicities to go and butcher one another. Alternatively, some suggest, one party should receive from another party several million rubles, levied on the populations of lands named Austria, Serbia, Bulgaria, or Turkey. At this point, a small number of individuals calling themselves the Russian government issue a declaration that they will be sending dozens or maybe hundreds of thousands of people to butcher those people who obey the people calling themselves the Austrian or the Turkish governments, unless those governments agree to the partitioning of the lands proposed by the Russian government.

All this is written in the most refined French, and—without a word being mentioned about the preparations for murder on which this all rests—is dispatched through an attaché of one government to another, published in thousands of papers, and read by millions of people who find it all quite natural.

It would seem clear that millions of people—creatures endowed with reason and moral feeling—could not go and kill people whom they don't know, without knowing why or what for, because some other people they don't know, called the government, order them to kill, readying them for the greatest deprivation and loss of all that is dear to human beings. And one can count on the fact that everything that the governments and their diplomats decide upon will be carried out with exactitude.[91]

Moreover—and this is astonishing![92]—nobody for a minute doubts that everything that the governments premeditate will be carried out. Everyone is as sure of this as they are when they send money to a butcher's shop to purchase beef that they will receive a certain amount of beef in exchange. The only questions they have are about the weight of the chunk of beef they will receive, the quality of the loin within the cut, and how much money to send. So, too, is it with the discussion in the ministries and the papers about the annexation of Bosnia and Herzegovina: The only questions are about how many people should be readied for butchery, who should be dispatched to butcher others, and what sorts of people will make the cut.

This was the first headline by which I was struck. I then read a second article, headlined "Work and Historical Heredity" ["*Rabota i istoricheskaia preemstvennost'*"].[93]

Whereas the first article was about international resolutions, about how sundry governments disagree among themselves and force their subjects to butcher one another in obeisance of aims that are as alien to the killers as to those killed, it also includes a discussion about something that has nothing to do with relations between international governments: namely, it talks about several individuals who regard themselves as members of the present Russian government and who rule over the lives of dozens of millions, and several other individuals who would love to be the government and who therefore consider all the resolutions of the present government to be bad.

In defending itself, the government says that "only the following division of people into groups is clear: those who strain their efforts to benefit the growth and development of the Russian statehood and those who struggle against its foundations." The author of the article objects to this, saying that to be able to act for the benefit of the growth and development of the Russian statehood, those with an alternative vision of its development and growth ought to be given as much leeway to act as the governing party. They complain that this

---

91 Either the editors of the *Jubilee* or Tolstoy omitted the auxiliary particle "ne" before "*sovershit'sia*" to indicate the intended double negation, meaning in the emphatic constructions of Russian usage that the impossible becomes possible.

92 "*Udivitel'noe delo*," the marveling narrator's refrain, is repeated four more times in this section of the article.

93 To date, it has been impossible to trace these mentions to specific authors and periodicals. The usual archival sources and manuscript holdings recording routine on-site work, such as the day notes by Tolstoy's domestics and secretaries, do not provide leads.

is not the case, that those with alternative views of how to grow the state are having their style cramped when, etc . . .

Again—astonishingly!—those individuals who regard themselves as empowered to govern millions and who would like and hope that they will accede to government if they persist in their restless struggle, are as certain that they can dispose of the lives of dozens of millions of people in their nation as we are certain that the sun will rise every day. The debates and arguments go on only about how best to order these millions of people; nobody doubts that these people will live as they are instructed to by the laws of a few individuals called the government. Even more astonishing still is that millions of human beings—reasonable moral creatures living by the fruit of their labor and therefore not only not standing in need of anybody's aid but in fact supporting with their own labor many thousands of leisurely individuals—slavishly obey the arguments presented by the feckless governors, individuals who are governed by petty foul passions, and certainly not by their proclaimed goal, which is the welfare of the people.

Following this is a third long article, "The Constitutional Budget." Its author deliberates about how much annually should be taken away in taxes from the products of labor of every individual working for himself and his family and remitted to the disposal of the individuals called the government. It would seem obvious that the toiling millions have neither want nor good reason to give away the products of their labor to individuals who have until now invested this money only in the most evil and immoral of ventures: in producing weapons of murder, in prisons, fortresses, vodka imports, the corruption of the populace by means of the army draft or falsely professed religion. It might then seem obvious that there should be no budget and no occasion for a discussion of how to tax and invest this money. So it would seem. But the incumbents and the government wannabes are so completely sanguine about the fact that they are pocketing the money that all they argue about is how to collect more of it and how to split it among themselves. And so it continues to happen—isn't this astonishing?—that money gets raised and then channeled: the frequently hungry toilers, who lack the most basic things, hand over their savings to idlers, who live an insane life of luxury.

Up next is an article titled "The Question of Treasonous Crime at the Moscow Congress of Criminology."[94] This article describes how some people

---

94 Coverage of the meetings of criminologists was one of the profile themes in the Russian press at the turn of the century. They were regularly discussed at the Moscow Psychological Society and in the pages of its journal, *Voprosy Filosofii i Psikhologii* [*Questions of Philosophy and Psychology*]. Of the ten International Congresses of Criminologists that had taken place

got together at an assembly in Moscow to discourse about clauses that allow for the deprivation of freedom, the plunder (through the imposition of fines), the torture, and the killing of people, which clauses disallow such things, how to make better use of these clauses, and so on. At first, it appears astonishing why these individuals, who apparently disagree with the government and are opposed to it, wouldn't have directly said as much. Every sane thinking person can see that—even setting aside Christianity for a moment, the religion we allegedly profess, given that our moral bar in that regard could not have fallen any lower—nobody has the right to plunder, torture, or deprive others of their freedom or their life, and that nobody should do such things, in the name of considerations of any sort. And so, you might think that, clearly, the anti-government opposition assembly must have uttered directly that which goes without saying for any sane thinking person: that one man has no right to do violence to another; no man has such a right. And that even if we were to allow that there might be considerations according to which some individuals can torture others—lo, this has always been the way—counter considerations could be found for others to apply violence against those who tortured them. But the "learned" assembly said nothing of the sort. Instead, they conscientiously cited subtle considerations about the "terrible consequences of the violation of the general court procedure in political trials," talking about "the necessity of studying treason from the sociological standpoint," about how "the main problem would only get bigger and bigger at group meetings," and about how "the impossibility of limiting oneself with concise theses on such a complex matter had become clearer and clearer still."

Again, I am astonished and bewildered: Why are both the current government and the aspiring incumbents who argue with it so cocksure that a populace that is ignorant of, and hasn't heard anything about, articles 120, 117, etc., of the constitution will nevertheless obey these and other such articles even when they command crimes against divine and human laws? Why would they obey these articles, when, luckily, they know other articles such as "don't do unto another what you don't want to be done unto yourself," and that "it is better to forgive not just seven times but seven times seven[95] than it is to take revenge" [Matthew 18:21-22]? Yet, most astonishingly, not only does the populace obey all these laws but they take on the roles of soldiers, wardens, jury, jailers, and

before Tolstoy's death, Tolstoy is likely referring to one of the regional meetings in Moscow, and not the 1902 Congress in St. Petersburg nor the latest Congress in Brussels (1910).

95 Translated as "seven times seven" [sem'iu sem' raz]. On Tolstoy's "77" and "seven times seven," see "Editor's Introduction."

henchmen to commit more of these crimes against themselves, contrary to their conscience and the law of God that they profess and pledge loyalty to.

The next and fifth article includes news about how a man—specifically, the Russian Emperor—expressed a wish for a recently deceased sweet old man who used to reside in Kronstadt[96] to be sainted. And the Synod—the gathering of individuals assured of their right and ability to prescribe to the populace which faith to profess—resolved to have a national celebration on the first anniversary of the sweet old man's death, so as to turn the old man's corpse into an idol of national worship. It is somewhat comprehensible (though even this is pushing it) that the populace might be taken in so badly as to believe that they are not so much human beings as they are subjects of a certain state, who should relinquish their human duties in the name of this idol called the state—as happens when people are coerced to be drafted as soldiers and participate in wars. One might even be able to wrap one's head around how people could be driven to giving up their savings that are taken from them in the form of taxes, to be used for deliberately evil doings. And however strange, it might even be understandable how a long and intensive cultivation of the evil feeling of revenge can lead people to obeying violent orders of all kinds, even to killing their brothers, under the pretext of punishing them. But it seems impossible to grasp how people living in the twentieth century, who know the gospels, can understand the purpose of their lives so perversely, believing in the necessity and benefit of worshipping inanimate idols.

It would seem that people who are Christians would not be capable of obeying other people to do such things, and yet—again, astonishingly!—such things are done all the time by the overwhelming majority of people: by the man who calls himself the tsar, by all of his servants, and by all those hypocritical or wayward people who call themselves the synod, who are quite certain that all of their resolutions about the celebration of the sainthood of a dead man will be embraced just as the entire populace previously embraced other relics, icons, and miracles, with their accompanying deceits. Lastly—how truly astonishing!—a million-strong populace calmly accepts these veneered legends with a sprinkle of holiness as orders to be followed, instead of turning away from them in revulsion. These legends take the place of the salvific Christian

---

96 The kindly old man whom Tolstoy intentionally and mockingly portrays as innocent and harmless is John of Kronstadt (1829–1909 [December 1908 Old Style]). Kronstadt embodied everything that Tolstoy despised in a cleric determined to influence the decisions of the state. He was also one of the prelates who advocated for and supported Tolstoy's excommunication.

truths known to the populace, ruining their lives, making these people irrevocably under the sway of the power of deceivers.

Yes, however terrible all the deceits under whose weight humankind suffers, this fideistic deceit, least noticeable by people, is the most terrible. It is terrible because on its foundation all the other deceits are piled and from it all disasters ensue.

Ask yourself: Why should reasonable and kind individuals get drafted when ordered to by strangers? Why should they put on uniforms, learn how to kill, and then go and kill other strangers, knowing all the while that man should not kill but should love all human beings? Why should they give away their savings to strangers, who use this money to commit deliberately evil deeds, when they agree that nobody should take another's property? Why do they go to court and demand punishment or submit to being punished, knowing all the while that nobody has the right to judge others, and that what is natural for man is to forgive his brother instead of punishing him? Why do people obey the resolutions of individual strangers when it comes to the most important thing for the soul: recognizing what is holy—the supreme goodness—and what is not holy, what is evil?

VII.

All these questions may be answered with one diagnosis: Those who commit such deeds—those who prescribe them, as well as those who fulfill them—are in a state of insanity. I mean this neither figuratively nor bombastically but in the most direct and definite sense of the word: to wit, they do not guide their life with the help of what should strike man as patently reasonable, that which we all have in common, and that which the teachings of the greatest sages of life have described. They follow incidental and patently anti-reasonable guidelines instead, as if they did not need to accept reasonable rationales as obligatory. How incorrect, really, is Pascal's idea that were our dreams as consistent as the events of reality, of life, we would not be able to tell dreams from reality? This is as wrongheaded as the thought that, were unreasonable activity universally accepted to be reasonable, we would not be able to distinguish unreasonable from reasonable activity.[97]

---

97 These are Tolstoy's interpretations of Pascal's thoughts on *"songe"* and *"rêve"*: Pascal writes on these topics in his objections to Pyrrhonism: see, e.g., "Contrariétès" (§§131/434); "Grandeur" (*"nous connaissons la verité . . ."* §110/282); and especially series XXIX of the unclassified sections, where he also writes on the Eucharist. On dreams specifically, see "Si

Both of these thoughts are erroneous because—putting aside the differences between dreams and the lack of universal acceptance of irrational activity—human beings have a key feature that allows them to tell true life from its fake likeness. The supreme quality of the human soul—self-consciousness—is that feature; moral feeling and moral effort stem from it. As a result—however consistent our dreams might be and however pervasive the general insanity—human beings can always distinguish dreaming and insanity from true life, for moral effort is absent from both dreams and insanity. One could even grant that the dreams of many nights were as consistent as the events of real life, or that, as happens to be the case for the majority of people in our "cultured" realm, people are in a state of complete insanity. Still, thanks to their self-consciousness and the moral feeling caused by it, along with the possibility of moral effort, everyone is always able to see and cannot help but see that a dream is a dream and that insane life is the life of insanity. It sometimes happens in a dream that we see ourselves and know ourselves to be committing the foulest of deeds, yet are powerless to stop ourselves. Yet we still have one option: we can get ourselves out of this scrap by calling on our self-consciousness for an emergency wake-up. So it is with our present insane life: If we feel that we are doing terrible filth and cannot stop from doing it, only self-consciousness—waking us up from insanity to a sane life—can rescue us.

Even if man's ravings are as consistent as they get and insanity unites all people, a healthy individual can always tell a dream from reality and insane life from a sane one. A healthy person can always tell a dream from reality and insanity from a rational state, because self-consciousness is absent both in dreams and in insanity; and with self-consciousness absent, absent are moral feeling and its consequence—moral effort. And so even if dreams were to perplex people with the strictest possible consistency and all people were possessed by one and the same insane bug, a healthy person would still be able to tell dreams from reality and insanity from sane living thanks to this one thing. As in a dream, in the state of insanity human beings are not conscious of themselves and are disempowered from making moral efforts. This is why it so happens that we can see ourselves in the middle of doing something filthy yet cannot desist, just as we often do not desist despite knowing that we are committing evil, following what everyone else is doing around us.

The difference between the two states consists in what Pascal supposed—consistency, the consistency of raving, of an insanity that has

---

nous rêvions toutes les nuits la même chose . . . " (§§803/386). In contemporary English editions of Pascal, see Blaise Pascal, *Pensées and Other Writings*. ed. Anthony Levi. trans. Honor Levi. (New York: Oxford, 1995), see especially pp. 146–47.

enveloped all or a huge majority of the people of our world. We live a life of insanity, a life contrary to the most basic, fundamental demands of rational meaning; it is only because all or a huge majority of people live such a life that we fail to see the difference between insane and sane life and accept the former for the latter.

Just as we do in a bad dream to rid ourselves of the terror happening to us in it—mostly, the terror of what we are doing in the dream—we must come to our senses, come back to ourselves to understand that it is a dream. And to rid ourselves of the nightmare that we are living through and in which we participate, we must come to our senses and call forth the moral feeling and moral effort characteristic of the sane creature called man.

VIII.

To say that we live insanely, that we lead a perfectly insane and mad life, is not simply a manner of speaking, a simile, or hyperbole: it is a simple statement of the fact.—I happened to pay a visit to two enormous asylums the other day. The impression that I got was that these institutions were founded for groups of mentally ill people who are not to be diagnosed homogeneously as one group of "the insane," sick from one and the same mass epidemic of insanity. The insane, victims of the epidemic, constitute a multitude of various classes, subsections, and kinds; there are motley forms of insanity. Their classifications have been put forward by Guislain,[98] Zeller,[99] Griesinger,[100] Krafft-Ebing,[101] Morel,[102]

---

98 As published in *The Jubilee* without any commentary, Tolstoy's list mixing Russian and foreign spellings is practically illegible. The list in this translation shows my attempt to restore the correct names using their correct international spellings: Joseph Guislain (1797–1860), father of psychiatric classification, author of *Traité sur les phrénopathies* (1833).

99 It is unclear whom Tolstoy may mean.

100 Wilhelm Griesinger (1817–68), the German neurologist and psychiatrist best known for his studies of the experience of pain and for reforms of the asylum system.

101 Richard Krafft-Ebing (1840–1903), author of the famous *Psychopathia Sexualis* (first published in 1886).

102 Bénedict-Augustin Morel (1809–73), specialist in mental deficiency, father of the theory of degeneration.

Meynert,[103] Lewes (?),[104] Magnan,[105] Kraepelin,[106] Morselli,[107] Clouston,[108] Hack Tuke,[109] Korsakov,[110] Ignatiev,[111] and many, many others. They all disagree about various things and work at cross-purposes. Every psychiatrist diagnoses different kinds of psychoneurosis, mania, paranoia, various forms of compulsive knitting, and catatonics, etc., ... psychopathia degenerative, and various others. As one learned author puts it, "no pathognomic and anatomic-pathological substratum (sic)[112] has been identified and no precise division can be therefore performed." The existing divisions might be useful for students cramming by rote, so that they have the words at the ready that they have heard from their professors. Once their diplomas are conferred, they can get an appointment with a salary that is 20, 30, or even 50 times that of a worker who produces something that is more surely necessary for other people. In essence, there is only one clear and comprehensible division of the mentally ill according to which patients are

---

103 Theodor Meynert (1833–92). An inspiration for Freud, Meynert is best known for his theory of cytoarchitecture.

104 As written, this name may best be understood as defunct. It is uncertain whether the English positivist G. H. Lewes is the person here intended.

105 Valentin Magnan (1835–1916), student of anomaly and degeneration, the author of *Art et l'hypnose* (1907).

106 Emil Kraepelin (1856–1926), best known for his "Kraepelinian dichotomy," a division used as the basis for modern classifications of psychoses.

107 "Morselli": Enrico "Henry" Agostino Morselli (1852–1929) was a eugenicist and author of a book on suicide better known by its English title, *Suicide: An Essay on Comparative Moral Statistics* (1881). In his later years, he developed a new classification of mental disorders.

108 Thomas Clouston (1840–1915) was a celebrated Scottish psychiatrist, professor at Edinburgh University, and author of *The Hygiene of Mind* and *Unsoundness of Mind*, among other works. Working on neuroses and mental diseases in adolescents, he was a key specialist at the Royal Edinburgh Asylum and founder of its charter hospitals.

109 Daniel Hack-Tuke (1827–95) was a well-known London psychiatrist and clinician as well as editor of *The Journal of Mental Science* and *The Dictionary of Psychological Medicine*. His name is badly garbled in the original.

110 S. S. Korsakov (1856–1900). Sergey Korsakov's clinic for the mentally ill in Moscow lay right across the fence from Tolstoy's Moscow home in Khamovniki. Korsakov attended Tolstoy's presentation "The Concept of Life" at the Moscow Psychological Society (see entry 43). His psychiatric specialty was alcoholic disorders, and his work identifying the disorders is now known as Korsakoff's syndrome and Wernicke-Korsakoff syndrome. While writing "On Insanity," Tolstoy was rereading Korsakov's course on psychiatry, and in his diary on June 27, 1910, he expressed his utter disgust for this work (58:70).

111 Although a common Russian last name, this mention has defied identification and is listed in *The Jubilee* as the "psychiatrist Ignatiev" (38:411). It could be the name of a doctor at the Meshcherskoe and Troitskoe asylums that Tolstoy visited in June 1910.

112 Appears as Tolstoy's "sic" in the original.

assigned in hospitals and this or that treatment is prescribed to them. This division is as follows:

1. the restless (previously called the 'unruly');
2. the semi-restless;
3. those at rest;
4. those undergoing testing.

This exact division relates quite accurately to the huge number of those at large, those possessed of the insanity of the so-called culture of our time.

63. Introduction to *The Path of Life*[113] [1910]

1. For a human being to live his life well, he must know what he should and what he shouldn't do. In order for him to know this, he must understand what he is and what the world where he lives is. This has been in the teachings of the wisest and kindest people throughout history. All of these teachings concur in the main, concurring as well with what reason and the conscience of every human being tells us. This teaching is as follows:

2. Aside from what we see, hear, touch, and what we know from other people, there is that which we do not see, hear, touch, and what nobody has told us anything about, which we nevertheless know better than anything else in the world. This is what life gives to us and which we call "I."

3. This same invisible element that gives us life we recognize as well in all living creatures and most vividly in creatures like us—in other people.

---

113 **Entry 63. "Introduction to *The Path of Life*"** [*Predislovie k knige* Put' zhizni] (1910). We include only the introduction to this final work by Tolstoy providing a summary of his views on life. The long book includes thirty short brochures on specific spiritual themes selected from the treasury of world wisdom and written for Posrednik, where it was published with substantial censorial excisions in 1911 after Tolstoy's death. Co-editors Ivan Gorbunov-Posadov and Nikolai Gusev restored the text to its original, which was published in 1956, sixteen years after Gorbunov died. The work constitutes all of volume 45 of *The Jubilee* (45:13-496), with extensive commentary by Gusev (45:521-90). The "Introduction" to this book translated for this anthology appears in the same volume (45:13-16).

4. We call "soul" the universal invisible element that animates everything that lives, of which we are conscious within ourselves and which we recognize in creatures like us, in people; in and of itself, this universal invisible element that animates everything that lives, we call God.

5. Being separated from each other and from God in the body, human souls strive to reunify with that from which they have become separated; humans achieve this unification with the souls of other people through love, and with God through their being conscious of their divinity. The meaning and happiness of human life consists in this greater and greater unification with the souls of other people by way of love, and with God—through being conscious of the divinity of life.

6. The greater and greater unification of a human soul with other creatures and God, and therefore the greater and greater happiness of man is achieved by the liberation of the soul from that which stands in the way of loving other people and consciousness of one's divinity: from sins, that is, from indulging the lusts of the flesh; from temptations, that is, from false conceptions about happiness; and from superstitions, that is, from false teachings that seek to justify sins and temptations.

7. The sins that stand in the way of human unification with other creatures and with God are the following: the lusts of the belly, that is, gluttony and drinking;

8. The lusts of lechery, that is, sexual debauchery;

9. The lusts of idleness, that is, self-exemption from the labor needed to satisfy one's needs;

10. The sins of profiting, that is, acquisition and hoarding of possessions that exploit the labor of other people;

11. And the worst sins of all, the sins of disunity from other people: envy, fear, condemnation, hostility, anger, and ill-will toward other people, in general. These are the sins that prevent the human soul from unification through love with God and other creatures.

12. The temptations that attract men to sins—that is, the false conceptions about their relationship with others are the following: the temptations of pride, that is, a false conception of one's superiority over other people;

13. The temptation of inequality, that is, a false conception about the possibility of dividing people into superior and inferior;

14. The temptation of legal regulation, that is, the false conception that some people have the right to organize the life of other people through coercion.

15. The temptation of punishment, that is, the false conception about the right of some people to do evil unto other people for the sake of justice or retribution.

16. And the temptation of vanity, that is, the false conception that it is not reason and conscience that can and must be the guiding principle of human deeds but human opinions and man-made laws.

17. Such are the temptations that attract men to sins. The superstitions that justify sins and temptations are the following: the superstition of the state, the superstition of the Church, and the superstition of science.

18. The superstition of the state consists in the faith that it is necessary and beneficial for a minority of idle people to govern the majority of working people. The superstition of the Church consists in the faith that the religious truth that is ceaselessly revealed to men was discovered once and for all and that certain people who have expropriated the right to teach the true faith to other people are indeed in possession of that religious truth once and for all expressed.[114]

19. The superstition of science consists in the faith that the integral true knowledge vital for all men consists in merely the fragments selected from the boundless sphere of knowledge, the miscellany of mostly useless knowledge, which, at a certain point in time, drew the attention of a small number of people who had liberated themselves from the obligation of labor necessary for human life and who therefore lived an immoral and unreasonable life.

20. By obstructing the unification of the soul with other creatures and God, sins, temptations, and superstitions deprive an individual of his natural happiness. So, for a human being to regain his happiness, he must combat sins, temptations, and superstitions. A human being must make certain efforts to do so.

21. These efforts are always within a human's power: first, because they always occur in the present moment, that is, in that timeless point wherein the past touches upon the future and in which an individual is always free.

---

114 Tolstoy places the superstitions of both the state and the church under the same rubric number 18.

22. Second, these efforts are within a human's power also because they do not consist in executing some unachievable feats but simply in exercising restraint, which is always possible for an individual: restraint from acts that are contrary to loving one's neighbor and the consciousness of a divine element in one's human self;

23. Restraint from uttering words that are contrary to loving one's neighbor and to consciousness of a divine element in one's human self;

24. And restraint from having thoughts that are contrary to loving one's neighbor and to consciousness of a divine element in one's human self.

25. It is the indulgence of the lusts of the flesh that brings man to sins, and man needs to make effort to exercise self-restraint from deeds, words, and thoughts that indulge the lusts of the flesh to combat sins—that is, he must make efforts to disavow the flesh.

26. It is the false conception of the superiority of some men over others that leads an individual into temptations, and man needs the effort of restraint from deeds, words, and thoughts that elevate their self over other people in order to combat temptations—that is, man must make the effort to be humble.

27. It is the admittance of the lie that leads men to entertain superstitions, and man needs the effort of restraint from deeds, words, and thoughts that are contrary to truth to combat superstitions—that is, man must make the effort to be truthful.

28. By destroying in man the obstructions to the unification of his soul with other creatures and with God, the efforts of self-disavowal, humility, and truthfulness deliver to man the happiness that is always available. Therefore, what appears to man as evil is only an indication that a human being understands his life falsely and does not act up to the natural provisions of his happiness. There is no evil.

29. And likewise: what appears to man as death is only what appears to the eyes of those who posit their life in time. For individuals who posit their life in what it truly consists, in the effort exerted in the present, to liberate their self from everything that obstructs their unification with God and other creatures, there is no death, and there never can be.

30. For an individual who understands his life in the only way it can be comprehended—as a greater and still greater unification of his soul with all that is alive through love and, through the awareness of his

divinity, with God achievable only thanks to an effort made in the present—, there can be no question about what is to become to his soul after the death of the body. The soul neither was nor will be but is always in the present. It is not given for a human being to know, and neither does he need to know, whether the soul will be aware of itself after the death of the body.

31. It is not given for a human being to know this so that he does not exert the powers of his soul for caring for the state of his individual soul in the imaginary world of the next life, but rather focuses on achieving in this world and now a quite definite and inviolable happiness of unification with all living creatures and with God. It is not necessary for a human being to know what will become of his soul, because if he understands his life in the way that it must be comprehended, as a ceaseless and ever greater unification of his soul with the souls of other creatures and with God, his life can achieve exactly what he strives for, the happiness that nothing can violate.

Section II

FICTIONS

PART 8

Exercises, Parables, Parodies, Satires, Tales, Vitae, and Visions

64. Apprentice's Writings[1]
[ca. 1839; but no later than 1840–41]

Fortune and the Beggar

There once was a beggar who would hang around towns complaining about his lot: "I don't get why the rich take no pleasure in their riches and end up going destitute seeking to acquire too much," he would say. "Such examples abound. I know a merchant who became very rich through trade. But however much he made, it was never enough; he always wanted more. So he freighted ships and sent them off to sea, but they sank with his riches and he was left even poorer than before. I know another man who made a million through tax farming.[2] But he bit off more than he could chew, buying up too many

---

1   **Part 8: Fictions**. **Entry 64.** **"Apprentice's Writings"** [*Uchenicheskie Sochineniia*] consists of 11 vignette pieces that must have been composed by Tolstoy in 1839 (though no later than 1841), based on the 1839 watermark on the 10 leaves on which the pieces are written. Thus, they were composed when Tolstoy was a 10- or 11-year-old boy. Not prepared for publication until 1939, these writings were not included in volume 1 of *The Jubilee*. Instead, they were published in combined volumes 35–36 of *Literaturnoe Nasledstvo* (Moscow: Akademiia Nauk, 1939), 271–75. Without going into any detail, V. S. Mishin, editor of volume 90 of *The Jubilee* in which "Apprentice's Writings" were reprinted in 1958 (*The Jubilee* 90:97-103), mentions that these pieces constitute both partial paraphrases of other literary works (for example, the fables of Ivan Krylov—themselves largely paraphrases of Aesop) and independent writings. See V. S. Mishin in *The Jubilee* 90:386.

2   One is struck by how knowledgeable the young writer is about a very complicated system of Russian land reselling, which falls under the umbrella of *otkupy* (i.e., the reselling of mortgage

exclusive franchises, and so he went bankrupt." One day, though, fortune showed up in front of the beggar and spoke to him thus: "Give me your knapsack, and I will fill it up with golden coins.[3] But I must warn you that any coin that falls to the floor will turn to dust." The beggar was so overjoyed that he could barely breathe. He opened his sack wide and fortune started to pour coins into it. "The sack is getting heavy," said fortune.[4] "Just a few more," said the beggar. "Won't it burst under the weight?" asked fortune. "Why?" said the beggar, "throw in a few more." Suddenly, however, the sack split and all the coins turned to dust. Fortune disappeared. Astonished, the beggar was left to roam about just like before.

Canine Friendship

One day, two watchdogs, Polkan and Barbos,[5] who were lying about side by side near the kitchen courtyard, struck up a conversation about friendship. Polkan said, "Why don't we, Barbos—you and I—form a friendship? It's unbecoming that two watchdogs from the same yard can't go a day without fighting." "To have a friendship would be beyond comparison," responded Barbos: "All right, it's a deal!" And so our new-found friends started embracing, scrambling to come up with names for each other: "You are my Orestes!" "And you are my Pylades!"[6] All of a sudden, though, a bone was thrown out into the yard from the kitchen. The new-found friends sprang into action, sprinting to get to it first.

---

licenses and acquisition of exclusive rental or ownership rights, both of which are included in tax farming).

3   Fortune promises *chervontsy* or 3-ruble gold coins to the beggar.

4   Fortune is also very ironic in the original: "The sack is getting heavy" [*suma to tiazhelen'ka*].

5   These are common Russian names of lowbred and mongrel male watchdogs. Although the etymology of "*Polkan*" may be lost in the history of Old Russian military nomenclature, the name likely designated the regimental watchdog (from "*polk*" meaning a wing of the army or regiment). The origin of "*Barbos*" is even more intriguing. The modest and ubiquitous Russian name Barbos and its diminutive cousin Barboska may indicate a family relation to the picaresque short-bearded canines of European literature (referring to *barba* and its derivatives in French, Italian, Spanish, and Portuguese). Even less magnificently, this name's origin may simply be the verb "*brekhat'*" (previously, "*barakhat'*") or "yelp," which is used figuratively in Russian to describe a compulsive liar and chatterbox. Another possibility is the relation to "barbarians" or to all foreign-sounding and therefore so-called useless or incomprehensible speech (from the onomatopoeic "bar-bar" representing foreignness as gibberish). Whatever the case, Barbos as a watchdog is not a very reliable signaler of danger.

6   The names of the mythological cousins Orestes and Pylades who are raised together (Pylades was the son of King Agamemnon's sister Anaxibia) are commonly used to indicate inseparable friends.

Soon, our Orestes and Pylades were growling and fighting with one another over the bone, and someone had to pour water onto them to break them up.

Daytime

One bright day, I was enticed into the yard by the fine weather. From there, I went into the forest and sat beneath a luxuriant tree: its thick boughs protected me from the hot rays of the sun. I stayed for a long time, enjoying the charms of nature. In the middle of my contemplations, I heard the sound of a flute resounding in the distance. Curiosity goaded me into approaching the place from where the sound was coming, where I saw a young shepherd playing songs with a pipe. Having listened at length to his pleasant music, I headed into the vale, where everything was aflush with life. Some peasant men and women were raking the hay and singing merry songs, some were resting after arduous work, while others were on their way to lunch singing merry songs. I came upon a wide valley that was irrigated by a fast-flowing river. Sitting on the bank across from me was a fisherman looking at his bob intently, which was floating gently, moved by a light breeze. I wished to stay and walk a little more amid such pleasant objects.[7] But then I remembered that I was expected for lunch, and so I started home, filled with pleasant sensations.

Autumn

Autumn is coming—when everything starts dying slowly. The trees turn yellow; the meadows turn white. Only the pine tree stands tall and proud among the other trees, as if it feels no change. At this time, you can no longer rest under the tree boughs but must hide inside your home.—Nature presents a sad sight.—Everyone is sorry about the passing of summer and starts to prepare for the winter. The wind wails mournfully and beats against the windows, as if it, too, feels sorry about the passing of the nice weather. Fine drizzle falls on the ground, arousing a kind of sadness in the soul. Bitter frosty mornings and evenings remind us that strolls in the open are, for now, over.

---

7   Pleasant objects [*priatnykh predmetov*].

Spring

How pleasant is the spring! How everything comes back to life! Naked trees begin to dress themselves, donning lush green robes. The birds announce the joy of the coming spring with their harmonic singing. Storks (and other birds) have flown back to their warm dwellings where they weave nests.—One morning, when the weather was fabulous—the clouds roaming around the sky, the sun shining hot—I could not keep myself inside, and so I went out to enjoy the pleasant weather and to delight in the pleasant sight of nature. I searched for a tree under whose shade I could rest. At last, I saw a pine tree under which a young shepherd was sitting, a large herd of sheep in front of him. I sat next to him and watched the sheep with pleasure: some were frolicking, some were resting, some were grazing on the grass, and other frisky ones were intermittently prancing around and resting on the grass. I turned my gaze to the right where I saw a waterfall running quickly from the hump of a hill. I rushed to the spring, where I gulped thirstily from its cool and refreshing water. By the time the sun had hit its zenith, inducing flabby relaxation with its excessive heat, I was already back at home.

Night

The night was throwing its cover on the vales, hills, and the woods, an occasional ray of moonlight shining through the clouds that roam the sky. It seemed that the moonlight and darkness were trying to exterminate each other: one moment the moonlight tore the clouds apart, while another moment the clouds wrapped themselves around the moon. All was quiet. The stillness of the night reigned everywhere, with interruptions only from the occasional cries of a hooting owl, the sound of the hooves of horses, who were obeying the voice of their master, or the occasional singing of a journeying coachman, cursing his "dear horsies." Amid this slumbering nature, I found myself sedated by its magic effect and did not feel the flow of time. The stars started to disappear as the dawn began to show. It was then that I remembered that it was time to return home, where my long absence might have caused much trouble. Yet, hearing in the distance the song of a nightingale, I approached this place and stayed all through the sunrise, listening to this singer of nature. Filled with pleasant daydreams, I went home intending to take these pleasant strolls every evening.

The Kulikovo Field

When [Prince] Dmitry Ivanovich[8] learned that [Khan] Mamai was advancing toward Moscow to quash the rebellious Prince, he immediately went to the Holy Trinity Monastery[9] to receive the blessing of the reverend elder Sergius.[10] Having bid farewell to his spouse and children, Dmitry held a parting prayer service before going to Kolomna. There, he joined with the other princes, inspected the troops, and went off to face the enemy, who were lying in wait, pleading for reinforcements from the traitor [the Prince of] Litovsk and Ryazan.—At Kulikovo Field, the armies clashed. Inspired by courage and love of the Fatherland, Dmitry rode his horse up to every regiment that was preparing for battle, ready to win victory or die for the freedom of the Fatherland. He convinced them not to be afraid of Mamai's horde. Mamai stood on top of a hill, observing every movement of his troops. The regiments at the front sweated during the opening of the engagement, but little by little, the battle was unleashed and blood poured like a river. [Prince] Donskoy remained at the front, but was gravely injured in the heat of the battle and fell off his horse, under a tree. Having lost consciousness, he did not get to see the end of this great battle.

Fire

What a lachrymose sight it must have been when fire spread rapidly across the entire area of Tula, this rich and populous city becoming victim to the flames. Wealth, magnificent buildings, works of art, and craftwork all perished from

---

8 Tolstoy is here providing an accurate yet succinct account of events in the glorious year 1380 of Prince Dmitry Ivanovich Donskoy (1350–89), the Prince of Moscow and Grand Prince of Vladimir. Son of Prince Ivan II Ivanovich (Ivan Krasny), Dmitry built the first stone structure in the Kremlin in 1367. After a series of successful campaigns from 1368 to 1378 that ensured the rise of the power and prestige of Moscow, Dmitry formed and became head of the Princes' coalition against the Golden Horde. He defeated the Tatar Khan Mamai in the battle on Kulikovo Field at the rivers Nepriadva and Don on September 8, 1380. This event marked the beginning of the end of the "Yoke" of the Mongol and Tatar Khans and earned Dmitry the honorary title Donskoy (of the Don).

9 This is now the Trinity Monastery of St. Sergius.

10 Sergius of Radonezh (1321–92) not only gave Dmitry a blessing for victory in the battle against Mamai, but he also sent two of his valiant monks, the legendary warriors Alexander Peresvet and Rodion Oslabia, to join the Prince's army.

the ruinous power of the fire.—The moans and wails of the miserable victims could be heard everywhere. A mother, who only had time to save herself, wept bitterly for her lost child, abandoned in the flames. A father, who ran into the fire, trying to rescue his son, died in terrible torment. And how astonishing is this example of maternal tenderness: A mother rescued her son, who leapt out of the window of a building to where she was standing amid the horrific torments of the fire that was engulfing and gorging on her. In less than a day, all was turned to ash. The wealthy [town] lost everything—the accumulation of years of hard labor—in one day. Heaps of ash, houses in ruin, and people could be seen everywhere lamenting: one at the death of his father, another at the loss of his mother, spouse, or son. It was rare to find a family that suffered no loss. Thus it is that when God wills to punish, it takes him an hour to equalize the richest with the poorest.[11]

The Kremlin

What a great spectacle the Kremlin presents! Ivan the Great[12] stands gigantically tall amid the other temples and churches and reminds us about the sly thief of the throne. This ancient little Teremok[13] over here is witness to the tempestuous times of Ivan the Terrible.[14] These white walls reminisce about the great genius and hero, whose luck ran out, where everything collapsed. These walls saw the shame and degradation of the invincible Napoleonic regiments. They saw the dawn of Russia's liberation from the yoke of the invading alien race. A few centuries earlier, immured in the same walls, was the beginning of Russia's liberation from the Poles during the times of the Impostor.[15] And how

---

11 The boy Tolstoy is describing the recent catastrophic fire of June 29, 1834, that occurred in the largely wooden city of Tula, the capital of the province where his birthplace and patrimony, Yasnaya Polyana, is located. Tolstoy was not yet six when the disaster took place, which is just five or six years before he wrote his reflection.

12 Part of the Kremlin with a magnificent belfry tower named after Prince Ivan III (Ivan Vasilievich; 1440–1505), the prince most credited with developing the ensemble of the Kremlin and the city center Moscow. "The sly thief" is the False Dimitry (the Pretender). See note 16.

13 The traditional wooden palace of Russian princes and the site of marvelous hideaways in Russian fairy tales.

14 Ivan the Terrible (Ivan IV Vasilievich [Grozny], 1530–84).

15 Tolstoy means the False Dimitry [Gregory (Grishka) Otrepiev; birth details unknown], the self-declared Tsar of Muscovy who was killed at the Kremlin, allegedly during his wedding to Polish Princess Marina Mniszech (1588–1614) in 1606 (accounts of the circumstances differ).

beautiful is the impression left on the quiet River Moskva. She saw, in her reflection, a tiny village unbeknownst to anyone grow upward into the sky, transforming into a city. She saw all of its misfortune and glory, and waited to see its majesty.—And now this former village of Kuchko[16] has become the greatest and most populous city in Europe.

Pompeii

How mutable and inconstant is everything in the world. Pompeii used to be the second largest city of Italy (Europe) during its glory days; it was the blossom of its welfare. It is now nothing but ruins and a heap of ashes. The spectacle of the earth quaking at its foundation and belching fire from its entrails must have been terrible.—The frightened burghers had tried to flee from death, but the lava and the ashes overtook them as they ran, burying them mid-flight. As they toppled, the towers of the heathen temple and the houses buried thousands of victims under their ruins. The terror was contagious, spreading everywhere. An obedient son, who was not quite strong enough, tried to carry his old mother to safety, but lava, ashes, and fallen stones blocked his way. A mother, trying to carry three weak children, caving under the excessive weight of each step, eventually collapsed.—A tender father went to save his only child, hugging it inside his cloak. But one blow was enough for him to collapse, his son frozen in his arms. Some died from the fire, some were buried alive under ash and lava, and others died in the ruins of their homes.[17]

---

16 The young Tolstoy speaks of the patrimonial holdings of boyarin Stepan Ivanovich Kuchka (Kuchka or Kuchko was decapitated for insubordination by Prince Yuri Dolgoruky) in what is now the very heart of the historical center of Moscow. What Muscovites know as the "Kuchkovo" district or the Kuchkovo Field is the territory between Lubyanka Square and the Sretensky [Presentation at the Temple] Gates. By curious coincidence, the publishing house Kuchkovo Pole [The Kuchkovo Field] is currently one of the more active Russian producers of rare editions of the works on Tolstoy and members of his close network.

17 It is not known whether Tolstoy is commenting on Karl Bryullov's monumental canvas, *The Last Day of Pompeii* (1830–33) or is summarizing his own impressions based on reading other historical accounts of the Pompeii disaster. The older Tolstoy used anecdotes about Bryullov's painstaking attention to detail and his talent for imperceptibly correcting that ineffable "tiny something" [*chut'-chut'*] that changes everything in a work of art, such as in a famous example in chapters 7-13 of part 5 of *Anna Karenina*, chapter 4 of "Why Do Men Stupefy Themselves?" (1890), and used again in chapter 12 of *What is Art?* (1897–1898). Notably, in his fragment on Pompeii the young Tolstoy notices how contagious (infectious) the sensation of terror may be. The infectious terror full of the sublimity of the spectacle [*uzhasno bylo zrelishche*] keeps the young author enthralled.

Marfa Posadnitsa[18]

There exist not only great men but also great women.—There has never been more dispute and discord in Novgorod than during the reign of Ionn.[19] The more reasonable were willing to submit to Ionn, while others wished to seek the support of Casimir, the King of Poland.[20] Theophilus, the Chief Priest of Novgorod,[21] took the side of the former, while Marfa, widow of the posadnik Iakov[22] Boretsky, took the side of the latter. The bell of the *veche*[23] resounded all over Novgorod, and hearts were enthused as noisy crowds went running into the square.—Marfa stood there with her son Mstislav[24] at her side. She presented all the advantages of being Casimir's subjects . . . The populace wavered. To overcome the last remaining obstacle to her ambitious plot, she used all her eloquence to persuade the people that the Archbishop should be replaced by the pious elder Piman [sic].[25] The people, as if of their own accord, and as if remembering the elder for the first time, rushed into his monastery cell, and took the Archbishop by force to the square. Marfa took his blessing; the populace hearkened with piety to the words of the elder and spoke in one voice, imploring him and Marfa to assume governance over the laity.—"Let thy holy will be!," he said, turning his eyes up to heaven. "I have been living in seclusion and never thought I would be called upon again from my cave to

---

18 This is the historical name of Marfa the Governess (or Marfa the Governor's Widow). "Marfa" is the Greco-Russian version of "Martha," and *"posadnitsa"* means "the wife of a *posadnik"*—a governor of a Russian city-state, who was appointed by the prince or elected by the *veche*, the popular assembly in the cities of Old Rus'. Marfa the Governess is Marfa Boretskaya, widow of Isaak (Tolstoy's original has "Yakov" [Jacob] Andreevich Boretsky, her second husband, the *posadnik* (or governor) of Novgorod. Marfa ruled Novgorod de facto from 1471 to 1478 until its fall to Muscovy. After the fall of the city, she took the veil and died—or was killed—in Novgorod in 1503.

19 Ionn [sic]. Although I have retained the young Tolstoy's spelling, he means Grand Prince Ivan III Vasilievich of Moscow (for more on the Grand Prince, see the above note related to Tolstoy's comments in the sketch about the Kremlin). The spelling of the name of Archbishop Theophilus's predecessor, Archbishop Ionn, may have influenced Tolstoy's spelling here.

20 This is Casimir IV Jagiellon (Kazimieras Jogailaitis), the Grand Duke of Lithuania (1427–1492).

21 Feofil, Archbishop of Novgorod (?-d. 1484 in Kiev), headed the deputation to Ivan III to Moscow in March 1476.

22 On Tolstoy's variant of the name, see the first note to this entry.

23 On *veche*, see note 19. The noun *"veche"* derives from the verb *"veshchat'*," meaning "to announce", as was done in the cities of Old Russia by sounding a bell.

24 Mstislav Isaakovich Boretsky.

25 The more customary spelling of the name is "Pimen."

assume governance over the expansive laity of Novgorod. I am ready to do anything for my brave compatriots."—The bell grew quieter and the people started dispersing, returning to their homes as the darkness of night surrounded them.—The following day, the bell of the *veche* again filled the expanses of the city; the anxious people ran to the *veche* meeting. There, Ionn's envoy, Kholmsky,[26] stood to announce his will. Surrounded by the posadniks in charge and the commanders of the thousands of retinue units, Kholmsky tried to persuade the people to submit to Ionn:

> How can you not realize the happiness you have as Ionn's subjects? Can't you see that no state can remain standing without sovereignty? Can't you see that your liberty must perish, sooner or later? It is more profitable for you to submit to Ionn, the Orthodox Tsar, for he confesses the same faith as you, has the same customs and mores as you, than it is to submit to Casimir the Latinate, who knows nothing of the customs of the Holy Rus, none of the rules of our Church. Hasn't Novgorod been the domain and region of the great princes?

A tear ran from Marfa's eyes. The furious populace shouted, "Take him! Take him!," and were about to tie him up. But Marfa threw herself forward, imploring the people not to harm Ionn's envoy.[27]

---

26 Boyar Daniil Dmitrievich Kholmsky (birth date unknown, d. 1493) served as the right arm of Ivan III and his best commander: the Novgorod Campaigns (1471; 1477–78) that ended the liberties and the existence of the Great Novgorod were one of the high points of his military career.

27 The Feudal Republic of Novgorod (the Free City of Novgorod) ceased to exist after its defeat by the Muscovite troops on the River Shelon' in 1471 and the annexation of Novgorod to Muscovy in 1478.

65. A Tale about How Another Girl Named Varinka Grew Up Fast[28] [1857–58]

(Dedicated to Varinka)

"How come we have been so totally oblivious about the children?" Mother said after lunch. "The holidays are over, and we haven't taken them to the theater once. Please fetch me the performance calendar; there might be something charming for them to see."—Varinka, Nikolenka and Lizanka were busy playing the sirens, all three of them sitting in the same armchair, pretending that they were on their way to see an underwater fairy.[29] They were playing as if there were six in the game: mother, father, Eugene, Etienne, Sasha, and Milashka. Lizanka[30] was Milashka and was about to become a fairy who receives guests; at the same time, she was listening to what the grownups were saying.

—"Varinka! Us, to the theater..." she said and went back to her business blowing air and waving her arms, which meant that they were traveling under water.

---

28 **Entry 65. "A Tale about How Another Girl Named Varinka Grew Up Fast"** [*Skazka o tom, kak drugaia devochka Varinka skoro vyrosla bol'shaia*] (1857-58). First publication in Lev Tolstoy, *Neizdannye khudozhestvennye proizvedeniia*, ed. A. E. Gruzinsky and V. F. Savodnik (Moscow: Federatsiia, 1928), 213-28. Published in 1935 in *The Jubilee* (5:223-29). N. M. Mendelson notes that Tolstoy made a lot of corrections to the text (5: 330); this fact and the general quality of the prose all indicate that Tolstoy took great care when writing. The tale was written from the end of 1857 to early 1858 when Tolstoy lived with his younger sister, Maria Nikolaevna (Masha), and her three children in Moscow after her separation the previous summer from Count Valerian Petrovich Tolstoy (1813–65), her first husband since 1847, Tolstoy's acquaintance since 1838, and a rather distant relative. The tale is dedicated to Tolstoy's niece Varvara Valerianovna Tolstaya (married name Nagornova; 1850–1921), the eldest child of Masha and Valerian and Tolstoy's great friend for life. The other young heroes in the story are Nikolenka (born December 31, 1850; 1879, Old Style) and Lizanka, the youngest, aged five or six. Tolstoy adored all the children with whom he continued to be close. After his own children were born, the cousins were inseparable. Records in his diary for the winter of 1857–58 indicate visits to dance lessons, the zoo, the circus, and the puppet theater with the children, with or without his sister Masha. The names of Masha's children correspond to the names of the young characters featured in the tale. Tolstoy must be both the "uncle" and the "officer" in the tale. "Varinka" is the family spelling of Varvara's name; the regular diminutive form of "Varvara" (Barbara) is "Varenka."

29 The water fairy theme was very popular in the theater world in St. Petersburg and Moscow in the seasons following the premier of Alexander Dargomyzhsky's *Rusalka* [*The Mermaid*] in 1856.

30 Elizaveta Valerianovna Obolenskaya (1852–1935) was another kindred spirit for Tolstoy and her mother, Maria Nikolaevna, and she authored important reminiscences about her uncle.

—"Mommy?" Nikolenka asked.

—"Yes," said Varinka.

The game was starting to get dull—it was taking them too long to get to the fairy, and the children were eavesdropping on their mother's consultation with their uncle about where to go. To the circus[31] or the Bolshoi Theater,[32] to "The Naiad and Fisherman" . . . ?[33]

—"Go and get dressed!" Mother said.

The sirens suddenly vanished, as did the boat, the water, and Milashka, as if nothing was there anymore.

—"Do you mean us, Mommy?" Varinka, the eldest, asked, although she knew that it was they who were told to get dressed.

Nikolenka and Lizanka awaited confirmation, looking at their mother in silence.

—"Chop chop, march upstairs!"

The children flew upstairs, shrieking, screaming, stomping their feet, and pushing each other.

Half an hour later, their faces and hands washed, moving with caution lest they smudge or crumple their dresses, ribbons, or shirts, the children came down to the drawing room. They all looked very sweet, especially the girls in their muslin dresses with pink ribbons, but also the boy in his blue-gray shirt of thick Persian silk and his golden belt—that he so wanted to, but couldn't, gaze at all the time.[34]

---

31 At the time, theaters operated from rented spaces in Moscow, which had no stationary the-aters. The famous Alessandro Guerra, Carl Magnus Hinne, and Gaetano Ciniselli circus group of theatres were a slightly later development, resulting in the building of the 1877 Circus on the Fontanka. For a long time, the St. Petersburg Circus was just a wooden structure situated on the site of the present-day Mariinsky Theatre. Circus companies of mainly foreign-born circus masters toured in Russia and were extremely popular. However, circus performances suitable for children were still rare in the 1850s, hence the excitement. Tolstoy was a frequent visitor of the Moscow Circus that was unveiled in 1880 on Tsvetnoy Boulevard.

32 The Bolshoi Theatre experienced a great surge in 1856 following its reconstruction to repair fire damage. In this era of new beginnings, the company gradually expanded its opera offerings, and after graduating locally trained students, it began to break new ground in the ballet world.

33 The mermaid and water fairy games played by children in the story are also inspired by the ongoing popularity of this ballet, for which Tolstoy provides the Russian title. The celebrated European hit *La Naiade et le Pêcheur* (1846, music by Cesare Pugni with choreography by Jules Perrot and Marius Petipa) premiered at the St. Petersburg Bolshoi Kamenny Theatre on January 30/February 11, 1851 (soon after which it was also staged in Moscow) and stayed on the repertoire thereafter. Based on the novella "Undine" by Friedrich de la Mothe Fouqué (1811), this ballet comprised three acts, making for a long performance indeed.

34 Tolstoy owned a small collection of swords from his service in the army, from which he had resigned in 1856. Nikolenka (Nikolai Valerianovich) died at age 28 on June 12, 1879, of

—"Could it be that I am as pretty as Lizanka?" Varinka thought, strolling past the mirror to check. Dragging her feet, she stole a glance at her own reflection underneath the table. In the mirror, she saw a pretty girl standing sideways.

—"Lizanka! Take a look: some of your curls are not so neat," she said, and Lizanka came up to look at herself.

None of her curls were frazzled one bit. Varinka was just joking.

Nikolenka also came up to the mirror and took a look at his golden belt:

—"Just like my dear uncle's sword, sweet!"—

The nanny who had been standing behind the door, mittens at the ready, entered the room suddenly and took Lizanka aside.

—"Your Ladyship, your skirt is wrinkled all over again," she said, pulling down on her skirt. "You can't be taken out like this!"

But Lizanka knew this was just in jest.

—"Allez, prendre vos précautions avant de partir,"[35] said the governess upon entering the room, wearing a silk dress with red ribbons, which rustled as she walked.

—"Precaution-ions, precaution-ions!"[36] the children screamed, as Lizanka ran up first.

—"I'm good," said Nikolenka with pride.

—"Me too," said Varinka.

—"Awesome hoop-skirts!" Varinka said.[37]

—"You are so beautiful, Bissaultushka!" the children said as they jumped around Mlle. Bissault. She also took a look at herself in the mirror as if to see whether her transformation into a vision of beauty was for real.

Their mommy took a long time dressing and so the children had time for another game—playing doctors, during which they ruffled up their dresses and got them all tousled. For this they were scolded and told that they couldn't be given nice dresses, and that they must be left behind. But the children knew

---

typhus, having been married just a few months to Nadezhda Fedorovna Gromon (1859–1935) whom he had wed on October 8, 1878. Tolstoy was away at Kursk when a telegram from Sophia Andreevna arrived. Heartbroken, he replied to Sophia Adreevna in the wee hours on June 13, 1879, that this news was "terribly sad" (83:270).

35 "Go and take your precautionary visit before leaving."

36 In their excitement, the children make the Russian plural out of the French "precautions" that is plural already.

37 The arrangement of consonants provides various hints that children lisp because they are missing their milk teeth. Varinka must be saying something close to "Aweshome hoop-shkirts!" especially because these gently hissing sibilants echo the nickname "Bissaultushka" that the children award to Mlle. Bissault in the very next phrase.

that this was only in jest, and so they pulled sour mugs while yet feeling joyous at heart. All were seated in the carriage at last. Mikhaila gave them a rocky ride, tossing them in the air like balls at every bump in the road. The old nanny saw them off from the porch in the freezing weather, continuing to tell Lizanka that her hat had slipped to one side and that Varinka should put her hands in her mittens. Nikolenka was a brave chevalier who needed nothing.

They arrived at the theater and entered the lobby. Immediately, as strangers started walking in their way, and Mommy had to ask for directions for neither she nor Mikhaila knew where to go, the children began to feel very anxious, truth be told, although they would not confess to it. Lizanka even got to thinking that it was all over and that they were completely lost, that they would tire themselves out looking and would be led astray, and that this was all there was to the theater. Feeling frightened, she began to gasp for air and was on the verge of tears. I know that she would never admit to any of this, but this is how it was. Yet, as soon as they had found their box, the door to which was opened for them by a man wearing gilded-piped clothes who had demanded their tickets from their mommy—this despite her being the mommy!— everything became so unbelievably nice, if still a little scary. The music was playing, everything was bright, there were big golden chandeliers, and people, people, people! Heads, heads, heads! Above, below, people everywhere. Just like real people.

Mommy let the children in first and took her own seat at the back. And the children started looking around. Across from them, around them, and below them, people looked really life-like: they were moving, and there were even children among them—children as real as they themselves. A boy and a girl were sitting behind the partition next to their box, so pretty, looking magical. The girl, no older than Varinka, was wearing her permed locks all the way down to her bare shoulders, and the boy, who also had long curly hair, was wearing a fitted velvet jacket with tiny golden buttons; he looked so pretty, better than Fedya and Stiva, better even than Raevsky—truly, a magical boy.—

The magical boy and the girl were looking at the newly arrived children, and the children stared back at them, whispering among themselves.

—"Here, children, look this way, there at the stage," Mommy said, pointing down to one side. The children looked that way, but didn't like what they saw. The musicians were sitting there, all clad in black, with violins and trumpets, and there were lousy plain wooden planks above them, as if this were the floor of a country house; up there, people wearing loose shirts and red pointed hats could be seen walking and waving their hands. A girl in a very short skirt and without any pantaloons was standing there on the tip of her toe, her other leg raised above her head. This wasn't nice and the children started feeling sorry for this girl.[38]

—"Mommy, where is the theater?" Nikolenka asked.

—"This is it," Mommy answered, pointing at the girl at whom she was looking through her opera spyglass.

The children started looking in that direction; the girl was prancing, swirling, and others were prancing and dancing with her, but there was nothing funny about it at all. Well, one thing that was nice was that something behind the girl was made up to look just like the sea and some kind of crescent.

—"Are these real girls for sure?" asked Lizanka. She was feeling queasy and scared, and she wanted to cry for no reason.

—"It goes without saying that they are real!," Varinka said, "just look at how she is walking; when she goes behind those screens, you can see very well she's real."

At this Lizanka took offense.

—"I can see that those people sitting next to us are real, but I don't know about those others."

Varinka, for her part, found it more enjoyable to watch the boxes and the chandelier and especially the girl and the boy, their neighbors, rather than the theater. Their little neighbors were also watching them, though the grownups kept urging that they all look at the dancers. The show only became fun when everyone suddenly started clapping their hands, or when, right before the end, lots of people came out on stage with halberds and began poking at each other. Then there was a fire and one guy fell through a hole; it was such a pity that the curtain went down at that very moment.

Their children-neighbors got up and exited their box with the officer who was with them.

—"It's so hot!," Mommy said and also exited into the foyer for a stroll with her children. Lizanka clasped on to her lest she get lost, while the others walked on their own. The officer and the magic children were also taking a stroll. The children stared at each other so intently when they came face to face that

---

38 Starting in their teenage years, students in the choreography school at the Bolshoi Theatre would have performed on its stage in the corps de ballet scenes. Before her early stardom, the prima Praskovia Lebedeva was already a seven-year veteran of the stage since her debut at age thirteen. Empathy for exploited child performers is one of the cult themes of Russian realism.

they stopped looking where they were going, and Lizanka committed herself so much that she stumbled and fell over. Yet she didn't cry, only blushed and laughed instead. And our kids and the magic kids broke into a big guffaw. The magic kids looked even better when they were laughing.

—"They are so pretty and merry, especially the girl," Nikolenka was thinking to himself.

—"Especially the boy,"—Lizanka and Varinka were thinking to themselves.

—"Quels charmants enfants!," Mommy told the governess, but loudly enough that the officer with the kids could hear. In her heart of hearts she was thinking: "nice kids, but mine are better." The children were taken aback and even astonished at the daring with which Mommy resolved to say this; but she put it so well. Having strolled to the other end of the foyer, the officer said the same to his children.

—"Go then and make their acquaintance," he told them.

—"Go by yourselves if you want," he told them.

—"Why should I go?" said the boy looking up at the officer. "What should I say to them?"

—"Ask the girl if she has hurt herself."

—"All right, I shall say that!" the boy said with resolve.

—"I shall also say that," the girl said, and they started making their way toward the kids.

The boy kept staring at the girl who had fallen over, paused near her, and opened his mouth to say something. But he lost his nerve and began blushing all over, from his face to his neck. His new boots squeaking, he ran back to his folks and grabbed the officer's hand.

—"Failure and disgrace, sir?" the officer said.

Walking from the other end, the kids came face to face again. The boy stopped facing Lizanka, and she stopped also.

—"What is your name, sir?" she asked.

—"Sasha!"

—"Oh, Sasha!," Nikolenka, Varinka, and Lizanka exclaimed, laughing all together.

—"We play a game called Sasha," Nikolenka said.

—"And we play shuttlecocks," the magic girl said.

—"Is this your first time at the theater?" Varinka asked.

—"No, we've seen *The Corsair*[39] and we went to the circus twice—clowns were there[40]—and we've seen *The Magic Flute*[41] and we'll go again with grandma the day after tomorrow."

Varinka felt ashamed.

—"*The Magic Flute* must be nice."

—"Oh no, the circus is better, the best of all!"

—"Do you speak French?"

—"We do, and German, and we are learning English."

—"And what's your name?"

By now, fewer people were strolling in the foyer. Mommy went back to the box as the music started playing. But the kids were still chatting.—

—"Well then, you've met now, so let's go back to the box," the governess said.

—"Say your farewells and kiss each other," the officer said, smiling.

The kids started kissing. Only Varinka had no time to exchange a kiss with the magic boy, as she felt flustered. Back in the boxes, the kids watched each other more than they watched the ballet, smiling at each other like acquaintances.

The only boring thing was that the governess got angry at them for creasing their dresses. What's the big deal, we've made it to the theater.[42]

In the second intermission the kids came together again and, hand-in-hand, they walked around, telling each other everything. The officer bought them grapes and they dirtied their gloves eating them.

— <"We forgot to exchange our kisses,"—the boy said. They chewed on their grapes, spat out the skins, and gave each other a kiss.>[43]

—"When shall we see each other again?" asked Varinka.

—"At the theater, perhaps," the boy said—"can't you pay us a visit?"

---

39 The staging of *The Corsair* in three acts and five scenes using Adolphe Adam's score set to the libretto based on Lord Byron's poem premiered at Théâtre Impérial de l'Opéra de Paris and at the Bolshoi Kamenny Theatre in St. Petersburg in 1858. Jules Perrot staged the ballet in St. Petersburg on January 12/28, with Marius Petipa as Conrad. In March, Petipa took the ballet to Moscow. Inserted numbers from *The Corsair* as part of the Pas d'Esclaves in the expanded score by Duke Peter Oldenbourg (Grand Prince P. G. Oldenburgsky) were also performed. The twenty-year-old ballet star Praskovia Lebedeva performed the role of Medora in Moscow.

40 In the 1850s, Russian did not yet accommodate its own pronunciation of "*klòuhn*" (after "clown" in English), and the children use the English pronunciation, although forming the Russian plural (*klàuny*).

41 As has occurred elsewhere and despite its Masonic symbology, Mozart's *Die Zauberflöte* has remained a staple with a devoted following among younger audiences since its first showing on the Russian stage in 1797.

42 This sentence is an example of Tolstoy's use of free indirect discourse. It is implied that the children think: "What's the big deal, we've made it to the theater all right."

43 This sentence must have been provisional: Tolstoy enclosed it in angle brackets.

—"Well, we can if Mommy allows us, but when we are grown up, we will do what we want and shall get a ride to your place."

—"No, come visit with us, our ballroom is big."

—"You know, one of our acquaintances taught me how to become a grownup. Only I failed at it. You have to pluck your hair, tie it around your neck for the night or place it in such a way that it doesn't fall; if you do that, you will become a grownup."

It was so much fun—the most fun time ever.

—"Shall we always be friends forever?" the boy asked Varinka, as they were taking their leave.

—"Always," responded Varinka.

Nikolenka said the same to the magic girl.

And Lizanka also said the same to the girl.

—"We shall all, all of us be friends, always!," said Sasha summing up and cutting to the chase. And they all were very pleased.

After the theater, Uncle came to have tea with Mommy, and the children told him and the nanny all about everything that they had seen—telling him more about the children than about the theater. Mommy wasn't feeling well; she had grown tired, and her mood was sadder after the theater.

—"So, these kids were fine ones?" Uncle asked Lizanka.

—"Very fine," she answered.

—"And you made friends?"

—"Very big friends."

—"And they fell in love with you?"

—"Yeess!"

—"Despite missing teeth?"

—"One can love toothlessly!"[44]

—"There can be toothless love, obviously," Varinka confirmed.[45]

—"They all fell in love over there," the governess said.

—"Yes, I fell in love!" Varinka said with some lingering doubt.

—"Oh, you sweetheart!" Mommy said.

Varinka wondered why she was being praised.

—"And you want to marry him?"

—"I do," she said.

—"You could if you were a grownup," said Lizanka, "but right now, you can't."

—"It goes without saying that she may not. Time for bed, kids."

---

44 It must have sounded more like "One can love toothleshly!"

45 "There can be toothlesh love, obvioushly" is a legitimate way to render the sound.

The kids gave their mother the sign of the cross, and she gave the sign of the cross to them, everyone in the room kissed each other good night, and the kids ran upstairs. While they were getting undressed and taking off their pantaloons, and while they were saying the Lord's prayer, all they could think and talk about were the magic children. And for a long time the nanny could not calm them down, for every now and then they would speak to each other from their cribs. At last, they fell quiet. The nanny fixed the lamp under the icon and went out of the room.

—"Nikolenka!" Varinka hissed in the looming light coming from the icon, her nightshirt slipping down from her shoulder, her head sticking out of the bed canopy.

Nikolenka jumped to his knees.

—"I want to see Sasha in my dream."

—"And I want Masha," said Nikolenka.

—"And I want both of them in my dream," Lizanka squeaked.

—"I'm on my way to report you to Mommy," the voice of the nanny sounded from behind the door.

The kids grew quiet.

—"Better them all, all of them!" Varinka muttered into her pillow. She could see Sasha with his black curly hair and merry laughter. "Oh, if only I were a grownup! I'd get married to him, for sure."

As she thought about their magic hair, Varinka propped herself up on her elbow and started plucking her own hairs, clasping and pulling at a few of them. She hurt herself and shrieked.

—"What's up, Varinka?" Nikolenka whispered.

—"Nothing, bye!" she said.

—"Bye!"

With two hairs still between Varinka's fingers, she chose the longer one and gave it a try. It ran short of her neck. She tied both hairs together, made a choker, and lay down on her pillow.

—"But Lizanka and Nikolenka shall remain small kids," she thought, suddenly becoming afraid. "Well, it's all right; I will do the same for them; we shall take Sasha in and shall all live together." As soon as this thought had come into her mind, she fell asleep. All of a sudden, Varinka felt as if she were stretching and stretching, so much so that she could no longer fit in her bed. She woke up, looked around, and she was a grownup. Lizanka and Nikolenka were still asleep. She got up quietly, put on her dress, her fur cape, and her hat, walked out to the porch and ran straight to where Sasha lived. Sasha was still asleep, but she was let in. She came up to his crib, woke him up, and noticed a choker made out of hair on his neck, which was barely holding and was about to break and fall off. She quietly fixed the hair.

Suddenly, Sasha started stretching lengthwise, he stretched and grew, and he grew so big that his crib started to crack. His arms and legs grew so thick, and a mustache started sprouting. Sasha opened his eyes and looked at Varinka, but his eyes and his smile were so strange.
—"Ah, this is a surprise," he said, stretching.

At once and all of a sudden Varinka started feeling ashamed and afraid. Everything went dark before her eyes; she cried out and fell onto her back. Gradually, she opened her eyes and saw her crib, the icon lamp, and the nanny who was standing near her wrapped in her shawl and giving her the sign of the cross. Varinka tore the hair off her neck, turned over, and fell back asleep.

66–67. A Dream [1857–58, 1863][46]

[First redaction]

I stood tall, higher than all the people. I was standing alone. Around me, at knee level, were faces <flushed with attention>, <heads> pressed together like the rippling dark surface of the sea; a sea of heads could be seen everywhere <and in every direction>. I was wearing an ancient toga, which flowed in sync with the passionate and beautiful gestures <that I was making>. I was telling people everything that was in my soul and things that I had not

---

46 **Entries 66-67. "A Dream"** [from the Russian *Son*] is a rare but authenticated piece of attempted mysticism by Tolstoy. It seems to be a write-up of a dream that Tolstoy had shared with his brother Nikolai in 1857. On January 4, 1858, Tolstoy sent a sketch to Vasilii Botkin in Rome, but Botkin's opinion for which Tolstoy was asking remains unknown. Nikolai may have been the first to hear about the vision, yet Tolstoy took several years following Nikolai's death in 1860 to complete the fragment in the first years of his marriage. He returned to the story in 1863. Sophia Andreevna then rewrote it, signed it "N.O." and sent it to Ivan Sergeevich Aksakov, the editor of the Slavophile paper Den'. She presented the piece as the debut of a young aspiring writer from the provinces named Natalia Petrovna Okhotnitskaya—the hanger-on noblewoman who lived at Yasnaya Polyana as help to Tolstoy's aunt Tatiana Ergolskaya. Aksakov refused to publish it, feeling—correctly—that it was too contrived. The problem was not with the style but with the content. Tolstoy had planned to use the fragment for the beginning of *War and Peace*, featuring Nikolai Rostov as the narrator of this dream, and then for the chapters on Pierre's visit to Bazdeev's home at the end of Book II, but ultimately he never incorporated it. The critic Boris Eikhenbaum believed this fragment was related to Tolstoy's story "Albert" (*The Jubilee* 7:367-69).

known before. The crowd understood me joyously. <I felt astonished and admired everything that I was saying.> The inexhaustible stream of courageous thoughts rose higher and higher and poured forth an inspired measured word, and I was astonished at what I was saying. The sound of my voice was strong, firm, and [unusually] beautiful. I was delighted at this sound. When *involuntarily but consciously* I raised my voice, the crowd were collectively startled, as if one person. When I fell silent, the crowd took its rest to catch its breath with meekness. When I wanted it, one feeling would rustle through the crowd—like wind through leaves—causing a sickly but forceful murmur to rise in it. I could discern flushed faces of old people and adult men, and of young men near me, and all of them wore the same expression of hungry attention, submission, and exultation. <But I did not take notice of them. They were all parts of the same face that I have conquered.> All eyes were fixed on me and I was moved by them as they were moved by me. I would guess immediately what the crowd thought or wanted, and my word reciprocated all their wishes; and the crowd responded to my words with frenzied applause and in slavish compliance. I was the Tsar, and my power had no limits. The insane jubilation that burned in me gave me power, and I swam in the exaltation of this power. My insanity and that of the crowd made me happy. But the temporariness of my ecstatic situation bothered me. Yet the force of movement engulfed me further and further, and the stream of thoughts and words became stronger and stronger and seemed inextinguishable.

All of a sudden, amid the crowd that I had worked up, amid the indifferent stares and the passionate, excited gazes fixed upon me, I felt an unintelligible but calm power behind me that was insistently destroying my charm and commanded my attention. I turned against my will as I was finishing the concluding words of the thought that was piercing through me. There was a woman standing there, in the crowd but separate—a simple woman in plain clothes.—I don't remember her clothes; I don't remember what color her eyes or hair were; and I don't know whether she was young or beautiful; but I felt joy seeing her.
—There was in her a vague quiet force that commanded attention and that destroyed my charm. She turned away indifferently . . . and only for a moment I felt upon me her bright eyes welling with tears. There were <ridicule,> pity, and love in her gaze. I read everything in this momentary look, and it all became clear to me. She did not understand anything of what I was saying, and did not feel sorry about this, but instead pitied me. She listened to my words with loving

regret. She despised neither me, nor the crowd, nor my ecstasy; she was simple and quiet . . .[47]

Everything disappeared; the crowd, my thoughts, words, and ecstasy—all was destroyed by that look. There remained only power, one solitary wish . . . Only that one thing my whole being desired—to be soaked again by that look, to understand it, and live its life. But imperceptibly and without moving, she glided away and did not turn once. I called after her; I beseeched her to look at me yet another time, mockingly, and tell me . . . She glided away . . . She disappeared. I started crying about the impossible happiness, but these tears were sweeter than any former ecstasies."[48]

A Dream

[Second ["Finished"] redaction][49]

In my dream, I was standing on a white quavering eminence. I was saying to people everything that was in my soul, things I did not previously know. My thoughts were strange as in a dream, but involuntarily they took the form of an inspired and measured word. I was astonished at what I was saying but joyously listened to the sounds of my voice. I did not see anything but could feel that strangers were thronging around me, all of them my brothers. Their breathing was near me. Far ahead, the sea raged—dark as the crowd.

When I spoke, a wind rustled through the whole of the forest at the sound of my speech. And this wind inspired exultation in the crowd and in me. When I fell silent, the sea was breathing. Both the sea and the forest were a crowd. My eyes could not see but all eyes were on me.—I could feel their gazes. I would not be able to hold forth without the support of their gazes. It was hard and joyous. I was moved by them as they were moved by me. I could feel my power over them, and my power had no limits.

---

47 Compared with the second redaction, the first version presents more pronounced themes of fame and art.

48 Published in volume 7 of *The Jubilee* in 1936, posthumously to N. M. Mendelson, edited also by A. S. Petrovsky and V. F. Savodnik (7:118-19). This was Mendelson's last commentary for *The Jubilee* 7:361-63.

49 As a more finished version, also published in volume 7 of *The Jubilee* in front of the earlier version (Ibid, 117-18).

Only a voice within me was saying, "dreadful!" Yet quicker and quicker did I go, further and further. I could barely catch my breath. Repressed fear increased the delight, and the quivering eminence on which I was standing elevated me higher and higher. A little more, and it would be all over. But somebody was walking behind me. I could feel the sustained gaze of a stranger on me. I did not want to turn around, but I could not help it. I saw a woman; I felt ashamed and I stopped. The crowd had no time to disappear and the wind still rustled over it.

The crowd did not disperse, but the woman walked through the middle of it without mixing with it. I became very ashamed; I wished to continue to speak, quavering, but words failed me. I could not deceive myself. I didn't know who she was; she was everything to love and an overbearing power drew me toward her, as a sweet ache. Only for a moment did she look at me. She turned away indifferently. I could vaguely see the contours of her face, but her calm gaze remained with me. There was meek ridicule and a barely noticeable pity in her gaze. She did not understand anything of what I was saying, and did not feel sorry for it, but she pitied me. I could not remove her gaze from within me. She did not despise me. She could see our delight and pitied us. She was full of happiness. She did not need anyone and I felt because of this that one could not live without her. Tremulous dusk concealed her from me. I shook off all shame and cried about the irretrievable happiness of the past, the impossibility of future happiness, about the happiness that wasn't mine . . . But there was real happiness in these words, too . . .

N. O.

68. An Anecdote about a Bashful Young Man[50] [1868–69]

There once was a young man. He would have been considered absolutely lovely were it not for the timidity that consumed him when in the presence of

---

50 **Entry 68. "An Anecdote about a Bashful Young Man"** [*Anekdot o zastenchivom molodom cheloveke*] [1868–69]. Published in 1936 in volume 7 of *The Jubilee*, editorship posthumously credited to N. M. Mendelson, edited also by A. S. Petrovsky and V. F. Savodnik (7:118-19). Savodnik wrote the commentary to this story (7:361-63).

The anecdote was written on a half-leaf of in-folio grey writing paper with narrow margins. Three pages were written on, and the fourth was left blank. First published in 1936 with the title we have translated from the Russian "*Anekdot o zastenchivom molodom cheloveke*" in volume 7 of *The Jubilee* (7:137). The commentator V. F. Savodnik believed that the sprawling and clear handwriting indicated that the story was intended as a reading exercise for strangers, so badly indeed that he blushed at the sound of any word and could utter nothing in reply.

One day, the shy young man arrived for a name day party at the home of one of his acquaintances. There were lots of guests. Everyone was invited to savor some pierogi followed by some fish, treats courtesy of the hostess. The shy young man declined the pierogi. Knowing he was shy and that anything was enough to overtake him with fright, the hostess said, "Try some fish, sir" and pushed the entire fish toward him, lest he feel ashamed. The fish was a big sterlet sturgeon. The young man took a fork and hooked a piece of the fish, which he tried to detach. But the slice wasn't cleanly cut. Try as he might, all he could do was stretch the fish out, slice after slice. The young man began to worry, thinking: "If I put the fish down, they will stare at me and laugh; so let me quickly tear off a chunk." He pulled again at the fish with his fork. The fish slid off of the serving plate and onto the tablecloth. While trying to keep steady, the young man rashly pulled at the fish which ended up on his lap. His efforts to scoop the fish up ended in the fish slipping from his lap onto the floor. Half frozen, the man looked around, barely breathing, thinking: "I will be laughed at to death." But at this stage he could see that nobody had taken any notice of him: all the guests were busy with their own pierogi. "Perhaps they will not notice it's missing," he thought. So, pretending to eat, he clinked his plate with his fork, while kicking the sterlet farther under the table out of sight, more or less stomping it away. With the pierogi barely finished, the hostess turned to find the sterlet, which she was now going to serve to her guests. Lo and behold, it had vanished, not a bone left. The shy young man buried his nose in his plate, feeling his face burning as if stung by nettles, with all the guests looking at him. But just then one of the guests dropped his napkin, which he bent down to pick up. "Oh my," said the guest, "the sterlet swam away; here it is!" At this, the young man jumped to his feet and ran away without bidding farewell to his hosts.

69. A Fairy Tale[51]
[1873]

. . . and I lost consciousness. When I came to, I was no longer lying on the sand, nor was I in the desert; instead, I found myself in bed surrounded by living

---

Tolstoy's older children. If so, they must be Sergey and Tatiana, aged 5 or 6 depending on the exact year of the composition of the anecdote (for Savodnik's opinion, see 7:372).

51 **Entry 69. "A Fairy Tale"** [*Skazka*] (1873). First published in 1936 in volume 17 of *The Jubilee* edited by P. S. Popov, V. F. Savodnik, and M. A. Tsiavlovsky (17:135-36). This draft

creatures. Two such creatures were sitting on a bench next to me: one of them was basting butter in a bottle, the other was pleating what looked like hemp. A third was busy with something at the table. When they saw that I was conscious, they discussed something in a language unknown to me and indicated with friendly gestures that I need not be afraid of them. That day, I managed to get up and walk; the following day, I felt a surge of energy and was soon quite all right. I lived for two years in a town called Djulays[52] in an undiscovered part of Central Africa. I had enough time to learn the language, character, mode of governance, life, and the occupations of the people who lived there.—The first thing that struck me about the Djulays was their uncommonly pitiful life and its brevity. Everyone I saw was clearly carrying the embryo of death within them; in truth, they melted or rotted every day, every hour, every minute, before my very eyes. I observed every day how some of them shriveled, ossified into stupor, became hollowed, dry, lost their teeth and hair; every day, they were dying. Others who had not yet begun to become hollowed out and dry and were not yet rotting were undercut by an invisible hand in their embryos and then were soon dead. Despite that, all the Djulays obviously lacked the capacity to see that law of death under whose star they were born. They could notice many other things, including very subtle things—only they couldn't see that they were not living but only dying in different ways. Having learned their language, a couple of times I attempted to draw their attention to this, but they lacked any vocabulary for this whatsoever.

I have now lived a total of 18 years among these people and—in line with the hypotheses of ethnographers and geographers—found them primitive. However, and contra the superficial general opinion about primitiveness, I did not find them to be simply wild in their savagery, that is, lacking in complex life. On the contrary, I found their life to be rather complex, having arisen out of historical conditions that were centuries old. I consider them savage since— putting aside some material sides of their life which were rather complicated— they had only primitive concepts about science, philosophy, and religion, and so tangled and convoluted were these original concepts that it is only with great difficulty and after 10 years of living there and studying their language that I started to grasp them slowly. Here, I shall endeavor to narrate these concepts as they were revealed to me.—

---

is in the same notebook with records dated November 5–December, 1873, which enabled commentator N. N. Gusev to attribute the fragment to the same year. For Gusev's commentary, see 17:616.

52 This is an imagined ethnicity. Perhaps the name is related to "joule," a mathematical unit used to indicate a measure of energy.

1) Marriage and families; 2) property; 3) the courts; 4) administration; 5) commerce and commonwealth; 6) education; 7) science; 6) religion. The Djulays subdivide themselves into many different strata, castes, and estates, each of them possessing a distinctive mark of their own. This distinction consists in the color and number of buttons that they wear on coned caps. But these subdivisions are not essential. The following subdivision is essential, however: There are working Djulays, that is, Djulays who produce something new by means of their own labor; and there are Djulays who ruin and destroy.—The former live in the countryside predominantly; the latter reside in the cities. Contrary to what might be expected, the producers are held in contempt, and the destroyers enjoy great honor: the more they destroy, the more they are honored. So, the producers strive to reclassify themselves by joining the ranks of the destroyers, meaning that there is a drop in the number of producers. I have asked why this was so in my conversations with them. I was answered: so that consumers may live better lives. But who are the first to start rotting? The consumers.

Continues in the manuscript: A conversation with a scientist. We shall never know. To while away the time like this. Blushed, became angry. A conversation with a peasant. Such is the order. A conversation with an Epicurean. A conversation with a mother. A conversation with a priest. A conversation with a rich man. A conversation with a social figure. A conversation about property that is fake. A piece of paper.

Religion-progress.

What's the point?

70. The Vita and Martyrdom of Justin the Philosopher[53] [1874–75]

Justin the Martyr was born in the lands of Syrian Palestine, in the district of Samaria, in a town that in ancient times was called Shechem but is known in

---

53 **Entry 70. "The Vita and Martyrdom of Justin the Philosopher"** [*Zhitie i stradanie muchenika Iustina filosofa*] (1874–75). First published in 1936 in volume 17 of *The Jubilee* (17:137-38), the fragment occupies two uncut half-leaves of low-quality writing paper inserted into one another. Only two and one-half pages were written on, and the remaining leaves were left

modern times as Neapolis of Flavia. His paternal parentage was of good and distinguished stock, of Hellenic faith. Before his illumination by faith, Justin was also an idol worshipper.—He was sent to study with scribes at a very young age and, being of sharp mind, he quickly mastered Hellenic wisdom. Having become skilled in rhetoric, he lusted for philosophy and so turned to a Stoical philosopher, to learn from their ponderous conjuring. Since he had a strong desire to understand God, he stayed just a short time with the Stoic from whom he learned nothing about God (for the Stoics knew no God and gave short shrift to such knowledge). Justin thus transferred to another teacher, also a philosopher by rank, Peripatetic by name, and a man most wise.

In the first few days, however, this teacher began haggling over price, not wishing to waste his wisdom for free. Having seen his cupidity, Justin came to despise this teacher as a miserly usurer who was not worthy of the rank of philosopher, and so he left both the Stoics and the Peripatetics. Still desirous of understanding God through immediate love of wisdom, he turned to another glorious teacher from the Pythagorean group of wise men. This teacher ordered Justin to learn astrology, arithmetic, land surveying, music, and other teachings—teachings that, he said, provided for the most basic necessities of life. But Justin could see that it would be necessary to spend many years on these teachings, and they promised little for his soul: nothing of what he heard from this teacher could satisfy the desire of his heart and his desire to love God, which grew more and more every day. So, he abandoned this teacher, too, and was admitted to study with one of the Platonists, who were greatly acclaimed and highly esteemed at the time. He applied to study with a Platonist teacher who had promised to demonstrate the incorporeal likenesses of corporeal things and the celestial likenesses of earthly things, as well as to teach him God from the shadow likeness of reasoned ideas. For, the whole route of Platonic philosophy was to ascend from the ideas toward knowing God. Justin chose this route, for he was hoping to penetrate divine wisdom in order to know God and to be rendered complete by the will of grace.—He spent enough time with this teacher and was soon versed in Platonic rules and became a famed, perfectly Greek, philosopher.

---

blank. Sprawling handwriting with many corrections and inserts reflects Tolstoy's care for style. In his commentary in volume 17 of *The Jubilee*, V. F. Savodnik considers the fragment to be similar to the unwritten vitae of the Russian and early Christian saints for Russian Readers (17:617-18). This is Tolstoy's abandoned fragment intended to describe the life of Justin Martyr (ca. 100–65 A.D.), also known as Justin the Philosopher, a middle Platonist turned Christian apologist.

But Justin failed to learn the right knowledge of God because the God of Greek philosophy was not glorified as God; Greek philosophy transubstantiated the glory of the imperishable God with the likeness of the perishable man, and birds, and quadrupeds, and reptiles. Justin found solace in spirit, doing his thinking exercises in the godlike way, learning the divine science, as much as his non-illuminated mind could muster.[54]

One day, he was walking alone near the sea in a remote place out of town and was contemplating his philosophical wisdoms when he saw a dignified old stranger adorned with gray hair. Having noticed his intent stare, the old man said: "Do you know me if you stare at me so?" To which Justin responded: "I am not acquainted with you, but I am stunned to see you in this deserted place, for I expected to see no-one."

The old man said: "My family departed to the other side; I am expecting them back and came here to meet them half-way, to see them from afar. And what's your business here?" "I love solitary walks during which I can learn from philosophy without hindrances," Justin answered. The old man asked, "What benefit do you get from philosophy?" "What could be a better benefit than philosophy?" Justin responded.

71. A Colloquy of Idlers[55]
[1887]

Once upon a time, some guests gathered together at a wealthy home. And it so happened that they struck up a conversation about life.

They talked about people who were present as well as those who were absent, but they could not find a single person who was pleased with their life.

Not only was there nobody who could boast being happy, there wasn't a single person who considered their life to be truly Christian. They all confessed

---

54 Tolstoy alludes to Neoplatonic ascending in the hierarchy of the spiritual. He deliberately did not use the term "theology" here.

55 **Entry 71. "A Colloquy of Idlers"** [*Bededa dosuzhikh liudei*] (1887) had been a work in progress since 1884. It serves as a prologue to Tolstoy's story of the same year "Walk in the Light While There is Light" [*Khodite v svete poka est' svet*]. Although an independent dialogue, Tolstoy chose to connect it with the above story from the life of the early Christians as a prologue. Previous versions were published in English (1890) and Russian (1893), but they are not based on the master text and are negligible for their poor quality and inaccuracies. In 1936, volume 26 of The Jubilee provided the first definitive text (26:246-49) for which P. B. Bulychev wrote his editorial reading of the five extant manuscript versions (26:738-43). *The Jubilee* relied on the fifth version copied by Sophia Andreevna on which Tolstoy made his final corrections.

to living out their daily lives taking care only of themselves or their family; nobody thought much about their neighbor, and of God even less so.

The guests conversed among themselves like this and all were in consensus, accusing themselves of living a godless, unchristian life.

—"So, why do we live like this?," one young man exclaimed, "why do we do what we don't approve of? Is it not within our will to change our life? We are so conscious of how our lives are ruined by the spoils of luxury, by our wealth, and by our pride most of all, our self-imposed separation from our brothers. To keep our sense of dignity and our wealth, we must deprive ourselves of everything that brings joy to a human being: we throng together in close quarters in the city, pampering ourselves, ruining our health, and, despite all the amusements, we are dying of boredom, full of regrets about our life not being what it should be."

"Why live like this? Why ruin our entire life and all the happiness that God has graced us with? I will not continue to live like this. I am going to abandon my studies, which are going to land me precisely with this very tortured life— the very life about which we are now complaining. I will relinquish my inheritance and I will go to the country and live among the poor; I will learn how to work with my hands. Should the poor be in need of my education, I shall impart it to them directly—and not through institutions and books, but through living like a brother among them."

—"Yes, I have decided," he said, while giving questioning looks to his father who was right next to him.

—"Your wish is good," the father said, "but it is supercilious and rash. Everything appears so easy to you because you have no knowledge of life. You have had no shortage of everything that seems good to us! Everything comes down to creating that which is good, which may be difficult and complex. It is hard enough to tread steadily on a trodden path, but harder still to break new ground. The people who break new ground have matured and mastered everything within human reach. This new path seems easy to you because you don't understand life yet. What you express is the supercilious arrogance of youth. We, the older folk, are here to rein in your bursts of enthusiasm and steer your experience. And you, the young, must obey us to make use of our experience. Your active life is still ahead of you; you are now growing and developing. Get yourself educated, bring yourself up, gain a firm footing on the ground, have your firm convictions, and then, if you feel empowered, you can commence upon your new life. For now, you must, for your own well-being, break no new ground; you must simply obey those who guide you."

The young man fell silent, and the grown-ups agreed with what the father said.

—"You are right," said a middle-aged married man to the father. "It is true that a young man without life experience may make mistakes when looking for new pathways, that his decision might not be firm. But haven't we all agreed that our life is contrary to our conscience and brings us no happiness? One must not fail to recognize as true a desire to take exit of this life."

"A young man may mistake his dream for a rational conclusion, but I am no youth, and I shall speak for myself: the same thought crossed my mind while listening to our conversations tonight. It is obvious to me that the life that I lead brings neither peace to my conscience nor happiness to me. Both reason and experience demonstrate this to me. So, what am I waiting for? You wear yourself out from morning till night, and the upshot is that neither you nor your family live a godly life but get bogged down ever deeper in the quagmire of sin. You try for your family, but you do not help them because what you do for them is no good. I therefore think frequently that it would be better if I changed my life and did exactly what the young man has spoken about: stopped caring about my wife and children and thought only about the soul. It is not by chance that, as St. Paul puts it, 'a married man cares about his wife; an unmarried man cares about God.'"

The married man had barely finished speaking when all the women present, including his own wife, unleashed an attack on him.

—"You should have thought of this sooner," one of the middle-aged women said.

—"If you have already put your horse collar on, then you should keep drawing the cart. Anyone can say what you have said whenever it seems difficult for him to raise and feed a family: 'I wanna get my salvation.' This is deceitful and it's a foul thing to do. No, men must learn how to lead a godly life within the family. To save your sole self is easy. But to do so is, above all, to act against Christ's teaching. God commanded us to love others, yet you wish to insult them. No, a married man cannot avoid his fixed duties, and he must not scorn them. It is another matter when the family is well on its feet. Then, do what you will for yourself. Yet nobody has the right to coerce their family."

The married man did not agree to this. He responded: "I do not want to abandon my family. I am only saying that one should not lead one's family and children into the habits of living for the lusts of their flesh; one should teach children just as we were saying, weaning them on to the life of need, to working, to helping others, and to brotherly life with all, above all. And one must give up noble rank and wealth for this."

—"You have no business trying to correct the lives of others while not living your own in God," his wife said in a hot temper. "You have been living for your own pleasure from a young age, so why do you want to make your children and family suffer? Let them grow up in peace, and then let them do what they please; you should not force them."

The married man fell silent. Yet an older man who was also a guest in the room took his side and interjected.

—"Supposing a married man may not deprive his family of life with a certain income all of a sudden after having made them accustomed to it," he said. "It is true that one should complete the education of one's children once it is in process, and only then overhaul everything. This is all the more so the case given that grown-up children will choose the path they find best for themselves. I agree that it is difficult or even impossible for a married man to change his life without sin. But it's God's decree to us, the older men. I will speak for myself. I now live without any duties. I live, truth be told, for my belly alone: I eat, drink, sleep, and I feel disgusted and foul. It is time for me to give up living like this: to give away all of my possessions and, on the eve of my death, to live in the way that God commanded us—to live a Christian life."

But then there were those who disagreed with the old man, too. There were in the room the old man's niece and goddaughter, all of whose children he had baptized and given gifts to around the holidays, and his son, too. Everyone objected to him.

—"No," his son said, "you've worked your life's share; you must take rest and not torture yourself. You have lived 60 years with your habits and you cannot divorce yourself from them. You will only make yourself suffer unnecessarily."

—"Yes, yes," the niece confirmed—"you will live in poverty and will be out of sorts; you will whine and will end up committing more sins. But God is merciful and forgives all sinners, and not only kind people such as you, dear uncle."

—"And why should we?," added another man of the uncle's age. "It might be that we only have two days to live. Why should we change now?"

—"Ah, that's wonderful!," intervened one of the guests who had been silent until that point. "That's just wonderful! We keep talking about how good it is to live in a godly way, and we agree that we live badly, that we suffer in the spirit and the body. But as soon as it comes down to business, it turns out that children mustn't be coerced but should continue to be brought up in the same old way and not in God's way. The young must not transcend their parent's will but should continue to live in the same old way, not according to God. Married men must not coerce their wives and children and must live in the same old way, not in God's way. Old men have no business changing: they are out of the habit and they only have two days to live, in any case. Nobody can live their life well, it turns out. Instead, all we can do is hold forth about how to do so."

72. Three Parables[56]
[1895]

Parable the First

There once was a nice meadow that became overgrown with weeds. To get rid of the weeds, the owners mowed the meadow, yet the weeds only grew back

---

56 **Entry 72. "Three Parables"** [*Tri pritchi*] (1893–95). Based on the first publication in 1895, this version was published in 1954 in volume 31 of *The Jubilee* (31:57-65) with commentary by V. S. Mishin (31:271-74). Mishin explains that Tolstoy started writing the work as a fable titled "Non-Doing" about a man who had lost his way and exhausted himself after fruitlessly running in many directions. Tolstoy was himself running in many directions with the plot and took a pause from writing it on December 22, 1893, at which time only a variant of the second fable about real and counterfeit coins as well as a draft of the first parable about a clueless runner had been written. When Nikolai Ivanovich Storozhenko, literary historian, Professor at the University of Moscow, Chairman of the Society of the Lovers of Russian Literature, and Tolstoy's good friend of many years, asked the writer for a contribution for a literary collection planned by the Society, Tolstoy initially considered another parable on the theme of worker bees and parasites that had been in the works since the late 1880s and was also unfinished but then changed his mind and returned to the two unfinished parables described above. To these, he added the third parable and then changed his mind again, until two new versions were written, with the one on counterfeit food taking the place of the parable on counterfeit money. In sum, the three parables were composed of (1) the parable about weeds; (2) the parable about a housewife shaming food merchants for selling counterfeit delicatessen; and (3) the parable about the lost way that was updated from the original plan and bookended the other two. The parables were published in the Storozhenko edited collection for which they were solicited: *Pochin. Sbornik Obshchestva Liubitelei Rossiiskoi Slovesnosti na 1895 god* [*The Good Initiative. A Collection of the Society of the Lovers of Russian Literature*]. (Moscow: Tipo-lit. Vysochaishe utverzhdennago Russkago t-va pechatnago i izdatel'skago dela, 1895), 328-36. As was his custom, Tolstoy was harsh on himself in his February 17, 1895, letter to Chertkov (87:317) and in diary entries from February 21, 1895, about the alleged lack of "real divine heart" in these parables (53:8), and he kept correcting them: in all, four autographs, three sets of proofs, and eight corrected copies of his work on the parables remain in his manuscript papers.

On the principle of non-doing and on flour as "counterfeit food," see my "Editor's Introduction" in this anthology. For Tolstoy's earlier work for the Society of the Lovers of Russian Literature, see entry 18, "A Talk Delivered at the Society of the Lovers of Russian Literature" (1859) in this anthology. On Storozhenko and the protest note by Storozhenko and Tolstoy to the Mayor of Kishinev on the Easter massacre of Jews during the pogroms in

worse as a result. A kind and wise property master paid a visit to the meadow owners and gave them several pieces of advice, chief among which was that they must never mow weeds, for mowing only makes the weeds grow back worse; instead, they should pull them out at their roots.

Whether because the owners overlooked this particular piece of advice not to mow but to uproot the weeds, whether perhaps because they misunderstood him, or whether because they consciously decided not to follow the advice, the advice was not observed—indeed, it was almost as if the advice hadn't been given—and the owners went on with their mowing and the weeds kept growing. True, in years to come some folk would remind the owners of the kind and wise master's advice; but the owners wouldn't listen, and so things continued as before. So much so that it became more than just a habit but a sacrosanct custom to mow the weeds as soon as they cropped up, and the meadow became more and more polluted. Things got so bad that eventually nothing grew in the meadow except weeds. The owners lamented this and invented various means to set things right, except the one thing that had long ago been suggested to them by the kind and wise master. Well, it eventually occurred to a certain person who witnessed the pitiful state of the meadow to recall from among the old commandments of the master's advice to not mow the weeds but instead to uproot them. It then occurred to this man to remind the owners of the meadow of their unreasonable behavior, telling them that this had long ago pointed out by the kind and wise master.

What happened next? Rather than either checking whether this reminder was justified by ceasing the practice of mowing the weeds or proving the reminder wrong and judging the advice of the kind and wise master unfounded and non-binding for them, the owners of the meadow did neither. Instead, they took offense at the man's reminder and turned on him with abuse. They called him a proud madman who had gotten it into his head that he alone could comprehend the master's teachings; others called him an outrageous false interpreter and slanderer; and as for the third group, well, they called him a wicked man intent on cultivating weeds and taking the meadow away from the owners (somehow forgetting that he was only reminding them of the advice of the wise master, who was revered by them all).

"He's saying that grass shouldn't be mowed, and if we don't destroy it . . ." they'd say, deliberately ignoring that the man had never told them not to destroy

---

April 1903, see my commentary to entries 74-76 that follow in this part in the anthology. On Tolstoy's parable of worker bees, see entry 73, "Two Different Versions of the History of a Beehive with a Lacquered Lid" (1888/1900) next in this anthology.

the weeds, but rather to uproot rather than mow them. "The weeds will grow so bad that it will bring our meadow to ruin. Why then would a meadow be given to us if we were simply to use it to cultivate weeds?," they would say. And the opinion that this man was a madman or a false interpreter or that he bore ill intent toward the people, aiming to cause them harm—this view became established so firmly that everyone scolded and laughed at him. Regardless of how much this man explained that far from wanting to cultivate foul weeds he considered destroying weeds to be one of the main preoccupations of an agrarian (just as the kind and wise master understood it—his words, not mine, mind you), nobody listened to him, no matter how many times he reminded them of this. It was decided for good that this man was either a proud madman who misinterpreted the words of the kind and wise master, or that he was an evil man who called upon the people to protect and regrow the weeds instead of getting rid of them.

The same thing happened to me when I called out the gospel commandment about nonviolent resistance to evil. This rule was preached by Christ and by all of his true disciples throughout subsequent history. Whether they overlooked the rule, or misunderstood it, or whether perhaps because observing this rule seemed too difficult for them, the more time that elapsed the more the rule became forgotten, and the further and further away from the rule did the order of the life of the people become. Eventually, it came to pass, as it is now, that the rule began to appear to people as something novel, unheard of, strange, and even insane. What happened to the man who had called to people's attention the old commandment of the kind and wise master happened to me.

The owners of the meadow had purposefully ignored the fact that the advice given to them was not that bad weeds were not to be destroyed but rather that they had to be destroyed in a reasonable way; they had decided not to listen to the man who reminded them of this advice, dismissing him as a madman intent on preventing them from mowing the weeds. Similarly, people claim in response to what I say that I am preaching the cultivation of evil when I tell them that in order to destroy evil, according to the teaching of Christ, one should not resist it, but rather uproot it by way of love. "We won't listen to him," people say, "he's a madman; he advises us not to resist evil in order for evil to suffocate us."

My claim was that, according to Christ's teaching, evil cannot be weeded out by evil, that any resistance to evil only increases evil, and that according to Christ's teaching, evil is weeded out by love. Christ teaches you to bless those who curse you, pray for those who offend you, do good unto those who hate you, love your enemies, and you shall have no enemy (this is the teaching of the

12 Apostles). My claim was that, according to Christ's teaching, the entire life of a human being involves struggle against evil, resistance to evil through reason and love, and that Christ forbids any unreasonable means of resisting evil with violence—a resistance that would involve fighting evil with the very same evil.

These words of mine were understood to mean that Christ's teaching was not to resist evil. All those whose lives rest on violence and to whom violence is dear for this reason have welcomed with gladness this perturbation of my words and the words of Christ along with it, taking it for true that the teaching of non-resistance to evil is a teaching that is incorrect, inane, godless, and ill-intentioned. And people go on serenely, under the pretext of destroying of evil, only for its production to continue apace.

Parable The Second

People used to trade flour, butter, milk, and various other foodstuffs with one another. Desiring to receive the greatest profit and to get rich quick, these people got into the habit of mixing sundry cheap and harmful stuff into the products they put on sale: they poured chaff and powdered bleach into flour, melted margarine into butter, and mixed water and chalk into milk. And at least until these products reached the consumer, all went well: wholesalers would sell to retailers and retailers resold these products to small shops.

There were lots of barns and small stores, and trading went on with seeming success. And the merchants were satisfied. But for urban consumers, those who did not produce their own food and therefore had to purchase it, this practice was very unpleasant and harmful. The flour was bad, as were the butter and milk, and yet, since nothing but these modified products was available at city markets, urban consumers had to continue buying these products, blaming themselves and their poor cooking for their ill health and the bad-tasting food. And the merchants continued to mix still more of the cheap ingredients into the groceries.

This lasted a long time. City dwellers kept suffering, yet nobody dared to voice their displeasure.

One day, it happened that a woman who nourished herself and her family only on homemade food arrived in town. This village housewife had been cooking her whole life. Although not a famous cook, she could bake bread and prepare tasty dinners.

This woman purchased food in the city and set to baking and cooking. Yet, the bread wouldn't bake and would fall apart. Margarine-fried pancakes would turn insipid. The wife gave the milk some time to rest and separate: but the cream would not rise.[57] She guessed at once that her provisions were no good. She examined them and her guess proved right: she found bleach in the flour, margarine in the butter, and chalk in the milk. Having seen that the provisions were tainted, the woman went to the market and spoke out, exposing the merchants. She demanded that they either stock good, nutritious, unspoiled groceries in their shops or stop trading and shut their businesses down completely. But the merchants paid no heed to the village woman, telling her that they traded in first-rate goods, that the whole town had been buying from them for many years, and that they had even earned star medal awards, gesturing toward the medals on their storefronts. But the woman wouldn't let up.

—"I don't need any medals; I just need healthy foods from you, foods that won't give bellyaches to me or my children.

—"Sweet lady mother," the merchants said, "you have never seen genuine flour or butter, have you?" As they spoke, they pointed toward white, clean-looking flour in lacquered wood casks, at the yellow imitation of butter resting in beautiful bowls, and at the white liquid in glittering see-through vials.

—"I can't help but know," responded the housewife, "for all my life I have done nothing other than cook all the food for myself and my children. Your wares are spoiled. Here is the proof," she said pointing at the spoiled bread, the margarine in the pancakes, and the sediments in the milk. "You ought to dispose of all your wares by throwing them in the river or burning them, and you should restock with good wares!"—The woman kept shouting the same thing to all incoming customers without pause as she stood facing the storefronts, and the customers began to feel awkward.

Taking notice that this daring housewife might harm their trade, the merchants told the customers: "Behold this lunatic of a woman, gentlemen. She would have people famished. She is willing to have all groceries thrown into the river or burnt. What shall you eat if we listen to her and sell no food to you? Don't listen to her: she is a crude country bumpkin and knows nothing about groceries; she assaults you solely out of envy. She's poor and would rather everyone were as poor as her."

This is what the merchants said to the crowd that gathered, keeping quiet about the fact that the woman had no desire to destroy groceries, but only to replace bad ones with good ones.

---

57   Tolstoy means that the milk purchased by the woman at the dairy shop to make homemade cream would not separate well and form a thicker buttery layer on top simply because it had not arrived straight from the cow. And thus: Milk would not condense when the woman kept it out in the cold for it to separate and for the cream to rise to the top.

And the crowd fell upon the woman and began berating her. The woman went to some lengths to assure them that she had no desire to destroy groceries—that, on the contrary, she had cooked to feed others and herself for her whole life, that she only wanted for the people who assume the duty of feeding others not to poison them with harmful ingredients masquerading as food. However, no matter how much she spoke or what she said, the crowd would not listen to her. For, it was decided that she was intent on depriving people of the food they needed.

The same thing happened to me in relation to the science and art of our time. I have subsisted my whole life on this food. For better or worse, I tried to nourish those whom I could with it. And because, for me, this is food and not items of trade or luxury, I know for certain when it is genuine and when it's only an imitation. And so, when I tasted of the food that went on sale at the intellectual market of our time under the guise of science and art, and when I tried to nourish the people whom I loved with it, I saw that the majority of this food was not authentic. And when I spoke and said that the science and art in which they deal at the intellectual market is margarine or that it contains a considerable admixture of ingredients that are foreign to true science and art, and that I know this because the products that I had purchased there turned out to be unfit for ingestion either for me or for people close to me—not simply indigestible, but in fact quite harmful—they started yelling and hooting at me; they tried to impress it upon me that this owed to my lack of learning, that I can't handle such lofty subjects. I made the case that the merchants who deal at the intellectual market are exposing one another's fraud constantly, and I reminded them that at all times much of what was harmful and bad was traded to people under the guise of science and art and that the same danger exists in our time, too. I implored them to see that this is no laughing matter, that spiritual poison is many times more dangerous than bodily poison and that one should, therefore, examine with the greatest attention the spiritual products supplied to us that masquerade as food, and toss out everything that is fake and harmful. When I started saying all this, nobody—not a single person—offered to contradict these arguments of mine in an article or book. And yet, shouts came at me from all the storefronts, as they had been directed at that woman: "He's a madman! He is aiming to destroy science and art, the trades by which we live. Beware and don't obey him! Welcome to shopping with us! We've got the latest foreign imports!"

Parable the Third

Some pilgrims were on a journey. They accidently lost their way and instead of even ground were forced to traipse through the marshes, bushes, thorns, and over the fallen branches that blocked their way, which made it more and more difficult to make progress.

And so, the pilgrims split up into two parties: the first group decided to move ahead without stopping, following the same direction they had been following. This group assured themselves and the others that they had never lost their way before and would get to the destination eventually. The other party decided that since their current direction was clearly not the right one—for, if it was, they would have already arrived at their destination—they should look for another way. To find that way, it was necessary to split up further and, as quickly as possible, to try every direction, without stopping. The pilgrims were divided between these two opinions: the former decided to walk directly ahead all the way, and the latter decided to try every direction. But there was one among the pilgrims who agreed with neither the former nor the latter opinion: he said that before committing to the same course or changing course by moving quickly in every direction in the hopes of finding the right way, they should first stop and think about their situation; having thought it all over, they should then accept one or the other course. But the pilgrims were desperate to move; they were afraid of their situation, and were keen to console themselves with a hope that they had never lost their way, but rather just temporarily lost their sense of direction and could now get back on track again; above all, they were willing to muffle their fear with motion. Hence, the individual's opinion was met with universal indignation, with reproaches and ridicule from people from both groups.

— "This advice comes from weakness, cowardice, and laziness," some said.

— "A nice guide for reaching your destination: stay put where you sit and don't move!," others cried.

— "What are we made human for if not to fight and do the work of overcoming all hurdles instead of bowing to them faint-heartedly," exclaimed the third.

And no matter how much the trespasser from the majority spoke about the risk of getting further away instead of closer to their destination by following the wrong direction without changing course, he was ignored. Similarly, he implored them to see that they would never reach their destination if they simply thrashed from one direction to another; the sole way of reaching their destination, he said, was to choose the course according to the sun and the stars and follow it. They should come to a halt to do this, not to go on standing still, but rather to figure out the right way from which never to swerve henceforth, he claimed. But no matter how much he said all this, he wouldn't be listened to.

The first group of pilgrims headed off in the same direction as they had been walking. The second group started to thrash its course from side to side. Neither one nor the other got any closer to their destination; neither group managed to break free from the bramble bushes and thorns, where they are all still roaming.

The very same thing happened to me when I attempted to express my doubt concerning our current course, which had led us astray into the dark thickets of the labor question, into the swamping hole in which the world's nations see no end to arms race escalation. Might this course be not quite the right path? Might we have lost our way? Must we not pause in our movement, which is evidently leading us astray, and come to a halt to figure out whether we are on the path that was originally intended, as revealed through the universal and eternal foundations of truth? Nobody answered the question, nobody said: we did not fall into error, we are not wandering, we are sure of this, based on this or that. Not a single person said that we must have made an error all right, but that we have a foolproof means of correcting our error without halting our movement. Nobody said either of these things. Instead, everyone got angry, took offense and rushed to drown out my solitary voice with their univocal chorus. "We are lazy and retarded as is. And here is a sermon of sloth, idleness, non-doing!" Others even added: "nothing-doing." "Don't listen to him, follow us, forward march!" shouted those alike who think that salvation is found along the trodden path, whatever that is, and those who think that salvation comes from thrashing your course in every direction.

— "Why stand still? Why think? Fast, forward! It'll all take care of itself!"

As a result, people have been led astray and are suffering. The first and main energetic effort that should be made, it would seem, is not to escalate the race that has gotten us into the false quagmire in which we find ourselves now, but to arrest it. Only having come to a stop, it should be clear, can we assess our situation and find the course that we must follow in order to arrive at true happiness—the happiness not just of a single individual, or a category of individuals, but the true universal happiness of all humankind, toward which all people and each human heart taken separately are striving. And so? People think up all possible ideas except that one thing that can save them or at least mitigate their situation, if not provide salvation: to take a minute's pause so as to not aggravate their disasters with false activity. People can feel that their situation is disastrous and do everything possible to save themselves from it, except the one thing that would be sure to alleviate their condition. Indeed, the advice to do this one thing is precisely what irritates them the most.

Were it still possible to doubt that we have lost our way, this reaction to advice to think for themselves clearly proves just how hopelessly we have been led astray and how great our despair is.

73. Two Different Versions of the History of the Beehive with a Lacquer-Painted Lid[58] [1888–1900]

The first version of the history of the beehive with a painted lid was composed by a drone bee historiographer called Prouprou. The other version was drawn up by one of the hive's worker bees.

The history of the beehive composed by the drone opens with a list of materials and sources. The materials and sources are as follows: Memoirs of world-famous drones; the correspondence of His Highness drone Debe, Sr., with His Grace Cuckoo, Jr.; the daybook of the Court Majordomo (Hof-fourrier); the oral legends, songs, and romances of the drones; criminal and civil court cases between the drones and the other bees; travelogues about the journeys of beetles, moths, and drones from foreign hives; and statistics about honey deposits across different periods of the life of the hive.

---

58 **Entry 73. "Two Different Versions of the History of a Beehive "with a Lacquer-Painted Lid."** [*Dve razlichnye versii istorii ul'ia s lubochnoi kryshkoi*] (1888–1900). Published in 1952 in volume 34 of *The Jubilee* (34:321-24). The first publications of this work in 1912 had errors. See the commentary by B. M. Eikhenbaum in volume 34 of *The Jubilee* (34:590-91). The translation in this anthology is based on the publication in *The Jubilee*. Started around 1888, the parable was continued in the mid-1890s (1894-95). Although Tolstoy considered completing it for inclusion in the literary collection *Pochin* [The Good Initiative] by the Society of the Lovers of Russian Literature, he instead contributed "Three Parables" (1893–95) to the collection (see entry 72 in this anthology and my commentary in the previous note explaining the relation among the satiric fables). During one of several starts to what ended up as a light-hearted satire, Tolstoy was reading John Kenworthy's *Slavery: Ancient and Modern* (1895). On Tolstoy's compliments to Kenworthy, see my "Editor's Introduction" and entries 48 and 49 in this anthology. It was only in 1900 and during his writing of the longer essay "The Slavery of Our Time" [*Rabstvo nashego vremeni*] (1900) that Tolstoy completed his "Two Different Versions," for which the beginning of the completed version is located on the obverse of his drafts of "The Slavery of Our Time" (on this detail, see Eikhenbaum's commentary).

This history of the beehive with the painted lid by the historiographer Prouprou begins with the era of the original swarm and the appearance of the first drones. According to Prouprou's records, this period, from June 6 to St. Peter's Day, was the period of the blossomiest prosperity on record of the beehive with the painted lid. The might and wealth of the hive drew the attention of all the other beehives, inciting the envy of neighbors and luring celebrity visitors. The beehive was under the auspicious patronage of grandpa Anisim himself. All the beehives were at work at this time, and so were the inhabitants of the hive with the painted lid. The main distinction and advantage of the hive with the painted lid was that it was the first to bring drones into the world: their governance of the hive and the way they conducted external relations are what made it glorious. Yes, there had been, and still are, many prehistoric hives, but those bees are primitive; they live and die in obscurity. This was not the case with the hive with the painted lid. In the middle of the day, at 2 pm, with the worker bee burdened like a pack horse, in the midst of his ceaseless, lowly work hauling honey and pollen for the offspring, the drones flew out for the first time. Those who witnessed their exit are unanimous in their testimony: the world had never seen a more resplendent sight. Large drones—one more lustrous than the next, attired in satiny black and fuzzy plush—sprang into flight from the ledge of the trapdoor. Rather than following the lead of the plain worker bee, who would fly directly over the fence and into the forest and meadows to forage, the drones soared off, streaking through the air in circles, eagle-style, above the beehives. The sight was so striking in its splendor. One could not help but watch it with tears of emotion in one's eyes. Its deep significance was even more striking. Having exited, the drones each did a trumpet solo, buzzing aloud their individual views on the tasks of governance, forthcoming changes and improvements. The attention of the assembly was drawn for the most part to the state and activity of the worker bee, which was unanimously voted unsatisfactory, in need of correction and mentoring. The assembly divided into different spheres of governance and without delay proceeded to detail measures for rectifying the bees' labor. Elected immediately were governors and vice-governors; assistants to vice-governors; spiritual censors; observers; moral police; judges; high priests; poets and the intellectual set—with respective salaries and bonuses attached to each position. As their next step, the voting contingent and the aforementioned core of elected bees voted in the outstanding few for these positions. Those elected were all luminaries, a pack of glorious eagles, who affixed their seal of illustrious might on the times. They circled and trumpeted for a long time in front of the hives, sometimes bumping into the foraging bees, who were not capable of appreciating everything that was being done for them and their welfare. Frequently, the ungrateful and ignorant bees shared with each other, for their own sake, their displeasure at the activities of the drones.

The following day, the drones got down to fulfilling their duties. It might have seemed, from afar, that they were always after the same thing, but this is only the misconception of the uninitiated. They were at work on something very important and tough. Here is an excerpt from the diary of one of the drones' chief figures:

> I have been elected unanimously as the founding engineer tasked with figuring out the correct flight paths for worker bees. My duty is very difficult and complex; I am fully aware of its huge importance and will try to fulfill it in the best way possible, sparing no effort. This is too tough a job for one person and so I invited A to be my deputy, not least because my aunt's second cousin asked me to find a place for him. I did the same for B, D, and G. They, too, will need deputies and so our department will have 36 or 38 staff. I already stated at the board meeting that we would need two honeycombs worth of honey to do our work. The resolution passed without objection and we assumed our functions immediately, spending the night at the combs tasting honey. The taste is not bad, though one hopes that it will be perfected if we act right, especially if my proposal is accepted. "Gentlemen," said I, "we must think through measures that will allow us to work out the basis of a draft of our strategy program." Opinions were divided. Debe, Sr., who chaired, motioned a vote. But precisely what we were voting on proved insufficiently clear and it was resolved to elect a commission that would draft a proposal for voting that would be submitted by our next session.

The other active drones worked just as hard. It is thanks to their labor that the hive thrived and prospered. Every day the drone bosses took a flight outside, dancing around discussing and solving important matters of state, coming back to the hive by night, hitching the combs, and replenishing their energies on the honey that was stocked for them.—They prospered to the full of their ability, and so did the hive. One day, however, a minor unpleasant perturbation[59] took place: A group of worker bees found it necessary to take flight from the hive

---

59 "*Perturbatsiia*" [perturbation] is Tolstoy's word.

along with the queen and to swarm on the bough of a rowan tree. This flagrant disobedience on the part of these bees might have diminished the influence of the drones, had they not scripted their quick-witted resolution to order the bees' flight in progress, lest the bees presume that what they did was an act of free will and not at the behest of their governors.

The migrant swarm were then declared extradited defectors, though the remaining bees were supposed to continue to obey and to take care of their governors. Toward the end of August, we started to see signs of unrest. One day, the drones arrived at the combs after concluding a promenade flight, only to discover a worker bee there that would not let them approach! They retreated in indignation and flew to other hives. But the same thing happened at the other hives. The worker bees would not let the drones in. Obviously, everything was coming to ruin. The drones made one last attempt to enter their hive, but the worker bees blocked the upstairs and drove them down to the basement where it was cold and there was no food. The same thing happened on the next day and the day after that. The drones began losing weight, and soon began dropping dead, famished, one by one. However, not a single one of them demeaned themselves by starting to work for food.

The bees upstairs were busy doing something, buzzing on the honeycombs. The drone historians say that what was most likely happening was that, having lost their leaders, they were dying from the anarchy. The disobedience of the worker bees to the drones spelled their ruin. They perished. This is how the history of the beehive with the painted lid by the drone bee concludes.

The history written by the worker bee does not harmonize with the above history. The history written by this bee states that the life of the hive began one early spring when the hive was put out in the sun. Immediately after unburdening itself, the worker bee flew to the pussy willow that was in bloom, buzzing as it pollinated the willow, collecting pollen with its tender appendages and honey with its stomach. The life of the bee was one of never-ending joyful labor, according to this bee historian. On the apple trees, on the bushes, and in the fields, flowers blossomed one after another, and the enjoyment the bee received from work was compounded by the delight it took in this blossoming nature. The larvae of the worker bees, the drones, and of the queen received good nourishment and grew up fast in the hive and the combs filled with fragrant honey. There was such a plenty and plenitude of everything that a new expansion was necessary, and so the drones were let outside into the world, even though only one of them was needed to impregnate the new queen; and even though only one queen was needed, three were harvested. The vital time arrived when it became necessary to split up to avoid surplus reproduction. Intense work continued. Yet meanwhile, the drones had started taking off for half a day at a time, trumpeting loudly above the hives. The worker bees had no idea what the drones thought they were doing, never divining the importance that the drones themselves ascribed to this. Nevertheless, the worker bees decided to forgive the idleness and gluttony of the drones, thinking, first of all, that one of them would ultimately be of service, and secondly, that there was so much of everything that it just wouldn't be right to begrudge the drones some of the good stuff, idle and useless though they were. While the drones were convinced that they were the ones in charge, one of the worker bees had this to write in his log:

> The lords got out of hand today. For four-whole hours, they droned around and were a nuisance to the working people. They flew off only at around 4. They became so famished doing nothing that, on their return, they began gobbling up the chow. God save us from their ravage! We have enough, even for them; it's just such a downer that they get in the way of the work.

A great event took place at the end of May: The bees saw the old queen pass into the next kingdom leaving them with their newly impregnated young queen, who started laying eggs right away. Lime trees had begun blossoming, and the baby larvae needed to be fed, so much needed to be done to the bloom while it lasted—honey preserves needed to be hoarded for the winter. The flower was strong and not entirely beaten down by the rain, and so the bees managed to gather a lot, though much more was still needed to stock up for the winter. Yet the drones, who ascribed such uncharacteristic importance to themselves, thinking themselves essential workers, simply continued to devour the stock of honey. This went on for some time. But eventually, after the blossom period had ended and only thorns remained, domestic demand for food increased. And so—without drafting a plan or agreeing on a resolution—the worker bees started blocking the drones' access to the honey, driving the drones away, and even picking off and killing the most arrogant and useless. All of the drones were ultimately destroyed. Not only did the hive not perish but it was then ready to face the winter in a most prosperous state. Once winter arrived, the bees grew quiet, staying put in hibernation, keeping their offspring warm, waiting for the spring to come when the joy of life would resume.

74. Labor, Death, and Sickness[60]
[1903]

A Legend

The following legend exists among the native people of Latin America:

They say that God created people at first in such a way that they did not need to labor; they needed neither dwelling, nor clothing, nor food; and they all lived to a hundred and knew no illness.

Some time passed and God came to look at how people were living. He saw that everyone was taking care of themselves and quarreling with one another; they were living in such a way that instead of delighting in life they cursed it.

And then God said: "This is because they live apart, each for themselves." And for this not to be so, God made it impossible for people to live without labor. In order for them not to suffer from cold and hunger, they would have to build dwellings for themselves, plough the earth, harvest, and collect fruit and grain.

"Labor will unite them"—God thought—"one cannot chop and haul logs, and build dwellings and forge tools, and sow, and mow, and thresh, and weave, and sew clothes all alone. They will come to understand that the more collegially they work the more they will get done and the better they shall live. And this will unite them."

---

60 **Entry 74. "Labor, Death, and Sickness"** [*Trud, smert' i bolezn'*] (1903) published in 1952 in volume 34 of *The Jubilee* (34:131-33) (see comment for entries 74-76). Tolstoy intended to donate the three tales written on July 22-23, 1903, and corrected in August 1903 to *Gil'f* [Help], an illustrated collection edited by Sholem Aleichem that was published in Warsaw in Yiddish for the victims of the Easter 1903 pogrom in Kishinev and was then translated into Russian and other languages. Tolstoy wrote a short preface for the collection, explaining the substitution of parables eventually included in *Gil'f*. Sholem Aleichem preferred including "The Assyrian Tsar Asarkhadon" instead of "This is You," which was Tolstoy's preference, and Tolstoy obliged. Because the Asarkhadon tale is frequently published alongside Tolstoy's better-known fiction, I am including the third of the tales designated by Tolstoy as his gift to *Gil'f*. "This Is You." In addition to "The Assyrian Tsar Asakhardon," the three tales in entries 74-75 are the only fictions completed by Tolstoy in 1903. "After the Ball" was completed in 1904. For the correspondence between Tolstoy and Sholem Aleichem on this project, see volume 74 of *The Jubilee* published in 1954 and edited by V. A. Zhdanov. Tolstoy's letters on August 20 (74:165-66), 22 (74:166), and 25 (74:167), 1903, were addressed to Aleichem using his given name in Russian, Solomon Naumovich Rabinovich. In these letters, Tolstoy speaks of the desirability of adding the tale "This is You" and substituting "South American Indians" (translated here as the "native people of South America" for the original "Pathagonians") (74:167). For additional details, see "Editor's Introduction."

Some more time passed and God returned once more to look at how people were living.

People were living worse than they had before, however. They labored together (it couldn't be otherwise) yet not all together. For, they divided up into small clusters, and each cluster tried to steal the work of another; everyone clashed with one another, wasting their time and strength on this struggle. It was dreadful for everyone.

Having seen that this was no good either, God decided to design it so that people could die at any moment and would not be aware of the hour of their death. And He announced this to the people.

"When they discover that each of them can die at any moment and come to realize the care that must be taken of their fragile lives," God thought, "they will not get angry with one another, will not spoil what time is left in store for them."

But it came to pass differently. When God came back to look at how people were living, He saw that their lives hadn't improved.

Taking advantage of the fact that people could die at any moment, the powerful had subdued the weaker, killing some of them and threatening others with death. It had come to pass that while the powerful and their heirs labored not at all and despaired of idleness, the weak labored beyond exertion and despaired of having no rest. Both groups feared and hated one another. And the life of the people was still unhappier.

Having seen this, God decided to try a last resort as a remedy: He unleashed all kinds of sicknesses on the people. "When everyone becomes subject to sickness," God thought, "they will come to understand that the healthy must take pity on the sick and help them so that when their turn comes to be sick the healthy will help them."

Once more did God take leave of the people. But when He came back to take another look at how people were living, He saw that the life of the people had grown even worse since they had become susceptible to sickness. The same sicknesses that God had thought would have united people, had driven them even further apart. Those who forced others to work for them also forced others to take care of them when they were sick; these powerful people never tended to other sick people. Those forced to work for others and take care of the sick were so exhausted by this work that they had no time to care for their own sick, leaving them unaided. So that the sight of the sick would not interfere with the pleasures of the rich and so that the sick could not solicit pity, the rich set up care homes. In these homes, where the sick were transferred into the hands of hired caregivers who tended to them not only without pity but with disgust, the sick suffered and died. Furthermore, having realized that the majority of sicknesses are infectious, the healthy, who were afraid of becoming infected, not only did not get close to the sick but distanced themselves as well from those who had been in touch with the sick.

And so God told Himself: "If this design fails to bring people to the understanding of what their happiness consists in, let them arrive at it through suffering." And God left the people alone.

Left alone, for a long time people lived without understanding that they can and must be happy. Only very recently did some of them begin to realize that labor must not be a scarecrow for some and coerced and arduous for others, but must be a common deed of joy that unites people. In the light of death that threatens everyone at every moment, it dawned on these people that the sole reasonable deed of every individual is to spend whatever years, months, hours, or minutes are left in store for them in accord and love. Sickness, these people have come to understand, not only must not be a cause for distancing but, on the contrary, must inspire a loving communion among all.

75. Three Questions[61]
[1903]

Once upon a time, there was a tsar who had a thought: If he could always know the perfect time to begin everything, which people to engage with and which to avoid doing business with, and, in particular, what the most important things are, then he would never have a setback. Having had this thought, the tsar announced to his kingdom that he would issue a great reward to anyone who could answer his questions and teach him *how to recognize the best time to do things, which people are the most essential, and how to recognize what thing is the most important of all.*

Learned people started visiting the tsar, giving various answers to his questions.

Some answered the first question by saying that in order to know the right time for everything, it is necessary to draw up and strictly stick to a schedule for every day, month, and year. Only then, they said, would everything be done in its due course. Others said that one must not decide ahead of time what to do and when; one should not be diverted by idle amusements but always be

---

61 **Entry 75. "Three Questions"** [*Tri voprosa*] (1903). Published in 1952 in volume 34 of *The Jubilee* (34:134-37), it is based on the first publication in 1895; see commentary by B. M. Eikhenbaum in *The Jubilee* (34:554-56; on the history of writing, see 557-60) and commentary for entries 74 and 76.

attentive to what is happening and then do what is required. The third group proclaimed that however attentive one might be to what is happening, one person alone cannot always recognize when everything needs to be done; instead, he should hold a council of wise men, who should collectively decide what to do and when. The fourth group said that things would inevitably happen when there is no time to seek the counsel of advisers, and so the tsar would have to decide on the spot whether it's time or not to undertake the action in question. But in order to know what to do, one would have to know in advance what was going to happen. And only the magi can know this. Therefore, in order to know the right time for everything, the magi must be consulted.

The second question received answers just as various. Some said that the tsar's most essential people were his aides; others claimed that they were the high priests; the third group said that the tsar's most essential people were doctors; the fourth suggested that it was the tsar's warriors.

As for the third question—what affairs are the most important?—the tsar also received various answers. Some said that the most important affairs in the world are scientific; others claimed that the most important affairs concern the military; the third group said that divine worship is the most important.

All the answers were different. As a result, the tsar did not agree with any of them and so did not issue the reward to anyone. But, still wishing to find answers to his questions, he decided to ask a famously wise hermit.

The hermit lived in a forest, never appeared in public, and received only common people. So, the tsar put on plain garb, and, realizing it was necessary, dismounted from his horse before reaching the hermit's cell. Leaving his arm-bearing entourage behind, the tsar walked the rest of the way to the hermit's dwelling, approaching him alone on foot.

When the tsar approached, the hermit was ploughing the earth in front of his little hut to make bed furrows. Seeing the tsar, the hermit greeted him before immediately returning to his digging. The hermit was thin and weak, and each time he plunged his spade into the ground to scoop the small clumps of soil that it turned up, he breathed heavily.

The tsar approached and said:

"I have come to see you, wise hermit, to ask you to answer three questions: *How can I learn to do the right thing at the right time so that I never miss out and avoid feeling remorse? Who are the most essential people, and so whom should I engage with and whom should I avoid? And what affairs are the most important and hence what should I prioritize?*"

Having listened to the tsar, the hermit said nothing in response. Instead, he spat on his hand and went back to his digging.

"—You are tired, the tsar said. Give me the spade, and I shall work for you awhile."

"—Thank you," said the hermit. Having handed over the spade, he sat down on the ground.

Upon finishing two bed rows, the tsar stopped ploughing and repeated his questions. The hermit again said nothing in response, but got to his feet and reached out for the spade:

"—Your turn to rest, let me continue now," he said.

But the tsar did not return the spade and continued to dig. An hour passed, then another hour. The sun started sinking beneath the treetops. The tsar finally plunged the spade into the soil and said:

"—I came to you for answers to my questions, wise man. If you cannot answer, then tell me, and I shall be on my way home."

"—Hey, someone's running toward us," the hermit said. "Let us see who it is."

The tsar turned around and saw a bearded man running out of the woods. He was pressing his hands against his stomach, and blood was streaming from under them. As he was running toward the tsar, the bearded man fell to the ground and fainted. His eyes rolled up and he moaned feebly.

The tsar and the hermit lifted the bearded man's clothes. He had a large wound in his stomach. The tsar washed it as best he could and dressed it with his handkerchief and the hermit's towel. But the bleeding would not stop. Several times, the tsar removed the blood-soaked dressing and washed and rebandaged the wound.

When the bleeding slowed, the wounded man came to and asked for water to drink. The tsar fetched fresh water and gave it to the wounded man to drink.

Meanwhile, the sun had completely set, and it had become cooler. With the help of the hermit, the tsar carried the wounded man into the hut and put him into bed. Lying in bed, the wounded man closed his eyes and lay there quietly. The tsar had become so exhausted from walking and working that after finding a perch near the threshold, he too fell asleep and slept soundly for the whole short summer night. For a long time, upon waking, he could not understand where he was or who the strange bearded man lying in bed staring at him intently with his shining eyes was.

"—Forgive me," the bearded man said in a weak voice upon seeing that the tsar had woken up and was looking at him.

"—I do not know you and have nothing to forgive you for," the tsar said.

"—You don't know me, but I know you. I am that enemy of yours who pledged to take revenge on you for your having put my brother to death and seized my property. I knew that you were walking alone to see the hermit and I decided to murder you on your return. A whole day passed, and you were nowhere to be seen. And so, I left my place in ambush to find out where you were. But I stumbled upon your arm bearers. They recognized me, fell on me, and wounded me. I ran away from them. But I would have bled to death had you not dressed my wound. I was going to kill you, but you saved my life. And now, should I survive, and should you so desire, I shall serve you as your most loyal slave and will order the same of my sons. Forgive me."

The tsar was very glad to have made peace with his enemy so easily. Not only did he forgive him, but he also promised to return all of the man's property, and, moreover, to send his servants and his doctor to attend to him.

Having bidden farewell to the wounded man, the tsar walked out and stood on the porch looking for the hermit. For one last time before taking his leave, he wished to ask for answers to his questions. The hermit was outside, crawling on his knees next to the beds they had furrowed yesterday, planting seeds in them.

The tsar approached him and asked:

"For the last time, wise man, I ask that you answer my questions."

"—You've already been answered," the hermit said, squatting on his thin shins and looking up at the tsar standing in front of him.

"—Answered—how so?," asked the tsar.

"—Do you not see?," replied the hermit. "If you had not taken pity on my weakness yesterday, hadn't plowed these beds for me but had walked back, that brave fellow would have attacked you and you would have regretted not having stayed with me. That is, the most important time was when you were digging the beds; I was then the most important person, and the most pressing thing was to do me good. Afterwards, when that other fellow ran to us, the most important time was when you were tending to him. For, had you not dressed his wound, he would have died without making peace with you. That is, he was the most essential person, and what you did for him was the most important thing. Remember this: There is only one time that is important—*now*. And it's the most important because in it alone do we have control over ourselves. The most essential person is *the one whom you have just encountered*, because nobody can know whether he will have dealings with any other person. And the most important thing of all is to *do him good*, since for that purpose alone has a human being been sent forth into this life."

76. This Is You[62]
[1903]

A tyrant summons a sage to ask him the best way to take revenge on his enemy.

Tyrant: Name the cruelest, slowest torment by means of which I might torture a criminal to death.

Sage: Make him recognize his sin and relinquish him to his conscience.

Tyrant: So, it's conscience, according to you. Listen, a relative of mine has offended me bitterly and I cannot be joyous and calm until I take revenge. I have been thinking about the cruelest torments and have not yet found one that would match my ire.

Sage: You won't find a match. No torment can annihilate either the crime itself or the perpetrator. Only one thing is reasonable: Forgive.

Tyrant: I know that I cannot do anything to undo what has been done, but why do you say that I cannot annihilate a crime?

Sage: Nobody can do this.

Tyrant: What nonsense you talk. Surely, I can destroy a crime just as easily as I can destroy this lamp here, which now will never shine again.

Sage: Now you've destroyed the lamp, but you cannot destroy the light, because light is everywhere the same; it exists of itself in everything. You cannot kill a criminal because you are the same as the one whom you would like to kill.

Tyrant: You are either a madman or a joker.

Sage: I speak the truth. The criminal is—you.

Tyrant: So it turns out I have insulted myself and I ought to destroy myself to avenge the insult?

Sage: Not at all; no evil can be expiated with spilled blood. To avenge your insult, you'd need to destroy all of humankind, because we are all guilty. Even then, what's offensive to you would remain, for, as you rightly put it, one cannot do anything to undo what has been done.

---

62 **Entry 76. "This Is You"** [*Eto ty*] (34:138-41). Also see Eikhenbaum's commentary in *The Jubilee* (34:561), notes to entries 74 and 75, and my "Editor's Introduction."

Tyrant: However strange your words, there is a grain of truth in them. Speak more clearly.

Sage:　Look around you at everything that is alive and tell yourself: All of this is I. All people are brothers; they are the same in essence. In the face of supreme justice, no evil will go unpunished. When you raise an arm against your enemy, you strike yourself, for the offender and the offended are the same in essence.

Tyrant: I do not understand thee. I rejoice at the sufferings that I cause my enemy. How could this be if he and I were one?

Sage:　You rejoice at your enemy's suffering, which you do not feel, because you are cocooned in your imagined vengeful personal "I." But wake up to the consciousness of your true "I" and you shall feel all of his suffering.

Tyrant: This smacks of insanity. Show me: Make it such that I feel as one with a criminal.

Sage:　It is hard to grant your wish, but I shall try. I shall induce in you such a state that you shall feel the unity of humanity in all people.

Being in possession of that power, the sage induced in the soul of the tyrant the same impressions and feelings that had led his enemy to insult him. In this state, the tyrant recognized himself to be the one whom he hated; the urges that had compelled his enemy became clear to him. He could no longer find the foundation for his hatred, because he now understood that personhood is not the true essence of being human. Rather, he came to see that consciousness of the unity of all humankind is the true foundation for all individualities, which manifest themselves in different degrees.

When the tyrant returned to his previous state, he posed this question to the sage:

Tyrant: Shall I tell thee what I have found out?

Sage:　Do tell.

Tyrant: I saw the truth as if I saw through a veil. I have learned that underneath the veil all of humankind is one in essence; my friends and enemies are its members just as you and I are. When someone offends another, he offends all of humanity.

Sage:　This is the truth that I meant to inspire in you and which is expressed in the words: This is you.

Tyrant: How should one live in the world after this?

Sage: A laborer serves, a merchant trades, a warrior defends the state, a prince rules. Each has a range of duties according to his nature. But the enlightened are different. What is high virtue for others is crime and insanity for the enlightened. You have now become enlightened; you have seen the ray of light that shines on all but is perceived by few; there is no going back into darkness for you.

Tyrant: Help me find pure light. I do not want to be an I, do not want anything transient; I want to be timeless, impersonal, just like you ...

Soon afterwards, the tyrant made peace with his enemy, fathomed the meaning and aim of life, and walked the path toward eternal peace.

77. The Wolf[63]
[1908]

Once upon a time, there was a boy who was very fond of eating chickens and was very afraid of wolves.

One day, this boy went to bed and fell asleep. He dreamt that he was walking alone through the forest to gather mushrooms when suddenly a wolf leapt out from behind the bushes and charged toward him.

The boy took fright and cried out, "Aie, aie! He will eat me up!"

The wolf, however, spoke to him in a human voice: "Hold on, I won't eat you. But I shall have a talk with you."

"You are afraid that I will eat you," the wolf continued. "But what about you? Don't you like to eat chickens?"

"I do."

---

63 **Entry 77. "The Wolf"** [*Volk*] (1908). Posrednik first published the tale in the inaugural issue of its new journal *Beacon* [*Maiak*], which came out on February 23, 1909, in Moscow. It was reprinted in 1956 in volume 37 of *The Jubilee* (37:5), whose veteran editors V. S. Mishin and P. S. Popov used the commentary by their deceased co-editor V. S. Spiridonov (37:403): Tolstoy's handwritten original could not be found in his papers. Tolstoy composed the tale for seven-year-old Ivan and five-year-old Tatiana, the children of his youngest living son Mikhail Lvovich (1879–1944), who had been vacationing at Yasnaya Polyana. As confirmed by Tolstoy's secretary Nikolai Gusev, Tolstoy also dictated the tale onto a phonograph, a gift from Thomas Edison, around July 19, 1908. The machine-typed copy of the phonograph recording is the same version as was published in *Beacon* without Tolstoy's corrections. On Thomas Edison and Tolstoy, see also my "Editor's Introduction" and commentaries to entry 48 in this anthology. I thank the seminar Crime and Salvation (fall 2018 at The New School) for their comments on the earliest draft of this translation.

"Well, why do you eat them? For, the chickens are just as much alive as you are. Go and observe how every morning they are caught, how the cook carries them off to the kitchen, how their throats are slit, and how the mother hen clucks about her babies being taken away from her. Have you seen this?" asked the wolf.

"I have not," the boy replied.

"Well, go and witness it, if you have not. But now I will eat you up. I will eat you up because you are a little chicken, just like them."

The wolf leapt at the boy, and the boy was terrified, crying out "Aie, aie, aie!"

At this, the boy woke up in fits of tears.

But after the dream, the boy stopped eating meat. Never again did he eat beef, veal, mutton, or chicken.

Further Reading in English

Anthologies and Collections of Tolstoy's Thought

An Anthology of Tolstoy's Spiritual Economics. Kenneth C. Wenzer, ed. Volume II of the Henry George Centennial Trilogy. Rochester, NY: University of Rochester, 1997.

Classic Tales and Fables for Children. Translated by Leo Wiener and Nathan Haskell Dole. Edited and introduced by Bob Blaisdell. Amherst, NY: Prometheus Books, 2002.

A Confession and Other Religious Writings. Translated and edited by Jane Kentish. London: Penguin, 1987.

Government Is Violence: Essays on Anarchism and Pacifism. Translated by V. Chertkov and Aylmer Maude. Edited and introduced by David Stephens. London: Phoenix Press, 1990.

Last Steps: The Late Writings of Leo Tolstoy. Translated by R. F. Christian, Constance Garnett, Michael R. Katz, et al. Edited by Jay Parini. New York: Penguin Classics, 2009.

The Lion and the Honeycomb: The Religious Writings of Tolstoy. Translated by Robert Chandler. Edited by A. N. Wilson. London: Collins, 1987.

Leo Tolstoy. Edited by Dragan Milivojević. New York: East European Monographs of Columbia University Press, 1998. [Tolstoy's writings on Eastern religions].

Selected Essays. Translated and edited by Aylmer Maude, and selected and introduced by Ernest J. Simmons. New York: Modern Library, 1964.

Tolstoy as Teacher: Tolstoy's Writings on Education. Edited by Bob Blaisdell. Translated by Christopher Edgar. New York: Teachers & Writers Collaborative, 2000.

Tolstoy on Art. Translated and edited by Aylmer Maude. New York: Haskell Publishers, 1973.

Tolstoy on Education: Tolstoy's Educational Writings 1861–62. Translated by Alan Pinch. Edited by Michael Armstrong and Alan Pinch. Rutherford: Fairleigh Dickinson University Press, 1982.

Tolstoy's Writings on Civil Disobedience and Non-Violence. Introduced by David H. Albert, with a foreword by George Zabelka. Philadelphia: New Society, 1987.

Individual Works of Tolstoy's Philosophy

Tolstoy, Leo. *A Calendar of Wisdom: Daily Thoughts to Nourish the Soul, Written and Selected from the World's Sacred Texts by Leo Tolstoy*. Translated by Peter Sekirin. New York: Scribner, 1997.

———. *A Calendar of Wisdom*. ed. and trans. Roger Cockrell. London: Alma Classics, 2015.

———. *The Gospel in Brief*. Translated by Isabel Hapgood. Edited and with a preface by F. A. Flowers III. Lincoln: University of Nebraska Press, 1997.

———. *The Kingdom of God Is within You: Christianity Not as a Mystic Religion but as a New Theory of Life*. Translated by Constance Garnett, with a foreword by Martin Green. Lincoln: University of Nebraska Press, 1984.

———. *On Life: A Critical Edition*. Translated by Michael Denner and Inessa Medzhibovskaya. Edited by Inessa Medzhibovskaya. Evanston, IL: Northwestern University Press, 2019.

———. *What Is Art?* Translated by Richard Pevear and Larissa Volokhonsky. London: Penguin, 1995.

———. *What Then Must We Do?* Trans. Aylmer Maude. London: Oxford University Press, 1935.

———. *Wise Thoughts for Every Day: On God, Love, Spirit, and Living a Good Life*. Selected and translated from the Russian by Peter Sekirin. New York: Arcade Publishing, 2005.

Criticism of Tolstoy's Philosophy and Thought

Anniversary Essays on Tolstoy. Edited by Donna Tussing Orwin. Cambridge: Cambridge University Press, 2010.

Berlin, Isaiah. *Russian Thinkers*. Edited by Aileen Kelly and Henry Hardy, with an introduction by Aileen Kelly. London: Penguin, 1994.

Christoyannopoulos, Alexandre. *Tolstoy's Political Thought: Christian Anarcho-Pacifist Iconoclasm Then and Now*. Abington, UK: Routledge, 2019.

(A) Critical Guide to Tolstoy's On Life: *Interpretive Essays*. Edited, and with an introduction by, Inessa Medzhibovskaya. Toronto: Imprint of the Tolstoy Society of North America and Tolstoy Studies Journal, 2019.

Eikhenbaum, Boris. *The Young Tolstoy*. Translated by Gary Kern. Ann Arbor, MI: Ardis, 1972.

———. *Tolstoy in the Sixties*. Translated by Duffield White. Ann Arbor, MI: Ardis, 1982.

———. *Tolstoy in the Seventies*. Translated by Albert Kaspin. Ann Arbor, MI: Ardis, 1982.

Emerson, Caryl. Chapter 11, "Tolstoy." In *The Oxford Handbook of Russian Religious Thought*, edited by Caryl Emerson, Randall A. Poole, and George Pattison. New York: Oxford University Press, 2020: 184-204.

Gifford, Henry. *Tolstoy*. Oxford: Oxford University Press, 1983.

Gustafson, Richard F. *Leo Tolstoy. Resident and Stranger: A Study in Fiction and Theology*. Princeton, NJ: Princeton University Press, 1986.

Jahn, Gary. "Tolstoy and Kant." *New Perspectives on Nineteenth-Century Russian Prose*, eds. George G. Gutsche and Lauren Leighton, 60-70. Columbus, OH: Slavica Publishers, 1981.

Knapp, Liza. *Leo Tolstoy: A Very Short Introduction*. Oxford: Oxford University Press, 2019.

Kvitko, David. *A Philosophic Study of Tolstoy*. PhD diss., Columbia University, 1927.

Love, Jeff. *Tolstoy: A Guide for the Perplexed*. New York: Continuum 2008.

MacLaughlin, Sigrid. "Some Aspects of Tolstoy's Intellectual Development: Tolstoy and Schopenhauer." *California Slavic Studies* 5 (1970): 187-248.

McLean, Hugh. *In Quest of Tolstoy*. Boston: Academic Studies Press, 2008.

Matual, David. *Tolstoy's Translation of the Gospels. A Critical Study*. Lewiston: The Edwin Mellen Press, 1992.

Medzhibovskaya, Inessa. *Tolstoy and the Religious Culture of his Time: A Biography of a Long Conversion, 1845–1887*. Lanham, MD: Lexington Books, 2008.

———. *Tolstoy's* On Life: *From the Archival History of Russian Philosophy*. DeLand: FL and Toronto: Tolstoy Studies Journal, 2019.

Morson, Gary Saul. *The Long and Short of It: From Aphorism to Novel*. Stanford, CA: Stanford University Press, 2012.

Moulin, Daniel. *Leo Tolstoy*. New York: Bloomsbury, 2011.

Mounce, H. O. *Tolstoy on Aesthetics: What Is Art?* Aldershot, UK: Ashgate, 2001.

Murphy, D. *Tolstoy and Education*. Dublin: Irish Academic Press, 1992.

Orwin, Donna Tussing. *Tolstoy's Art and Thought, 1847–1880*. Princeton, NJ : Princeton University Press, 1993.

The Palgrave Handbook to Russian Thought. Edited by Marina F. Bykova, Michael N. Forster, and Lina Steiner. New York: Palgrave Macmillan, 2021.

Paperno, Irina. *"Who, What Am I?": Tolstoy Struggles to Narrate the Self*. Ithaca, NY and London: Cornell University Press, 2014.

Pickford, Henry W. *Thinking with Tolstoy and Wittgenstein: Expression, Emotion, and Art*. Evanston: Northwestern University Press, 2016.

Redfearn, David. *Tolstoy's Principles of a New World Order*. London: Shepheard-Walwyn, 1992.

Scanlan, James, "Tolstoy among the Philosophers: His Book *On Life* and Its Critical Reception." *Tolstoy Studies Journal* 18 (2006): 52-69.

Spence, C. W. *Tolstoy the Ascetic*. New York: Barnes and Noble, 1967.

Tolstoy on War: Narrative Art and Historical Truth in War and Peace. Edited by Rick McPeak and Donna Tussing Orwin. Ithaca, NY: Cornell University Press, 2012.

Walicki, Andrzej. *A History of Russian Thought from the Enlightenment to Marxism*. Translated by Hilda Andrews Rusiecka. Stanford, CA: Stanford University Press, 1979.

Zorin, Andrei. *Leo Tolstoy*. London: Reaktion, 2020.

Bibliographic Sources, Reference, and Context

Berman, Anna A., ed. *Tolstoy in Context*. Cambridge: Cambridge University Press, 2022.

Bulgakov, V. F. et al. *Biblioteka L. N. Tolstogo v Iasnoi Poliane. Bibliograficheskoe Opisanie*. [The Library of L. N. Tolstoy at Yasnaya Polyana: A Bibliographic Description]. Parts 1, 2, 3. Moscow: Kniga, 1972–2000.

Egan, David R, and Melinda A. Egan. *Leo Tolstoy: An Annotated Bibliography of English Language Sources from 1978 to 2003*. Lanham, MD: Scarecrow Press, 2005.

———. Leo Tolstoy: *An Annotated Bibliography of English Language Sources to 1978*. Metuchen, NJ: Scarecrow Press, 1979.

Medzhibovskaya, Inessa. *Leo Tolstoy*. Oxford Bibliographies. Editor in Chief Eugene O'Brian. Oxford University Press, 2021. Last Modified 24 March 2021; DOI: 10.1093/OBO/9780190221911-0104.

Index of Tolstoy's Works

Tolstoy's Works included in this volume (listed alphabetically)

Tolstoy's Works cited in this volume

Index of Names and Titles

[For Tolstoy's works, see Index of Tolstoy's Works]

Index of Terms

"Discovering any untranslated work of Leo Tolstoy is akin to finding buried treasure. Inessa Medzhibovskaya in this lovely volume unearths a cache of short writings and burnishes them for the reader in English with excellent translations and expert commentary. The collection shows Tolstoy's appreciation of life and quest for meaning from his earliest to his last writings. As a seven-year-old child in 1835 he noted observations about birds, and two years later wrote about patriotism—both essays are in the volume. The compendium concludes with a cycle of tales written for the relief of survivors of the Easter pogroms of 1903 in Kishinev, as well as the introduction to his final book, *The Path of Life* (1910). The writings, the introductory essay, and the notes make this an excellent companion volume for biographies of Tolstoy, but it also stands alone. The fluidity and clarity of translation will reward those who dip into sections as well as those who read straight through. Medzhibovskaya gives new insight into the life course and philosophical development of this marvelously perplexing man."

– Jeffrey Brooks, Author of *The Firebird and the Fox: Russian Culture under Tsars and Bolsheviks*

"A major contribution to Tolstoy studies. Medzhibovskaya's research, based on decades of scholarship and archival work on Tolstoy, is impeccable. She places the writings into the broader contexts of his life and thoughts. Many of the works appear for the first time in English translation. Tolstoy scholars, general readers, and philosophy specialists will benefit from the breadth of the writings and from Medzhibovskaya's erudition. She also highlights nuances of Tolstoy's language.

The reader can experience the joy of discovery from reading the many unknown writings on science; art; music; the meaning of life; justice; Tolstoy's question about why a tree grows; his views on psychiatry; on how to prevent suicide. He talks about tolerance; love; happiness; morality; ethics; how to avoid the causes of war; politics; religion. The writings span Tolstoy's life, from what he wrote as a young boy, to what he wrote, at 80, about vegetarianism, for his young grandchildren."

– Ellen Chances, Professor of Russian Literature, Princeton University

"In this mix of Tolstoy's short works on philosophical questions, his readers will find the unadulterated essence of the questions on life and on death that he novelizes in *War and Peace* and *Anna Karenina* and explores elsewhere in his writing. This anthology is treasure trove for students, scholars, seekers, and all interested in Tolstoy's thought and thought processes. ranged chronologically, the volume shows that Tolstoy began his quest to understand the meaning of life as a boy and never gave up.

As compiler, translator, and annotator, Inessa Medzhibovskaya has done a masterful job. She draws on her comprehensive understanding of all Tolstoy's oeuvre and on her unparalleled familiarity with his philosophical works to make this anthology especially valuable."

– Liza Knapp, Professor of Slavic Languages, Columbia University

"Those who read Tolstoy only in English – and many who read him in Russian – are used to thinking of him as first a writer and then, in old age, a political and religious thinker and a social activist. This unique volume includes writings, most of them translated for the first time, that together comprise a 'biography' of the development of his thought from childhood on. They range over many genres, from maxims to letters to fiction to memoirs to hybrid forms and much more. Meticulously translated almost entirely by editor Inessa Medzhibovskaya and, just as importantly, annotated and commented upon in great detail by her, they make available a new tool for English and Russian readers alike for understanding both him and his art."

– Donna Tussing Orwin, Professor, University of Toronto and Fellow of the Royal Society
of Canada

"This book presents the truly philosophical material that has never been translated. The inspiring academic dedication of Inessa Medzhobovskaya and her hard and enduring work in the archives and libraries of the Leo Tolstoy Museums in Moscow and Yasnaya Polyana brilliantly resulted in this volume of Leo Tolstoy's works, *An Anthology*, translated, edited and introduced by Prof. Medzhiboskaya. The volume, accompanied by *Further Reading, Index of Names and Titles, Index of Terms*, makes the edition immensely valuable not only for the academic readers but for the general public interested in Tolstoy's work and life. My sincere congratulations to Inessa Medzhibovskaya on behalf of the Yasnaya Polyana researchers who know Prof. Medzhibovskaya as a dear friend and a recognized Tolstoy scholar."

– Galina Alekseeva, PhD, Academic Director, The Leo Tolstoy Museum-Estate at Yasnaya
Polyana

About the Author

Inessa Medzhibovskaya is Professor of Liberal Studies and Literature at The New School for Social Research and Eugene Lang College in New York City. She is the author of *Tolstoy's* On Life *(from the Archival History of Russian Philosophy)*, 2019 and *Tolstoy and the Religious Culture of His Time* (2008; paperback 2009); and a book-long online bibliography of Tolstoy's publications and Tolstoy criticism in the Oxford University Press Bibliographies series (2021). She is the editor of the critical edition of *Tolstoy's* On Life, co-translated with Michael Denner (2018), and editor of two more volumes: *Tolstoy and His Problems: Views from the Twenty-First Century (2018),* and *A Critical Guide to Tolstoy's* On Life: *Interpretive Essays* (2019). She also served as the academic advisor for volumes 267 and 289AC of Short Story Criticism from Gale/Cengage that focused on Tolstoy (2019, 2020). Her forthcoming monograph, *Tolstoy and the Fates of the Twentieth Century*, is a big archival project solicited by Princeton University Press.